"Endowed with a vivid sense of time and place . . . the characters are wonderfully drawn and the dialogue is sharp and colorful. At the heart of *Fast Greens* is the game itself, whose lore and wisdom are lovingly imparted."

—*The New York Times*

"A compelling, emotional story of a golf match among some motley characters, so rich that—pardon the cliché—we couldn't put it down. Do yourself a favor and order one or more. . . . It may be golf's best buy."

—David Earl, *Golf Journal*

"A must-read for every golfer or anyone who just likes a great Texas story."

—*Austin Chronicle*

"Turk Pipkin's hilariously poignant novel . . . is an absorbing, very funny book, told with skill and insight. Golfers will be particularly delighted by it, but you do not have to know much about golf to enjoy it."

—*Houston Chronicle*

"Turk Pipkin proves that something very close to perfection on the golf course may be achieved in fleeting moments of grace and glory."

—*Dallas Morning News*

"Enough Lone Star golf talk to satisfy those of us whose libraries include the collected works of Dan Jenkins and Harvey Penick."

—*Golf Digest*

"Great! If he'd learn to putt, he'd really have something."

—Lee Trevino

"This funny, fast-paced, picaresque romp features plenty of heroic shot-making, world-class hustling, some impressive creative cheating, a classic high-noon shootout on the finishing hole, and even a flashback cameo appearance by the immortal Titanic Thompson."

—*Golf* magazine

"A dead-on ear for Lone Star State dialogue."

—*Kirkus Reviews*

"A joyful romp through the weird and wondrous world of Texas golf."

—Bud Shrake (coauthor of *Harvey Penick's Little Red Book*)

"*Fast Greens* is a funny, sentimental story of golf and love and life, not necessarily in that order."

—*San Angelo Standard-Times*

"To the engaging characters of *Fast Greens,* golf transcends the task of getting the ball into the cup. Honor, courage, and money are at stake, not to mention salvation itself. Anyone who has ever invoked divine intervention on the green will understand and enjoy the plot's entertaining undulations."

—*The Austin American Statesman*

FAST GREENS

Turk Pipkin

St. Martin's Griffin ⚲ New York

www.stmartins.com

ISBN 0-312-34268-3
EAN 978-0312-34268-5

First published in the United States by Softshoe Publishing

First St. Martin's Griffin Edition: May 2005

10 9 8 7 6 5 4 3 2 1

JUST PLAYING THROUGH

A decade after the publication of my debut novel, it occurs to me that there are now two key stories to *Fast Greens*. The first is the tale of young caddy Billy Hemphill and his search for the secret of golf and life, and perhaps for a father to help him with both. You'll find all of that and a good deal more about old-school Texas golf in this new edition of *Fast Greens,* and I don't think Billy, Beast, Jewel, March, and Roscoe need any more help from me with their tale.

The second story of *Fast Greens,* on the contrary, has never been told. That is the saga of a much bigger kid—six feet, seven inches tall and forty years old to be precise—who laid all his cash on the line in the wild hopes that his modest novel would reach out and touch the hearts of golfers and nongolfers alike.

My wife and I were told over and over that we were crazy to self-publish any novel—much less a coming-of-age story about golf—but I believed in *Fast Greens* and decided to roll the dice. For an underemployed writer with a three-year-old daughter, this was quite a leap of faith, but with a little help from family and friends, the book eventually made its way to a printer who started to crank out a ridiculously large order for twenty thousand books.

The first bound copy was soon shipped for my approval, and I promptly sent copy number one to David Earl, the editor of the USGA's monthly magazine *Golf Journal*. I'd never met David, but was a fan of his magazine, plus he'd read an early version of the manuscript and had encouraged me to press on.

Not long after receiving the book, David called me from a pay phone just before boarding a plane to France for the World Amateur Team Championship. He was calling to tell me to look for his review of *Fast Greens* in the new issue of *Golf Journal*. I thanked him profusely, and we promised to talk again as soon as he returned to the States.

The review was all I could have hoped for and more. In addition to saying I'd done a great job with plot, characters, and pace, David called *Fast Greens* "a compelling, emotional story of a golf match among some motley characters, so rich that—pardon the cliché—we couldn't put it down."

These complimentary words were accompanied by the cover in full color, plus an address for ordering the book, which was not yet available in stores. Curious to see if we had any orders, I promptly drove to the post office and found nearly a hundred envelopes, each with a check for one or more copies of the book, with many of the checks wrapped in David Earl's review. (A high percentage of these first readers would later reorder copies as gifts, including one gentleman who had me sign nearly a hundred copies, one for each of his golf buddies.)

David Earl's review was just one of many good notices that would follow in *Golf* magazine, *Golf Digest,* and *The New York Times,* but David's was first, and I knew that the love we shared for the game of golf had changed my life in ways that I could so far only imagine.

A decade later, as I prepared to write this preface, while looking through my files, I found my copy of a letter of thanks I'd mailed to David—a letter that he never had the opportunity to read. Walking through the airport in France, David Earl had a sudden and massive heart attack. Dead at the age of forty-eight, he left behind a wife and a young son.

There are many things I could say about the evolution and further developments of *Fast Greens*—that the name of the hit man Fromholz was stolen from Texas songwriter Steve Fromholz; that a large percentage of readers make the assumption that young Billy's story is actually my own; or that the novel began as a movie for Willie Nelson (a movie that may ultimately be made by someone reading this preface).

But the trivia of *Fast Greens* pales in comparison to the story of how one person can so dramatically change the life of another, even if they've never met. That ability is truly an awesome power, one each of us should strive to remember. In part because of David Earl, *Fast Greens* was soon hailed as one of the great success stories of self-publishing, and was later reprinted in numerous editions by publishers around the world. Because of David Earl, I've been able to spend a good part of the past decade writing all over the world about a game that I love. Not bad for a skinny caddy from West Texas.

Two years ago, my life was again changed by another person's words, this time by my father, Pip (and how great to go through life with a name from Dickens). In what would turn out to be our last conversation, Pip told me that he wished we'd played a round of golf together at Pebble Beach, from where I'd just rushed back to see him.

After Pip's funeral—filled with regret at not having spent more time with him—I dedicated a year of my life to playing golf in his memory (a year chronicled in my book *The Old Man and the Tee*).

Amazing things happened to me in that year; not only did I become a better golfer, but I believe I became a better person and a better father as well. More important, I learned that I had not lost my father at all, that Pip would always be with me, in my heart and in my mind.

As *Fast Greens* circles back into the world, I cannot help but reflect in awe at how, from beyond the grave, two amazing men were able to reach out and work miracles in my life. For that reason, I'd like to dedicate this reissue of *Fast Greens* to David Earl and to my father, Raymond Pipkin, the ever-smiling Pip.

To both of you, I wish endless fairways and fast greens.

INTRODUCTION

It was the summer I turned thirteen, and it had been a fat year in Texas. The mild winter was followed by a succession of tall booming thunderstorms, black with sweet-tasting rain, and the country, lush and green, smelled like the gardens of paradise.

It was a funny time: Not long after man entered space, a Texan entered the White House, and though my pals stayed up late listening to the Beatles, they still wore their hair in flat-tops and spent envious hours in the company of their fathers.

Having no part in that, my days were spent in toil and grace on playing fields of green, hallowed grounds where one man, seeking his own salvation, would reach out his hand and change my life forever. Almost thirty years later, both the perils and the miracles that befell me on that incredible day shine as brightly in my mind as the Texas sun of my youth.

Tanned to the bone and sporting long, unruly hair, they called me the Wild Indian, but it was really just a joke. I didn't know about the world around me the way an Indian would; about the meaning of the stars, or how to follow forgotten trails and unravel the truth of hidden signs.

In actuality I didn't know much of anything but the game of golf; neither love nor hate, envy or pride, jealousy or revenge. I didn't know, but I was about to learn.

BOOK ONE

Hope springs eternal in the human breast;
Man never is, but always to be blest.
—Alexander Pope

1

FOR THE THIRD TIME IN FIVE MINUTES, THE BIG GUY CALLED ME Skinny.

"Hey Skinny! Your foot's in my line!"

He had ten years and a hundred-pound advantage, plus one thick eyebrow that stretched all the way across his bony forehead. I moved the foot.

Beast drew back his putter smoothly, impossibly straight, like he was pulling a sword from a scabbard without the blade touching the sides. The putter face was square to his line at the back of the stroke and still square as it accelerated the ball toward the hole some eighteen feet away. His head remained perfectly still as the ball rolled a showering arc through the early morning dew, cutting a track that led to the edge of the hole, and disappeared into the bowels of the earth.

The ball plinked solidly in the metal cup. Without looking up, Beast dragged a second ball onto the same spot directly beneath his right eye. A long ash dangled precariously from the cigarette in his mouth as he repeated the putt perfectly, the ball rolling through the same damp track as the one before, and the one before that.

"Toss 'em back, Skinny! Before they get cold."

The words crawled out of the side of his mouth without disturbing the cigarette ash.

"My name is Billy," I told him.

Hoping to screw up his concentration, I scooped the three balls out of the hole and rolled them back at angles slashing through the single line in the dew.

Over on the first tee at the Pedernales Golf Club (pronounced Purd-n-Alice, because that's the way LBJ said it), my friend Sandy Bates cleaned his golf ball, paced, then cleaned the ball again. Sandy was a top-notch golfer, likely to play on the professional tour against Arnie and Fat Jack, and oh how I wished I were carrying for him instead of for this ugly putting machine. For once in his life, Sandy really needed my help. When he'd driven me to the course in the predawn darkness, for the first time I'd seen that he was afraid of a game of golf. Now to make matters worse, his partner March was only minutes shy of forfeiting this big match for both of them.

"He welshed, I tell you! Chickened out!" spat Beast's partner, Roscoe Fowler.

Roscoe was a snub-nosed, potbellied, sixty-year-old parody of all things Texan. His khaki pants were worn so far under his gut that you expected them to fall to the ground at any moment. And in the hazy morning light, his pockmarked face reminded me of NASA's lunar landscape photos taken from orbit around the earth.

"I know March; known him since nineteen and twenty-nine," said Roscoe. "Hell! He's probably halfway to Méjico right this minute."

Roscoe spit a big glob of brown tobacco juice—mostly on the green grass and partly on his handmade Charlie Dunn cowboy boots with golf spikes and little side pockets for tees. Unable to look away, Sandy gazed at the dark stain on the grass. With his stomach already tied into sailor's rosettes and other obscure knots, his blond face began sinking to a ghastly green.

Another man, known only as Fromholz, was there to referee this big match. Fromholz was not a man that you would mess with, and though I was afraid to stare, I found it hard to look away. His face was chiseled and tough, with one eye partially but permanently shut. His rattlesnake-skin boots and embroidered Western jacket probably cost a thousand dollars, but the New York Yankees cap on his head and the rolled bandana tied loosely around his neck were faded and worn. Turning his head to give his good eye a fair opinion, he glanced once around the deserted golf course.

"Be cool, Pops!" Fromholz scolded Roscoe. "Don't get your vowels in an uproar! I'm the man in charge and by my watch, it's two minutes till seven."

Plop went another of Beast's putts. Sandy winced at the sound, but his focus was still glued to the brown tobacco stain on the grass.

"Hell, Fromholz!" grumbled Roscoe as he limped over on a bum knee and compared his watch to the ref's. "You don't know shit from shinola! My Rolex says he's got exactly thirty seconds. And that's set to the atomic clock in Switzerland—*noocular* time!"

Like clockwork himself, Beast stroked another ball into the hole. Those balls didn't want to fall into the hard metal cup. No ball *wants* to go in. You've got to coerce them in, sternly but lovingly, the way Beast was doing it.

Again I dug the three balls out for Beast as nearby, Sandy gave a slight retch. For the second time in less than an hour he could taste the truck stop's greasy *huevos rancheros*—undercooked eggs with peppers and hot sauce—which were contemplating a jail break from his stomach. Worse yet, he could taste another bitter defeat at the hands of Beast the golf monster.

5

Just as Sandy started to gag, we heard a car gunning over the hill to the near-empty parking lot. Sandy swallowed hard and the *huevos* went back down to *huevos* land. Roscoe swallowed too; an eye-opening, belly-aching gulp of liquid chew. On the green, Beast's head jerked up as he hit another putt. The long ash from his cigarette fell softly to the earth as the ball spun off the edge of the hole.

"Shit!" we all said in unison as, wide-eyed, we saw it roaring at us: a shiny new finless and *driverless* '65 Coupe de Ville, its gunning motor racing with the devil. Without slowing, the big car jumped the curb and plowed through the wet turf that was our only miserable defense. I tried to run but my legs refused to obey, leaving me frozen in the path of the out-of-control car. It was already too late to scream.

A vision of road kill flashed into my mind—all the putrefied deer, skunks, and armadillos I'd seen bloated by the side of the Texas roads. The vision vanished when at the last possible moment the car braked hard and slid sideways, skidding smoothly to a halt beside our huddled group.

I checked the front of my pants, then breathed a sigh of relief.

The window was down and Hank Williams was singing indifferently from somewhere inside the empty car. Then, like a jack-in-the-box, a shaggy gray head popped quickly into view from below the dash.

"Dropped my donut!" the man said. "Darn thing started rollin' on me."

The heavy steel door glided open and out hopped Mr. William March, flashing eyes, smart mouth, and grinning like a fool.

"The years came down, in crawling pain," sang March, twisting Hank's song with his own words. *"You lied and lied, I went insane."*

"Morning gents!" he intoned loudly above the music. "Looks like you all got here early."

The four of us stared openmouthed, dumbfounded, happy to be alive.

I'd met William March only twice, both times at the urging of my grandmother Jewel, and I had yet to come to any understanding of his true nature. There was some mystery behind his tired and smiling eyes, something devious or devilish, or both. It was like he knew what no one else knew, some nugget of knowledge that he could use against the rest of us whenever he chose.

He tossed me a half-dollar.

"Get my sticks, kid."

Slipping the coin into my pocket, I dragged his monstrosity of a bag from the trunk and strapped it to a gasoline golf cart. March leaned in the open window of the Cadillac, shut up the radio with a yank at the keys, and pulled out a greasy paper bag.

"There's mine," March sang. "Twenty grand! And what a grand twenty they are!"

March handed the bag to Fromholz, then snatched it back.

"Hold on, cowboy! I almost forgot."

He reached into the bag and pulled out a partially squished jelly donut with a hundred-dollar bill stuck to it. Peeling them apart, he shoved the bill back into the bag.

"That was close," he said. "I damn near bet my donut!"

Fromholz peered in at the jelly-covered money. "I don't think it needs counting," he proclaimed.

In the meantime, Roscoe Fowler was fumbling through the pockets of his own bag, which I'd already strapped to another cart. Without disturbing the little blue-steel automatic that I had glimpsed in the side pocket, Roscoe pulled out two fat bundles of bills and flipped them one at a time to Fromholz, who snatched them from the air: two lateral completions; crippled quarterback to one-eyed juggler.

I had caddied before for what I thought were big money matches, hundred-dollar Nassaus with automatic presses, and Bingo Bango Bongo where pink slips for pickups passed from hand to hand and losers went home on foot. But the moulah in this match seemed more like Monopoly money than the real thing.

"Hold it!" said Roscoe. "How do I know our ref is honest?"

"Hell, you can shoot craps with him over the phone," said March. "Let's play."

Gathering round, the golfers assembled in natural affinity; March and Sandy standing tall at one side, Fromholz in the middle, and the blackhats Roscoe and Beast on the other. Unable to take sides beyond reluctantly carrying Beast's bag, I stood to myself.

"Nine holes. Best ball. Winners take all," said Fromholz.

Then he pulled out a yellowed scorecard that looked a hundred years old. Squinting his good eye at the faded nine holes of figures scrawled on it, he came to a decision.

"Roscoe, you won the last hole, so I do believe, after twenty-seven years, you still got the honors."

Subtracting quickly, twenty-seven from 1965, I came up with the year of the last hole: 1938. Unfortunately, I was not as strong in history as I was in math, and I was unable to place any particular event with the year in question. Likewise I had no conception of the clothes, the music, even the cars. With regards to 1938, I was nearly blank. The only image that would form was one I had first seen just one week earlier, an image that I could not get out of my head.

William March's secretary tilted her head down, peered over the top of her small wire-rim glasses, and looked me over from head to toe. Apparently I passed her inspection, for she told me to wait in the hall, then she turned and disappeared through a heavy wooden door.

The walls of the hallway were covered in framed photographs, all of people standing near drilling rigs and oil wells, all except one. Raising on my toes to the level of that faded photo, I saw two men dressed in dusty cowboy clothes: wide-brimmed hats, leather chaps, bandanas around their necks. One of them was holding the flag from a golf hole while the other putted. In the background stood two horses with worn leather saddles, and hanging from each of the saddle horns was a golf bag.

"Golf on horseback?" I whispered to no one. I'd never thought of that.

My grandmother Jewel had let me off here on her way to the beauty parlor—though for the life of me I could never figure out why Jewel needed to be made more beautiful. We'd moved to Austin less than a month before, and already she had her choice of several suitors. Despite that, her only interest seemed to be in Roscoe Fowler and William March, two men she had not seen in almost thirty years.

Shortly after arriving in Austin, Jewel told me she'd run into an old friend who'd asked if I would caddie for him. She assured me that William March would make me laugh, and was a big tipper to boot, an important point because I was saving every penny to buy myself a new set of irons.

I had already carried for March at the Austin Country Club on a beautiful Sunday afternoon. Jewel had been right; he did make me laugh, at least until he and Roscoe Fowler began to bicker and quarrel, exchanging deadly verbal darts the way I imagined desperate men might fight with knives. The round had started pleasantly enough, but on the back nine, with March three holes up, things started to get ugly.

"This friggin' heat makes my goddamn knee hurt!" Roscoe complained as he knelt awkwardly for a better look at a do-or-die two-foot putt.

"I thought your knee hurt in the cold," March answered.

"It hurts in the heat *and* the cold!" Roscoe shot back. "And it's your goddamned fault. It's all your fault!"

"My fault?" March protested. "You sorry bastard! After the way you screwed up our company, you ain't laying the blame on me!"

"Up yours!" said Roscoe, giving March the old one-finger salute.

I was beginning to think they'd go at it this way all day long, but Roscoe lost the match then and there by jabbing the two-foot putt about four feet past the hole.

True to Jewel's word, March was a big tipper. He even gave me a ride home and bought me a chocolate milkshake at Dinty's Hamburgers on the way. We pulled up to our little rented house in South Austin, and March seemed pretty disheartened when I pointed out that Jewel's car wasn't in the driveway. I got out, thanked him for the tip and the milkshake, and went inside. A half hour later, I peeked out the window and March was still sitting there in his big Cadillac, just staring up at the house.

That night at the dinner table, I hadn't even said grace before Jewel started pestering me for details about the game.

"It was okay," I told her. "But I didn't understand what they were always arguing about."

"Well, they're probably just being pigheaded," Jewel told me. "But if you really want to know, ask March. You might find it . . . interesting."

The pause as she considered that final word, combined with the slightest hint of mystery in her voice, suddenly seemed proof positive that March would allow me a glimpse of some secret of the adult world that lay beyond my imagination. And that was all it took for me to find myself staring at old photos in the hallway of an oil company.

The tall door of March's office swept aside and the secretary led me in. I'd never been in a real office before and it was different than I expected, darker, a little scary. The curtains were drawn tight and the room was lit only by a desk lamp that threw tall shadows onto the bookcases and walls.

Only half in the light, March was barely discernible from his big leather chair. Approaching slowly, I rested a hand on the big desk; it felt solid and heavy, and compared to the stuffy room it was cold as chiseled marble. The way it grew out of the floor reminded me of a tombstone. There was an odd odor in the room that reminded me of science class formaldehyde and dissected frogs, and I wanted to run away.

Looking older than his years, March produced a quart of Scotch from the desk drawer, opened it, and poured a glass halffull. Then he scooped in two heaping teaspoons of bicarbonate, stirred the concoction into a murky cloud, and drank it down.

"Scotch and soda, kid. That's what it comes to sooner or later. A man spends a lifetime washin' down greasy chicken-fries and jalapeño pinto beans with a hundred dry wells and it all comes down to Scotch and soda."

He held the bottle out toward me.

"You want a taste?"

I shook my head.

"Suit yourself," he said. "Have a sit."

Releasing his death grip on the bottle, March's focus swung involuntarily toward the cloudy dregs in his glass. I couldn't imagine what he saw in there, but his gaze reminded me of the snow scene in a crystal that Jewel had given me. When I shook it and stared through the swirling snow, I liked to think I could see through the windows of the tiny house to a happy family gathered around a dinner table, the father saying grace before he carved a big golden turkey.

"Tell me, kid," March finally said. "A good caddie can really make a difference, can't he?"

I looked up at his eyes and noticed he was smiling now. It was as if the very mention of golf had lifted the pall from the room.

"Yes Sir!" I told him. "A good caddie can read the greens like a book, and he knows the grain and the yardages, lots of stuff."

March leaned forward.

"You like golf, don't you kid?"

"More than anything," I answered.

"And for you—tell me if I'm right—for you golf is a pure game: physical and mental, joined together without any questions of right and wrong?"

I wasn't sure I understood but I nodded yes anyway. Golf is a noble game, a combination of uncertain skill and specific laws, untainted by ethical dilemmas or moral quandaries. The first twelve years of my life had been spent in hot dry West Texas, where the only snow was in my crystal jar, so golf was for me the one thing pure.

"What would you think of a man who cheated in a golf match?" March wanted to know.

I didn't hesitate, not on the one thing in the whole world that I knew to be true.

"A guy that cheats is lower than a skunk or a snake or a scorpion, Sir. I mean I've seen lots of people tee it up in the rough or miscount their strokes after a bad hole, but they're not golfers, they're just people with bags of clubs."

He shifted his weight, leaning closer across the big desk until his face was full in the light.

"I want you to help me cheat in a golf match, son. Would you do that for me?"

Not wanting to believe my ears, I looked away to the rows and rows of fat leather-bound volumes on the bookshelves.

"No Sir," I said, silently counting the books to avoid his gaze. "I couldn't cheat at golf, not to save my life."

2

WE MOVED TO AUSTIN, MY GRANDMOTHER AND I, IN THE SPRING of 1965, and celebrated my thirteenth birthday on the day of our arrival. I had long hoped to trade the slow and easy small-town life of San Angelo for the excitement of a big city like Austin. My main desire, though, was to escape the memories of my mother Martha, who had gone out for cigarettes six years earlier and never come back.

Martha was only fifteen herself when I was born, a teenager with bangs and curls. Perhaps if she had sported long hair instead, I might have been able to hold her close. But my arms were too short and my cry too soft for me to grasp her young heart. Instead I turned to Grandmother Jewel, who fed me, changed me, loved me, and scolded me as her own, while Martha assumed the role of disinterested older sister. And since Jewel had been for many years without a man in her life, that was a role I was destined to fill as well. Ignored by a teenage mother and cradled by a grandmother still in her thirties, I was already the man of the family.

As I grew into my toddler years and beyond, Martha continued her life as before, idling away her time with dating and gossip, and sometimes caring for me while Jewel taught school. Among the few memories of my mother during those years is of Martha constantly yelling for Jewel because I needed something or because I was misbehaving.

"Jew-el! The baby won't quit playing with the tee-veeee!"

Even when I was six years old, Martha still persisted in calling me "the baby."

"Jew-el! The baby's messing up my clo-set!"

Jewel would then come to correct the situation or else she'd yell to Martha to handle it herself. The latter approach generally elicited more protests until Jewel finally did arrive, or until Martha simply left the house, the town or the state, depending on how put-upon she felt.

"Stay out of the backseat of those boys' cars!" Jewel would shout after her as Martha bounded out for an evening of pleasure or work.

The only job my mother was qualified for was as an underage cocktail waitress in the one real nightspot in town, the Enlisted Men's Club at Goodfellow Air Force Base. There she continued to grow wild and restless until she eventually flew the nest, leaving her "baby brother" far behind.

Martha had been gone two years when she wrote from California to say she missed us; and would Jewel mind sending her clothes. That's when I knew I would never see my mother again.

Now Jewel and I had also left West Texas, and the only thing I regretted leaving behind was my nickname. While the other kids still wore the stupid crew cuts and greasy butchwax stubbles that their dads demanded, my long hair and dark tan had made the Wild Indian alias seem natural. But it did not follow me to Austin, and I soon discovered it is not an easy matter to rechristen yourself with a heathen name among strangers.

Sitting in William March's office that day, I suppose it was the Wild Indian side of me that felt so certain I could never cheat.

"Oh hell, I knew that already," March told me. "I mean you are Jewel's kid. That says it all right there. I was just testing you."

I smiled at him uncomfortably, not sure what he was getting at.

"No, what I really need is an honest caddie, not for me, but for the other team. There's a big match coming up, and I promised to find a bag-shagger for Roscoe's partner. The guy's a player."

"Who is it?" I asked.

"None other than Carl Larsen, state amateur champion."

I sat up straight. Carl "Beast" Larsen was the longest hitter in Texas, and he'd actually played against the pros.

Trying not to look too eager, I asked March about the pay.

"Oh, that's between you and your golfer," March said. "But if he pays you less than twenty, come see me about it."

Twenty dollars? The going rate was six bucks plus a tip that *might* get you up to ten. This was too good to be true.

March picked up a silver dollar off his desk and absentmindedly began to roll it one-handed across the backs of his fingers, sliding it back in a circle with his thumb.

"So whadaya say, son? Can I count on you?"

I was about to say yes, but hesitated for a moment. There was something in that last question I didn't quite understand. If I was caddying for the other team, why would March be counting on me? Then I remembered the twenty bucks, and I knew that at the very least he could count on me to do my job.

"Yes Sir," I told him. "Count me in."

For the first time since I'd been there, March smiled at me. He had a very memorable smile.

Now that we had come to that simple agreement, March seemed eager to talk about the big match and its participants. About the only thing he didn't tell me was who his own partner would be. Had I known he would be playing with Sandy, I'd never have agreed to caddie for Beast.

Soon Jewel was honking for me out at the curb. It seemed I had been there only minutes, but I looked to the big clock on the wall and was surprised to find that it had been exactly one hour, just as she had promised. Saying a quick good-bye, I bolted for the door before March could even get out of his chair.

I was climbing into Jewel's car when March came running down the sidewalk, arriving out of breath and almost out of words as we were about to pull away. Resting his arms on my half-open window, he knelt down so he could look straight across at Jewel who, after her trip to the beauty parlor, looked like she'd come right out of some movie magazine.

Not a word passed between the two. From either side of me their gazes met, and there on Cedar Street in Austin, Texas, in June of 1965, time stood still. I heard no ringing of church bells nor the sound of passing cars. It was almost as if the sun stood motionless in the sky. In front of my eyes the second hand of the heavy gold watch on March's wrist was frozen like a ship in ice.

Across from me, I noticed for the first time that Jewel's hair was different than I had seen before, though my mind raced to photos I had seen from her youth. I realized then that William March was lost in the sights and smells and sounds of a sweeter day, when life had been good and love easy. At first there was only sadness in his eyes, like sails hanging limp on a ship becalmed at sea. Then somewhere on the far horizon of their lost youth, a breath of sweet wind came rushing to the rescue of that floundering ship, flying across the blue and unfurling his eyes in a glorious recollection of a girl and a dress and a place so far away; and yet so close.

If that same memory shone in Jewel's face, it was also adorned by a single tear, which emerged slowly from the corner of one eye and slid down her cheekbone. Finally the tear fell free in the slowest of motions, then landed with a tiny splash on her hand in her lap. The deafening sound of that splashing tear was enough to jump-start time again, and as I glanced back at March, the second hand of his watch was ticking yet again.

"Glad I caught you," March told me softly, no longer out of breath. "You forgot your picture."

I didn't know what he meant at first, but I took the big folder he passed in through the window and there inside was the framed photograph of the two golfers on horseback. Unable to find my voice, I gazed at it in total disbelief that such a treasure should be mine.

"Golf will never be like that again," March told me, "and now you're part of it."

As we drove home, Jewel remained pensively quiet. During the drive, and through much of the evening, I studied the photo closely, wanting to discover everything about this wonderful joining of golf and horses—a new game from out of the old West. There was both mystery and magic in that photo, though I did not know how, or why.

I was reminded of a western I'd once seen on TV. A white man tells an Indian that the whites must rule the land because they know much more than the red man. With his spear, the Indian draws a circle in the sand.

"This . . . what red man know."

The Indian draws a larger circle.

"This . . . what white man know."

The white man nods in smug self-assurance.

"And this . . ." says the Indian, sweeping his hand across the vast horizon, "this is what neither of us know."

3

T HAT NIGHT, UNABLE TO SLEEP, I LAY IN MY BED GAZING AT THE photo, trying to take myself back almost thirty years to that place. The story March had told me of playing golf on horseback was clear in my mind, but now the pictures were filled out by the moonlight outside my window.

"It was the fall of 1938," he had told me, "and the course practically glowed in the light of the harvest moon. The hard edges of the scrub oaks and scrawny mesquite trees were showing their softer sides, and there was no place I would rather have been.

"We considered it a private affair, a challenge between two drunken friends. What with looking for the balls in the darkness, it had taken us most of the night to play only eight holes, and with one par three to go, we were dead even. Roscoe stepped up to the ball on the tee, but halfway through his long, drawn-out preshot routine, the ball disappeared. The damndest thing: without Roscoe swinging the club, without the ball even moving off the little mound of sand that we used as tees in those days, it simply disappeared! I looked up to see if Roscoe was trying to pull a fast one, but he had vanished too."

March's voice, as if telling a ghost story, began to gather a hissing speed.

"A chill ran across my flesh, then it dawned on me. The moon had sunk like a stone into the gathering fog, dropping a pitch-black cloak over us, our horses, and the whole course."

To March, in the black of the moonless, starless night, it seemed futile to continue, but Roscoe wasn't having any of that. Lighting one of his stubby Camels, Roscoe smoked it down to a bright ember and set it next to the golf ball, which glowed in eerie red reflection. Then with the sudden sharp sound of forged steel on hard rubber cover, the ball again disappeared. Where Roscoe's shot in the dark had landed was anybody's guess.

They were contesting, March told me, for the position of chairman and head honcho in their own oil enterprise. And with that burgundy leather chair came the right to name the company. Damned determined to call it March Oil, he placed his own ball next to Roscoe's still-glowing cigarette. Guided by the scent of the lantana blossoms that surrounded the little adobe clubhouse beyond the green, March swung a smooth six-iron, knocking the ball out into the blackness where he thought the hole might be.

As I envisioned the story from my bed in South Austin, I could smell the lantana blooming outside my own window. And in my mind I could see that clubhouse perched on a hill above the Dry Devil's River.

March had described the sound of his shot: the simultaneous *whoosh* and *whack* vibrating outward only slightly faster than the actual flight of the ball. He told me that the sweet haunting sound of his clubhead making contact with the glowing ball was something that he'd never forgotten. He knew, and would always know, that his own shot had sailed more true than Roscoe's.

Finding his ball on the putting surface, March picked up a heavy iron roller and, in the dim light of the coming dawn, he smoothed out the sand between his ball and the cup. That's right, sand! In a futile attempt to find irrigation water for their new nine-hole course, March and Roscoe had drilled nine more holes, bored 'em deep into the earth; but instead of life-giving water, one by one the wells had come in gushing oil. Each one gave up a daily supply of West Texas crude, good for a growing country but hell on growing greens. With no other choice, they installed putting surfaces made of hard-packed sand. And to keep the sand from blowing away in the constant West Texas gales, they *watered* with a light mist of oil.

March's ball was one sandy putt from victory, but Roscoe's ball was nowhere to be found. I had witnessed Roscoe Fowler's perpetual complaining when I carried for March, and now I could picture Roscoe's increasing bitterness and panic, picture him stooping close to the ground, groping blindly for the ball, searching with desperation in the right rough, the left rough, short and long. I can almost hear him now, Roscoe the original curmudgeon, cursing the sun for coming so slow, the moon for setting so early, and the fog for staying so long.

"Oh mama!" Roscoe had cried out as he tripped over a root or a rock or a deaf armadillo, and landed on a prickly-pear cactus. "I'm in a world of shit now!"

But it was March who was really in a world of shit, because March was about to win control of Roscoe's life, and that could not be allowed. The senior partner picks the wells to drill while the junior partner picks his nose.

"Hey March," cried Roscoe. "Git out the Bird! Let's have us a drink!"

The Bird: Wild Turkey, Kentucky whiskey. March knew Roscoe was stalling but didn't mind giving his friend time for the light to dawn.

"I moved to the horses and groped in my daddy's oiled saddle-

21

bag for the bottle," said March, turning to catch my eye. "Those horses were my pride and joy, a necessity born of Roscoe's leg and my own invention. They liked to carry golfers, and waited untied while we hit our shots. My Appaloosa was born wild. I found her dying of thirst near a wildcat we were drilling in Big Bend; put out water and hay every day for a week till she'd eat right out of my hand. She never let Roscoe ride her either. When it comes Judgment Day and St. Pete wants to know did I have any friends, I'm gonna tell him about that Appaloosa.

"We huddled together, Roscoe and me, beneath a mesquite tree not much taller than ourselves, and passed the bottle back and forth. The gray-streaked dawn arrived before long, but didn't reveal Roscoe's missing ball. He took one last look around, planting his footsteps in the sand of the green in the process, and finally he conceded that the ball was lost.

"Fair enough, I thought as I stepped up to stake my claim. Two putts would have won, even three; but hell, I rammed it right in the cup for a birdie and the only key to the executive washroom of that soon-to-be-renowned ground-poking enterprise, March Oil! Hallelujah, brothers and sisters, hallelujah!

"Kid, I literally waltzed across ten feet of Texas to fetch my ball from the hole and, goddamn! There were *two* balls in there! We'd never thought to look in the hole, not in the middle of the night, on a dark par three? Who in their wildest imagination would have ever dreamed that Roscoe could've knocked his tee shot dead in the cup for a hole-in-one?

"Roscoe Fowler, the luckiest man alive: president and supreme head honcho of *my* company. Fowler Oil! Even the name was a bad joke."

. . .

Twenty-seven years after that historic shot, march saw the look of disbelief on my face as Roscoe Fowler, the very same golfing magician who had made a blindfolded hole-in-one, prepared to hit the first shot of their rematch. Roscoe's quick back-swing was followed by an even quicker forward lunge, and he topped the ball so that it bobbled ignominiously to the ladies' tee.

"Christ, crud and crapola! I done drilled me a dry hole!" he said, letting loose a mighty gusher of tobacco juice that flew almost as far as his tee shot. "I don't suppose I get a mulligan?"

Pretending not to have seen, I averted my gaze and stared blankly at the long, untied laces of my high-top tennies. I was lost in a den of thieves. Roscoe could never have made that hole-in-one; it was impossible. Shoot, Roscoe couldn't even compete in a kids' competition. In the San Angelo caddies' tourney, any kid hitting a shot that failed to clear the ladies' tee was compelled to finish the hole with his fly down and his willy waving in the wind. Not a comforting thought, but a good cure for a jerky swing.

Not having received any more answer than his request for a mulligan deserved, Roscoe stepped away, happy just to have his fly in the raised position.

"Well sir!" he trumpeted. "That's why I got me the best partner!"

Roscoe, it seemed, was not wagering on his own game, but on Beast's. And by wagering on Beast, of course, he was also wagering on me, betting a king's ransom that I would do my job honestly. And that's exactly what I intended to do: take the straight and narrow; carry the bag, clean the clubs, and keep my damn mouth shut. The first step of that task was to hand Beast his driver.

Wow! That thing's heavy, I thought. I'd be a dope to screw around with a guy who could swing that.

Though I had told March that I could not cheat, somehow I got the feeling he was still expecting my help. But it wasn't like I could simply step on Beast's ball when he wasn't looking. Golf balls will land in some pretty weird spots, but they don't fall into dimpled indentations exactly the shape of the ball. I could give him bad advice about the greens or the yardage, if he ever asked my advice, which he probably wouldn't. Beyond that I hadn't a clue, and that was final: I couldn't cheat; I didn't want to, and I didn't know how. March was on his own, and so was Sandy.

That was the best part of it.

4

WAY OVER IN ONE CORNER OF THE SKY A FEW CLOUDS STILL shone soft and pink, but they were just nature's little joke—the last illusion that the day would be anything but hot. As the rising sun began to show a growing speck of gold at the horizon, only Sandy had yet to hit his opening tee shot. His furrowed eyes showed how badly he wanted to start the match with more than a good drive, more than a great drive. Sandy wanted nothing less than to hit his ball just six little inches past Beast's tee shot, now cooling its round heels in the middle of the number one fairway, two hundred and seventy-five yards away.

Beast hadn't gotten it there with finesse. He'd simply flexed his big biceps and bullied the ball almost out of sight. Sandy intended to do it the hard way—with grace and skill. As he brushed by me on the tee, he spoke to me under his breath, like Babe Ruth making a home run promise to little Johnny Sylvester.

"Six inches past him," Sandy said. "Just six inches."

Gripping his driver lightly, Sandy squinted at the sloping green a quarter of a mile away. Allowing himself one wasted motion—a dry swallow—he set his mind to the execution of the longest possible shot with the smoothest, purest swing. The first move was contrary to all logic: a slight forward press of the right knee that effortlessly recoiled backwards, initiating the unlikely synchronized movement of the hips and shoulders, arms and hands, grip and shaft so that the clubhead moved straight back from the ball, conducting his turning body in a low-angled arc. His weight shifted imperceptibly to the right foot as the left knee bent toward it. Through it all, his head was still, his left eye fixed in an even glare on the ball.

It was impossible to identify the moment that the clubhead changed direction and the downswing began. Sandy's left hip had already begun to turn back toward the target, shifting his weight to the left side and accelerating his arms and the club with the potential—so far only the potential—of incredible power.

As the clubhead rushed toward the ball, Sandy instinctively performed one last crucial move: releasing all the wound-up power of his hands, arms and shoulders so that the moment of greatest speed was also the moment of contact with the ball, the moment the ball ceased to rest comfortably on its wooden throne, the moment the flattened-to-oblong sphere was suddenly flying at two hundred miles an hour toward its target.

The ball climbed above the full sun at the horizon while the clubhead continued its arc till it had circled his still-turning body and whapped him rudely on the right cheek of his butt. I knew he liked that little slap on the ass. It meant that he'd hit the ball the way he intended: perfectly.

When the ball began its reentry and descent, it had long resumed its round shape so that it bounced hard, then skidded down the middle of the fairway.

Perhaps my greatest asset as a caddie was my vision: I could see my employer's ball under almost any circumstance, a talent that never ceased to amaze me, since I did nothing to cultivate it such as eating great fields of leaf-topped carrots. Whatever confounded the vision of the other golfers and caddies—a background of white clouds, the blinding glare of the sun, a sky thick as soup with minuscule particles of Texas dust—they only made me look more closely and let me see more clearly. All of which meant that I was the only one to see Sandy's ball skid through the dew on the fairway and come to a rest just six inches *behind* Beast's shot.

But why should this contest have been any different from the hundred matches he'd already played against Beast? Since he was ten years old, Sandy had been competing head to head with his own personal golf demon, Carl "Beast" Larsen, and other than a few unimportant pro-ams or practice rounds, Sandy had been cruelly vanquished every single time. If it wasn't Beast's long drives, it was the crisp irons that landed ten feet past the pin and clawed backwards toward the hole. If it wasn't the snake putts from forty feet, then it was the smart-ass demeanor, that twisted sneer or the constant dangling cigarette. Sandy hated it all; the whole overwrapped package that mocked his own weaknesses, that made him look small, that exposed him for what he was to anyone who cared to see. Here he comes down the fairway, tail between his legs: Sandy Bates, loser!

Sandy badly needed to win this match; if not for the self-esteem, for the cash. The Professional Golfers' Association had announced that in August 1965—less than two months away—they'd be holding the first ever PGA qualifying school. The winners of this grueling 108-hole marathon would be given the dubious privilege of competing on Mondays for the available spots in that week's Tour event. Sandy intended to succeed at this tortuous rite, and to do so he needed cash. Ten thousand dollars—his potential share of the day's winnings—would do nicely indeed. But his dreams of the tour must have vanished abruptly as he arrived at his ball and was brought back to harsh reality by his opponent.

"Just six more inches, Sand!" trumpeted Beast as they stood over the two balls. "Six more inches and you'da had me. Shit!" he laughed. "Might as well've been six miles!"

Sandy sighed; it was going to be a long nine holes.

Six inches was nothing on a practical level, but to their egos it seemed all-important. Besides, Sandy would now hit first and Beast would gather valuable information from watching Sandy's approach shot.

Pulling his seven-iron from the bag, Sandy tried to muster his concentration, then failing that, he put his swing on automatic pilot. Once you've hit it sweet a few hundred thousand times, it's not that hard for muscle memory to hit a good shot. Sure enough, Sandy's muscles made a nice move at the ball, which sailed onto the green about thirty feet from the pin.

"Dumb-butt!" he cussed himself softly. "You gotta do better than that!"

I handed Beast the eight-iron he requested, and without so much as an apparent second thought, he smote the ball a burning blow that cut a hole in the air. The ball landed fifteen feet long, then spun back furiously toward the hole.

"Wow!" I blurted out. "How'd you do that?"

"Well Skinny," Beast replied, "you just got to keep the grooves clean."

He handed me the new Wilson iron and a small metal file from his pocket.

"Every time I hit a shot with my irons, you're gonna clean out the grooves with this doodad."

The file had a square tip on it that fit neatly into the groundout grooves of the clubface. I began to run it back and forth.

"Always perpendicular, Skinny; not at an angle, got it?"

"Billy," I said. "I got it."

March and Roscoe, in the meantime, were zooming back and forth in their carts, bouncing up and down across the rocky right rough in search of their balls. Roscoe had already sacrificed any chance of bettering his partner's score on the hole by chili-dipping his second shot and shanking his third. It was a pitiful display.

When March finally found his errant tee shot behind a stubby live oak tree, Sandy yelled to him, asking if he had a shot.

"No problema!" March hollered back. "All I got to do is catch this five-iron clean and get the ball up quick to clear that little tree."

Doing none of that, March jerked fast and hard at the ball, blading it on the sole of the club so that it rocketed straight at the tree trunk and ricocheted right back at him. With shortstop reflexes betraying a natural talent for the wrong game, he quickly dodged, leaping into the air and coming down splayed on one leg and one hand.

Hiding in a crouch behind his own cart, Roscoe burst out laughing.

"Ha! You almost shot yourself in the foot, old Poot! Lucky we got us a couple of sharks to help us out."

But the sharks, now strolling toward the green, were too perplexed by this inept display to even circle the bait, much less each other. In a partner's best ball, the team uses the lowest of their two scores on each hole. The higher score is disregarded. If Beast made three, it didn't matter if Roscoe shot nine or sixteen or withdrew, just as March needn't even tee one up if he was certain Sandy could make an eagle. The chances of Roscoe or March bettering their partners on just one hole seemed about as likely as snow on the Fourth of July. So as far as we could tell, it was just one more head-to-head match between the two young guns; only this one was worth ten thousand bucks to the winner.

For me, it was worth something less. But even with the usually crummy pay, caddying was a job I took with great seriousness, even when it was not entirely pleasant.

Jesus! I thought, trudging along like a pack mule. This bag must weigh sixty, seventy pounds. I bet Beast has got a hundred balls and ten jillion tees in here.

To make matters worse, in the excitement on the first tee I had neglected to shorten the bag's strap and it was all I could do to keep it from dragging the ground. Beast, Sandy and Fromholz all moved quickly toward the green, and though my legs were long, their strides were longer. I slogged along as best I could, despite the heavy morning dew that coated the grass and soaked through my high-top sneakers and my socks. Both Beast and Sandy wore leather Foot-Joys, a fine waterproof golf shoe that could be taken off your foot and floated on a pond like a Volkswagen bug. Foot-Joys shed water like alligator skin. Roscoe's boots, by the way, *were* alligator skin.

The sun was just high enough for the long shadows of the trees to stretch across the fairway like giant fingers that clutched at my wet feet. I hefted the bag higher onto my shoulder, tried to speed up, and wondered if I'd ever dry out, or catch up, or understand any of this mess. I was a fool for participating at all: caddying *against* the only golfer I truly admired, caddying *for* the only golfer I truly feared, and perhaps still expected to cheat by an old man I hardly knew.

Near the green, when the others slowed for March to hit again, I caught up in time to hear Beast—who seemed anything but a philosopher—pondering the true meaning of the day.

"Why in hell would these geezers offer me a sure shot at one half of twenty grand just to replay some dumb-ass match from thirty years ago?"

"Mayhaps . . ." said Fromholz, "they figgered you needed some fast green, Slick."

The locker-room scuttlebutt had it that Beast had recently lost a fortune in personal markers on Benny Binion's craps tables at the Horseshoe Lounge in Las Vegas. March had mentioned that Fromholz was from Vegas, and I wondered if our ref might also be Binion's bill collector. Then I wondered if Beast, suddenly silent, was thinking the same thing.

"Maybe it's not that much money to old March and Roscoe," said Sandy.

Beast positively cackled. "Who are you kidding? The word is out their company's in the shitter."

Handing Beast his putter at the green, I took a chance with my own guess.

"Maybe it's not about the money."

Fromholz, the one-eyed laughing bear, had words for that opinion. "Kid, don't ever forget this: When a guy says 'it's not about the money'—it's always about the money. But keep up the clean living there, Boy Scout."

I was a Boy Scout. I liked being a Boy Scout. But I hated being called one.

31

5

I WAS SEVEN YEARS OLD WHEN I FIRST SAW SOMEONE STRIKE A GOLF ball. At the time I was knee deep in the muck of Sulphur Draw, a pleasant but smelly creek that trickled and splashed over small rock dams and harbored a never-ending bounty of red ear perch, box turtles, and crawdads. From its bubbling springs near the elementary school where my grandmother Jewel had long taught classes, the creek meandered twenty blocks through the oldest residential area of San Angelo and dumped into the North Concho River directly across from the Santa Fe Municipal Golf Course.

On the day of recollection, each of my slender hands had a careful grip on a fat crawdad, their four pincers reaching desperately but hopelessly over their heads to lock onto their captor. The struggle was futile. Like bare-handing bumblebees off of flowers and jamming them into a jar, or snaring horny toads without being struck by the blood spit from their eyes, holding crawdads was a skill I had fully mastered.

Looking up, I saw a man on the opposite riverbank swing a skinny bat at a skimpy ball that ricocheted off a concrete park bench and bounced into the water with a splash.

"Goddammit!" the man shouted.

I thought this was marvelous—a game in which my mother's favorite curse played an instrumental part. I clapped my hands in glee, momentarily forgetting the two murderously aggravated crawdads who suddenly found purchase for their pincers, each grasping tightly to my opposite hand. Releasing them with a scream did not encourage them to let go of me, and there I stood—sinking in the mire—my arms flying willy-nilly, like an epileptic swatting yellow jackets, the two miniature lobsters holding on for dear life. As I was about to go under, either dizziness or my shrieks finally disoriented the crustaceans and they loosened their grips. One after the other they flew thirty feet into the air, each landing in the river with a splash of their own.

Sucking on one sore thumb and one finger, I stifled my sobs while the man tossed down a second ball and took a poke at it. Alas, this one was doomed as well, hitting both the picnic bench and a pecan tree before splashing into the river like the crawdads and the first ball.

"Goddammit!" he shouted again, hurling the bat after the ball.

The bat made by far the largest splash of all, and the man gave a little cry.

"Oh nooo!" he moaned. "My five-iron!"

I was very good at interpreting the bad moods and hangovers of my mother, and I quickly concluded that the man wished to have his bat back. Plunging headlong into the murky water, I demonstrated that the YMCA's lessons had not been wasted. Swimming thirty feet to the middle of the river and diving to the bottom, I miraculously came up with the man's five-iron on the very first try. Then waist deep on the golf course side of the water, I tossed him the club.

"Thanks," he said. "Say, you didn't happen to see either one of my balls down there, did you?"

33

I had not, but I knew where they had fallen. Within two minutes I was standing in front of him holding two mucky balls.

"Well, these aren't mine, but I guess they'll do," he said, handing me a dollar. "Boy, you sure earned that one!"

It was absolutely the very first dollar bill I had owned in my life and I stared at it in wonder, as if George Washington had strolled up and handed it to me himself. As the man picked up his bag and walked off, I yelled to him.

"Hey, mister, whadaya call this game?"

We owned no television on which I might have seen a tournament, so for all I knew it was called goddammit.

"Golf," he answered. "If it's good to you, you call it golf."

A few minutes later my friend Mick wandered up. In the same grade as myself, but a full year older, Mick was impressed by the dollar but allowed as how I was going to get my behind warmed for the mud on my clothes. This thought did not deter me for one minute. I still knew—approximately—where two golf balls worth hard cash were resting in the mire. It took me no longer on the second dive than it had on the first to return with two balls.

"How do you know those are the same ones, Creep?" Mick asked me. "Maybe the river's full of them balls."

I was awestruck by the beauty of his logic. We fished out balls for hours and sold them for a quarter a pellet to the passing golfers, making a total of five dollars each (plus my original buck, which I refused, under threat of frog knots and burnout, to split with Mickey).

Bright and early that Saturday morning, while Jewel graded her students' papers and my mom slept the day away as usual, I took my six dollars down to Santa Fe Golf Course and purchased one well-worn club-a five-iron no less. The golf pro cut the shaft down to my size with a hacksaw, then added a few wraps of masking tape to reattach the grip to the shaft.

"You need to buy balls?" he called as I ran out.

I didn't even answer. I was already swinging wildly at the thousands of fat pecans lying on the ground, waiting for another foulmouthed golfer to bounce one into the river.

6

SANDY LIPPED OUT HIS LONG PUTT ON THE FIRST GREEN, AND BEAST
had only an eight-footer for birdie and a win. After his incredible
display on the putting green I didn't see how Beast could possibly
miss, even though he hadn't consulted me on the break (almost
none) or the speed (very slow). Caddies hate not being consulted
because it means the golfer thinks he knows more than the caddie,
and that's often the case.

In this instance, however, it was definitely not the case, and Beast
left the ball hanging on the front lip. "A freckle short," as March
described it.

"Yeow," said Roscoe. "You shoulda eat more beans."

Without looking up, Beast elevated a middle finger in his partner's general direction.

"'Cause that one ran out of gas," Roscoe explained.

What Beast didn't know, what Roscoe didn't know, what I
didn't know either was *why* the putt came up two beans short. Although the course was closed for weekly maintenance, the grass on
the practice green had been mowed incredibly short and the base
had seemed dry and firm. But this green was almost mushy, as if it

had been soaked overnight, and the grass was grown out like three days of scruffy beard. Confused, I looked toward March. He was wearing another of his big grins and shaking hands with Sandy as if it were all a part of his plan.

"After one hole," proclaimed Fromholz, "the match is even-steven."

7

ONCE I HAD DISCOVERED THE GAME AND PURCHASED MY FIRST precious club, I began to study the wide variety of golf swings at Santa Fe Golf Course. I loved the very idea of golf, the spiritual image of the ball in flight: each shot a tiny sputnik—the golfer both the astronaut and the rocket—hurtling through space and overcoming, however briefly, the grasping hands of gravity, breaking free as the earth passes below in a blur of trees and water.

The reality of the game, however, turned out to be quite different. The simple truth is that the crystal-clear image of a ball in flight is achieved only through boring, plodding work: long, monotonous hours of trial and error highlighted by exhilarating glimpses of success. The ball does not wish to leave the earth and has no interest in defying gravity. In truth, the ball is perfectly content to just lie there. Or, when struck a glancing blow by a young golfer of seven, the ball tends to scoot along the ground letting friction do its job. Friction, of course, produces heat, the result being a ground-hugging hisser then known as a "worm burner" but now referred to more often as a "bug fugger."

Our French becomes more proficient, but the dilemma remains

the same: the reality of golf has no more to do with the idea of the game than a vista does a painting. Just as an artist may move paintless brushes on a canvas, a golfer may swing the club without a ball or target. But a canvas without paint, despite artistic intentions, remains empty, with no measure of the artist's skill.

So this cratered pellet, like a palette of paint, is really no more than a measuring device, an indicator that registers the degree of perfection of a golfer's every swing (not neglecting, unfortunately, the golfer's wayward thoughts in making that swing). To make matters more difficult, the ball also measures the wind, the water and even the specific gravity of the ocean's shore, commonly known as the dreaded sand trap. And for a proficient golfer swinging smoothly in a groove, more than anything else it indicates proper club selection.

Hole number two at Pedernales was what the locals called a little old par three. Nothing tough about it except that from the tee the green looked somewhat larger than a postage stamp but considerably smaller than an envelope.

Roscoe promptly threw out his honors and his back by topping another shot with a swing that reminded me of the one I employed back in my first year of play. When he lurched at the ball, Roscoe looked like a guy trying to fly cast a frozen turkey. You got the vague sensation that he once had a better swing, but perhaps couldn't remember where he kept it.

"Don't let it bother you," said Sandy, a nice enough guy that he even complimented his opponent. "You got a good short game."

"Yeah!" said March with a snicker. "Off the tee!"

"My partner, the jack-off king!" said Beast, enough of an ass that he even insulted his partner. "You could open a whorehouse and run it by hand!"

It was clear that Beast didn't view anyone as being on his side, not even his partner or his caddie. This seemed a lonely way to go about things. From the local scuttlebutt, I knew some of how he'd come to be that way, and even through my fear of him I couldn't help but feel just a little bit sorry for the big ape. No father was bad enough, but one who beat you must have been a hundred times worse. Though I craved attention, there are limits to all things, especially in what passes for love.

Roscoe had returned Beast's single-digit salute, but it did not stop the insults.

"What's your handicap, Roscoe: hemorrhoids?" taunted Beast.

"Why'on't you eat my shorts?" said Roscoe. "But first, hit your shot—*partner*!"

Without asking me for a club, Beast reached silently into the bag and pulled out his six-iron. Then he casually stepped onto the second tee and once again hit the ball a few feet from the hole. It looked like the simplest thing in the world.

Kissing his club and hugging it to his chest, he didn't wait for compliments.

"Oh you sweet little five-iron, you!"

Five-iron? Confused, I looked back in the bag. He hadn't hit a five; it was a six. Then it dawned on me. Glancing up, I saw Sandy—a funny look on his face too—as he exchanged his six-iron for a five. Sandy knew better than to choose a club by watching another player, but Beast was more than just another player.

Sandy made his usual sweet move at the ball; it almost took my breath away. The ball sailed as straight as a string, looked down into the hole for a moment as it passed overhead, and flew the green by twenty yards.

"Shit!" said Sandy.

"Shit has been mentioned," noted Fromholz.

Sandy fumed on. "I knew it was a six-iron! Beast, you must not've got all of yours."

Beast painted a shocked look on his hard face.

"I'm sorry, buddy. Did I say five? I hit six. Oh well, an honest mistake."

Jeez! I thought. These guys have got more tricks than a magic convention.

Simmering in his own juices, what Sandy needed now was for March to save the hole for their team with a solid shot right at the flag. What March gave him, unfortunately, was a Texas leaguer—a quail-high lob that bounced short and failed to roll on. Part of the problem was March's swing. Actually, all of the problem was his swing. March swung like the ball was a hand grenade with the pin pulled out. He had a choice of throwing his body over it or hitting it fast before it blew up. This time he chose the latter.

"Grow legs and run!" shouted March.

The ball did neither, stopping in the frog hair just short of the green.

"Hell, I think that ball's deef!" he said to me with a wink.

Sandy slammed the five-iron back into his bag and stomped off toward the green. Beast hurried to catch up and I hurried to catch up with him.

"Hey, Sand ol' bud!" Beast called after him. "Wait up!"

Against my better judgment, Sandy slowed and Beast drew up alongside him. "Say . . . you're not still mad 'cause I beat you in the state amateur, are you?"

Sandy was silent.

" 'Cause it was just luck; like the high school finals at Muni. Hey, remember the Peewee play-offs when I chipped in from fifty yards?"

"Don't push it, Larsen!"

"Okay Sand, whatever." From behind I saw Beast turn his head to Sandy and flash a wicked grin. "So I got lucky and made a couple of forty footers."

"I said: Don't push it!"

"Calm down, Blondie. It ain't my fault you never beat me."

Sandy dropped his bag and wheeled on the big man, poking him in the chest with a sharp forefinger. Considering that Sandy was outweighed by thirty or forty pounds, this did not seem like a smart thing to do. Beast's Popeye forearms looked as if he could wring your neck like a dishrag, while his bony, stubbled jaw could bite off one of your limbs. Worst of all, the evil, smoldering fire in his eyes made him look like he was contemplating horrible butcheries on your vital organs.

But Sandy, acting so completely against his own personality, had taken Beast by surprise.

"Never," spat Sandy, "is a long time."

Without pushing his luck any further, Sandy withdrew his finger from Beast's sternum, turned, and was gone before the big man knew what had happened.

While we waited for Roscoe to hit his second shot, I picked up Sandy's abandoned bag and carried it over to where he was conferring with March. Sandy's bag, I noted, weighed about thirty pounds less than Beast's.

"He's right, March," Sandy complained bitterly. "I never beat that big shit. Either he gets a lucky break or I lose my confidence and fold in the stretch. Why'd you pick me to play him anyway?"

"Hey mama's boy!" said March. "You're supposed to be kicking his butt, not yours. I picked you as a partner because this is a grudge match: winner take all. And I wanted a guy on my side who's gotten the short end of the stick, someone that knows how to carry a grudge."

Indeed, Sandy's face was inflamed exactly like a guy who knew how to carry a grudge.

"Are you pissed?" March asked.

"Yeah, I'm pissed," Sandy told him.

"Good. Stay that way!"

Being pissed, unfortunately, was no help on number two. Sandy made a decent chip to the green, but he still had a four-footer for par. When Beast bent over to repair the deep hole his own tee shot had made in the green, he made a wisecrack about the divot reminding him of his ex-wife.

"You and every other two-handicapper in town," Sandy told him.

In a flash Beast was eye-to-eye with the source of the insult. I thought they might swat it out with their putter blades like samurai, but they just continued to stare. A fly buzzed around their heads, and still they stared. Long after Sandy should have turned tail and run, he *still* stared. And then I noticed their feet: one of Beast's oversized shoes was trodding heavily on one of Sandy's size nines. Sandy couldn't back off because somewhere under that massive steel-clad hoof at least one sharp spike was impaling him to the ground. Something needed doing.

"Beast," said Fromholz dryly, "I think that guy's trying to get your goat. Now let's play some golf."

The big foot came up slowly, like heavy machinery, and as Sandy's stare abated I realized that his face had just been frozen in pain. He limped away, two spike holes in the toe of his shoe, both showing spots of blood, bright red against the white leather.

Beast cackled a similar warning to the rest of the group.

"You guys think he's funny, don't you? Well, see how funny this is."

Replacing his ball on his mark, Beast putted out of turn. This was just the kind of rash action that Sandy had hoped to push him into. But that's where the plan went astray; Beast knocked the putt right in the hole.

"With seven holes to play," said Fromholz, "the team of Fowler and Beast are one up."

"Shit!" said Sandy.

"Shit has been mentioned!" added Fromholz.

8

SHIT WAS SANDY'S ONE AND ONLY CUSS WORD. HE ALSO HAD A weakness for Tammy Wynette music and double orders of chicken-fried steak. His girlfriend's name was Darla. Like any true golfer's gal, she didn't play the game herself. One set of heroic feats per household, please. Otherwise dinner would never end.

I'd met him while caddying in the quarterfinals of the Texas State Amateur. To avoid playing Beast in an early round, Sandy had entered in West Texas. He'd asked around the San Angelo Country Club pro shop for a good caddie who worked cheap and they referred him to me. Since I was only twelve, he doubted my abilities but found the price just right.

Even at twelve I took the job seriously, unlike a lot of boobs who carried the bag backwards on their shoulder and cast their shadow on the hole when tending the flag. Partially guided—I like to think—by my expertise on the local greens, Sandy won his match five up with four to go.

In the quarterfinals at the Midland Country Club, he'd drawn a local oil-money favorite named Preston Deforest-Hunt, Jr. Having played at the course daily since he was seven years old, Junior knew it well enough to be a formidable opponent, even for a much better golfer. Unfortunately though, Junior was the occasional victim of a serious duck hook, the result of having learned the old-style hickory-shaft swing from his aging and doting father. A duck hook to a serious golfer, in case you don't know, is the golf equivalent of a Baptist preacher developing Tourette's syndrome, that dread and little understood neurological malady that makes one involuntarily spout the foulest profanities and bark like a dog. I once heard a respected golfer-slash-doctor claim that the only cure for either was a double dose of Thorazine, a shot of Old Crow, and a glass of Budweiser. Simultaneously.

Deforest-Hunt Senior was one rich oil-pumping son of a buck, but he had yet to find the right golf professional to cure his own infernal hook. To make matters worse, he'd taught his own weak game to his young son. Then having handicapped the kid. almost beyond recovery, Dad had pinned all his hopes on Junior winning a prestigious tournament like the state amateur. So on the day of the match with Sandy, Junior was clearly out for blood.

Carrying Sandy's clubs, I was astounded at the consistently high quality of my employer's golf. Throughout the round he ignored the unlikely means that Junior utilized to get the ball in the hole. Sandy didn't panic, didn't choke, and didn't get demoralized by the miraculous recoveries from certain doom that his opponent hit on the odd holes or the long putts that he snaked in on the even ones.

"Well!" said Junior in his pseudo-British accent. "I *have* been everywhere on this course dozens of times."

Sandy ignored all this, negotiated the course with long drives and crisp irons and trusted in the fact that, since he was the better golfer, he was bound to win. He was two down with two holes to go when Deforest-Hunt Senior showed up to watch the product of his loins and inheritor of his own faulty golf skills kick some lower-class butt. But Dad's very presence reminded his offspring of all those early golf lessons, and Junior suddenly remembered how to duck hook the ball. Sandy won the last two holes and the playoff on number one.

The semifinals were at Fort Worth's famed Colonial, a long trip on the train that still carried passengers twice a week east and west from San Angelo. Jewel had a teacher's seminar that weekend, but put her trust in me by letting me go alone (with Sandy meeting me at the station in Fort Worth).

I didn't get a chance to study the course because the train arrived only the evening before, but it mattered little, as Sandy's opponent was a stiff, unable to work the ball under the big oaks (now dead but not forgotten) that used to overhang Colonial's greens. On the way to winning seven and six, Sandy taught me more about golf than I'd ever known there was to learn.

He taught me how to read the grain of the greens by the angle of the sun and the cut at the cup, how to tell the differences between bent grass (slick putting but lots of bite) and Bermuda (slow putting but bounding approaches), how not to be fooled by the mower cut, and on short putts how to listen for the ball to drop before moving my head. He told me to chip uphill with less loft and downhill with more, and never to hit a driver from the fairway when the grass is leaning toward the ball and away from the green.

Sandy could name all of the great Texican golfers and he occasionally did so when walking down the fairway, as if he were in a trance: "Guldahl Nelson Hogan, Mangrum Thompson Trevino, Sanders Zaharias Rawls . . ." chanting their names over and over like a mantra.

"Who was Trevino?" I asked.

"*Is* Trevino," Sandy corrected. "Who *is* Trevino."

"Okay. Who is Trevino?"

"The guy who taught me how to fade the ball."

"A fade is easy," I told him.

"Not a slice, Brainiac, a fade," answered Sandy. "There's a big difference. A fade is intentional; a slice is a curse."

According to Sandy, the reasons why Lone Star golfers win so many tournaments include the diversity of the courses in the huge state, the ability to play in the constant coastal and western winds, and having to putt on both bent and Bermuda greens. More important, they have that infernal sense of moral and physical superiority that's brainwashed into all Texans at an early age, and a Texan's commitment to a life's pursuit that doesn't take place behind a desk or in a store.

In learning all this, I had no doubt that one day Sandy would join the ranks of those chanted greats himself. And he saved the best for last, finally informing me that he'd also learned to play the game by caddying. So there was hope for my game yet. I was in caddie heaven.

But my elation was deflated somewhat when Sandy returned to Austin for the finals at Morris Williams, a course named for the most charismatic and heroic Texas golfer of his day. Morris Williams was a Harvey Penick student who was the only player in history to win the Texas Junior, Texas State Amateur, and Texas PGA championships, and he did it in one twelve-month period. Sadly, his career was cut short when he was killed while flying a training mission during the Korean War.

Knowing this, unfortunately, was no help in convincing Sandy to take me to caddie at the finals.

"It's too far from San Angelo, and there's no train," Sandy explained. "Plus you don't know the course."

True, but not the real reasons I didn't get to go. Just as Sandy had known in his previous matches that he was the better golfer and would certainly win, he also knew that Beast was the better golfer and would beat Sandy in the finals. He simply didn't want me to see him lose to Beast. In a way, I suppose I didn't want to see it either. I had never seen Sandy lose.

Now I'd ended up a traitor, caddying for his archenemy, the evil Beast. Luckily, Sandy carried only one grudge and it wasn't against me. He'd proven that by picking me up long before dawn and fueling me up for the big match with breakfast at the Big Wheel truck stop. As we made the drive through the hills to the course in his beat-up Plymouth Valiant, we talked about everything but his chances that day.

When the early hour overcame me, I leaned my head against the window and watched sleepily as the black sky was imposed upon by a slender turquoise wedding band of dawning light, creeping ever upward from beyond the hills in the east.

I was jolted to attention when Sandy pumped hard on his brakes to avoid hitting a red-tailed fox that scurried across our headlights and off the road.

Wow, a fox! I thought. That's a good sign.

"Almost hit him," Sandy said. "That would've been bad luck."

I glanced at Sandy, his face lit up green by the dashboard lights. He looked spooked.

9

BEAST WAS TO SANDY AS A TIMBER WOLF IS TO A CLEVER CIRCUS dog. Back when Beast was still called Carl, his old man owned a driving range, which is to say Pop drank a lot of beer and collected the money while young Carl picked up the balls. When you're in your preteen years and picking up and washing ten thousand golf balls a day, retrieving an extra thousand balls you hit yourself isn't much worse. So Carl grooved his swing by hitting balls till his hands bled.

When Carl was fifteen, Pop went out in true white-trash style, going on a three-day stinker and taking a folding buck knife in the gut (unfortunately, it was unfolded at the time). The bank took the driving range and Carl took to hustling golf for a living. No matter how much money he won, and it was plenty, he couldn't escape his trailer-trash heredity and always lived in a cheap motel. And no matter how much he lost (he often played the best at Hundred-Dollar Low Ball with equal side bets on greenies and sandies), he never carried his own bag. He'd picked up so many range balls as a kid, he didn't even like to pick 'em up out of the hole. A caddie I knew once followed him at a safe distance around the Austin Country Club where Carl was playing a solo practice round. My pal picked up eighteen brand-new Titleists that Carl had left in the holes.

In typical Texas-schoolboy style, Carl got passing grades, despite the fact that he rarely attended class; the schools needed all the winning athletes they could muster. Thanks to the curve of the grade and to some nifty work with a one-iron, Carl was medalist in the state high school championship as a junior, but he was disqualified for gambling on the tournament. To make matters worse, that meant he lost the bet he'd placed on himself. Maybe it was the bookies who turned him in. In any event, the treasured first prize was passed to the second-place finisher, Sandy Bates. I heard Sandy threw the trophy into a pond at Morris Williams. He knew who'd won.

A couple of years later, in Knoxville, Nashville or Gatlinburg—one of those faceless, reporterless stops on the Southern beans-and-rice tour—Carl met a golf groupie with substantial backspin and bite of her own. It must have been lust at first sight, for after winning his first tournament against the semi-big boys, Carl married her on the eighteenth green. Not long after, so the story goes, Carl's new wife started playing midnight driving range with a number of other golf pros who began to refer to her as the Dragon Lady (supposedly in tribute to her fiery talents with lips and tongue).

It was the Dragon Lady who rechristened big Carl as Le Beast. Apparently they were quite a team. If Beast was in the finals of a match-play tourney, she'd slip him a late-night mickey, sneak over to the opponent's motel room, and screw *his* lightbulbs in and out all night long. Beast, having slept like a baby, never understood why he was winning all those final rounds against tired guys with limp putters, till one of them—desperate to get back in the match—confronted the jealous husband with the bare-assed truth.

It was a rare day in the history of match-play golf. Since neither of the players in the final eighteen actually completed the round, the winner of the consolation match was awarded the five hundred dollar first-place prize. Beast was resting comfortably in the county jail and his opponent was in guarded condition at the local hospital. The other guy's memory lapses cleared up after a few weeks, but his hearing was never the same. Beast had bitten off much of the guy's right ear but, lucky for them both, the crowd pulled him off before he could get the other one.

10

ONE UP," SAID ROSCOE AS WE WAITED ON THE THIRD TEE FOR THE greenskeeper to finish mowing the fairway. "Wanna press the bet?"

"You seem pretty confident," answered March.

"Confident? Hell, we gonna kick your butts! You *and* your pretty-boy partner."

"In that case," said March, pulling a sheaf of folded documents from his golf bag, "let's bet the whole kit 'n' caboodle." March handed the papers to Fromholz and the girth of our circle tightened considerably.

"What's that?" asked Sandy.

Fromholz cocked his head and held the papers in front of his good eye to look them over.

"That, Miss Curious, is the deed to a golf course, a clubhouse, a house, a barn, and some very old and tired oil wells."

"Don't leave out my daddy's grave and headstone. They're part of it," said March.

Beast perked up his ears. "Did I hear something about a golf course?"

"The Dry Devil's Golf Club," said Roscoe. "We built it."

"On *my* land!" said March.

"Aw hell, March! Don't start that doo-dah again. That land was a company asset from the very first, just like my drilling equipment. We each made a capital investment."

"Your drilling equipment wasn't handed down to you by your father."

"How could it have been? I was a bastard. You gonna hold that against me now?"

"If you keep acting like one, yeah!"

March grabbed the papers back from Fromholz and waved them in Roscoe's face.

"Just sign the deed and we'll play for it."

On the big oak desk in his office March had rolled out a map of West Texas to show me what this match was all about. By myself I picked out points nearer to San Angelo, places I knew well: the parks with swimming holes and rope swings at Christoval and Knickerbocker, a railroad trestle high over the Concho River that I'd jumped from on a dare, and the abandoned U.S. Cavalry station at Fort McKavett. But March had to point out the dot indicating the golf course he and Roscoe had built in a crazed attempt to duplicate the links-style courses of Scotland, where they had learned to play the game.

"We went to Scotland in nineteen hundred and thirty-eight," March told me. "We were hunting for oil. A fat cat Scottish lord had come to Texas looking to shoot some big game. Roscoe and me, we steered him in the right direction. One night we were all drinking and telling oil wildcatting stories when his lordship informed us they'd been mining shale oil in Scotland for sixty years. Mining, but no drilling. I found that curious!

"We walked across Scotland for days. It was hell on Roscoe's knee, so we sort of limped from pub to pub across the Lothians into Fife, searching for seepages and uplifts and smelling the air for the faintest one-millionth of a whiff of oil."

I didn't believe you could smell oil beneath the ground, but March insisted I was wrong. They'd taught us similar such stuff in San Angelo at Santa Rita Elementary, which was named for Texas's first major oil well and where—Jewel's classes excepted—the three R's became four: readin', 'ritin', 'rithmetic, and royalties.

One day an old man came to our school and demonstrated the use of a doodlebug or divining stick. Holding the forked branches of the stick with upturned palms, stem pointed to the sky, he crossed our schoolyard until the base of the stick shot mystically toward the earth. The stick had found water, he told us.

The first graders were impressed, but we sixth graders knew better: we put our faith in science. That is, until Coach White gave Tommy Story one end of a long tug-of-war rope and sent him to the water meter at the street. Another kid took the other end over to the water cutoff at the side of the school, and they stretched the rope tight to find the run of the school's main water line. The rope crossed the exact spot indicated by the old man's doodlebug. He'd found water all right, a pipe full of it. Even the sixth graders were impressed. And with a branch from a beech tree, he told us, he could just as easily find oil.

Now March was telling me he could find oil with his snoot. He claimed that traces of iron inside our noses act as a compass—like a salmon's homing device—but due to evolution most people no longer notice.

"I'm just less evolved," boasted March. "To me the smell of oil is as strong as rhubarb pie."

A geologist is a great one for maps. March soon covered the one of West Texas with an old chart of Scotland; then he carefully traced their journey from Edinburgh around to the north side of the Firth of Fife, past the hamlets of Alloa, Dunfermline, Pittenween and Crail.

They were in the ancient town of St. Andrews when March finally picked up the scent. Triangulating with his nose and the very same map he was showing me, March got a bearing from the south of the ancient town and another from the north. On his last day of searching he planned to find a third and final bearing from within the boundaries of the town itself.

"I was so excited," March told me, "that Roscoe could hardly keep up."

Still waiting at the third tee for the mower to finish, I heard a second, more abbreviated version of the journey and how it led to the building of a golf course. But Roscoe's recollections were not so pleasant.

"It was cold as a well-digger's ass that day," Roscoe said. "Which was about the warmest it got the whole time we were there. Between my bum knee and three layers of wool I could hardly move, but March just hopped an eight-hundred-year-old stone fence like it was built yesterday. He waded across a road full of puddles and strolled onto a big green meadow that stretched all the way down to the waves. Then March sticks the ol' sniffer into the air and says he smells oil, lots of it!

"'How lots'? I ask him, and he says, 'More than you can even imagine.' 'Well, where is it?' I say. And this joker points straight out at the cold ocean.

"Hell, he was pointing at the North Sea, and I *knew* we couldn't drill out there! Now here it is twenty-five years later and next week I'm going to the North Sea to drill for that same damn oil. When it makes me rich, I guess I'll have the last laugh, huh?"

"Well, Roscoe," March said. "The way I see it, you already got the last laugh. Don't you remember whiffing the ball?"

"Oh, hell, March, don't tell that again!"

Suddenly impatient, Roscoe began to yell at the greenskeeper.

"Hey, Manuel! Manuel Labor! We're waiting here like a bunch of hogs for slop. Fore, goddammit, fore!"

Over the loud roar of the mower, the man could hear nothing and just kept mowing. The course was, after all, closed for the day. The fact that March had slipped the pro a hundred bucks to let us play didn't mean anything to the guy who did the real work.

So Roscoe hobbled back to his cart and March told us about the big whiff.

"We're standing there staring at the North Sea when suddenly . . . *Yeow!* Roscoe grabs his shoulder and lets out a yelp like you never heard before. I think he's been shot for trespassing. We look around for our attackers and all we see is this odd white ball laying by us on the ground.

"'What the hell is that?' says Roscoe. 'Some kind of aigg?' And I swear he turns his gaze straight up, searching for some giant Scottish bird. Hell, we were just a couple of hillbillies, but even I knew what a golf ball was. I knew St. Andrews was the spiritual home to the oddball game that had swept the States during the twenties. I just thought the game was a waste of time, but hell, so is life."

"That's the first damn thing you said was true," hollered Beast, who was pissing loudly into a growing puddle just off the tee.

March ignored him. "But Jesus, to hear Roscoe howl, to see that purple bruise, I was impressed. The ball must have been struck with an incredible force. And sure enough, out of the mist came four Scotsmen dressed like they were heading to church. And tagging along behind them were four little tykes with bags on their shoulders."

"Caddies!" I blurted out like some damn fool.

March gave me a look, then he continued.

"Roscoe, doing a little St. Vitus' dance with the pellet in his hand, is about to spew some vile Mescalero curse on the Scotsmen when they beat him to the punch. 'Ha'e you no sense, lad? Ye mooved me ball froom its prooper place. Are ye trying to spoeyl me game, or are ye merely daft, eh?' "

It was a fair to middling Scottish accent that March affected, but Roscoe wanted to get to the point.

"I threatened to turn his hide bass-ackwards, that's what I did!"

"Yeah, Roscoe, you were always quite a scrapper. So when the Scotsman figures out Roscoe wants to fight, he starts in with the brogue about how he don't 'ken the coostoms' of our own land, but there in Links Land gentlemen settle their differences with a match of 'gowf.' But of course, the fella says it wouldn't be fair for a seasoned 'gowfer' to complete against a 'rank rookie' like Roscoe!"

Just telling the story is beginning to make March snicker.

" 'Rookie!' shouts Roscoe. 'Give me one of them sticks! How hard can the damned game be?'

"So they show him the basics of the overlapping grip, and we watch the Scotsman hit a shot that bounces onto what I figure must be the target, a big green area adorned by two waving flags."

"*Two* flags?" I ask.

"At the Old Course," Sandy had to explain to me, "some of the holes going out share big double greens with holes coming in."

I shrugged; how was I supposed to know?

"So Roscoe takes a mighty swing at the ball, almost drilling himself into the ground. He looks toward the green, then at the sky, and finally at his feet. Ignominies of callous fate, curses of obdurate execration, O scourging plagues of malediction–and goddammit too! He'd missed it."

"Big deal," says Roscoe from the cart. "So I missed it."

"Yeah, Roscoe, but you swung harder when you missed it the second time. I lost count about fifteen swings later when I fell on the ground laughing with the Scotsmen. Finally Roscoe hits the ball for the first time, a little top that sends it maybe twenty feet ahead. 'There!' he says. 'I told you I could do it.'"

"Tell 'em the rest of it!" Roscoe demanded. "I learned to hit it. I learned in *one* day."

"Well, you stayed up all night to do it," countered March.

Even Fromholz took an interest in the story. "Sounds like you were hooked solid Pops, hooked through the gills."

"We were both hooked," said March. "And that's how we came back from Scotland more interested in golf than oil. Since there wasn't a course within a hundred miles of home, we built one ourselves. Which brings us back to the deed. Whadaya say, Roscoe?" March pushed again. "Do we bet the course?"

"Not a chance. There's still oil under that land."

"Roscoe, it's all played out," insisted March. "Drained! Sucked dry! *¡Perdido! ¡Ya no hay más!* All that's left is my land."

"*Our* land."

"My father's buried there! What the hell are you worried about, anyway? You're one hole up and you got nothing to lose."

"Forget it; let's play."

Roscoe pulled a club from his bag and we looked down the third fairway. The mower was gone.

.   .   .

Easier on the eye than it is to play, the third hole at Pedernales Golf Club is a classic example of the strategic design theory of golf course architecture. The strategic theory, the wolfsbane of the casual golfer, was developed and refined by a long line of masochistic architects who were obsessed with their mamas and hated their papas. In order to punish the latter, they built golf courses which guaranteed that a golf shot lacking proper planning, let alone near perfect execution, would end up in a place from which the hole looked like a flickering star as seen through the windblown branches of a bare tree. On a strategic course the duffer has to go around the trouble and thus ends up playing a much longer layout than the pro. Sounds fair enough—if you're the pro.

What it meant here was that this short dogleg hole had a large pond yawning across the left corner of the fairway. The front side of the water was only about two hundred and twenty yards from the tee; the far side about two-fifty. Strategic intelligence tells the few who have it that they're not likely to fly the ball two and a half football fields. So the prudent course is to lay up short with a shot that lands high on the right side of the fairway and rolls down the slope to the bank of the pond. Any shot foolishly landing in the middle of the fairway might as well be bouncing off the end of a diving board because it's just as certain to get wet. On the other hand, a bold long knocker who successfully navigates his tee shot to the far side is faced with an easy wedge instead of a long iron to the bunkered green.

Beast, I figured, was considering all these pros and cons as he stared long and hard down the third fairway and scratched loudly at the stubble on his chin.

"Have a shot somebody," interjected March. "But don't hit the ducks on the pond."

"I don't see no friggin' ducks and neither do you," said Beast flatly.

"Right you are, Mr. Larsen," answered March. "I don't see 'em. I *smell* 'em."

"Bullshit!" mumbled Beast, testing the wind with a lofted pinch of grass. "Roscoe, you hit first, and don't whiff it!"

Some people shed life's capricious insults and embarrassing moments like a duck sheds water, while others are forever burdened by the heavy wet feathers of these past vagaries. Because Roscoe's mightiest blows had once been spurned by a lowly Scottish golf ball, he had taken great pains to learn to hit the ball properly. And a perfectly placed shot from the third tee at Pedernales finally proved that he could still do it.

With Roscoe's ball as insurance, Beast was free to go for the other side of the pond. Standing to one side, I could sense Beast's toes gripping the ground through his leather Foot-Joys. I could see the veins bulging in his forehead; each muscle and tendon tightened toward one object: power. It occurred to me then that I was caddying for the biggest, meanest, ugliest golfer that ever came out of Texas. When he swung I was sure that the clubhead had broken the sound barrier, but that mini-sonic boom we all heard was just the sound of wood on ball, a scorching blast that soared in screaming flight. Turning slightly to the left as if it had eyes, the ball landed safely on the other side of the pond, and bounded up the hill toward the green. From where the ball stopped Beast could probably toss it into the hole for an eagle.

Around the tee there was the smell of burning air, as if the devil himself had grabbed a driver and tried to knock his ball into a hole where it could nestle a little closer to home.

Once again, the pressure was on Sandy. Looking at his clubs, he considered the task facing him. His hand hesitated, this time between the five-iron and the driver: safe or maybe sorry.

March cheered him on softly. "Swing away, Sandy. Show him how it's done."

Sandy took out the driver.

It was a lovely swing, but just as he hit a light breeze came up in our faces. It was a lovely swing, but there was no sonic boom, no burning air. It was a lovely swing, but he wasn't Beast. The ball flew almost on the same track as Beast's, but it came down a few feet short of the opposite bank with a splash. The noise scared up a small flock of mallards who circled toward us, flashing their iridescent green and blue wings in a banking turn as they headed off in search of a course with better golfers.

"Po' little ducks," said Fromholz.

It was up to March. He pulled out a three-wood with a little apology.

"Us short knockers gotta use a wood just to lay up."

Taking the club back slowly as if he was in no hurry to win, March made his prettiest swing of the day.

"Most beautimous," said Fromholz.

But Sandy knew better. "Hit soft," he whispered. "Hit soft."

It didn't hit soft. The ball hit hard on the sloping fairway and bounced left, picking up speed and barreling toward the water.

"Whoa ball!" yelled March. "Whoa! Hold up now! Take a rest! Grow hair!"

But the ball didn't grow hair. It just kept rolling.

"Have a wreck! Hit something! Stop!"

It hit something—the water—and sank like a stone.

March began to holler at the ball as if it had stepped heavily on his bunions.

"That's a crock of fig-plucking rat-spit! Hey, ball! Why don't you take a flying—"

March might have given us an interesting tirade if he hadn't been cut short by a fit of coughing that blew up his face like a red balloon until the muscles in his upper body were constricted to rigor, his strong right hand squeezing the life out of his driver. We stood frozen in tableau as the color drained from his face, the muscles gave way, and the driver dropped to the ground. Gasping for breath, he stumbled toward his golf cart and pulled out his medicine. Somehow he managed to get a couple of pills in his mouth, and within moments the attack was over, and March was once again looking and acting his own self.

"Goddam bum ticker, that's what I got." He took a deep breath and let it out. "Whew! Sweet Mother of Jesus, I hate that! Good thing we're just playing nine."

"Hey, old-timer," said Fromholz. "You look like you been ate by the coyotes and shit off a cliff."

Sandy pushed Fromholz aside and put an arm around March to support his weight.

"You okay?"

"Son," said March. "I'm just trying to hit every shot like it's gonna be my last."

"Listen," Sandy said as he climbed in to drive March's cart. "Why don't we toss in the towel?"

"Forfeit? What about your going on the Tour?"

"March, the game's not worth dying over!"

March forced a doleful smile. "Maybe not, but why don't you play like it is."

Just then, Roscoe sauntered over to check on March.

He ain't so mean, I thought.

"March. I been thinking," Roscoe said. "Let's play for it all."

"Roscoe, I as good as lost this hole already. That means I'm two down with six holes to go, my chest can't decide whether to explode like a well or cave in like a mine, and now you wanna play for my land?"

"Exactly."

"You're on," March told him. "Sign the deed and give it to Fromholz."

"Not so fast," said Beast. "Does the winning pro get a share of this crummy ranch or golf course or whatever the hell it is?"

"Pro, my ass!" scoffed Roscoe as he signed the deed. "I don't see no pro! Nobody around here but sharks and duffers and mama's boys. And I don't even know which one you are. So don't get greedy, boy—we ain't won yet."

11

MARCH WAS ONE OF THOSE GUYS WHO EVEN IN A GUSHER
year could never stroll past a golf ball in the water without trying to
fish it out. With Roscoe's tee shot sitting pretty and Beast's almost
on the green, you'd have thought his main concern was to take the
penalty, get a good drop, and pray to Jesus H. Christ His Own Self
for some wild hare of a hope at tying the hole.

But as the rest of us headed toward the pond, we were treated to
the sight of March leaning out over the water, a wedge in his right
hand, his left entrusted to Sandy who anchored him to terra firma.

"Hah!" snorted Beast, who didn't like golf balls and did his best
to hurt them bad. "Gonna be two down for twenty thou and he's
sweating over a used Titleist. What a rube!"

Of course, I could have gone in after the ball, but I had already
learned that a kid carrying a bag doesn't become a caddie until he
assumes the decorum of the game. I would no sooner have waded
in than I'd have told Beast I thought he was an a-hole. Golf is not a
game about succumbing to temptation.

So, with Sandy proving himself at least some sort of capable partner, March successfully snared the ball and dragged it to shore through the goop on the bottom of the pond. Muck and all, he tossed it to me for a quick cleaning.

"Hey kid," he called. "What's your name again?"

I answered even though he knew it. "Billy."

March chewed my name the way Roscoe chewed his tobacco.

"Billy. I like that. Just like when I was a boy. Billy, you know why the pond holds water?"

"No Sir. No Sir, I don't."

"Duck shit! It coats the bottom."

I frowned at the slimy goop that the ball had left on Beast's towel and toyed with the idea of wiping some of it on his grips. Then I saw Beast fixing me with his evil eye as if he'd read my mind. The thought of him biting off my ear replaced the idea of doctoring the grips, and I turned to toss the clean ball back to March.

But then I noticed that something about March had changed. Both his cavalier attitude and his concentration on the game had suddenly vanished. He wasn't even considering the shot he was supposed to make. Instead he was staring toward the third green, almost in a trance. I looked to Sandy to see if something was wrong. Maybe March needed his medicine again. But Sandy's attention was focused on the green as well. The same with Fromholz, Roscoe, and even Beast.

And then I knew.

Standing next to the third green, silhouetted against the blue sky and motionless except for her cotton dress billowing in the gathering wind, was a very lovely woman. Even with my young eyes I could see that she was an exceptional vision of beauty. She was shaded against the hot sun by a slender parasol and her long fair hair was gathered loosely in a bun except for a few wild strands that played about her face.

For a long silent moment, the six of us stood sweating through the goose bumps on our arms, waiting for the mirage to disappear.

A low whistle issued from Roscoe's pursed lips, but it was March, speaking in reverential awe, who gave a name to the vision.

"Miss Jewel Anne Hemphill."

I could tell by the tone in March's voice, and by the look in both men's eyes, that to the two of them she looked exactly like the budding beauty of seventeen they first remembered from thirty years before. And the true wonder was that to me, too, this timeless woman looked just as she did in my earliest memories. I can see her still, leaning over my crib, her sweet smile stifling my infant sobs, her hair, long then as always, dancing into my stubby fingers, which squeezed tightly in an effort to keep her close.

Then another tender memory of Jewel rushed back upon me like a perfect dream. She had taken me on a picnic in the Hill Country one fine April day—April I know, because in Texas that is the month of bluebonnets. I was a little boatman surrounded by a sea of wildflowers: bluebonnets salted in patches of yellow and black Mexican hats, deep red Indian blankets, and stalks of purple coreopsis, all wavering like a painted canvas drying in the breeze. From my ship of quilted cotton, transfixed, I watched Jewel atop an island hill, a trick of the eye making her appear waist deep in flowers so that she seemed to grow out of the blossoms, her own floral-print dress floating among them like the living sail of a prairie schooner.

And ten years later I looked at Jewel beside the third green, still wearing one of her silken floral dresses, and the smell of those flowers and the sleepy hum of the bees came back upon me in such a flood that I almost began to cry.

God knows what visions rushed back upon March and Roscoe, but they were powerful enough for March to decline his shot and climb in his cart, leaving behind the ball he'd worked so hard to retrieve from the pond. He intended to get a closer look at the dream, but Roscoe cut him off.

"March, you prick! I still ain't hit."

"Who cares?" March shot back.

But Sandy had not hit his shot either. March snorted like a bull penned next to a pasture full of cows, but he managed to stuff his hands in his pockets while Sandy knocked his ball onto the green not ten yards from where Jewel stood, applauding softly as the ball landed.

Then Roscoe, no doubt inspired by the new gallery, hit his best shot thus far, a four-iron that sent the ball flying to the banked front edge of the putting surface. Though the ball appeared to be farther away than Sandy's, Jewel applauded more enthusiastically.

After rounding the pond with their carts, both March and Roscoe had to wait impatiently as Beast, his mighty drive resting a half wedge from the green, checked his alignment at least three times and flew the ball straight at the hole. A nanosecond after the ball left his clubface, both carts were racing toward the green.

"Christ! Give a guy a chance to follow through!" Beast called after them.

Whatever was about to happen at the green, neither Fromholz, Sandy, nor I wished to miss it. I quickly shouldered Beast's bag and the three of us hurried up the hill, leaving only the big man behind.

"Hey, kid!" Beast yelled at my backside. "How about my divot?"

Thirty feet in front of him I bent over as I passed the big clump of dirt and grass and tossed it back at him.

"Let him replace his own dang divot," I mumbled, opening perhaps the first crack in the floodgates holding back my dislike of the caddie's subservience. Those heavy tournament bags would never feel the same again.

12

BOTH RUSHING TO REACH JEWEL, MARCH AND ROSCOE SKIDDED
to a halt just below the green, jumped out of their carts, and started
up the little slope. It was both childlike and wonderfully funny; one
moment Roscoe ahead, only to be tripped up by March surging
past, merely to be dragged back himself by Roscoe. Because of my
long arms, one of my favorite kids' games had always been King of
the Mountain. Coming off the starting line in the fifty-yard dash, I
might have looked like a slow giraffe, and playing tackle football I
was nothing more than a target for some overgrown linebacker
who had failed a couple of grades. But once ensconced on top of a
big boulder or sandpile I could not be easily dislodged. So it was
with great merriment that I observed this adult version of the game
between these two old rivals. I had heard country songs about playing the fool for love, but until that moment I'd never known the
meaning of the phrase.

The greatest comedy was that somehow, after all their senseless
jousting, both men arrived in front of Jewel at exactly the same moment. Standing side by side, their lungs trying to exact some pur-

chase on the damp air, they doffed their hats, bowing low to what was obviously the single object of their hearts' desire.

"Miss Jewel," said Roscoe as March continued to battle for his breath. "Might I say that you are looking as purty as a picture postcard."

"Why, thank you, Mr. Fowler," she answered, turning to March for his compliment.

March took a short breath and let loose with one florid word.

"Likewise," he panted.

It was as clear as the smile on her face that Jewel loved it all.

"You gentlemen make me feel like I'm seventeen and the queen of the ball all over again. Now stand up straight and behave yourselves. You've no more manners than a couple of pig shoats; you haven't even introduced me to your teammates. Let's see, it shouldn't be too hard. Young Billy I know already, and you . . . you must be Sandy. I've heard a lot about you."

Sandy was clearly puzzled; he'd met Jewel several times and knew she must remember him.

"And this must be Animal," Jewel continued.

"Beast," he corrected her.

"Of course. Please forgive me; I'm not accustomed to such ferocious names."

Though it was obvious to me, somehow the others didn't seem to notice that she was kidding them with this act of Southern graciousness and aplomb. Of course they didn't know her as well as I did. March and Roscoe had not seen her from 1935 until just weeks earlier, an absence of almost thirty years. Of the other three men, only our ref seemed to grasp the game at hand.

"Fromholz," he said with a gallant tip of his cap. "No mister required."

"Well, Fromholz, to which team do you belong?"

"I'm the referee."

"How charming!" she gushed. "And who, pray tell, is winning?"

"The way I figure it, Roscoe and Mr. Beast there are fixing to go two up."

"May I watch?" she asked.

"Damn right!" "You bet!" said Roscoe and March.

So far Jewel had yet to say a word to me. And I was too surprised to say anything to her. I hadn't the slightest idea that she was coming to the match, and though I knew of her long-lost link to March and Roscoe, I'd never seen them all together, with the exception of another of the photographs lining the walls at March's office.

Not far from the horseback golfers had been a photo taken in front of an old wooden oil derrick: two grimy, smiling young men and a spotless woman between them. Where the years had been kind to Jewel, they'd been positively devastating to Roscoe and March. One crippled and the other all eaten up on the inside, they now seemed almost shadows of their younger selves, both beaten down by dry wells, broken hearts, and inside straights that didn't fill. In the photo they all looked close to the same age, but now you'd never really guess that Roscoe and March were only ten years older than Jewel.

As I contemplated all this, Roscoe, Sandy and Beast examined their putts.

"You want me to line it up for you?" Beast asked his partner.

Roscoe snorted. He'd rather have missed the putt than accept advice in front of Jewel.

"Suit yourself, old-timer," said Beast. "I'm gonna make mine anyway, and we only need one birdie to win."

But in Jewel's presence Roscoe was not an old-timer. Feeling his oats, he snaked a long putt up the slope that broke left two feet for every ten it moved ahead, straightening out only when the ball hit the bottom of the cup.

Jewel applauded with excitement, the fingers of one hand patting quickly in the palm of the other. March looked away in disgust, not so much at losing the hole but perhaps at being so obviously bettered by Roscoe.

"Just once," March said to Sandy through gritted teeth. "I'd like to run in a long putt like that when it really means something!"

Sandy would have liked to make one as well, especially the one he now needed to halve the hole. His line was more straight up the hill than Roscoe's, and he should have known that his putt would break less. He should have known, but did not, and the ball slid past the high side of the hole.

"Two up with six to play," pronounced Fromholz.

"I could have made mine," said Beast as Jewel congratulated Roscoe with a peck on the cheek. "I could have made mine easy."

March dropped his ball and the babble and went all slack and sad-eyed as Jewel entwined herself arm in arm with Roscoe and the pair walked away as one.

"Honey, I just love a winner!" she said to Roscoe. "Do you know, you're shining just like when we ran off together in 1935."

"I could've made mine!" Beast said a little louder; but if anybody heard him besides me, you really couldn't tell.

73

13

On the thousand and something nights that my mother Martha stayed out till all hours toting drinks to flyboys for tips and squeezes, Jewel filled some of the parenting gaps by cooking, tending, and tucking me in.

"Hush, Squirt. Go to sleep," she had told me till I grew too big for my britches and her little affections.

"It's too early!" I'd whine. "Can't I wait till the sun goes down?"

"Oh, you rascal! The sun's been down for hours. How about a story?"

Being a schoolteacher and well-read to boot, she knew all the traditional wolf, sheep, and prince stories, and by the time I was six, so did I. That's when I began to realize I could actually ask for whatever story I wanted. It didn't have to have a moral, and it didn't have to be out of a book.

Jewel just reached into her past and her family's past, pulled out whatever she thought was of interest or instruction, and wove a spell over me with her words. I still remember it all. Her grandfather, Adoniram Judson Hemphill; Adoniram, the Old Testament's

Lord of Height; Adoniram, Civil War hero, Indian fighter, pioneer settler of Texas; Adoniram, who begat Elisha Judson Hemphill.

Elisha Judson Hemphill, self-anointed prophet, Baptist circuit rider, pioneer radio proselytizer, and Jewel's father; a stern man who followed the twentieth century from horseback to airwaves without changing his moral tune or his mind about heathens, sinners, adulterers, liars, cheats, back stabbers, or drinkers of backsliders' wine.

Despite being a preacher, Elisha Judson Hemphill was not a man of belief, being more of the disbelieving type. The list of things he didn't believe in was almost longer than my wakefulness. He didn't believe in dancing, drinking or the worshipping of idolatrous devils. He didn't believe in purposeless joy, ready compassion or the singing of anything but hymns on Sunday. He didn't believe in ice cream, root beer, penny candy, or swimming, any more than he believed body heat was meant to be shared in the winter or aired in the summer.

And of course, more than anything else, he didn't believe in fornication. So when Elisha Judson begat Jewel Anne, she was living proof of the single sinful lapse of his life, one failed misstep intended to produce a male offspring. Though he had fallen from grace with a taste of evil fruit, and been punished with a girl, he became not a saint among sinners, but a sinner among men, determined to find the right track, to ignore his wife's cursed desires, and to raise a child more perfect and less sinful than himself.

So Jewel, begat of Elisha, begat of Adoniram, was admonished for sixteen years of Sunday sermons and dinnertime harangues on the major and minor disbeliefs: avarice and sloth, jealousy and greed, alcoholic fortification and bestial cohabitation. To me, the things he didn't believe in were like a roll call of shaggy unicorns, scaly-winged griffins, and long-toothed dinosaurs. Jewel loved to tick them off to me one by one, laughing all the while at how she had once plotted secretly to violate each of his disbeliefs, starting with the world's number one and number two evils: dancing and drinking.

By 1935, the residents of both Del Rio, Texas, and its sister village of Villa Acuña, Mexico, had all had a bellyful of Elisha Judson. There was nothing the sinners would have loved more than to trumpet Jewel's fall in her daddy's face, nothing they'd have loved so much as to get his rantings off Acuña's 500,000-watt radio station, XER. So powerful was the station that its signal bled through onto every band of the radio. For six hours each day and night the only damned station you could listen to was that raving Baptist maniac, when all anyone wanted was a little bit of dancing music from New York, Los Angeles, or Mexico City.

At least in the evening you could hear the brash nerve of XER's owner and primary broadcaster, Dr. Brinkley—the goat-gland surgeon. Brinkley entertained with his advertisements for transplants that guaranteed "renewed potency for the male patient and satisfaction for the wife who panteth for the running brook."

But no, it was Elisha Judson's god-awful preachin' all day long, and no choice but to leave the radio off, which, for some folks, still brought no peace. The unlicensed Mexican station was so strong that some people with a mouthful of cheap metal fillings could pick up the broadcast through their bridgework. More than once one of them just went insane from all that screaming in their brain. So Jewel knew better than to fall drunk into the street anywhere nearby, lest the locals paint her as Jezebel, people's exhibition number one in the trial of Elisha's self-righteousness.

Jewel's Cinderella ball would have to be in another kingdom, ninety hard miles away, in the town of Sonora, Texas. With four of her friends, Jewel set out from Del Rio one hot summer afternoon in a borrowed jalopy, willing to endure the rutted, unpaved roads in order to simply have some fun. And it was only when they topped a big hill, passing an iridescent turkey gobbler standing majestically beneath a sign marking the Sutton County line, that Jewel finally felt free of her father's foul breath and well-aimed accusations.

As they came up the valley of the Dry Devil's River into Sonora, bouncing along the dusty road and breathing through handkerchiefs, she began dreaming of the Prince Charmings who awaited her at the Wing Ding, southwest Texas's finest example of switching off the preacher and switching on the fun.

It was a big hoo-hah, too big for the county courthouse, too big for the high school auditorium, too big even for the town square. Only the largest buildings within fifty miles would suffice: the Western Star Wool and Mohair Warehouses numbers one and two. Each summer, right after all the smelly spring goat and sheep shearings had been shipped off to markets east and north, the ranchers of West Texas paraded into Sonora and begat a reverberating din of celebration and iniquity.

One of the barns was primarily for families: kids, old ladies and little babies. The main attractions were music, social games, lemonade, and a hundred yards of homemade food. To get in, you had to bring a covered dish of edibles. Twenty plates of sliced tomatoes and goat cheese or thirty hominy casseroles were not uncommon. There was apple bobbing, watermelon-seed spitting, and a thousand other activities, each of which, to an aspiring young woman of the world, was more boring than the next.

The second barn was for couples, ex-couples, would-be couples, confirmed bachelors, gamblers, whores, and other sinners too numerous to mention. To get into the main barn, you had to pony up a case of beer or a bottle of liquor, usually homemade. Though

Prohibition was two years gone, West Texans went on as they had for years, making it and drinking it and paying no mind whatsoever to whether the law or XER's Elisha Judson felt it was a good idea.

None of Jewel's friends had the requisite booze or looked old enough to get in. They didn't really care, though, for they were happy to listen from outside with a hundred other young people in the same situation. Jewel looked the age, or at least by proud beauty and sheer determination she looked unstoppable, except she lacked a bottle. No problem: she just stood there in virginal radiance listening to the strains of Bob Wills and his infernal Texas Playboys as they tuned their instruments inside.

Before the band had played a single waltz, a man walked up to Jewel with two bottles in his hand, two bottles because his partner had intended to be there too. But their oil well, the sum total of their future financial prospects in and on the earth, and yet to hit pay dirt, was behaving strangely. Leaking a variety of noxious gases, the well required careful tending.

The whim of a single cut of the cards had left one sorely disappointed partner back at the drilling site, and sent one, both bottles in hand, straight into Jewel's tony white arms at the entrance to that barn. Her skirt was scandalously scalloped just above her knees and her hair was cut above her bare collarbones in a loose Gibson the way she'd seen Joan Crawford's in *Grand Hotel*. It was a stunning combination of cowgirl, virgin and movie star. To a lonely oilman she looked like fun in a pair of boots.

Her new escort whisked her straight through those gigantic double doors into a whirling cloud of dancers and sawdust, ten thousand dizzying turns an hour, drinking and laughing and dancing like the dickens to a West Texas waltz. Several hours and too many drinks later, Jewel lay back on the seat of the man's pickup truck. Half passed out as he tugged at her clothes, she stopped him in a panic because she couldn't remember his name, and then allowed him to complete her indoctrination into a whole new set of beliefs when he reminded her for the twentieth gol-dang time that his name was Roscoe.

14

As I stood on the fourth tee and watched my grand-mother flirting shamelessly with Roscoe Fowler, I could not help but wonder, was he my grandfather? Though I'd never known my own father, I'd at least known who he was, known by my mother Martha's childish vitriolic reminders that if he'd only taken the time to marry her before he got killed in Korea, we'd have been rolling in Air Force pension money. But Jewel had never identified my grandfather in her many stories, and I'd always hoped it was because he was still alive and would one day step forth and assume his rightful role at Jewel's side.

But Roscoe Fowler—crippled, pockmarked, tobacco-drooling grouch—could he possibly be the one? I'd refused to believe it from the moment I heard his name and connected it to Jewel's confession of her defloweling. He couldn't be my grandfather. I refused to accept the possibility. At least until I saw them cooing and wooing and carrying on like young fools. Then I wasn't so sure.

Why do I need a grandfather, anyway? I thought.

After thirty years, it was pretty damn late to step back into shoes that long vacant. To hell with him.

Jewel must've seen my scowl because, after some moments of questionable merriment, she left Roscoe and came to my side.

"I brought you something, Squirt," she said.

I flushed with embarrassment at the baby name as she pulled a brown paper sack out of her large straw handbag. In the sack was a tall bottle of Dr Pepper and a bag of Tom's salted peanuts.

I opened the bottle with the buckle on Beast's golf bag, ripped open the peanuts, and poured them into the soda bottle. Before the resulting fizz could surge out of the top, I took a huge swig. It was cold, wet, salty and crunchy, and more heavenly than tasting stars, which is why we called it caddie champagne.

"Thanks!" I said, releasing a rush of air from my lungs.

Jewel took off my cap and straightened my hair.

"You look almost like one of the men, Billyboy."

Smiling halfheartedly at her idea of a compliment, I messed up my hair a little, took the cap back, and replaced it in its natural cock-eyed position.

"What about me?" came Roscoe's voice from just over my shoulder. "Didn't you bring your sweetheart Roscoe nothing cool to drink?"

I hoped that she hadn't brought him a thing, but even so I had no intention of sharing mine.

"As a matter of fact, Mr. Fowler, I did bring you something," she said.

His paper bag, smaller than the Dr Pepper sack, was the kind you get in liquor stores. The thing that amazed me most about this new and wondrous city of Austin was just how darned many liquor stores there were. Everywhere I went it seemed I was passing a liquor store. I figured it must be something to do with the legislature, which met infrequently and drank continuously here in the state capital.

It wasn't so easy to get a bottle in West Texas. San Angelo was—and is to this day—a dry town, which doesn't just mean they suffer from a shortage of rainfall. Being a dry town means you can't sell booze in the city limits. This prohibition does not apply, however, to beer or wine, which can be had by the bottle, quart, six-pack, case, jug, keg, or truckload on about every fourth corner of town.

And the prohibition did not and does not apply to the county in general, although there are plenty of dry counties in the Baptist areas of Texas. In San Angelo all you have to do is drive twenty feet outside the city limits and you'll find a whole slew of liquor emporiums, "package stores" as they're known, because they wrap your bottle tightly in a brown paper sack. It was much easier to make such a purchase in Austin, unless of course you were thirsty on Sunday, God forbid. Suffering and misery awaited the Texas heathen with a faulty Saturday memory, and since it was now Monday morning, Jewel had remembered to make her purchase at least two days earlier. I disliked her planning such a show of affection.

The bag Jewel handed to Roscoe, by the way, was pint-size, and so was the bottle of Jack Daniel's inside.

"Whoo-eeee!" said Roscoe, taking a peak at the label. "Jewel, you beauty, you sure know how to get a man's attention!"

Roscoe unscrewed the cap and held the bottle almost to his lips.

"Hooch for a smooch," he said, lowering the bottle for a moment.

Jewel gave him a wet one and as I walked away Roscoe must've taken a big swig because I could almost hear his eyes swell up with the first taste.

"Goddamn! That curls my shorthairs," he said. "I'm about as happy as a dog with two dicks."

The rest of the group had waited patiently while Jewel talked with me, but this was carrying things too far.

"Roscoe!" hollered March. "Quit screwing around and have a shot!"

"Hell," said Roscoe, ambling over to his cart for a club. "I never seen a man in such a hurry to get his butt waxed."

I handed Beast his big black-headed driver and was chugging down the rest of my soda, when—whoosh!—I felt the wind from a mighty practice swing as it passed within an inch of my ear.

Spitting out a fountain of Dr Pepper and a trail of peanuts, I saw the club coming back for me again.

Whoosh!

Still mad at being superfluous, Beast was taking it out on the air and anything else that got in his way. If I hadn't ducked, he'd have thumped my head like a pumpkin.

Whoosh!

The club swung forward and—whoosh!—it went back again. I jumped back two giant steps and took refuge in the company of March and Sandy.

"Sandy, it's time to pull out all the stops," March was telling him in measured confidence.

"What!" Sandy hissed. "You think I been holding something back? I'm playing as hard as I know how."

March looked at him with a stone face. "I ain't talking about *play!*"

"Nice shot, Roscoe!" March added a little louder. Roscoe had whapped it out about two hundred yards right down the middle. "One more of those and you'll have it out to where Slammin' Sammy hit his tee shot in 'forty-eight."

Beast, stepping into the batter's box, perked up his ears at that.

"Where'd Snead hit it to?" he asked.

Having hooked his fish, March had only to reel him in.

Number four was a long dogleg par five with some sizable oak trees protecting the corner about two hundred and sixty yards away. March told us that Snead had cut the corner by going over the trees, leaving himself a mere middle-iron to the green while the other players had to feather in a three-wood or a fairway driver.

"Course Slammin' Sammy was a *long* hitter," concluded March, implying that Beast was not.

It was a valiant effort, perhaps the best of the three incredible drives Beast had hit thus far. Still, my heart cheered as his tee shot came up short of his goal, slammed into the ten percent of tree that wasn't air, and fell down beneath the overhanging branches.

"Son of a bitch!" yelled Beast. "Snead never hit it over those trees!"

"Sure he did!" boasted March. "Of course, those trees were just saplings in 'forty-eight, probably a lot shorter then."

Beast's face began to rage into shades of scarlet. We all stepped back, except Fromholz—Dr. Cool—who stepped toward Beast, but not before slipping one hand into the bulging pocket of his jacket. It was not the pocket he'd stuffed the wads of cash into and it was not too hard to guess what he had in there. This guy took the referee job very seriously, carrying it so far as to provide protection for the participants. But March didn't really need protection. He wasn't even done yet.

"Oh, hell!" March said. "What a stoop I am. My memory's all screwed up. I don't think it was this course at all. Come to think of it, I can't even remember if this course was here in 'forty-eight. I must be goin' crazy—crazy like a bat."

"The expression is crazy like a fox," said Roscoe.

"Whatever."

If the first confession had served to pump Beast up, the second had taken all the wind out of his sails, and then some. He exhaled a mighty blast of disgust and even I could see that the physical danger was past. Beast simmered back a few steps, Fromholz withdrew his hand from his pocket, and March stepped up to hit his own shot.

The trick had been a marvel, but despite his tactical triumph, March hit his ball deep into the right woods. A minute later, the most unimaginable event of the day happened: Sandy hit his shot and I didn't see where it went. I was too busy watching Roscoe slip a hundred-dollar bill into Fromholz's hand.

"Ride over there and keep March honest, ref," said Roscoe in a pseudo-whisper, which wasn't much under a low roar.

Roscoe knew full well that March was little or no threat on this long par five, so I figured his main intention was to distract Sandy during his swing. But if Sandy had been bothered, he certainly didn't let on. Instead he picked up his bag and started down the fairway without complaint.

Guys whose concentration can't be broken never cease to amaze me. I carried once for Don Cherry, a famous Texas singing golfer who hit the ball sweet despite a lot of attractive requests for autographs and an occasional jealous husband. When I asked him how he avoided distractions, Cherry told me he used to hit practice balls with a lady friend sunning nearby in her birthday suit. Once he got used to that, the rest was easy.

"Jewel darling!" drawled Roscoe as they sat in his cart in the middle of the fairway. "Ol' March there is knee-deep in shit and coffee break's about over. And we know what that means. Back on his head! He ain't never gonna find that ball. Maybe you and I should run off to *Foat* Worth to celebrate."

Tilting his bottle, Roscoe toasted March's lost balls and then waited for March to give up the search. That Dr Pepper had run through me pretty quick, and with Jewel ten feet away I had to excuse myself for the woods. By the time I reached the nearest bushes,

March had found his ball. From my new position I had a good view as he studied his dismal prospects, blocked from the others' view by the same cover I was using, blocked from the green by a row of trees and blocked from a rat's-ass chance of reaching the fairway by all of it.

Since neither March nor Fromholz saw me standing there conducting my business, it was almost like being the proverbial fly on the wall.

"How much did Roscoe give you, Ace?" March asked Fromholz.

"A hundred."

March took out his wallet. "Here's *five* hundred."

"You want me to move it?" asked Fromholz.

"Move it?" says March. "Hell, I want you to hit it!"

March handed Fromholz what looked to be a four-wood.

Alarmed, I turned back to the fairway to see if the others were watching, but they couldn't see a thing; I was the only witness. I didn't even know if Fromholz knew how to play golf. Even for a pro, getting the ball over those trees would have been tough with a wood. Fromholz took a couple of powerful practice swings, free and loose, then stepped up to the ball.

"Fore!" yelled March.

The group in the fairway jerked their heads up in unison, kind of like cows in a field. Jewel had taught me to think in such pictures, but I don't think she'd have been humored to be a part of that one.

Fromholz made a move at the ball exactly like each of his perfect practice swings, and the ball jumped off his open clubface and soared out of sight. I couldn't tell where it went, but when it cleared the trees Sandy started hollering and screaming from the fairway.

"Yeah! Yeah! Great shot, March! Go! Go! Yeah!" Sandy was only about four words away from being speechless.

When you see a golfer with a great swing, it sticks with you forever. To this day I've only seen about a dozen truly great swings, and they belonged to Sandy, maybe to Beast, to a handful of guys out on the Tour (not all of whom have been successful), and to Fromholz. Later on I learned that our ref had shown a lot of golfing promise until he'd been hit square in the eye by a golf ball. I'd hate to be the idiot who hit a ball that destroyed something so fine in a man as tough as Fromholz.

Zipping up my fly, I ran back to the fairway as fast as I could. By the remarks I surmised that March's ball was either on or very near the green; in two shots, putting for eagle. And Roscoe just couldn't imagine how that duffer March could have managed such an incredible shot.

15

I WAS BY NATURE NEITHER A FIGHTER NOR A FINK, FALLING SOME-
where in the middle ground of these dubious childhood achieve-
ments. I'd always made too good of grades to be hip, and I teetered
precariously on the line of being a Goody Two-shoes, but I could
usually be counted on to participate in a little group mayhem as
long as it didn't cause me any physical pain. Most notable among
these escalating instances of delinquency in San Angelo was a
boredom-induced rock fight among a group of my sixth-grade
classmates. I hadn't really wanted to take part, primarily because in
the prebattle negotiations I was appointed captain of the geek team,
which consisted of myself, fat Donny Ratley, and Clyde Eckhardt,
the stutter king.

The three of us were sure to get pulverized, tenderized like a
bad cut of meat. My ego was already injured by not being included
on the team of the genetically cool, but when somebody screams
"Go!" and the rocks start flying, there's not much you can do but
dive for cover, gather an armful of ammunition, and start lobbing a
few long, deadly bombs between the incoming salvos.

One of the reasons I liked golf so much was because the rules were so specific. There ain't no rules in a rock fight. Hopelessly outgunned, my army bruised and battered, and one of my troops crying shamelessly, a ray of hope broke through the clouds. A seventh kid walked up in a lull between volleys, and, unable to comprehend the murderous sincerity of the game, he wanted to play. Even though Larry Seebers wore thick glasses and threw like a girl, an extra body on my side gave us a remote chance of not dying a horrible death before the end of recess. But it was not to be. As I jumped from cover to claim him as ours, I was immediately buried by a barrage of rockwork.

"Larry's on our side!" the other team yelled. "You guys outweigh us!"

It was true. Weight was our only advantage. And never having been on any sporting team with the cool guys, Larry fairly beamed with complicity. My protests were answered with another volley of rocks and I was driven back into my hole. The only thing that kept the game going was that, mad as I was, no one in their right mind was gonna get within thirty feet of my long slingshot arm. Nobody, that is, except a geek in glasses who didn't know the game. Nobody but Larry.

"Here's what you do," his new teammates explained as they handed him his first rock. "Run straight at Billy, screaming as loud as you can. We'll do the rest!"

What a rube this kid was. Not questioning this idiotic directive, Private Larry ran at me, screaming for all he was worth. Just like his throw, he also ran like a girl and screamed like a girl. When he was twenty feet from me, I hopped out of the hole, took aim and hurled a ragged stone straight at his head. Thank God for safety glasses. I cracked the left lens into a dozen sections and he went down as if I'd shot him with a howitzer.

That's about it. When Larry regained consciousness, he staggered to the school nurse, crying all the way. Only one question was asked: "Who threw the rock?"

For me there followed long hours in the principal's office awaiting the eye doctor's verdict on permanent blindness.

"As far as blindness goes," I contemplated telling the principal, "I'm against it."

No, that would never do. Maybe I could raise the money to buy Larry a seeing-eye dog like old man Parker's fat Lab that peed on everyone's leg. Maybe I could donate one of my own eyes. I finally settled on trying to pass for seventeen, joining the Marines, and shipping off to Vietnam as an adviser. Anything, just as long as they didn't make me stay after school for the rest of my life.

In the third grade I'd been unjustly accused of scratching a dirty word onto the wall of the cafeteria. In fact, I'd been playing a childish game of make-believe with a toy car, but the principal didn't fall for the truth and sentenced me to a week of staying after school. I was like a wild animal chained, serving time without end, each tick of the clock like Chinese water torture on my brain.

My transgression was more severe this time and I was now old enough for corporal punishment. For throwing rocks, I got five golf-swing swats from the principal's maple paddle (we called them "licks"). For being a smart-ass ("As far as blindness goes," I told him), I got five more. This from a man who really enjoyed his work. He busted my butt; worse yet, he broke Jewel's heart. She was just down the hall listening to each echoing blow while pretending to teach second graders how to read. Looking back on it, I realize that this was the event that started our move away from San Angelo the following year. Jewel didn't believe in beating children, especially her baby.

I cried softly on five of the swats and howled like a dog on the rest. During the week's enforced vacation that was added on for not telling who else was involved, I played a lot of golf and found that much more enjoyable than sitting on my sore ass.

16

T HAT LYIN' SUMBITCH!" SAID BEAST. "HE'S GOT A LOT OF BALLS TO pull that crap on me."

March's medicine had not set well on the big man's stomach. Not only had Beast's tee shot ended up under an oak tree on number four, but the ball had dropped down so that the trunk of the tree stood between the ball and the spot where Beast should have been standing to make a swing. He could take a left-handed stance and rotate one of his long irons so that the toe of the club pointed straight down at the ground, swing like a southpaw and probably hit it a hundred yards. But hell, March was putting for eagle. Beast had to do more than hack it back into play. He had to pull something out of his hat.

He snatched his one and only fairway wood from out of my hand and began to experiment with various stances: both feet ahead of the tree, both behind it, standing on one foot or the other, and finally bear-hugging the trunk with both arms as if he were humping it. But it was just no use; he couldn't see the ball for the tree.

The best option, at least the one he chose, was to stand with the tree between himself and the green, his body aiming to hit the ball way left, and the face of the three-wood opened to hopefully slice the ball back in the proper direction. He also had to start the ball low to avoid hitting the overhanging oak limbs, *and* he had to stop his follow-through dead or he was likely to carry the club and possibly his hands into the trunk of the tree.

It was cool there in the deep shade, a pleasant spot to watch him consider each of these options as his attention turned step by step from being duped by March to the business at hand.

Taking the club back faster than usual, he tomahawked the ball, carving hard and furious at its upper right corner. Launching out from under the tree like an artillery fusillade, the shot exploded as the clubshaft slammed into the hardwood trunk and snapped cleanly into two pieces.

"Son of a bitch!" Beast screamed as he threw down the short end of the stick. "Son of a bitch never sliced!"

I couldn't believe it. He wasn't cursing about the broken club or the pain that must have vibrated through his hands to his brain. He was pissed off because the ball had failed to do exactly what he wanted, furious because he'd hit it straight when he wanted it to slice.

"Son of a bitch! I should have hit it left-handed!" he said as he stomped off.

The ball's straight flight path had taken it into the woods left of the green—out of bounds. Beast declined to take the penalty stroke and drop another ball beneath the tree, so he was out of the hole— and so was I.

I picked up the two pieces of the three-wood, marveled at the sharp edges of the broken steel, and put them both in the bag.

"Them new shafts break a mite cleaner than the old hickory clubs."

I jerked my head up and saw Roscoe sitting in his cart nearby.

"I used to break a club or two myself, but I got tired of picking them hickory splinters out of my hands so I had to give it up. But like the man said, 'It's better to break one's clubs than to lose one's temper.' "

I had to laugh at that one.

"Now you're laggin' behind, Spud, so quit lollygaggin' around and climb your butt in here."

The passenger's seat was once again empty, Jewel having abandoned Roscoe for a closer look at some wildflowers in the far rough. I thought about telling her to watch for snakes, then remembered that she could handle herself.

"I said haul your butt in here. There's nothing wrong with riding now and then. Hell, I been doing it ever since March blew a hole in my leg."

I looked at him wide-eyed, my face a slow green waiting to be read by an old caddie. I was sure of what he'd said, but unable to believe it.

"Oh yeah, it's true. March was jealous of me and Jewel, so he crippled me with his thirty-ought-six. But never mind that. That's all in the past. Bygones are gone by and all that stuff. Now climb in here and let's have us a chew."

Burying three fingers and a thumb into a pouch of Red Man, Roscoe withdrew a gigantic wad of tobacco and stuffed it into his cud.

"Dig in!" he said, extending the open pouch in my direction.

I looked closer at the jumble of stems and leaves, and the smell about knocked me out of the cart.

"Just pick a cheek and shove it in!" he said. "Jewel tells me you're her blood. I hadn't figgered that. We're gonna be great friends, you and me."

Taking a small pinch, I placed it gingerly into one cheek. It burned like the dickens.

"Hell, boy! We ain't gonna have none of that pussy-style chewing around here. You ain't got enough to taste. Come on! Make like an outfielder: grab yourself a fistful!"

Aw, what the hell! I crammed my right cheek with the stuff and felt an immediate wave of giddiness.

While we drove slowly to the green, Roscoe began to tell me a little story about golf tempers—his own, that is. Shortly after he and March moved Fowler Oil to Austin, Roscoe goes out by himself for a practice round. But he just can't get it together: one shot a hook, the next a slice. Finally he comes to a dreaded par three, a long shot over water. Fearing the worst, Roscoe takes a big cut at it, and damned if he doesn't hit a nice high shot that soars toward the green. But halfway there a friggin' bird dives at the ball; the two collide and both fall dead in the water. He can't believe it. Of all the damned luck!

Somehow Roscoe avoids losing his temper. Instead—very calmly, according to his reckoning—he decides to quit golf forever. This is not a rash decision. He simply knows it's over. Taking all the balls from his bag, he tosses them down and hits them one at a time into the lake, his only aim a tiny island of pampas grass. His target might as well have been Mars, because each shot is worse than the last: a slice, a duck hook, fat, topped, a shank. Each shot fills him with joy because he's one ball closer to the last damn shot he'll ever have to hit.

"The last ball! Hallelujah, just one more crummy shot," Roscoe told me. "So I take a half-assed swing at the ball . . . and it cuts through the air like a bullet, lands dead in the center of the pampas grass—a virtual hole-in-one! Holy moly! I was stunned. It looked just like the pros! Trying to remember exactly how I did it, I start searching like a madman for a ball, any ball—in the thick grass, in the rough, in the bushes—nothing! Finally, I remember where there's plenty of them balls. So I wade into the pond—damn near drown when my boots fill up with water—and find me a couple of golf balls so I can keep playing.

"You can't quit this game, son!" Roscoe concluded. "It's the game that gets to quit you!"

Either the story or the chew was very moving, for at that moment I hopped out of the cart and upchucked in the flowers by the green.

17

THESE GUYS REALLY HAD IT IN FOR THE YOUTH OF AMERICA. FIRST
March offers me a glass of Scotch and a golden opportunity to cor-
rupt my morals, then Roscoe makes a play for my grandmother and
forces a wad of tobacco down my throat. Did they want my help,
my affection, or my soul? Whatever it was, they sure had a funny
way of going about it.

For all I knew, Roscoe's leg could have been the result of childhood polio; I'd seen kids just a few years older than me who had
that same kind of limp. Maybe Roscoe was conning me by blaming
March. Roscoe had a history of that sort of thing, or so March said.
Who was I to believe? Had March entered into a partnership with
all of a valuable ranch and left it with half a worthless one? Or had
Roscoe come into the deal with two good legs and gone out a cripple? The only answer was that neither was to be trusted: they were
both a couple of hustlers.

They used to be partners, not just in the oil business but in golf
as well. While March drove me home after that first round, he told
me that in the early fifties, when their swings were smooth and the
oil business easy, he and Roscoe would travel around Texas laying

the sandbaggers' hustle on unsuspecting country clubbers. On the hunt for some winter prey along the Gulf Coast, they'd been set up by the pro at Corpus Christi Country Club with a Mr. Thompson, an out-of-towner who appeared to be an easy mark.

Thompson didn't look anything like a golfer; instead of slacks and a cap, he wore a suit and a gray fedora. March and Roscoe quickly got him into a hundred-dollar Nassau six ways: a hundred on the front nine, two hundred on the back, and three hundred on the total. And Thompson was going to play against March and Roscoe's best ball. It must have seemed like money from home.

Once the bet was set, Mr. Thompson called over a caddie.

"Run out to the black Cadillac," he told the kid, "and fetch my golf clubs for me."

The kid returned empty-handed.

"Did you want the left-handed clubs or the right-handed ones?" the caddie asked.

Mr. Thompson scratched his neck for a minute while he thought.

"Get some of both," he answered. "I need the practice."

"We knew we were screwed," March said. "But we'd have been damned before we'd turn tail and run. I shot 79, Roscoe shot 80, and the man in the fedora took us for four hundred apiece—driving right-handed, chipping from the south, and putting with a two-iron 'cause the caddie forgot to get a putter out of the trunk.

"After the round we found out Mr. Thompson's first name was Ti, as in Titanic Thompson, the king of the cons; and man, he sunk us but good. He took our money and then we all got drunk in the bar and laughed about it. What a grand old scoundrel he was!"

Later, I asked Roscoe if it was true they once played Titanic Thompson, and Roscoe said it was all gospel except for one thing: "March got it backwards as usual: I shot 79 and *March* shot 80."

18

WHEN MARCH CHIPPED IN FOR AN EAGLE FROM JUST OFF THE fourth green, it no longer mattered that Beast had hit his second shot out of bounds. And Beast could reach the only remaining par five with a driver and a one-iron, so it didn't even matter that he'd broken his three-wood. Nothing mattered except that March bounced his ball into the hole with a little chip shot learned, he said, "from an old Chinaman."

"Well, you can't lose 'em all!" he declared.

"One down with five to go," said Fromholz. "This is getting interesting."

I'd had enough of riding, chewing, and upchucking, so I fell in line with those afoot and started the climb up the hill to the fifth tee. Jewel, siding with the winner again, hopped into March's cart for a ride. Watching this, Roscoe mumbled something that sounded an awful lot like "goddamn her hide," then climbed into his cart and sped off after them.

"This is getting interesting," said Fromholz.

Now that the sun had burned off the morning dew, we began to suffer under the not-too-pleasant delusion of golfing in a gigantic steam bath. None of us was quite to that point in Texas summer golf where the sun starts burning a hole in your eyes, but it was only a matter of an hour or two.

Needing relief, we lined up at the water well next to the fifth tee. I was last. Jewel, of course, was first.

"William March!" she called out. "You cut out that nonsense and have a cool drink before you keel over dead."

March, in hopes of knocking down a fat pear for his lady love, was tossing a golf club up into the limbs of a big fruit tree that shaded the well. But rather than a pear coming down, his club stayed up, lodged in the branches. Attempting to knock it down, he hung a second club with the first. For a while it looked as though he might lose his whole set to the squirrels, but eventually they all rained down—the clubs, that is. He never did dislodge a pear.

"It's a fine day in Texas," he said. "Blue skies. Gulf breezes. Money on the line!" He turned to me. "A momentous event, Billy. A day you aren't ever going to forget. Lots of big things are gonna happen in your life; you'll have kids. I guess before that you'll probably get married. And if you're lucky, before that you might even get laid!"

I blushed a bright red and Jewel came to my defense.

"William March!" she said. "You be nice to that boy or I'll whip you with an ugly stick!"

"Too late for that," Roscoe snickered.

"Okay! I'm nice. I'm nice. See how nice I am?" March cut in front of Fromholz, filled the long-handled tin cup under the stream of well water, and handed it to me.

"Drink up. A man needs ten glasses of that a day in this sun. Enough to make you sweat. Right, Roscoe?"

"Nobody does it better," Roscoe answered, tilting his whiskey bottle for relief and showing us the dark expanding sweat stains that threatened to conquer his entire cowboy shirt.

"Golf is like sex," March said. "You have to take a shower after both."

"I used to think that joke was funny—twenty years ago," said Roscoe.

"It was—then," said March, not the least insulted. "But we got older. And so did the jokes."

"Kid, if it's wisdom you want," Roscoe told me, "I'm your man: never trust a queer or a golfer who wants you to give him strokes."

"Roscoe!" commanded Jewel. "We don't need that kind of talk."

Much to my surprise, Beast came to Jewel's support. "My old man told me to watch out for a guy with a gimp leg who wants to play for money!"

"Amen to that!" said the guy with the gimp leg. "Watch out for ol' Roscoe; I'll jump on you like ugly on ape!"

"My turn," said Fromholz. "Golf advice," he told me, "ain't worth the wind it's written on. You want to enjoy life like a true bohemian? Get yourself a fat girl: warm in the winter and shady in the summer."

"Very educational," Jewel scolded the whole shameless lot of them. "And oh-so-kind: advising this youngster about the trickeries and meanness of life. Well, here's one for all of you: 'I've lived some years on this planet and I have yet to hear the first syllable of valuable advice from my seniors.' Henry David Thoreau."

They all looked at her, dumbfounded. She was always talking that way, quoting some dead guy that you couldn't remember who he was. I was used to it, but those other guys didn't know whether she was coming or going. Still, they were so taken with her radiant charm and generous smile that they'd have put up with rickets, hives, or the quoting of Scripture just to be near her. Men had been barking up her tree for as long as I could remember, scratching on the screen door like cats in heat, but Jewel just fended them off with a glass of sun tea and a sprig of fresh mint.

Some women have the knack of capturing men, and others master the fine art of keeping them at bay. Jewel's tools in these conflicting tasks were charm, mystery, and me, which greatly increased my stock with her suitors. Jewel's beaus were always taking me out for milk shakes and burgers or dropping off a wrist-rocket slingshot, a baseball glove, or even some fancy new putter, all in hopes that I'd put in a good word for them.

Even there on the golf course, my relationship to Jewel was increasing my stock to the point that the golfers were beginning to include me almost as a participant in the game. Being the closest to Jewel made me in some ways the most respected of the group.

"Kid, you seem to know a lot about bag shagging," said Roscoe. "Can you play?"

"Can he play?" answered Sandy. "Heck, yes! I've seen him working out on the range, hitting three, four buckets a day, right?"

"Yeah, I guess."

"You guess? Once you beat that slice, you'll be darn good."

I hadn't known Sandy was such a great believer in me.

"Slice, huh?" said Beast. "You'll never be nothing with no slice. I bet you got one of them long, loose, loop-de-loop back-swings with all the power at the top and no finish. I could cure that in a minute. Answer me this, Skinny: How long is the backswing?"

This had to be a trick question. Nevertheless, I moved my hands from in front of where my belt buckle would have been—if I'd owned a belt—to above and behind my shoulder at the top of my swing.

"That long?" I asked him.

"Just what I figgered. You're all turned around like a dog after his tail."

Beast pulled a club from his bag—only the second time he'd done so all day—and handed it to me. The club felt heavy, but it felt good to grip it like a golfer instead of like a caddie. And it also felt powerful, like I could do no wrong.

"Do it again," he said.

I turned my body and shoulders once more, careful not to take the club back so far.

"Here?"

"Wrong!" He made a little buzzer noise like the ones game shows use when you miss a question. "Wrong, wrong, wrong!"

With everyone watching, this was quickly turning into the most intimidating lesson of my life. Sandy had already helped me with my swing, strengthening my grip and helping me to feel rooted to the ground. He'd also told me about Ben Hogan's "pane of glass" theory concerning swing planes along an axis from the ball through your heart.

"That's the plane the club travels through," Sandy had said. "Actually there's two planes. One going back and a less steep one as you come down to the ball."

That had helped me to get away from my all-arms-no-body swing, but it had, just as Beast guessed, given me a big loop when the clubhead changed direction at the top.

Beast grabbed the club from my hands and set up to hit the ball. "Where's my left shoulder?"

Another trick question. "Right there?"

"Square and level, right?"

I nodded as he took the club to the top of his swing. "Where's my shoulder now?"

"Under your chin."

"Riiiiiight!" He drew the word out over the full length of his takeaway. "So how long is the swing?"

I still didn't know the answer.

"Eight inches—less for a kid. That's the distance the shoulder travels from square to just under your chin. Don't wrap the damn club around you like a vine. Take it back and put it in the slot. Got it?"

"Got it."

I wasn't nearly so sure as I sounded; I just wanted the lesson to be over. But I was not to be so lucky. Advice hung in the air like clothes on a line.

"And don't forget," said Roscoe, taking over the pulpit. "Golf is ninety percent mental, ninety percent skill, and ninety percent luck."

"What's the other thirty percent?" Beast asked in all seriousness.

We did our best not to laugh out loud. Beast was such a good golfer, maybe he didn't need to add past even par.

March had been uncharacteristically quiet through all of this, but he didn't intend to let his archrival get away with being the sage of the group.

"Roscoe," he said, "I always knew you were an unabashed ego-tist, but I didn't know you were also golf's primary authority."

"Hell, I'm so smart you wouldn't believe it."

"You got that right!"

"Screw you!"

"You been doing that for years, every time I turned my back."

These two couldn't carry on a conversation for ten seconds without coming to an argument. It was hard to believe that they'd put up with each other for so long. This time it was Jewel who came to their rescue.

"Don't you want to see if Mr. Larsen's lesson was functional?"

"Lady," said Beast, "what are you talking about?"

"I think it's time you let Billy hit a ball. You can see if he learned anything."

I protested the best I could: I wasn't warmed up and I didn't have my clubs. But Sandy handed me his driver and offered his shoes.

I looked down at his size nines, still sporting two holes with spots of dried blood from Beast's spikes. I already wore a size twelve; Jewel always said I'd have been seven feet tall if there wasn't so much turned under. Hopping on one foot and then the other, I pulled off my tennies and then, embarrassed by the big holes in the toe of each sock, removed them as well. The grass felt good under my feet.

"Barefoot?" asked Roscoe. "You gonna hit it barefoot?"

"In San Angelo they called him the Wild Indian," Jewel told them.

Everybody had a laugh over that one while March teed up a ball for me. The whole thing was like the customers massaging the masseuse. I gripped the club lightly, stepped up to the ball and closed my left eye into its usual concentrated squint. The rest—as with most good golf shots—was a mystery. The next thing I remember the ball was soaring down the middle of the fairway with a slight draw, then bounding over the ridge out of sight, a near-perfect shot.

There followed an open-mouthed silence.

"How's that?" I asked.

After a beat, they all began talking at once.

"How'd you do that?"

"What were you thinking about?"

"How tight was your grip?"

"See, you put it in the slot . . ."

I did my best to feign nonchalance, but I think they knew.

"Heckuva shot, Billy," said March. "That makes me real proud!"

"Yes Sir!" came a new voice in the group. "That was an admirable endeavor you struck upon there, mister."

Turning our heads in unison, we were surprised to see that our group had grown. From out of nowhere, or so it seemed, a mysterious little man—ninety years old if he was a day—had appeared on the tee.

"A very admirable endeavor, indeed."

I supposed he had walked up the path from the fourth green, but we didn't see him till he was right on us. His clothes were different than any I'd ever seen, Scottish or Chinese or somewhere in between, and I think he wore a beekeeper's helmet on top of his head. The flimsy canvas bag on his shoulder held three or four clubs, one an ancient wood with a hickory shaft. He withdrew the wood from the bag and turned to us with a wrinkly smile.

"Morning," he said. "Mind if I play through?"

We all stood there, dumbfounded. Finally Fromholz took charge.

"All yours, Pops! Hit it good."

The old guy teed up a ball with a Texas tee—meaning he scuffed the sole of the club down into the ground, creating a little peak of turf on which to set his ball. The ball itself was rather yellowed and appeared to be of an entirely different make from anything then in use. He took no practice swing, just stepped up to the ball, took it back effortlessly, made flawless contact and a nice finish. Even with his limited power and antique equipment, the ball flew at least two hundred yards.

"How's that one?" he asked Fromholz, mimicking my own query.

"Solid, Pops! Solid!" replied Fromholz.

"Well, it didn't go far," the old man said with a twinkle. "But I can find it!"

Find it? There was a long narrow indentation *exactly* in the center of the fairway where the ground had sunk along the irrigation pipe. The old man's ball had to come to rest in that depression.

"Thank you, young'uns," he concluded, and before any of us could utter so much as a word of reply, he was gone. I felt as if I were in a trance or something. One minute he was there, and the next he was unshouldering his bag down in the fairway.

"Mother, Mary of Jesus!" said Roscoe. "Did you see that? He split the goalpost! First the kid; now the old geezer. Jewel, you wanna hit one?"

19

I HAD NOT YET DISCOVERED THAT THE BASIS OF LIFE IS TO BE afraid, though Jewel already had me reading my Faulkner, so it was there before me as plain as the nose on my face. But I had not seen it and did not yet know that once I truly accepted fear, I would at last be able to ignore it. And so I walked in the timidity of the young: afraid that Jewel would leave me the way my mother had, afraid of Beast's intimidating demeanor, afraid of the bullies in school who twisted your spine to wring out your tears, afraid to hit the ball from the sand for fear of leaving it there, afraid to do what I knew to be right for fear of being wrong.

But as I bent over in the fifth fairway and picked up the ball that I'd hit there by choking down my fear, a burst of pride welled up in me and I saw for the first time that the track was open, the sky was blue and the way was clear. And I was not the only one to see. March pulled up next to me in his cart and looked me in the eye.

"Like I said on the tee, you make me proud, Billy, real proud."

I did not know why, but I blushed.

"You want some gum?" he asked, holding out a package of Juicy Fruit.

When I reached out to take a piece, he touched my hand. We'd never even shaken hands before, but I will never forget that he touched me then. He also unwrapped about three sticks of gum for himself, shoved them all in his mouth, and sped away in the cart.

I swung my sock-stuffed tennies over my shoulder and hustled off on my tough bare feet to catch up with Beast. The ball I'd picked up felt warm in my pocket. That was a lucky ball if I ever saw one. And March had put it on a red tee for me too. I wished I'd kept it. A red tee was considered very lucky, but I'd been so excited at the shot that I'd forgotten to pick it up.

Sometimes I wonder if Jewel ever walked in the timidity of the young. For even though she feared Elisha Judson, she refused to let that fear stand in the way of what she felt she must do. Jewel had learned that if there comes a time when the rules or the beliefs that govern your life can be broken then there must follow a time when you learn to no longer need rebellion. That time must come or you are lost. Back in that fateful summer of 1935, it was a full week before Jewel could get a ride from Del Rio back to Sonora. A full week during which her father locked her in her room as punishment for her post–Wing Ding daylight return, a week during which she came to look upon her night of rebellion with great horror. Jewel realized her moments of debauchery hadn't improved her situation at home, or her life in general. And that is the reason, I suspect, that she eventually told me the rest of her story: so that I wouldn't do what she had done.

Jewel's situation was complicated by her sense of fear and honor: fear that her new beau would come howling like a hyena in heat at her father's back door, and honor that it was her duty to get out of the mess she'd gotten herself into. For there could be no doubt that she was not the least bit in love with Rodney or Roger or whatever his name was.

He'd drawn her a crude map to his well site, and she was determined to go there and tell him that what had happened could never happen again. Telling her father she was visiting friends, Jewel embarked on the hot and miserable bus ride from Del Rio to Sonora. The driver let her off where a bald rubber truck tire hung in a tree to mark the faint sidetrack into rough country. As the bus rumbled away, she picked her way down the packed caliche road, presumably toward the well.

Topping the ridge of a hill, her handbag hanging limply at her side, she halted, wide-eyed with wonder at the noisy clanging of the salvaged and borrowed drilling rig that whip-snaked a rusted cable through a protesting crownblock and down into the violated ground. The crooked drilling tower was lashed and welded together from mismatched timbers and steel scavenged from broken-down tractors and wrecked trucks and stolen from other wells. Cowering beneath it was a wood-fired boiler that was patched and rusted and patched again, hissing and belching like a giant snake about to explode from inhaling too many rats.

It put her in mind of her father, who often preached that oil was the God-given source of fire and brimstone and was used to fuel the furnaces of Hades. If those damned oilmen didn't cease the withdrawal of the oil from the earth, they might cause the fires to go out. In his eyes they were evil, wicked men, extinguishing the all-important threat of eternal damnation.

Two small, dark-skinned Mexican men, who looked in no way evil, were chopping and tossing cedar stumps into the boiler fire. What's-his-name was nowhere in sight, and neither was the dusty red pickup in which she'd made her bed.

"*¿Dónde está Señor Roger?*" she asked the Mexicans, yelling over the noise.

"*¿Cómo?*" they replied.

"*¿Señor Roger? ¿Dónde está?*"

"*¡Lo siento! ¡No hablo Español¡*" one of them answered, flashing pearly teeth studded with a variety of metal and stone fillings.

Having had their joke, they directed her to another man as he stepped clear of the crownblock atop the drilling platform. Spotlessly clean amid the all-pervading grime, he was studying the copper-colored tailings that streamed out of the hole. When his men yelled to him, he turned to see a stunning mirage in a long dress and sun hat. Dropping a heavy wrench on his own toe, he limped and climbed and leapt down to greet her.

Beneath his clean clothes he was tan to the bone and his eyes shone brightly through the sweat that beaded on his forehead. He came over and extended a hand that was hot to her touch. As she shook the hand and looked into his bright, clear eyes she fell instantly and madly in love with him. His name, I know now, was William March.

20

G ET *OWN* UP THERE!" SAID MARCH AS HIS BALL FLEW A HUNDRED
and fifty yards down the fairway and bounded up the slope in front
of the fifth green.

Not that I'd noticed at the time how he pronounced words like
"on." It wasn't until years later, after I'd spent some time out of the
state, that I realized how funny and wonderful we Texans talk. The
lazy combination of two words into one (Sa-nangelo), three words
into two ("Haw yew?") and the even lazier tongue that turns "fine"
into "fahn," all require a more removed perspective before they really come home to roost. It's like eating a chicken-fried steak all
smothered in cream gravy—you really have to miss it awhile before
you begin to 'preciate it properly.

"Fahn-lookin' shot, March!" said Roscoe, outdoing March's accent by a power of five. "Ah bulieve wur both puttin'."

"You are right as rain!" replied March. Their tee shots had been
side by side in the fifth fairway and, incredibly, their second shots
were nearly kissing on the green.

"Hot damn, this is almost fun!" said Roscoe.

"Just like old times," said March. "You know, it's not too late to shake hands, pool our cash, and go someplace godforsaken to drill a well."

Roscoe looked him up and down in amazement. "Sun getting to you, March?"

"Nah! Don't you remember when we stood together and took on all comers, butt to butt against the sunrise and the sunset, so those other bastards always had the glare in their eyes?"

March grabbed the bottle from Roscoe. "Here's to us; to hell with them!"

Then came the most unimaginable occurrence of the day: Roscoe's perpetual frown relaxed for a moment; his squinty eyes opened just wide enough so we could see they were brown; his tight, cracked lips separated a bit; and, ever so slowly, some fond memory came blooming across his face. It almost made you want to smell him; the sheer epiphany of some forgotten adventure long since misplaced in that attic full of mostly rotting memories of their mutual past. It only lasted a few moments, then Roscoe's mind began to wander into darker corners. The blazing rose just shriveled back into the same old grouchy curmudgeon who chewed and spit and scratched his ass, and had long since forgotten that life could be basically good with just a bit of shit thrown in rather than the other way around.

Roscoe snatched the bottle back from March.

"And all I got to do to make us unbeatable again is just stick out my hand and say the word, right?"

"Yeah," said March, extending his open hand. "Why not?"

"Aw hell, March!" said Roscoe. "That's a bunch of crap if I ever heard any! We ain't been friends for thirty years, not since the moment we both set eyes on Miss Jewel Anne Hemphill there. I got her. You wanted her; then you got her. Then she didn't want you anymore and I got her back."

Through all of this talk, Jewel had stood quietly to one side, weaving the wildflowers she had picked into the sun hat which she often carried in her bag. Now she placed the hat on her head and stepped between the two men. "Nobody's got me now," she said.

"That's true enough," said Roscoe. "But March and I aim to change that, don't we, March? And that's why we ain't calling off nothing: a bet's a bet. Play ball!"

It looked like the good part was over, so I hustled along to catch up with Beast. My tennies bounced and swung from my shoulder as I stretched out my strides in the direction of the left rough where my boss was stomping around looking for his ball. Always trying to get that extra edge, Beast had actually tried to drive the green by bounding one down the road that paralleled the fairway. I guess the ball must have taken an asphalt hop in the wrong direction because it was nowhere in sight. But before I could get to him, Beast began raving like a madman.

"Aigghhhhh!" he screamed. It was an awkward shriek, like he hadn't had much opportunity to express fear.

I ran toward him; with each step the big bag bounced off my shoulder and slammed down on my hip, while the flopping tennies kicked me double-time in the back and chest. I tried to find some kind of smooth canter, but both bag and the tennies continued to rattle my bones.

"Yeee-aigghhhh!" hollered Beast again. His screams were improving with practice and had now attracted everyone's attention. March and Roscoe were driving over in their carts, but I was the closest, about twenty feet from him when he finally got out an intelligible word.

"S-s-snake!" he hollered as if it were biting him in his private parts. "S-s-snake!"

Hearing the reference to slithering reptiles stopped me in my tracks. There was no use carrying this Wild Indian thing too far. I unslung my tennies from the bag, and by the time the others arrived, I had the shoes on my feet.

March, Roscoe and I walked up together and, sure enough, we found Beast darn near cornered by a snake—a diamond-back rattler, to be precise. We couldn't tell how long the snake was because it was coiled around Beast's ball as if it were hatching an egg. Beast's behind side was backed up against a barbed-wire fence, and as he moved to get away, the snake pulled back its head in indication of striking at him.

"Somebody kill it," begged Beast. "Please somebody kill it!"

"Ease on out of there, son," advised March. "Nice and slow-like."

"I cain't. My pants are hung on the bob wire. You gotta kill it."

Roscoe strolled closer, nonchalant. "Well, I've seen a snake-milking, a toad-roping, and a duck fart under water," he said. "But I'll be damned if this chicken squawking don't beat all!" He turned back to March like he'd discovered something marvelous. "I think the big man's afraid of snakes!"

"Hell, yes, I'm afraid of snakes!" Beast whimpered. "Somebody kill it."

"Calm down, big guy," said Roscoe. "No reason to panic. You get a free drop, right Fromholz?"

By this time Fromholz, Sandy and even Jewel had arrived to survey the situation. Fromholz stepped in next to Roscoe, about six feet from the snake and just out of striking range.

"A drop? For a rattlebug?" said Fromholz. "Not a chance. A snake is a natural hazard."

"Aw, hell, of course he gets a drop!" argued Roscoe. "You look in that dang rule book! There's gotta be something in there about snakes!"

"Forget the damn drop and kill the snake!" pleaded Beast.

"Hell, no, we won't forget the drop! We ain't counting you out of the hole, pawd-no!" Roscoe turned back to Fromholz. "Ref, this just ain't fair!"

"Maybe not, but that's my ruling," said Fromholz.

"I don't believe this!" said Beast. "I'm about to get eat up by a snake and you guys are arguing *rules*!"

The three of them would have bickered over that rattler till they were blue in the face if one sane voice hadn't risen calmly above the din.

"Give *me* a golf stick."

We all turned slowly to look at Jewel, who was holding out her hand for a weapon.

"Give me a club," she repeated. "I'll kill it."

I was about five years old. Jewel was showing me the ruins of the Mission San Saba, an eighteenth-century Spanish outpost on the San Saba River that lasted a dozen years before the Indians drove the heathen Catholics back to Bejar.

Walking a few feet ahead of her, I was about to climb the stone steps into one of the roofless buildings when Jewel told me to freeze. I'd never heard her speak with such a chill and it frightened me bad. I froze in my tracks and stayed there.

There was a snake, she said, a rattlesnake, coiled just in front of me. I couldn't see it; my eyes were darting all around in search of the snake, but all I could focus on was Jewel's hand edging ever so slowly toward a heavy oak log in the dry leaves. She steadily closed the gap till at long last she had her flattened palm against the log, and then her fingers around it. Just as slowly, that thick timber came up into the air, rising above my head, and exactly as it crashed down from the sky like an instrument of God, I saw the snake, coiled on a little stone ledge not eighteen inches from my face with its cold eyes fixed on mine. The snake struck forward and a hand's width from my eyes, the log came down squarely on its head. I jumped back, and Jewel screamed as she pounded that snake's head over and over and over until it almost became a part of the stone path.

"You son of a bitch!" Jewel screamed through her tears as she continued to swing the log. "You son of a bitch! You leave my baby alone!"

She just kept pounding and screaming and crying until finally I had to wrap my arms around her leg and tell her the snake was dead.

"Jewel!" warned Roscoe. "You stay back!"

"Yeah," said Beast. "Skinny, you kill it."

"Billy?" said Fromholz in disgust. "Why, you pantywaist!"

Having heard all he cared to hear, Fromholz reached into the pocket of his jacket—actually I think he reached right *through* the pocket of the jacket. From somewhere beneath it he withdrew a large six-shooting pistola and nonchalantly blasted that snake's head off with one loud, terrifying shot. Then with a second shot he blew off its rattle. We all jumped when the gun went off, but none higher than Beast who leapt straight into the air, tearing his pants on the fence.

"Souvenir for you, kid," said Fromholz, pointing to the still-quivering rattle.

I picked it up gently. The rattle twitched on my palm as I counted the sections—eleven of them—one for each skin the snake had shed during its life. I collected stuff like that: little things that meant something to me. They were all at home in an old wooden cigar box with a warped top that wouldn't close: arrowheads and flint scrapers, old-timey marbles made of clay, two stamps from Tanzania showing gigantic white birds in flight, and even a harmonica with *Herb Shriner's Harmonicats* engraved on it. But this rattle was the best of all.

"Six-iron always was my best club," said Fromholz, putting the pistol away as quickly as he'd produced it.

"Damn! I ripped my pants!" complained Beast.

"That ain't so bad," answered Roscoe. "We thought you was going to wet 'em! Now have a shot."

The others backed away from the messy snake while I selected a seven-iron and handed it to Beast. He didn't even look to see what club it was. As he addressed the ball, I could see his hands quivering like the snake's rattle. After a long time of just standing there, he backed away and called to Roscoe.

"What the hell is that guy doing with a gun?" he whispered in a shrill voice.

"Protecting you, evidently. What's the problem?" said Roscoe.

"He's not protecting me!" said Beast in a panic. "He's here to get me. I owe Binion a lot of money. If we lose, that guy's gonna kill me, ain't he?"

Roscoe didn't answer.

"Ain't he?" repeated Beast. "Ain't he gonna kill me if we lose?"

Roscoe pursed his lips together and rubbed his tongue around the inside of his mouth. Either he'd lost his chew or he was searching for something to say. Finally it came to him.

"Don't lose."

21

WHEN THE MONEY'S ON THE LINE, GOLF BECOMES LIKE POKER: you can play to win or you can play to not lose. Or, if you don't have any real idea what the difference is, you can do what most golfers *and* poker players do: play to lose. They don't know that's what they're doing, but the loss is just as inevitable as if they had drawn four cards to a deuce kicker or used a putter off the tee.

Shortly after buying that first five-iron at Santa Fe Park, I learned that golf is much harder than it looks. So after a lot of frustration and a good deal of pleading, Jewel finally enrolled me in a junior golf class.

I was by far the youngest student in the class. The course covered everything from driving to irons, chipping to putting, and even included a little lecture about common courtesy. It was complete in every way except one: the coach hardly touched on the rules. Oh sure, they told us about a number of penalties: stroke and distance for out of bounds, two strokes for hitting the pin when putting, and a whole variety of strokes for encountering water, lateral or otherwise. All examples of how the rules worked against us, but nothing about how the rules might work *for* us. They told us what to do if you lost a ball, but they never told us anything about what to do if you found a ball, but couldn't figure out how to hit it. And on the very first hole of the class graduation tournament, that was exactly what my drive rolled into: an unplayable lie.

It was Bermuda grass, about eighteen inches deep. For most kids the ball would have been lost, but I knew it was in there. My eyes did not deceive. And when I found it nestled at the bottom of that jungle, I knew right away that I could never hit it out. But I'd never heard of an unplayable lie, that I could just take a one-stroke penalty and drop the ball out within two club lengths. I pulled out a seven-iron—having already graduated to a larger mismatched set of clubs—and I began to whale away.

Two, three, four; hit it some more. Five and six; change sticks. Seven, eight, nine; let out a little whine. Ten, eleven; bad-mouth heaven.

By fifteen the ball still hadn't moved, but I was digging a nice tunnel toward it. How high can an eight-year-old count anyway?

I got the ball out of that patch of grass on the twenty-second stroke. Then a kid who was a couple of years older than me came over laughing and told me I could have dropped it out with one penalty stroke. I stood on my tiptoes and punched him in the nose.

My final score was one hundred and thirty-eight, for which they gave me a trophy in the shape of a boxer for fighting the course (not to mention the other golfers). Just like Sandy's consolation trophy when Beast was disqualified for gambling, I refused to accept it. A trophy is for the winner. The awfully adult lesson I learned is that it's often not that important if you win, only that you don't finish last.

My third-grade pals and I used to tell a riddle about a two-man Olympic race won by an American (of course) and lost by a Russ-

ian. The headline in Russia read: RUSSIAN SECOND. AMERICAN NEXT
TO LAST.

Unfortunately, Sandy and March still seemed more likely to come
in second than next to last. After Roscoe's admonition about not
losing, Beast hit his shot from next to a headless-but-still-squirming
snake to the front of the fifth green. I tended the pin while he
stalked the putt for the kill. He studied it from all sides, plumb-
bobbing it from back and front, then bent over it with the usual
cigarette dangling from his mouth.

"Don't be short," warned Roscoe as Beast was about to putt.
Beast tilted his head menacingly in Roscoe's direction, then looked
back down at the ball and stroked it hard up the slope.

I was surprised how fast it was coming at me. Hurriedly I pulled
on the pin. Nothing happened. Confused, I pulled again: still nothing. The pin was stuck in the cup.

"Pull it!" yelled Beast.

I pulled harder. Nothing.

"Pull it!" hollered Beast and Roscoe.

At the last second I yanked hard, dragging both pin and metal
cup up out of the hole. It happened so fast I didn't even know I'd
done it. The ball barreled straight at what should have been a hole,
struck the raised cup, and bounced about three feet away.

With the pin and cup still in my hand, I looked up in horror and
saw Beast charging at me. His putter was cocked back behind his
head like a baseball bat, and a scream of rage was issuing from his
mouth. It didn't occur to me to run. After all, I was guilty. I had
pulled the cup up. I had kept him from winning the same hole on
which he'd nearly been killed by a snake. Whatever he did to me—

and it looked as if he was going to lop my head off—was certainly my due.

About ten feet of the charge and two seconds of my life remained when Fromholz stuck out a foot at the same time that he cuffed Beast on the back of the neck with the six-shooter. An elephant gun wouldn't have brought the big man down any faster.

While Beast was coming to his senses, Fromholz proceeded to investigate the stuck pin and quickly discovered that someone had put chewing gum in the bottom of the cup. Chewing gum? I quickly swallowed mine and glanced over to March. He no longer seemed to be chewing his, either.

That's twice, I thought. That's twice he cheated.

Beast was learning some hard lessons. His three-wood was broken, his pants were torn, and there was a knot on his head about the size of one of the smaller British golf balls. On top of that, the putt was not considered good.

Fromholz kindly waived the penalty for striking the pin with a putt from on the green because, technically, the ball had struck the cup. But the ball was not in the hole and the birdie had flown the coop. With Fromholz's help I separated the pin from the cup, and replaced the latter in its hole so the others could putt. But still no birdie putts went in, and number five was halved by pars from both teams.

"No blood," said Fromholz. "Well, not much anyways. Four holes to go, gentlemen. Fowler and Larsen are still one up."

"Not for long," said March with a grin. "Not for long."

22

THE BUMP ON HIS NOGGIN WAS SUFFICIENT TO DETER BEAST FROM beheading me, but it didn't keep him from methodically yanking open each of the ten or twelve zippers on his bag, turning it upside down, and dumping the clubs, balls, tees, cigarettes, matches, and miscellaneous junk in a pile on the fringe of the green.

"Pick 'em up!" he ordered; then stomped off cursing. "What the hell kind of crummy course is this? Bunch of damn cheap greens!"

I gathered up the mess, trying to remember whether the extra shoe spikes went in the pocket with the tees, and if the divot-repair and club-cleaning tools had a place of their own. At the same time I was feeling guilty for what I'd done, and inwardly, I guess, I was blaming March, who must have been the cause of it all.

Twice now he'd cheated, and that was only what I knew about. Who knew, maybe March had put that snake by Beast's ball. And even if that theory was a little far-fetched, I also suspected that he had something to do with the weird cutting of the greens, which continued to be alternately slow and fast.

And then I noticed that March was standing there by my side. Whether he'd come to apologize, bribe me, or beg my forgiveness, I didn't know. He removed his hat—a straw version of LBJ's Open Road Stetson—and wiped the sweat from his brow. I realized that now was the time to come clean and confront him. But as I opened my mouth to speak, his words came first.

"Found something you might take an interest in, young'un."

He held out his closed hand and unwrapped his leathery fingers to reveal an ugly rock just a little smaller than a golf ball. It was a burnt reddish-brown color and it appeared to be both exploded like a kernel of popcorn and melted around the edges.

"Take it."

He dropped the rock in my hand in the same manner as the stick of gum. I was astonished at its weight. It seemed more like lead than a rock.

"I figgered a guy that keeps a snake rattle in his pocket needs some good ju-ju to go with it. And that's what you got there: ju-ju, magic, good vibes, as Fromholz would say."

I didn't know what he was talking about.

"It's a meteorite," he told me. "A moon rock. I found it back there in the rough. Must've been a giant meteor hit here hundreds of years ago. We're probably standing in the crater."

I looked around at the large bowl depression surrounding us and the green.

"Yeah?"

"Moon rocks are magic, you know. You hold 'em tight in your hand and concentrate heart and soul on what you want."

He had to be pulling my leg.

"You mean I wish for a Frito pie or to get out of doing my homework?" I asked him skeptically.

"No! That ain't it at all! Nothing selfish. Moon rocks are very perceptive. They know the difference between a grabby little piss-ant and someone in true need. You think magic is about a Frito pie, son? No, sir! Magic is the most basic form of nature. You wanna learn something in life, you hang on to that moon rock and you think for a while about what it takes to make a miracle."

I looked down at the heavy pellet in my hand. A major interest in seventh-grade science told me it had probably been snatched from a passing asteroid cloud by the earth's gravity. Most likely it was comprised primarily of nickel and iron that had been melted when speeding through our atmosphere. Once on earth it had re-mained undisturbed until March found it and handed it to me with this far-fetched tale that only a kid would believe. And yet I did be-lieve it. I believed it because he'd given me something special, be-cause I was a kid who wanted to believe. Because he'd made it magic. My magic.

March patted me on the head and left me to finish my cleanup. It wasn't till I put the rock in my pocket that I realized I'd forgotten to confront him about cheating.

Beast's bag finally reassembled, I caught up with Jewel and we walked up to the sixth tee. She saw the worried look on my face and told me not to feel bad about yanking up the cup.

"If one person was cheating," I asked her, "and another person knew it, should he rat on them? I mean, are you cheating too if you know about it and you don't tell? Or are you just a snitch if you do tell?"

"Hypothetically?" Jewel asked me.

"Oh, yes ma'am!" I told her. "Hypothetically. Definitely."

We walked on a ways to the shade beneath a large cluster of live oaks, our feet rustling through the small brown leaves of years past. In the top of the trees two cicadas buzzed back and forth to each other.

"No. I don't think you should tell," she said. "Hypothetically or otherwise."

"Why not?"

She didn't answer at first, so I gathered my courage and took the plunge into the great unknown.

"Just because March is my grandfather?" I asked her.

I shifted the bag higher onto my shoulder and the cicadas grew silent.

"No. Not because of that."

I bit softly on my lip. Here was final confirmation of what I had suspected since Jewel first sent me to caddie for him weeks ago.

"Not just because March is your grandfather, but also because I'm in love with him. Because I've always been in love with him. And because he needs to win. You're asking about something being right and something being wrong, Billy. Well you look in those two men's eyes, then you tell me who is right and who is wrong."

23

AFTER ALL THIS TIME, IT'S HARD FOR ME TO SEPARATE WHAT I knew then about Jewel's early time with March and Roscoe from what I learned in the time that followed that amazing day. During my junior and senior high school years, Jewel would sometimes get a faraway look in her eyes, and the corners of her mouth would crawl slowly upward. I knew that meant she was going to tell me about some picnic with March on the Dry Devil's River, or of the letters she'd written that he'd never answered. The odd part was that she never seemed bitter to have lost those thirty years with the man she fell in love with that day at the well.

Since Jewel had come all the way from Del Rio with the honorable intention of letting Roscoe down easy, she managed to convince herself that suddenly falling in love with March was not a problem. Roscoe had been off fetching the mail and supplies when she arrived, so she didn't actually have the opportunity to tell him the original purpose of her visit. Surely the right time and place would present itself, she thought. Unfortunately, the right time and place never arrived.

March and Jewel became fast friends and soon-to-be lovers. Because of what had already transpired between Jewel and Roscoe, neither of them was immediately eager to take the ultimate step of intimacy. A true courtship ensued. Traveling to Del Rio as often as he could get away from the well, March would formally request the honor of Jewel's company from her father the preacher. That Elisha Judson would grant this permission indicates just what a smooth talker March must have been.

There being little or no nightlife in Del Rio, March and Jewel would head across the river for dinner and dancing in the festive town of Villa Acuña, Mexico. Their favorite place was Ma Crosby's, where they ate fried catfish fresh from the Rio Grande, washing it down with ice-cold Carta Blancas drunk from small, often-refilled glasses barely four inches high. The idea was that the beer go down fast and cold and easy.

There were *cantadas* and *bailles* under the stars in the main plaza and numerous *bandidos* of Pancho Villa's former employ singing ballads and telling heroic tales of the Mexican Revolution. To appease Roscoe—and because he was more fun back then than later in his life—they sometimes invited him to come along.

Jewel gave little thought to Roscoe's feelings in all this. It wasn't as though he had been in love with her, or as if they'd spent five sober minutes together. But March knew better. He'd seen another side of Roscoe and he knew that it was only a matter of time before his partner's jealousy erupted in a violent rage, much like the well they were still hoping to bring in any day.

After two months of this uncomfortable situation, March left one night without telling Roscoe. Driving down to Del Rio in the very same truck in which Jewel had forever misplaced her virginity, March found Jewel waiting for him across the street from her father's Victorian mansion.

They drove slowly over the rickety bridge that barely spanned the muddy Rio Grande, and waved at a new friend who guarded the international border from a comfortable seated position, leaning way back on two legs of his chair. After convincing a local merchant to reopen her dress shop, they strolled arm in arm to Villa Acuña's main cathedral. There—in the presence of a priest, a nun and a half-wit—they were married.

"For long as you both should live," pronounced the priest in his broken English.

It was the first time either of them had been in a Catholic church.

Their honeymoon took them all the way back to Sonora, where they spread a blanket beneath the brilliant night sky on a point of land that would in three years become the ninth tee of a strange new sporting field, but which that night was a vantage point to a whole new universe.

Imagining them when they were young, it was easy for me to picture how March and Jewel would have lain together, would have rolled and tossed among the thick woolen blankets, Jewel grasping at tightened muscles, and March with fistfuls of hair, both sighing at the joy and wincing at the pain of being in love. Neither would have the slightest idea that the son of the daughter they begot that night would only be able to compare their tryst with a night he spent forty years later atop a building in Paris with a girl who knew just three words of English.

The red wine and baguettes that kept that beautiful French girl and myself going till dawn tasted to me like the warm beer and cold tacos that March and Jewel bought from a vendor in Mexico and carried to their wedding supper on the hill. My gaze wandered over the city of lights and I thought of the meteor shower Jewel told me they saw that night. The honking of Parisian horns became the hooting of owls, and whatever type of creatures were scurrying about, be they rats or cats, were to me a kit of young foxes come to bask in the glory of the night, to roll and tumble together in scratching, nipping, biting yelps of pain and innocence.

As we awakened with the coming dawn, perhaps like March before me, I wondered if that wondrous girl and I had conceived a child. To this day I wonder still, because I never saw her again.

24

THERE WAS A LITTLE OUTHOUSE IN THE MIDDLE OF THE GOLF course, and from the sixth tee we could all hear Beast in there exercising his temper and his golf shoes on the sheet-metal walls and wooden throne.

"Whooo-eee!" said Roscoe. "Glad he's not mad at me!"

Sandy was swinging his driver to stay loose, and Fromholz just sat still and watched us all, buzzardlike, from his perch on the stump of an old rotted fruit tree. If someone were to fall over dead, I thought, it wouldn't take him long to hop over and peck out one of our eyes to match his own.

Jewel and March stood close to each other at one side of the tee. Jewel was speaking softly to him. I couldn't hear her words, but March's sad blue eyes were staring in my direction all the while.

When she'd had her say, March came walking over toward me. Again he held out his closed hand as if to give me something, but when he uncurled the fingers, there was no chewing gum or moon rock. This time there was only an open hand reaching out to me. It was my turn to put something in his hand. I extended my arm and opened my clenched fingers slowly and we shook hands until a tear appeared in the corner of March's eye.

"Jewel tells me you're a good boy," he said.

"She thinks so."

"Well, Jewel's an excellent judge of character," he said. "Except in Roscoe's case . . . and mine. I guess there's no denying that I let her down sadly. I hope that hasn't cursed me forever. I'm not a bad guy. I've always tried to get some enjoyment out of life. I try to take care of my business and my friends. Now I'm trying to take care of my family."

I gave him a weak smile.

"I feel bad when I make the wrong decisions," he continued. "And I forget to notice when I make the right ones. I don't hit a guy when he's down. And I'm just beginning to learn that when somebody knocks me down, I'm gonna get right back up again. I been down on my knees a long time, but never again. However long I got left, I'd like to spend it with my head held high. I'd like for you to be proud of me. I'd like for the two of us to be friends. And I wish I had a little more time. There's a lot of places and things I'd like to show you."

"I'd like to see 'em all," I told him, fighting back a tear of my own.

"Someday, everything I own'll belong to you. My daddy's ranch will be your ranch, my golf course yours too. It's a beautiful land. My heart left with Jewel, but my soul is out there on that unforgiving land."

The *Llano Estacado*—"staked plains" it means in Spanish. Supposedly the conquistadors marked their way across the Indian country with stakes so as to find their way back to the gulf, laden with the gold of seven cities. But secretly they expected death at every turn, and believed that their souls—lost angels—would need the stakes to guide them back to a civilized afterlife. Then, as they traveled farther into the country, their actions grew more and more barbarous and they thought less and less of becoming angels.

From the estuaries and intercoastal tide pools of the gulf, there's no way to tell just how God-almighty big or how unbelievably dry this land can be. The early settlers, from the Spanish all the way through March's Irish ancestors, entered this vast scape through the mouths of its rivers—rivers that run neither wide like the Mississippi nor deep like the Columbia.

Instead, numerous small rivers meander back through the sunken coastal plains to their time-eroded cuts of the elevated Balcones Fault and beyond into the hostile canyons, draws, and creeks where ancient man made his home. That habitation of thousands of years is still given witness by stacked-rock burial mounds, spent or discarded tools of work and war, and limestone cliffs painted in the glyphs of their written language.

If, like the original inhabitants, you continue to follow the water to its source, you'll eventually find a limestone crevice, grown all around in ferns and sweet watercress, with a freshet of cold spring water gushing out, gathering with other trickles and founts and warming slowly as it heads to the sea. But if you follow the riverbeds farther inland, beyond the springs, you'll find the isolated pools that remain from the last rain and river rise; the catfish trapped in ever-dwindling puddles as they flounder in panic until raccoons or bobcats feast on their flesh and drink the last of the water. Only bleached skeletons remain on the baked and cracked soil which cries out for rain farther upstream.

And still the canyons continue on, past any signs of water but their own eroded existence, cutting into country that survives by hoarding more, by needing less. The prickly pear cactus, fat even through the drought until the cattle or the buffalo, dying for water, eat them thorns and all. The mesquite trees, with tiny leaves catching little of the hot sun and providing minimal shade; the thin-bladed grass growing lush in the violent spring storms and waiting patiently, brown but standing tall, through the passing of the other seasons. The wildflowers springing forth in brilliant rainbows after the storm, then burning brown till their seedpods explode, scattering future life to the southwest winds. The snakes, the lizards, and the horny toads, all living as can on gathered dew and, like the larger animals, keeping one eye cocked to the sky and one ear to the ground for the hopeful sound of distant thunder.

And then there is man, greediest of consumers: grudgingly adapting through conservation, then lowered expectations, and lastly by insanity. Postponing the inevitable by digging wells or drilling, by constructing dams to hoard in times of plenty, by defending their impoundments against the downstream thirsty with ancient yellowed papers, bribes, or guns. By hiring charlatans: white-whiskered old men, crazy Indians, fireworks experts, aviators, scientists, and quacks of all denomination; each promising to make it rain, each coming on the happy rumor of success and leaving on the sad fact of failure, so all that continues unchanged is the vastness of the land and the smallness of man; never conquering but sometimes adapting; looking alternately reddened and browned, increasingly cracked and tanned like a discarded hide, becoming in apparition more and more like an organ or appendage of the living land; and ending up as dust, blowing on the hot breeze, sighing contentedly at the sound of soothing thunder, waiting like all the land for the rain to come, waiting to be washed back to the distant sea.

These were all things I learned and confirmed in the years after I met William March, but I first saw them in his lined eyes and felt them in his calloused hand as it dawned upon me that, if Jewel had become my mother, then he had become what I had never had, and always wanted, a father.

March and I sat down on the grassy slope next to the sixth tee, leaned back on our elbows, and looked up at the sky. The wind had begun to blow hot like a furnace, a sure sign that summer was here to stay. The sun blazed down, an ill-defined orb suspended in a perfect pale-blue bowl that had been inverted dead center on top of our group. How curious that no matter where you stand on earth, your single-point perspective testifies that you are the center of the universe.

I started to speak. I wanted to ask him what was going to happen to us, but March shushed me into quiet attention. After a short silence I began to hear what he heard: bees searching out a blossom, a woodpecker hard at work, the wind rustling the cedars that lined the course, and way off in the distance, a truck whining up a big hill on the Llano highway, then shifting into a lower gear.

A funny bird with two long, skinny tail feathers flapped and glided over our heads, then flapped and glided again. Dipping and twisting his auburn-colored tail feathers gracefully like a rudder, the bird steered itself away from our upturned gaze.

"Scissortail!" said March softly. "That's my favorite bird!"

I thought he'd said the same thing about a mockingbird that had pestered the group earlier, and I imagined that he probably said it about all of them.

"You got a girlfriend at that new school of yours?" he asked.

"No Sir," I lied.

"Well, treat her good, son. You won't regret it."

25

WHEN WE MOVED FROM SAN ANGELO, JEWEL HAD JUST SENT HER twenty-third class of students on to the third grade, and I had moved to the eighth. Since I'd started school a year younger than the other kids of my grade, I'd long lagged behind my pals in ability at contact sports and interest in girls, so I really hadn't bothered with either.

When we arrived in Austin I discovered, to my absolute horror, that school was still in session. Jewel, always the teacher, insisted that I finish out the term in my new school, essentially graduating from the seventh grade all over again.

"Haven't you heard of double indemnity?" I asked her.

But Jewel's natural wisdom was at work in its usual wondrous way. Rather than spending a friendless summer in a new town, I had a little time to get acquainted. And my best consolation turned out to be that the end-of-school dance had not yet been held. Much to my surprise, I was asked by a girl to be her date. She was completing the ninth grade but she invited me to be her escort because, unlike the boys her age, we saw eye-to-eye. After all, I was descended from Adoniram, Lord of Height.

Jewel drove us to the dance while I nervously tried to pin a gigantic corsage to a slender shoulder strap on my date's dress— about as humiliating an experience as a young teen is gonna find.

The similarities to Jewel's Wing Ding were few. The kids were seventh-to-ninth graders, and the copy band played 1965's rock-n-roll favorites, including what seemed like an awful lot of slow tunes, during each of which my date held me closer and tighter while my body temperature rose about five degrees per song.

The funny thing is I don't even remember her name. But I'll never forget that while we danced close—cheek to cheek, pelvis to pelvis—every time her hip swayed out to the right it gave a little bouncing pop as it shifted in the other direction.

Curious to discover whether this was some sexual secret about which I knew nothing or whether she merely had an artificial hip in need of lubrication, I just kept pushing her hip out there with my own. I pushed and we swayed and my date popped in time to the music until, soaked to the skin, I danced us over to the refreshment table. We drank three quick, cold glasses of punch, not knowing that it had been spiked by some smart aleck with 180-proof Ever-clear. Outside the gym we gleefully and groggily leaned against each other face-to-face. Our lips touched and she so completely surprised me when she slipped her tongue into my mouth that I must've jumped three feet into the air.

When summer was over she'd be moving up to high school where all the boys were tall. So I knew I only had three months to figure out some way to make it happen again. As it turned out, March's advice to treat her good was perhaps the single greatest pearl of wisdom I would ever be given.

· · ·

"Are you gonna marry Jewel?" I asked March.

"Far as I know, we are married," he told me. "It's been a long time, but I haven't heard any mention of divorce."

"I mean, are you gonna live with her like you were married?"

March laughed. "I don't rightly know, son. I been single most of my life, just staying out late and hanging around with my bad habits. Fear and whiskey kept me going. I haven't run out of whiskey yet, but I about used up my ration of fear. What I'm trying to say is, it's up to Jewel. And you, of course. It's up to you and Jewel."

He gave me a smile and I smiled right back at him. The bees were still humming sweetly and I laid back on the cool grass and closed my eyes for a few seconds to think about how my new life was going to be: French-kissing with older girls, going fishing with my dad March, and playing golf with Sandy until it was too dark to find your ball.

The next thing I remember a shadow came across the face of the sun. I opened my sleepy eyes and blinked up at a gigantic figure.

"Skinny, get up off your bony ass and hand me my driver!"

I scrambled to my feet, noticing that March was already back at his cart.

"Billy!" I said to Beast. "My name is *Billy!*"

While I had napped, Sandy had evidently stayed loose by swinging his driver to and fro. I looked into his blue eyes and saw that he'd found some kind of electric golf groove. It was funny about Sandy's eyes. They changed color with the sky and his emotions; clear blue now, where earlier they had been hazy and gray with the morning overcast. At night they deepened to a dark royal blue, and if you sneaked a close enough look, you could almost see the stars in the little flecks of his irises. In San Angelo he once hit his number ten tee shot into the murky South Concho River. I'd never seen him lose his temper and I felt sure this would be the time, but it only affected his eyes, which assumed the musty hazel color of the water until we left the hole and the river well behind with an eagle on the par-five eleventh.

Along with his fair-haired fraternity-boy good looks, those mysterious eyes made Sandy a bull's-eye target for women wherever he went. But he didn't even seem to notice how their heads turned slowly to follow after him or how they got that distant, dreamy look in their own eyes when he came close. Like a lot of good golfers, Sandy was just a big kid who found a game he didn't have to give up and who never really wanted to grow up at all. The two of us played miniature golf with our dinner once—peas for balls and carrot sticks for clubs; I nearly beat him too.

Now Sandy's blue eyes were flashing. He'd seen Beast lose his temper and he sensed that opportunity was at hand. With a giant, arcing swing of the driver just in front of Beast's nose, Sandy issued a challenge.

"Come on, Larsen. Let's see what you got." He swung the club again, harder this time. "How 'bout a little game of chicken?"

Beast cracked his knuckles loudly.

"You're on, weenie!"

I didn't even know what they were talking about.

Sandy stuck a tee into the ground between them and they both stepped into a wide-anchored version of their golf stances, facing each other about six feet apart. They waggled their clubheads and set them face-to-face on opposite sides of the tiny wooden tee, golfers and clubheads both staring at each other intently.

Finally I figured it out. It was like playing chicken with cars, where two idiots drive straight at each other and whoever turns off first is the chicken. Only the golf clubs would be moving a lot faster than speeding cars. This seemed like an exceedingly stupid thing to do. I ducked down behind Beast's bag and peeked around for a look. Everybody else, including Jewel, stepped *way* back.

They both took a little warm-up; feeble swings about like wedge shots. The clubheads passed by each other safely, but it still looked plenty scary to me.

"You ready?" asked Beast with a wicked grin.

"Let's do it," answered Sandy.

Just as they started to swing, Roscoe interrupted: "A hundred on the Beast."

"Covered," said March.

Fromholz took the money from each of them, and now that he'd been made the ref in this contest as well, he stepped forward to insure that everything was in order.

"Don't kill yourselves off," Fromholz told them before scampering safely away.

Working up their nerves again, both took their clubheads back. With no worries as to where a ball might go and their only concern whether or not to chicken out, they were free to swing as hard as they wanted or were able. That's exactly what they did: two huge, powerful, simultaneous swats.

Neither chickened out. Instead both screamed mightily as the clubheads met head-to-head in an incredible explosion of wood and steel. Splinters of persimmon and hot metal shards flew in all directions. Sandy bent over with a groan while Beast merely grimaced, his hands vibrating like church bells.

"Well, I'd have to rule that a draw," said Fromholz. "How about two out of three?"

Neither of them seemed so inclined (or had another driver), so Roscoe snatched his money back.

"Don't worry about it, partner," he said to Beast. "Some days you eat the chicken; some days you eat the feathers."

Smelling something like burnt flesh, I looked down at Beast's bag and found two finger-size holes where flying hot metal from one of their shafts had torn through the leather.

Sandy still had ahold of his grip, with most of the shaft attached, but the head of his driver was no more; it had completely disintegrated. He spiked the shaft into the ground and shook off his pain the way basketball coaches told you to after you'd broken a couple of fingers or had your nose flattened. Then he took out his three-wood and hit a great shot up the fairway of the long par five.

"Oh! That's how you do it!" complimented March. Then he teed one up, swung easy, and hit his straight down the middle as well.

Beast stuck his big paw in my face. "Gimme my three-wood," he growled.

I hesitated, not sure I'd heard him right.

"Gimme my goddamn three-wood! Are you deaf?"

Taking out the two pieces of his three-wood that he'd smashed against the tree on number four, I held them out to him. He looked at the pieces like they were from Mars. I guess between the snake in the grass and the cup popping out of the ground, he'd forgotten all about breaking his fairway wood. A wave of understanding swept his face as he realized what Sandy's game of chicken had really been about.

"I'll beat you with a one-iron, smart-ass," Beast said to Sandy. But I got the feeling he didn't believe it.

26

I HAD A HARD TIME KEEPING MY MIND ON THE JOB AT HAND AS WE walked up the sixth fairway, climbing a long, slow hill like all the holes on the course. It's hard to figure how, but somebody built that course so you'd always be walking uphill. It felt like we'd end up about a mile higher than we started, but I didn't give a hoot 'cause I was just about tickled pink with the way things were turning out.

I believed then that a golf course was some sort of magic spot. The only places I'd ever been happy were sitting down at Jewel's dinner table or walking on the golf course. Seemed like everywhere else I went, either some kid was bragging about the neat stuff he'd been doing with his dad, or people were talking about something shitty that had happened. To me it sounded like there must be a lot of crummy goings on, and I had begun to suspect that the world was not as nice a place as everyone would have a kid believe.

From what they told me, Texas was supposed to be just about the greatest place on earth, but that hadn't kept Jewel from being lonely—sometimes I used to hear her crying softly in the night—and it hadn't even kept my mother Martha from going to some other place where she didn't have to think about me or any of her other troubles—and she always had plenty. Seemed to me like no one ever had enough rain or money or good times, but there was always plenty of trouble—trouble at school, trouble at home, trouble with a bunch of nosy neighbors who were having trouble with the bill collectors who were having trouble with their wives and girlfriends who were all having trouble finding a good hairdresser or a Mexican housekeeper to do their dirty work for them.

I didn't understand why, if Texas was such a great place, all the Mexicans had to live in such crummy houses in neighborhoods that really were on the other side of the railroad tracks. Everybody called it Mezkin town. There weren't any paved streets or sewer lines, so when it rained the whole place just turned into a mud hole, and if it rained enough it turned into a shit hole. Then everybody on this side of the tracks would start complaining about the gawdawful smell coming from Mezkin town and how can them people live like that?

About the only answer anybody ever had for that question was that "those people wouldn't live any other way if they could." That was just the way they were. Hell, if you put in a bunch of paved driveways and fancy toilets, they'd still go right on parking their cars in the grass and doing their business in the bushes or the outhouse, at least that's what folks said. Besides, if you gave 'em an inch, they'd start wanting to live in the regular neighborhoods and send their kids to the regular schools where they wouldn't know how to speak no English and they'd just cause a bunch of trouble anyway. And the last thing anybody needed was any more damn trouble!

That was what I could never figure. If the world was such a fine place to live—especially our corner of the world—then how come everybody had so darn much trouble in mind?

Now all of a sudden I was looking at the other side of the coin. Everything that had been tails was about to come up heads. Beast was licked; you could tell it by the way he talked. Before when he bragged, it seemed as factual as if you had read it in the newspaper, and there was a chance that you would read it the next day.

Now it sounded sort of hollow. "I'll beat you with a one-iron," he said, but it sounded more like, "If I don't beat you, nobody can blame me. All I got is a one-iron."

The tide had definitely turned. Roscoe was about half looped on Jewel's whiskey, so there wasn't a doubt in my mind that March and Sandy were going to win the match. Sandy was going to take his winnings, go out on the Tour, and make a potful of money. He'd be famous and I'd probably be his caddie at the Masters and the Crosby out at Pebble Beach, and at the British Open at St. Andrews where March had learned to play.

March and Jewel were finally going to be man and wife, and since Jewel had been my mother, that meant March was going to be my father. I could call him Dad if I wanted, but I wouldn't 'cause March was the coolest name going.

Maybe we'd all move out to Sonora and drill some oil wells and open up that old golf course again. If Sandy was too rich and famous to be the head pro, then maybe Fromholz could take the job, or maybe someday I could. In the meantime March could take me horseback riding and camping, and on New Year's Eve and the Fourth of July, the three of us—my family and I—could drive down to Villa Acuña for a big celebration with fireworks and mariachis.

It was all going to be great fun, and I wasn't gonna have any more trouble in mind, that's what I decided. I was all through with trouble in mind.

BOOK TWO

Walk tall and loose, carrying your club
at your side, as you go toward your ball.
—Count Yogi

27

IN TRYING TO UNDERSTAND WHAT HAPPENED THEN, I'VE GONE "own and own" (as March would've said) about who I used to be, but I haven't even hinted at who I am now, these twenty-five years later. Perhaps the point is, who I am now is the product of what happened to me then. Suffice it to say that I've never been able to get any of it out of my head or my heart, and I guess the truth is, I never really wanted to.

I dreamed of March last night; of what he told me and what I learned in the too-short time that I knew him. In my dream March was young, like in the photo with the horses that he'd taken down off the wall of his office and presented to me as a gift that day it all began. Even in the dream I remembered that March's horse was the Appaloosa. Jewel was with him, and her age was undefined—timeless—just the way I always think of her; her cheeks like roses and her hair like fine silk. March kept trying to tell me something; it was terribly important but I couldn't understand what he was saying, and Jewel brushed my hair back out of my eyes and repeated over and over, "That's right. That's exactly right. You'll find out sooner or later that he's right." But I never did understand what they were trying to tell me.

It was raining when I awoke; the middle of the night. I heard the water dripping from the roof, dripping, it seemed, in sweat upon my brow, then running a salty trickle down my nose like a tear. I knew it would be quite a while before I could sleep again.

I thought about March and Jewel and the love they shared; undying in both their hearts through thirty years of separation and in my own mind for another twenty-five years after, and I wondered how it is that man survives the misery of circumstance and the burden of regret. March would have said that it was like surviving the scarcity of rain: by hoarding more, by needing less.

A distant flash of lightning illuminated the room for a moment, and I considered getting up to check on my son, five years old and just learning a fear of thunder. But it wasn't loud enough to wake him, so I decided against turning on the light and bothering my wife, a sound and happy sleeper. Insomnia is not an affliction to be shared.

As the rain grew heavier I wondered how I'd ever be able to tell my boy what March had meant to me. I figure I owe that much to both of them. I've already told Squirt parts of it; shown him the photo and explained about playing golf and riding horses, but none of it seems real to him—they're just bedtime stories. Sometimes, though, he'll be about to doze off and some detail will fascinate his idling mind and pull him back from Sandland.

"Poppy! You were an Indian?"

"No, Squirt. I just looked like one. Now hush up. If you get some sleep you can go out to the course with me in the morning."

"Can I take my golf club?"

"You bet you can."

The game goes on: his one treasured club, a cut-down ladies' five-iron. He whales away at the ball, and though it doesn't go far, like the shot of a very old golfer, it often sails straight and true, demanding that you marvel at the miraculous flight.

The thunder began to move away and with it the chance of a real soaking rain. In Texas the best part of the storm is always somewhere else. I lay quietly in the dark and in my mind I played a near-perfect nine holes of golf, nine holes at the Pedernales Golf Club just the way it was, and just the way it is now, essentially unchanged this quarter-century later, though perhaps the greens are no longer as fast. Each shot was crystal clear in my mind. My drives split the fairways and my crisp irons bit nicely at each and every pin. The making of the putts, if I paid the proper attention to a light grip and a square putter face, were mere formalities.

Nine under through eight holes, with only the long par four remaining, I began to wonder what the course record was for an imaginary round. And though the south breeze at the end of the storm blew fresh in my face, the fluid swings were rapidly sending me from insomnia to dreamland. I stood over the ball, driver in hand, and lazily dragged the clubhead back. My legs were already asleep, so I blocked the shot, cutting a huge bending slice right out of my childhood, my drive soaring from the fairway into the driving range. With my ball lost among thousands of range balls, I waded through them searching for that single pellet without a stripe, desperate to finish a perfect round of golf that only my mind kept from completion. But before I found the ball, I was fast asleep.

"Even a blind hog finds an acorn once in a while."

That's what Roscoe said when he hit his ball up close to the sixth green from what he called "the seven-iron pole." Actually the big telephone pole he was talking about was way over on the far edge of the rough, but Roscoe had been lying about even with it.

"It's the only place on the whole danged course I know what club to use."

If he'd been twenty-five yards inside the seven-iron pole, he'd probably have chipped backwards so he could hit that seven-iron with some confidence. Golf does strange things to the brain.

Now Roscoe was hitting a little chip shot, and from the look of things, he really was rooting around for acorns, 'cause he looked up, chili-dipped, burped and farted all at a time.

"Same damn dummy hit that shot as the last one," he said, again taking a long pull on the bottle of whiskey Jewel had brought him.

"And all your other shitty ones too," added Beast.

Sandy was next. He'd flown in a long, high four-wood that just caught the top edge of a trap at the front of the green. The ball was buried so completely in the sand that we'd first thought it lost.

"You might be able to chip it out sideways," suggested March when he discovered the ball, which showed itself only as a nickel-size circle of white peeking out from the sand.

"No time to play it safe," answered Sandy.

Wedge in hand, his right foot down in the trap and left foot up on the lip, Sandy cocked the clubhead and lifted it straight up to ear level. Then, without uncocking his wrists, he moved the club, his arms and his shoulders as one powerful unit into the ball. As the clubhead came up, it was accompanied by a giant gouge, not just of sand, but of the entire lip of the trap: grass, dirt, beach and all. The ball lofted to about ten feet from the pin and stuck like a lawn dart. After a beat, the giant divot landed next to the ball.

"Aye, laddie! Be ye digging for pirate treasure?" asked the one-eyed Fromholz.

"You bet he is," said March.

Beast's birdie attempt was from fifteen feet. He must've been losing confidence because he threw his cigarette away before he putted. Then he licked his lips and lipped the putt out as well.

"Son," says Roscoe, "you been gettin' lots of nibbles but not many fish!"

I don't think March even lined his up. A lot of golfers swear by the plumb-bob method: holding the putter loosely below the grip with thumb and middle finger, then extending the arm so that the lower part of the dangling putter is in line with the ball and the hole. All you have to do then is close one eye, look through the other, and see whether the upper part of the putter shaft indicates to the right or left of the hole. Take into consideration the grain of the grass, the lawnmower cut, and maybe even the wind, and then you know *exactly* where to putt the ball—about a third of the time. March had his own method: aim right at the hole and hope for the best.

This putt must've been a straight one because it looked perfect all the way to the hole and even more so after it dropped. Perhaps not trusting his own eyes, March glanced around in surprise. When it dawned on him that he'd actually made a birdie, he tossed his putter aside, knelt down, and did a little frogstyle headstand on the green, singing another of his twisted songs.

"Grab your goat and get your cat. Get the puppies off your doorstep—"

"With three holes to go," interrupted Fromholz.

"Let them do their deeds—"

"The match is even."

Before March could finish his song, he lost his balance and fell over on his ass.

"You okay?" asked Sandy, leaning over him.

March opened his eyes and picked up the beat: *"On the other side of the street."*

I thought his act was even better than Ronny and Donny, the Siamese twins I'd seen at the rodeo sideshow in San Angelo. "They were born to die, but God let them live!" trumpeted the banner. It cost me fifty cents to get in and all they did was eat donuts, watch *Gunsmoke* on TV, and make fun of my big ears. Truly I didn't mind being awkwardly skinny and tall, but I loathed my gigantic ears and dreaded being called Dumbo, which was, of course, the name that either Ronny or Donny hit upon for me.

Beast could have hit me two-for-flinching when he stomped up to me with his putter, but for once he was mad at someone else. Easing the putter into the bag, he strolled over to Roscoe's cart and violently wrenched the almost empty whiskey bottle out of his partner's hand.

"Are you nuts?" screamed Beast. "Twenty grand on the line and you're blotto!"

I figured Roscoe was fixing to go for the little pistol I'd seen peeking out of his bag, but being a drilling boss, he must've handled guys like Beast before.

"How dare you yell at me, you fat ape!" he hollered in the big man's face. "You're my trained monkey, remember? My dumbass jerk of a hit man. And why is that? Because I put up the cash! So when I want to have a drink, I have a drink. And when I say 'Hit it at the pin,' you hit it at the pin! Otherwise keep your ugly mouth shut!"

Beast stared coldly at his partner. There weren't many possible responses to a lecture like that. It looked to me as if Beast was deciding between keeping his mouth shut or killing Roscoe right then and there.

But before Beast could do anything, Roscoe turned his back as if to say "dismissed," then sat heavily in his cart.

"Come on, Jewel, hop in."

Jewel looked somewhat disinterested.

"You go ahead," she told him.

"Then hop in with me," said March. "I got a spot on my dance card."

"Gentlemen," she said. "Just now, nobody seems to be winning. I think I'll walk a spell."

Then she latched her hand onto the crook of Fromholz's arm and the two of them strolled on beneath the shade of her parasol, while Roscoe and March fumed in the hot Texas sun.

28

Now that march and sandy were bound to win (i could smell it), they no longer even needed my help. Shouldering Beast's bag, I dropped two dutiful paces behind him, glad that I could quit worrying and just enjoy the day. The seventh tee had been built atop the highest hill on the course, and the view that was afforded us there was thirty miles in all directions.

On two quarters, east and south, was the winding body of Lake Travis, named for Colonel William B. Travis, defender of the Alamo. You remember the Alamo, don't you? Well, it is Lake Travis's job to make sure we remember the colonel. And that day he was pretty unforgettable. Several miles across and too far away to reveal the shimmering of the waves or the wakes of the few sailors and bass fisherman, the lake instead showed us a deep indigo blue, motionless, as if it had been painted there.

To the north and west were the river basins themselves, the Colorado (the *Texas* Colorado) and its tributary, the Pedernales: immense valleys spotted to their horizons in the various greens of oaks, cedar, and grasses that would within a month be burned to a crisp by the summer sun.

From our distant vantage you'd never have known that the entire vista was populated not just by the normal array of ranch animals—cattle, sheep, and goats—but also by millions of wild animals: white-tailed deer, wild turkeys, javelinas (a south Texas peccary with big teeth and a nasty disposition), beavers, bobcats, badgers, porcupines, possums, raccoons, and prehistoric armadillos. The four hundred species of birds varied from majestic bald eagles and great blue herons to the tiny black-capped vireos and colorful painted buntings. And of all these animals, only a small minority would ever be seen by a human.

Yet we call that land our land. We issue covenants that bestow and convey the right to occupy and utilize it according to our need, to subjugate and cultivate according to our want, and to obliterate or ameliorate according to our whim. Then we convey that right according to our lineage, our greed, or to the roll of the dice or the drop of a curling putt.

A man dreams of owning such land because the use or abuse of it is one of the truest tests of his character and disposition. That, coupled with how he treats his family, friends, partners and enemies, in the same manner that the ball indicates the measure of the golf swing, indicates the measure of the man.

March, having missed nearly a lifetime with what should have been his family and his land (far across those hills to the northwest), had apparently one day taken his measure and come up sorely lacking. Although somewhat late, he was now on the verge of changing all that, reclaiming what was his no matter what the cost. Deep inside me I could feel my breath swelling up and lifting my heart to him. Somehow I just couldn't help but love him.

Roscoe obviously didn't share my emotion. As March drove his cart leisurely toward the seventh tee, Roscoe pulled his own buggy up tightly against March's back bumper and stepped on the gas.

Hoping to outrun him, March also stepped on the gas, but Roscoe's cart was faster and both carts raced forward in tandem.

"I'm on your butt, cowboy," Roscoe screamed like a madman. "Now git outta my way!"

We all jumped back as the two carts sped by, hooked together like two dragonflies in passionate copulation. Rounding a curve in the path, first March's cart, then Roscoe's, leaned out on two wheels. Just as I thought they were goners, both carts straightened up and slammed back down on all fours.

"Yeee-high!!!" screamed Roscoe.

Coming to the elevated tee, Roscoe stomped on the brakes of his cart and screeched sideways to a halt. March's cart rocketed forward over the ridge and launched into the air.

We were running toward him when the cart bounced twice and March wrestled it to a halt at the edge of a precipitous drop-off. He looked over the edge at his near fate, then drove the near-crippled cart back up the hill to the tee where Roscoe was roaring with laughter.

"Whoooeee! March, you flew further than your average drive!" laughed Roscoe. "I was watching you like you wuz a hawk!"

March laughed along with Roscoe for a moment, then both slowed their laughter till nothing was left but their heavy breathing and a mutual stare. Roscoe wasn't sure what March was going to do.

March smiled broadly. Relieved, Roscoe smiled too.

Then without warning, March coldcocked Roscoe with a gigantic sucker punch to the nose. Roscoe went down as if a pickpocket had lifted his spinal cord. March just stood there over him, breathing hard, exhausted, unnerved, and wrenched by tiny spasms as his hand reached slowly to his chest.

"I owed you that, Roscoe," he said through the pain. "I owed you that for thirty years."

I never knew exactly what March owed Roscoe for thirty years. Was he literally talking about a punch in the nose? Or was he figuratively talking about the fact that Roscoe had so brazenly screwed March out of their company and his own land? Neither of them denied that March had shot Roscoe in the leg, near crippling him for life, and you'd think that an additional punch in the nose after all that time would have had little effect on the score they seemed to be keeping.

But when Roscoe came groggily to his senses on that lofty seventh tee, the two of them began a deadly downhill momentum that would finally bring them head-to-head over the bitterness they'd harbored through the years. Empty insults and verbal back-stabbing would no longer suffice. Nor would settling their case through a couple of golfing surrogates like Beast and Sandy. This time it was for real. And even though I didn't understand all of what transpired—not just then anyway—it wouldn't take long for me to get a grasp on the big picture, to finally realize why Jewel cried out for them to just *stop!* Stop the fighting, the arguing, the animosity. And stop the eternal quest for revenge and one-upmanship that had come to define a once-great friendship that had simply turned to shit.

The problem was—those thirty years ago in West Texas—that Jewel fancied herself such an independent young woman, that March was downright stubborn, and of course that Roscoe was such a prick.

The problem was that Jewel didn't want to have the baby she

was carrying, despite the fact that March professed to be tickled pink about the situation. So Jewel lied; telling March that to avoid any chance of gossip getting back to her father, they should cross the border and visit a Mexican doctor for a check on the health of their unborn. March must have been naive to drive her to Mexico and wait patiently in the dirty reception room while Jewel's so-called examination began. I can imagine him there, blissful in igno-rance, musing on being a father—things he'd do with his child; things to teach; things to learn.

And I can also see his eyes opening wide for a real look at the squalid clinic, the realization of what the place was and what they were doing there. A locked door wouldn't stop March, not to save his child, and perhaps to save Jewel as well. Apparently he barged in with only moments to spare, and over Jewel's protests, March car-ried her and the tiny life inside her to safety.

But a flimsy door was less of an obstacle than Jewel's determina-tion, which remained unswayed. Was it that she felt too young to have a baby? Did she fear the wrathful judgment and accusing fin-ger of her father? Or did she just not want to be tied down?

No, the problem was that Jewel wasn't sure whose baby it was. Perhaps she told that to March as he carried her from the clinic; I don't really know. It would have been like him to say he didn't care—but it would have also been like him to have cared very much.

Not a single word passed between the two during the three-hour drive back to Sonora. And during that long and oppressive si-lence, both knew that something between them had changed. So when March and Jewel arrived back at the well, with the procedure aborted instead of the baby, Jewel did the only thing her white hot rage at March would allow: she asked Roscoe if he was sick of that smelly dry hole they'd been pumping. When he said "Hell, yes!" the two of them—Jewel and Roscoe—climbed into the same dusty pickup in which the trouble had all begun and drove away. I don't know if Roscoe punched March before they left; maybe that was what March owed him. All I know is, Roscoe took Jewel away, and March didn't see her again for thirty years.

That was the problem.

29

Whether Roscoe deserved it or not, March had given him one heck of a bloody nose, and it just wouldn't stop running red. He sat there between the blue markers of the seventh tee, soaking his handkerchief in blood, and sputtering how he hadn't asked for any of this. The only thing he did wrong, he mumbled, was to cheat at the cut of the cards so he could go to the Wing Ding instead of March.

This didn't even get a raised eyebrow from March, who had sagged down next to Roscoe. They looked like a pitiful pair of aging boxers, too weak to punch or even to get back to their corners. The one thing they had in common was that they both looked worn-out to the point of extinction.

When I met them, they'd only looked a little over the hill, and that was in relation to my tender years. Now, in addition to being bloody, Roscoe's face was yellow and puffy, not just from the punch, but from the emotion, the whiskey, and perhaps from the faint idea sloshing around in his pickled brain that he'd lived long enough in that damned Texas sun.

March, besides being pale and clammy, looked sort of shrunken and withered. I'd fetched the little bottle of pills from his golf bag, quickly given him two, then returned the medicine to its proper place. But March was not reviving the way he had earlier. The both of them looked like death's rejections, leftovers from the pickings of the devil that only a buzzard would touch.

I turned to Jewel to see if she'd noticed as well, and for the first time I had ever seen, she wasn't all beautiful and shining. She just looked very, very sad. And instead of stepping closer to be a part of things, she stepped back where she wouldn't be noticed, I suppose to hide the tears that were slowly rolling down her cheeks.

"It's a good thing we're only playing nine," March gasped.

"Nine holes is for babies," said Beast, trying to reignite the game and his possible fortune. "We oughta be playing eighteen."

"Son!" said Fromholz. "The gods made the game eighteen holes because the first nine you play against the course and the second nine you play against yourself."

"So?"

"So you don't have to play eighteen 'cause you've already played against yourself."

"Up yours!" said Beast. "Let's play some golf."

Roscoe finally stopped his nosebleed by stuffing a plug of chewing tobacco into his damaged nostril, and March climbed up off the ground with only a little assist from me. Neither of them, however, was in any shape to swing a club. Sensing that he'd lost control of the match, Fromholz ruled that the pros would play the hole alone. Then Beast and Sandy both hit good shots down to the bottom of the big hill.

Trying to referee for March and Roscoe was like orchestrating an insane asylum. Just the technical details were beginning to test Fromholz's patience. March's cart was now sitting seriously askew—the landing from the trip aloft having bent the axle beyond repair—so Fromholz shifted March's clubs to Roscoe's cart. Roscoe refused to ride with March, who was in no condition to walk, so Jewel was enlisted to be March's driver.

"Hold up!" Roscoe hollered to Jewel as she passed by us in the fairway. "Forgot my chew."

Roscoe limped over to the cart and I handed Beast his eight-iron. Then I remembered that Roscoe had used his tobacco on the tee and hadn't returned to the cart since. I turned around, and for a brief moment I could've sworn that he was digging around in March's bag instead of his own. I would have said something—oh, how I wished I had—but when I looked at March to see if he'd noticed, I lost the thought. For March's mind had wandered to greener pastures and fairer shores, one final aimless journey of heart and soul, marked only by a faint mumbling delirium.

Drawing closer, as if in a dream myself, I gazed into his sad blue eyes, and I became his witness, an involuntary eavesdropper on the final tally of his life, the way it had been, and the way it might have been as well; March shivering in a stream of icy water, at last a well spewing artesian life instead of smelly oil. It must have tasted sweet as he pursed his lips, tasted sweet like a long putt topping a rise, gathering speed, and rushing toward the heart of the hole. He was humming to the *norteño* music playing in the background, and Jewel must have been radiant in her white-lace Mexican wedding dress. Lovingly, Jewel had once taken the dress from her closet and shown it to me, telling me its story. The sleepy *señorita* who owned the shop had held a lantern as Jewel twirled and spun, her hair and the hem of the dress all whirling with dancing, dervish shadows that reflected in March's eyes. And then he was looking out again from the Scottish Lowlands to the brooding sea. And the bagpipes resounded from off the stone (or perhaps from within it), and he recalled the nun's funny little accordion as it sang "Here Comes the Bride" in a minor key while the unshaven Mexican priest beseeched the Lord on high in Latin and in Spanish. March's murmuring was racing in a stream of unconsciousness that had his sad-eyed alcoholic father looking down from the back of the chapel upon his son about to be wed, and for the last time March would ever envision, his father smiled. Smiled so that March could feel the tears streaming down his face as Jewel gripped his hand tightly and said, "¡Si! I do take this man. I do." And in his reverie they were lying together in the coming dawn, lovers, wrapped in a huge pile of Mexican *serapes* and colorful handwoven blankets, lying soft upon skin that moves softly on skin softer still. And somewhere his numbed brain or tired soul began to glow, the light approaching from the east to the top of this sacred hill. The darkness fled from their touch, Jewel sighed with the wind, and March knew for the first time since his father died that the God in heaven can also be found on earth. . . .

And suddenly Jewel's voice is saying, "William, oh please, William, are you all right?"

His eyes, still without focus, flickered with a little smile, then his lips moved like the wind on a calm day, and the highest leaves of the tallest trees rustled a faint "I love you."

Jewel put her arms around his neck, hugging for all the lost hugs, then spoke softly back to him, her words seeking out the place where he'd gone to hide.

"William March. You come back here this minute; there's people here that love you." Then after a pause to sniffle back a tear, she added, "I love you."

He was more than one foot down in that grave; both legs were in and sinking fast, but he summoned a wildcatter's strength long forgotten and pulled himself up out of the dead earth just as surely as he had so many times sucked up long-dead dinosaurs or eons of whale urine or whatever it was he'd spent his life pumping up from out of the old rock. When his eyes began to focus, he breathed deeply, smelled the hot dust on the living wind, and almost smiled.

He still didn't know where he was, not at first. He looked at us like the strangers we mostly were, and slowly it came to him that he was seated there in the cart next to Jewel on the seventh fairway of a long road home. And for each of his tears, there were tears on Jewel's cheeks to match.

Sandy stepped up close. "March, you okay?"

"Sure," he said. "I'm fine." He turned to Jewel. "It's just that I been a long time alone. A long time. But it won't be long now."

30

THINGS DID NOT IMPROVE AFTER JEWEL AND ROSCOE ABANDONED March that day at the well, because none of them had actually gotten what they wanted, a sad state of affairs they all seemed unable to admit.

For starters, Roscoe's lotharial conquest had been just that, a victory, much as losing Jewel to March had simply been a loss. Spending the first fifteen years of his life in a Galveston orphanage had given Roscoe a sense of the score. Those who slept in top bunks and ate at the head of the line were winners. Those who slept on the bottom and scraped the pail were little more than bed wetters and beggars. Life was not meant to be spent on the bottom bunk.

A semifamous wildcatter like Roscoe drew occasional attention from the Texas press; after all, he was successful local color. One of the newspaper interviews—in Roscoe's own words—told how at age fifteen he'd broken into the office of the orphanage that dared to call itself his home. Discovering whose monthly checks were paying his bill, he escaped his toy prison and hitchhiked to Houston. There he confronted H. R. Hughes: inventor, oilman, and founder of the Hughes Tool Company (which made millions manufacturing the rolling cone drill bit, invented by H.R. himself).

Being smart and tough himself, it wasn't hard for Roscoe to conclude that he was indeed sprung without consent from the loins of the famous manufacturer, but there was a complication. H.R. already had a son, Howard Hughes, Jr., future aviation pioneer, moviemaker, and proverbial chip off the old block. Not knowing that Howard junior would eventually become an emaciated, germ-fearing billionaire-recluse, H.R. was somewhat less than ecstatic at Roscoe's arrival.

Denying knowledge of any young bastards, H.R. offered the teenager two choices. Have the crap beat out of him before being tossed out on his ear. Or have the crap beat out of him, then work as an apprentice welder and tool dresser. H.R. had in mind an unproved test well in Big Lake, Texas, which was about as far from Houston as you could get and not be under the legal jurisdiction of another state where Hughes didn't own the law.

If keeping score wasn't already the dominant influence in Roscoe's life, it didn't take long as bottom boy on Santa Rita Number One to tattoo it into his soul. The experience must have hardened him like steel. Even for a seasoned roughneck, the work was long, tough, dirty, and dangerous. For a boy, it must have been almost inhuman.

Santa Rita Number One eventually spewed a million gallons of the creamiest crude the world had ever tasted.

"Its specific gravity was so high," Roscoe boasted decades later, "that a refinery was redundant. One day the foreman's truck ran out of gas, so I put in a couple gallons of crude right off the wellhead, and it *ran*, better than before!"

He could burn it in the boss's truck, but that was the closest he'd ever come to owning it. Not that Roscoe or his bone-tired fellow workers wanted to change the natural order. No, they weren't in-terested in none of that commie labor organizing. Oh no, the way to make things better was to tell the boss to shove twenty feet of casing in an alternate location where the sun don't shine, then get the hell out and drill your own damn well!

That's what took Roscoe, then in his twenties, to the hills above the Dry Devil's River, where William March swore there was oil beneath his very own land, known since March's dad's lonely and booze-laden final years as the Devil's Sanctuary.

It was there that Roscoe and March founded a business based on that famous Texas sentiment that a man's word is as good as his bond. Their deal was sealed by a handshake, less between geologist-owner and drilling contractor than between two men who were bound to act as honestly as they expected to be treated. Of course, that was before they made the acquaintance of Miss Jewel Anne Hemphill. That was before March really knew Roscoe at all.

Once Jewel abandoned March in favor of Roscoe, the score be-came two to one in Roscoe's favor. As far as he was concerned, the contest was over. After a few weeks, Roscoe got bored with his amour. And when he found out she was pregnant, he walked out on her. Where did Roscoe go? Where else? Back to the oil business. Back to March.

But things change. In Roscoe's absence, March had somehow managed to keep the crew working without pay. He worked double and triple shifts himself to cover for those who did leave, and he kept the whole operation going twenty-four hours a day. Every minute of it, they were firing that old boiler with mesquite and cedar stumps so they could keep sinking the bit, adding a pipe, and sinking the bit, ad infinitum. The only break in the routine was when the time came to pull the bit and remove a pipe—over and over for the whole damn drilling string—so that they could sink more casing to chase their progress downward. There was no due date, no known gestation period for this baby, indeed no guarantee that the damn well would come in at all. Nothing really to know for sure except that Jewel was gone and that the hole wanted deepening, was practically crying out for another length of pipe. All the while, March schemed to float the food, tobacco, and whiskey bills, and kept drilling so that he didn't have to think about anything but landing that bit in gumbo, which, with a lot of cursing and coaxing, he finally did.

The well didn't come in a showy gusher the way March had hoped, but it was a steady flow; a moneymaker sitting in a potential field of moneymakers. And as far as March was concerned, not a penny or a drop of it belonged to that back-stabbing bastard Roscoe.

Some folks call it a timeless land; some think of it as behind the times. In any event, the Indians hadn't been murdered or run out of West Texas until the late nineteenth century, and most of the folks of the region hardly noticed the twentieth century arrive. In the Sutton County of the early thirties a horse was often more reliable transportation than a car, and a gun was just another of the tools, like a hammer or an ax, that you grew up learning to use. So when Roscoe returned to demand his share of the well, there was only one way to settle their differences: the old-fashioned way.

March selected a lever-action .30-30, not real fast but deadly accurate, and Roscoe foolishly ignored the shotgun in favor of the traditional Colt six-shooter.

It was an affair of honor. The referee was Uncle Piggy, the alcoholic nitro man who had days earlier blasted the well into production with a nitro torpedo—loading a metal canister with twenty gallons of liquid nitro, dropping it into the well, and running like hell. Ten seconds of free-fall silence was followed by a deep, rumbling explosion that fragmented the subterranean rock in all directions and allowed the nearby oil to come to the surface under the pressure of the field.

Like all nitro men, Uncle Piggy's problem was his persistent headaches—brain damage really—brought on by breathing glycerin, and temporarily relieved only by massive and steady doses of alcohol. Between the melted brain cells, decaying liver, and your occasional accidental explosion, the career expectancy for a nitro man was about four years. Uncle Piggy had been at it for fourteen.

He did his damndest to load the wrong bullets into the right guns, and then tried to reverse it and load the right bullets into the wrong guns. At last Roscoe and March each loaded their own—one bullet each—then the pair declined to shake hands and impatiently walked several paces apart.

Uncle Piggy tried to count to ten but kept having to start over at four. Roscoe fired first and missed. With the leisure of time on his side, March drew a steady bead on Roscoe's hard heart, but at the last minute, he just didn't have it in him. As he pulled the trigger, March jerked the gun down toward the ground. Though he was attempting to miss, he still blew off Roscoe's kneecap.

It was months before Roscoe was able to walk again (and even then with a hobble he'd never shake). In the meantime, March's guilt took over. Maybe it really wasn't Roscoe's fault. After all, from the first night at the Wing Ding, Miss Jewel Anne Hemphill had been the foundation of a house divided. By virtue of countenance and deed, by way of innocence and vanity, she had driven a festering wedge between the two friends.

God, what had he done? March had almost killed his pal; he'd crippled him for life over some kind of horrible jealous love or infatuation. It was like a sickness both of them had contracted, an infection of the heart, a poisoning. That was it: they'd been snakebit.

There was no righting the kind of wrong that March had done to Roscoe, but he did the best he could and gave back half the well, indeed half of that well and all future wells. They'd be partners again. And they'd be friends. At least they'd try.

As for Jewel—well, March only wanted her if she needed him, or cared for him. She was bound to write, he thought, but he received no word.

31

THE SHADOW OF A SMALL, BILLOWY CLOUD, THE MID-MORNING edition of what would later be a rumbling thunderstorm, floated toward us and momentarily cast its cool relief across the seventh fairway. The shade wasn't much, but it was enough to bring March back to life. Or perhaps he'd simply come to a decision that would finally bring things to a conclusion one way or the other. Pulling an iron from his bag, he tossed a ball down in the fairway.

"What the hell are you doing?" asked Roscoe.

"I thought I'd get back in the hole," March answered.

"Well, it's too late for that, honcho! You tell him, Fromholz. No scramblin'! No mulligans! No damn cheatin'!"

March hadn't even hit a tee shot, so for once Fromholz had to agree with Roscoe.

"What's up, March?" Fromholz asked.

March told Fromholz to bring out the thirty-year-old scorecard from the first match and Fromholz produced it.

"Notice anything funny about it?" March asked.

"Yes sir! I been meaning to ask you about that. Roscoe won

with an ace on the last hole? That would have to be the most miraculous shot in the history of golf!"

"Oh, it was more than a miracle," March assured us.

"What the hell's that supposed to mean?" Roscoe demanded to know as he limped toward March with just a little more hobble than usual. "You saying I cheated? After all these years, you're saying I cheated?"

"Hold it! Just wait a dang minute," said Beast. "How does a guy cheat to make a hole-in-one? Either it goes in or it don't go in. What, were you guys blind?"

"Well, big man," said March, "as a matter of fact we were blind, 'cause it can get real dark when you're playing at night."

"At night!" Beast threw up his hands in surrender. "You're both looney-tunes!"

"I don't get it either," added Sandy. "Why would you play a big match at night?"

"That's when we thought of it," said March.

"And it was too damn hot to play in the day," added Roscoe. "It'd been a hundred and ten every day for weeks. The glare was bright enough to sunburn your eyeballs."

"Besides," added March, "that way, Roscoe could cheat."

"You want me to admit it? Is that it? Okay! Fine!" trumpeted Roscoe. "I did cheat! I fixed your pants good, didn't I, March? And there's nothing you can do about it now, you dumb hillbilly. I found that ball in a patch of prickly pear and just dropped that sucker in the hole!"

March must have been waiting a long time for this confession, not just wanting to get even, but hoping to finally satisfy the doubts in his mind.

He shook his head sadly. "Christ, Roscoe, of course you cheated! We've played golf together once a week for twenty-seven years and you've cheated every damn time. If you weren't teeing it up in the rough you were finding out-of-bounds shots in the fairway. If you weren't neglecting to count a topped shot or a scooped chip, you were on the green marking your ball over and over, each time moving it a foot closer to the hole. It's the only way you've been able to stay in the game."

"Screw you!" said Roscoe.

"And you had to live with it, you sorry bastard! Just like you're the one that has to live with having run our company into the ground. It wasn't my field reports that bankrupted us. It was you trying to screw everybody in the oil business a second time after you already bent 'em over and poked 'em once before. And now we're just oil bidness history. It'd bother me if I knew I screwed the pooch, but since I was just along for the ride in your own little donkey show, I really don't shiv a git."

For the first time I'd ever seen, Roscoe was speechless.

When March had finished his little rant, he took a swing at the ball he'd dropped and caught it with a giant yanking hook that sent it farther left than ahead.

"Would you look at that! I'm a pitiful excuse for a sad sonuvabitch myself. Like taking candy from a rube! I talk myself into a free shot and I blow it."

The rest of us just looked on helplessly while March laughed at his own sad self, then coughed and choked and laughed some more.

It was Jewel who calmed him, who took his hand and held it to her own soft face, who soothed him with gentle words as if he were a sick child or an injured dog. And it was Jewel who had a solution.

"March, it's not worth dying over," she told him. "Just drop it. Walk away. Come with me and start all over. Even if we can't be young, we can still manage carefree. But please, God, don't just stand there wasting away a little bit at a time. That's not what you want, is it?"

"No," said March, hanging his head.

"Well, it isn't what I want either. I'm tired of you two fighting over me anyway. In case you two old coots haven't noticed, I still have a certain amount of choice in the matter and my choice will always be you, March. So if I'm all you're fighting about, it's settled. Let's get out of here. Let's get out of here right now and start our lives over."

March took her hand away from his face and kissed it.

"That's good enough for me," he said.

For a moment the two of them might have been a little porcelain portrait of ageless love, then March led Jewel back to the cart and gallantly brushed the dirt off her seat.

"Sorry, Sandy. You're on you're own! But you don't need me to whip these mugs, anyway."

"Jewel!" ordered Roscoe, pushing her lightly to one side. "You stay out of this! It was never about you; it was always about him and me."

He pointed a stubby finger from March to himself.

"The better man, the tougher, the smarter, the meaner; and by God, it's just about over and I aim to see it through. March, after all these years, don't you even want to know who won?"

"You poor bastard," March said softly. "That may be what you thought it was about, but as far as I'm concerned, it was about Jewel. I never did get her out of my heart or my head. Every day and every night, I missed her. I miss her right now 'cause you're standing between us like always, you and your sense of being wronged. Drop it, man. Leave it alone. It's over. Finished. Done. Go drill your damn well in the North Sea or marry that woman Rowena who's always following after you, but get it through your head that whatever you do, it ain't gonna have nothing to do with us."

March tipped his hat to the rest of the group.

"Gentlemen, it's been interesting!"

"Hold it, hoss," said Roscoe. "I got something for you."

Roscoe moved to his bag at the back of the cart, opened a zipper, and stuck in his hand. I knew that little gun was in there and suddenly I realized that the only way out of this humiliation, the only way for Roscoe to preserve his twisted sense of honor, was to kill March.

"No!" I yelled.

All heads turned slowly and looked at me in surprise. Then Roscoe, muttering in disbelief at the general level of insanity, instead of a gun pulled out a wrinkled, faded envelope and waved it at March.

"I promised to deliver this to you," he said. "And if you leave now I might not see you again. I wouldn't want to go back on my word, ol' buddy!"

Jewel looked at the envelope like she'd been struck by lightning.

"Roscoe, you son of a bitch! You dirty rotten bastard! Thirty years! You ran off and left me, a homeless pregnant woman in the middle of the Depression, and all I asked was that you deliver this letter to March. You swore! You *swore* you'd do it."

"That's right," Roscoe admitted. "But I didn't say when."

Jewel took the letter from Roscoe and held it bunched in her hand.

"Oh, William!" she sobbed. "I'm so sorry! I kept waiting for you to come. I was just a girl and I didn't understand why you wouldn't come for me. Finally I decided you didn't want me. I would have come to you sooner or later, but not if you didn't want me."

March just looked at the letter blankly, like the rest of us, trying to understand what had happened.

"When Roscoe found out I was pregnant, he started packing and I wrote this letter for him to take to you."

Jewel tugged on the flap of the envelope. The decayed or broken seal flopped open and the letter tumbled out onto the seat of the cart. March picked it up and began to read.

" 'My dearest March, how can you ever forgive me? How could I not want to keep your child, our child—' "

"That's not what you told me it said!" Roscoe yelled. "You swore just like I did, but you lied too! And you kept writing those lies to March, didn't you? For months you wrote, but ol' Roscoe always picked up the mail. It was the only job fit for a cripple! You both thought I was some kind of fool you could just treat any way you wanted, but I showed you different, didn't I? Didn't I show you different?"

Jewel sobbed softly and March just stared at Roscoe for a long, long time.

"I can't leave yet, Jewel," March finally said, "not till I see this heartless bastard beat to the bone, and hear him say he's sorry."

32

MAYBE ALL THREE OF THEIR LIVES WOULD HAVE TAKEN BETTER turns if Jewel had been certain who the father was; perhaps she'd have wanted that baby all along. But after Roscoe left her alone, some change came over Jewel. March became more important than her situation, and her baby became more important than anything.

There was one large Catholic convent in San Angelo, populated mostly by Latinas who had exchanged the harshness and poverty of the outside world for the harshness and boredom of a poor convent. When she walked up the dirt path to the heavy wooden gates, Jewel told me, she didn't know that the nuns hadn't taken in pregnant girls since times got so hard in 1930. Hers was a hope devoid of foundation, a plan lacking in fact. But while Jewel waited there to see the Mother Superior, she was visited by the one miracle of the entire affair. Not much showing her pregnancy and being better dressed than most supplicants of the day, she was mistaken as an applicant for the low-paying job of English teacher for the Spanish-speaking nuns, a job the Mother Superior had advertised in the *San Angelo Standard-Times* that very morning.

It was a good day for miracles. The front page of the paper was emblazoned for the first time in months with a page-high imprint of a large rooster, so big and red you could almost hear it crow. This same rooster has always appeared in the San Angelo paper on a morning after the miracle of rain. That day it was overprinted on black ink stories of hard times beginning to soften to good, of a panhandle family once torn asunder and now reunited in the relative plenty of California, of the dawning hope of what was being termed a New Deal.

"It was Christmas Eve, turning cold, and I didn't have a penny to my name when out of the heavens arrived not only food and shelter, but an income and a purpose to fill my life."

Jewel told me all this a couple of Christmases after the big golf match. Christmas had always been an introspective time for her, a time when her thoughts turned away from others, the only time that her expansive personality was insufficient to fill her many parental roles. Even at age ten, I wondered why it had long been up to me to play Santa. About the time I entered high school, I finally asked her.

"I was smart enough to keep quiet about the baby," she said. "The Mother Superior would find out about that sooner or later, but in the meantime, I would be a teacher. And when March came for me, I would still be a teacher. Perhaps I was afflicted with my father's talent to instill, but I would not disseminate blindness as my father had—I would spread light."

Growing up in Del Rio, Jewel's Spanish was second natural. While she taught the nuns to speak English, she also increased their knowledge of Spanish grammar, and taught them to read and write in both languages. By the time Jewel could no longer hide her condition, not only would it have been inhuman to turn her out, it would have been impossible. The convent had begun to depend upon her.

Besides, Jewel told herself, she would only be there until March came for her. Roscoe would take the letter to March, and March would come. It wouldn't be long. He was bound to come. But Jewel grew larger and larger, and March did not arrive.

In despair, Jewel decided that she would wait for the baby's arrival, then notify him one last time. She felt that if the baby was born much more than nine months after she met Roscoe at the Wing Ding, that if she could keep that baby inside her by sheer will until enough weeks and months had passed, then it couldn't possibly be Roscoe's child, and could belong only to March. It was a matter of inner strength, of refusing to let go. And it was a feat she accomplished with ease.

"I had some small contractions and a couple of false alarms," Jewel told me. "But I made it past nine months, and I was sure that everything would be okay.

"The convent had a musty library—just a dim room with stacks of old books. Every day I'd sort through some of the mess and try to get things organized. Books in English I'd arrange on one wall, books in Spanish on another. One morning I came across a medical book in Spanish. The true measure of a pregnancy, it said, was not nine months, but forty weeks.

"Feeling faint, I leaned back against the wall, and dropped the book to the floor. A spasm pulled at my stomach. Then another. 'No!' I cried out. 'Not yet! It's too soon.'

"Unable to walk, I laid down on the floor. Alone, in a room no bigger than a closet, I fought to keep your mother inside of me. Sister Elena found me—I don't know how long it had been—and they put me in bed for the baby's arrival. They told me to push, and I pulled. They told me to pant, and I held my breath. They told me to relax against the contractions, and I fought them with every ounce of strength. I *knew* that it was March's baby, and only I could prove it."

It was a battle of nature against will, a battle that two weeks later still had Jewel refusing to push until she could refuse no more, until a baby girl forced her way into the world as March's rightful child.

And that was my mother, Martha Anne Hemphill, who, no matter how much affection and reassurance she was given in her life, never felt wanted in her home or in this world at all. Sometimes on the coldest nights of winter, even after all these years, I listen to the January winds howling through the bare trees outside my window, and I wonder what became of her.

33

Sneak around in the bushes eavesdropping on any regular golf foursome and you'll hear them talking about the random breaks of the game. If one golfer lips out eight putts in a row, his partners and opponents will just shrug and say the cup's too small (in fact, the ball lips out because the cup is round and not square). If the weird breaks and unlikely bounces start rearing their ugly heads to another in the group, it's explained that the unlucky golfer didn't go to church on Sunday (of course he went to church, he played golf). And hitting one tree or barely catching the lip of just one trap is a sure invitation to repeat the disaster over and over again.

"The golf gods just weren't with you today," console the playing partners. "You must have pissed off somebody upstairs."

If you stop to think about it, these players are describing the true nature of the game. Golf is more religion than sport, a religion with a very tiny and unforgiving goal: perfection. As in some groovy Eastern religion, the golf gods have a habit of rewarding the believer who approaches that perfection with a yin/yang philosophy of both diligence and indifference. Work your tail off to learn each and every shot that may confront you, but try not to give a hoot about any of them. The way to golf in the groove is to not worry about the ball going in the hole, but rather to just get in the groove and stay there—the golf gods allowing, that is.

When I was caddying for Sandy at one of the Texas regional qualifiers, he started off by telling me he'd been hitting the ball great, never better.

"I don't know," he said, half talking to himself. "I been in the groove for weeks. Every shot seems sweet and pure. I can feel it, twenty-four hours a day. I can feel it at breakfast, I can feel it at dinner. I can feel it in my sleep."

"That's super!" I told him.

"Yeah, I guess. Except . . ."

"Except what?"

"Now I don't feel it. I woke up this morning and it was gone. I can still chip and putt. I been out here practicing for hours and I can still hit the shots, but I can't *feel* it anymore."

He was right. It was gone. Poof! Vanished like a genie after the third wish. And there was nothing Sandy could do about it. He was damned lucky to beat some yo-yo with a swing worse than my own.

"God, I want it back," Sandy said to me after the match. "I want it back so bad!"

What was the problem? Was he trying too hard? Had he offended the golf gods? Or did he just have too many sticks in his bag? That was March's theory.

"The problem with golf," March told me, "is you got too many tools. You give a carpenter fourteen hammers all different weights and lengths, and I guarantee he'll come home with his thumb beat to a bloody pulp. We don't half know how hard this game is. Fact is, we're lucky to come back alive."

The fact is, golf is a fickle game: alive, but only in myth; marvelous, but only in theory; generous, but rarely in practice. I don't know why we curse and pray to the gods of golf. Do they live only in our minds, or are we, the mortal golfers, the products of their invention? No one really knows, of course, because it's a question meant for keener minds than those who take up sticks and balls as an unwitting form of worship.

And speaking of those without keen minds, Beast had been casually rewarded one of the worst breaks in golf. His approach shot to the seventh green backed all the way from the hole to the front edge of the green, and finally came to rest against the first cut or ridge between the short grass and the longer fringe. In such a case it's nigh on impossible to get the flat blade of the putter onto the full face of the ball. Either the flat iron hangs up in the thick grass behind the ball, or it sweeps over the grass and tops the ball. To compound matters, there was a twisting, double-helix break between his ball and the hole. For once I was glad he didn't ask me for assistance in reading the putt. Instead, he asked for his wedge.

I'd long heard of a Texas sand wedge—using a putter from a sand trap—but the other way around—a wedge from the green— that *must be* what an overly proud Texan would call an Oklahoma putter. Beast, with an already difficult putt, hoped to sweep the sole of the club over the deep fringe and square into the middle of the ball, which was just peeking at him over the lip of grass. Getting the ball near the hole would have been quite a feat. Knocking it dead in the heart for a birdie would have been a true miracle. And that's exactly what Beast did. Some days chicken; some days feathers.

"Hot damn!" said Roscoe. "My animal came to play!"

"One up," said Fromholz. "One up, two to go."

The golf gods had certainly come down upon Sandy, who sunk his head into his hands as if the whole match was over. But you wouldn't have known it by March. Having rejoined the game, he tried to recharge Sandy's spirit with another song.

"Oh, there's free beer tomorrow,
But there's heartache today!
Now we're filled with sorrow,
But tomorrow we won't pay!"

In wonder, Sandy turned to look at his older partner, whose boundless optimism seemed incapable of giving in.

"It ain't over till it's over," March told him with a wink.

Knowing that in golf one never abandons ship, Sandy nodded his head in reply.

Beast, meanwhile, walked cockily up to the hole, stuck his wedge into it, and popped the ball straight up into the air. Instead of catching the ball in his hand, though, he bounced it several more times on the flat blade of the wedge.

"That's quite a little circus trick, Bobo," said March. "Bet you can't bounce it fifty times without missing."

Beast quickly caught the ball and turned to March. "How much?"

"Fifty bucks!" said March. "A buck a bounce."

"Done," said Beast, with a loud crack of his knuckles. Holding the wedge just below the grip, he began to bounce the ball up and down easily as if it were on a tennis racquet.

Everyone paused to watch. Around bounce forty, he nearly missed and the ball went off at a sharp angle, but Beast deftly extended the club and brought the errant orb back into its vertical hop.

"Forty-eight, forty-nine, fifty!" counted Beast and Fromholz.

"Pay up, doofus!" added Beast. "You owe me half a c-note."

March already had in his hand the engraving of Grant looking green.

"Tell you what, big man," March told him. "I'll bet you can't do five hundred bounces for five hundred bucks!"

"Money from home," said Beast, turning toward the eighth tee. "Somebody help me count."

And with Fromholz trailing behind, Beast strolled casually across the green, whistling off-key as he bounced the ball on the wedge over and over and over.

In addition to playing both left- and right-handed, links hustler Titanic Thompson had quite a few other interesting golf bets: that he could chip a ball into a hat from thirty feet; balance a driver, a golf ball, and a tee on his nose; or hit a drive half a mile at the place of his choosing (he chose a frozen lake).

My favorite of his short cons, like Beast's trick wedge bounce, wasn't really a golf bet at all; it just took place on a golf course with golf equipment. Having reamed his suckers right-handed, left-handed, one-handed, and possibly even no-handed (he could putt with his foot), Ti would generally say he felt sorry for his opponents and suggest some wild and wonderful wager so they could win their money back.

Back at the car, having already untied his golf shoes, he'd take out his putter and hold it by each end. Then he'd wager that he could jump out of his shoes, pass his bare feet over the putter held horizontally in his hands, and land his feet back in his golf shoes. This was clearly impossible, and I doubt that anyone ever declined the wager.

It was said that Ti won a quarter of a million dollars a year for fifty years with his original short cons. And I wouldn't be surprised if half of it was with that single impossible feat, a stunt that he could accomplish each and every time. How did he do it? He was a natural athlete, he practiced for hours a day—after all, hustling was his job—and what the heck, maybe the golf gods were just on his side.

34

Beast was already on the four hundredth bounce when he arrived at the eighth tee. Fromholz, still counting, eased up next to me.

"This guy . . ." Fromholz said to me softly. "Four-o-eight, four-o-nine . . . This guy pisses me off! Four-eleven, four-twelve . . ."

"You missed one!" yelled Beast, still bouncing. "You started jabbering and you missed one!"

"No I didn't," answered Fromholz, missing several more.

"Yes you did, you missed one!" Beast insisted.

"Are you sure?" asked Fromholz, no longer counting at all.

"Damn right I am!"

"Okay. You ought to know. Four-thirteen, four-*fifteen*," skipping forward one bounce in correction, by then having missed at least twenty others.

I expected Beast to be pissed about Fromholz's tactics or for March to jump in there and distract Beast himself, but the fact was March had made a bad bet. As if to prove it, while the ball bounced toward five hundred, Beast explained to us that he had learned the trick by picking up balls on his dad's range: bucket in one hand, wedge in the other, he'd slip the blade of the wedge under a ball, pop it into the air and bounce it into the bucket. If he had to walk to the next ball, he continued bouncing the first one until it was time to lift the next.

"It's been a few years," boasted Beast, "but I've done at least a million bounces!"

"Four-ninety-nine, five hundred," Fromholz concluded.

"Too bad I didn't get a buck from some sucker for every one of them. Come on, March, pay up! You owe me five hundred!"

"Yes I do," agreed March. "But you'll have to be patient 'cause my money's in the car."

"It better be!" crowed Beast. "I don't like a guy who welshes on a bet!"

"Nobody does," added Fromholz, shutting the Beast up cold.

Jewel slid up next to March and took his hand. I'm not sure if it was a sign of affection or if she was just checking his pulse.

"Nice bet, William," she said. "Are you still going to have a little money left when this thing's over? Three don't live too easily on a teacher's salary."

"Well, Jewel," piped March, "let's don't worry about that. When life deals you lemons, you just gotta make whiskey sours."

This put a frown on Jewel's face. Now that she had March, the challenge was not only to keep him alive but also to mold him into some sort of respectable head of a household. Her prospects for accomplishing the latter, I viewed as slim. Roscoe, on the other hand, just wanted to get the whole thing over with so he wouldn't ever again have to watch Jewel and March talking soft and sweet.

"Beast! Your shot!" he barked.

Beast asked for a six-iron and stepped onto the tee. As soon as he moved into his stance I could tell something was wrong. He was gripping the club kind of funny and there was a slight tremor to the clubhead, as if we were in a small earthquake.

Being a seasoned veteran, Beast backed away. He cracked his knuckles loudly, then regripped the club and stepped back up. If anything, the shaking had grown worse. I saw him tighten his grip to a choke-hold, a terrible mistake common to duffers and high handicappers. As Roscoe might have put it, the true golf grip is no tighter than a prostitute handling a teenage boy.

"What's wrong?" asked Roscoe. There was a note of panic in his voice as Beast backed away again.

"I don't know," said the big man. "My right hand feels screwy. I guess I was gripping my wedge and bouncing that ball too long at a time."

March, like the March of old, was grinning from ear to ear, winking at Sandy and making goo-goo eyes at Jewel, all at the same time.

"My partner the dumb-butt!" said Roscoe. "I swear, if we wuz to shove a bowling ball in your brain, it'd bounce around like a BB in a boxcar! Hell, if you wait much longer, Fromholz'll probably penalize you for slow play. He don't really seem to care much for you anyways, so you better swallow your medicine and hit it."

Beast was so shaken that he sculled the top half of the ball and it flew like a wounded quail only halfway to the green. To his credit, I must add that Beast had learned one thing: he didn't break his club. There was one hole left in the match. Instead he squinted his red eyes toward a white-tailed deer that his shot had flushed out of a shady midday bed in the left rough. Bambi had trotted out into the middle of the fairway, where she stood broadsided looking at us.

Beast tossed down a second ball. Puzzled at what he was doing, the rest of us watched as he again moved into his stance—his hands quivering with rage this time, as he shifted them forward, effectively turning the six-iron into a two- or three-iron of destruction.

I don't know whether he was trying to further prove his idiocy or his golf prowess, but before anyone could stop him, he took a flat, short backswing and smashed the second ball at the unsuspecting doe. The ball whistled through the air and slammed into her hindquarters with a sickening thud that sounded like a hollow-point bullet finding flesh. The deer actually went down for a moment, then leapt to her feet and sped off limping on three legs.

"Got her!" yelled Beast. "How's that for a shot?"

His gloating gaze panned over our wide-eyed horror and came to rest on Fromholz, now striding quickly toward him. Beast made as if to defend himself with the six-iron, but Fromholz deftly took it away from him and laid the big man out on the ground with some sort of jujitsu or karate maneuver. Then Fromholz raised the club above Beast's head as if to strike him dead between the eyes.

"How'd you like to get hit with a six-iron, you steaming sack of white-trash defecation? You a wimp! You know that? You some kind of wimp and a bum and an egg-sucking half-breed, diseased mongrel that ought to be sent to the glue factory in a little box. If you ever do that again, I'll kill you twice and enjoy it both times. What do you say, pussy, should I hit you?"

"I been hit," stuttered Beast, almost in tears. "M-my old man hit me, lots of times."

This was a good tactic. Our hearts softened almost immediately. Fromholz, his damaged eye about to pop out of his face, suddenly looked more like an animal than the cowering Beast. The ref even felt it himself.

"Sorry, Hoss!" Fromholz said, grabbing the big man by the forearm and helping him to his feet. "When you were a kid, huh? Man, that's tough. How old were you?"

"Thirteen," said Beast. But then he realized that this figure didn't seem that young for such a big guy. "Thirteen," he corrected himself, "the last time."

I don't really know what moved him to tell us this story. I don't even know if it was true. He might have been trying to escape Fromholz's anger, but just maybe he really was a great big scared and lonely galoot, haunted by his past and terrified of falling back into that hardscrabble life.

"When the driving range got real crowded on holidays and stuff," Beast began, "we'd run out of balls and my old man would make me pick 'em up while people was still hitting 'em. So he used to dress me up in this stupid padded jacket and football helmet, and I'd walk around out there with a bucket and a club picking up balls. So one day I'm out there with my four-iron and the people on the tee are laughing at my football helmet and they're hitting balls at me. It's not too bad to get hit in the jacket, but this one guy—I seen him—he beans me in the football helmet twice in a row. I mean he rang my bell. I got so mad I dumped all the balls down and started hitting 'em back at the tee. It was great! All them golfers yelling and screaming and running for cover. Man, they were getting in their cars and peeling out of the parking lot, and then I sorta accidentally hit one guy in the face with a ball. It wasn't even the same guy that had been hitting at me. It was just some guy and he got hurt bad. The ambulance came and took him away. Afterwards, my old man beat the crap out of me."

When Beast finished the story, there was a long, uncomfortable silence.

"Pop mighta killed me," Beast concluded, "if I hadn't of knocked him out with a shovel."

As he finished the story, his downcast eyes lifted long enough to check the reactions on our faces. And just as he turned his own face back to the ground, I thought I saw the slightest smile.

"Very interesting, Mr. Larsen," said March. "A good example of how cruel and unfair life can be." Then almost as an afterthought he said, "Fromholz. Lemme ask you again, how'd you lose that eye?"

We all turned to Fromholz.

"I was hit in the face with a golf ball," he answered. "On a driving range."

Beast shrunk back—rather ashen-faced I thought—and Sandy stepped to the tee box.

35

THE FIRST TIME I SAW SANDY HIT THE FLAGSTICK WITH HIS TEE shot, I thought it the most amazing thing I'd ever witnessed and I gushed like a fool. Sandy had to remind me that not only had the ball not gone in, but with the bounce off the metal post, it had actually ended up farther away than if it had just bit into the grass.

In subsequent rounds I managed to control my enthusiasm as he continued on a long string of almost aces. Once he nearly made two holes-in-one in the same round. It was incredible the way he was bouncing them off and lipping them out and hopping them over. And these near miracles didn't seem like good luck at all. To me, it seemed like every one of those shots should have gone in. They looked perfect; why shouldn't they drop?

Sandy explained to me that scoring well doesn't require many great shots. Even for a duffer, one good shot is all you need to make a bogey on a par four. Two good shots—say a nice drive and a good putt to go with it—will usually earn you a par. The problem with birdie is that it usually takes three good shots in a row, a feat beyond most golfers whose handicaps or ratings as excellent, fair, or pitiful players are generally just an indication of how consistently they strike the ball.

"You're not as good as your best shot," Sandy told me. "You're only as good as your worst."

And since Sandy didn't have a bad shot in the bag, he was darn good. I knew it was only a matter of time before he fired one of those middle-irons at the flag and left all the bad luck and crummy bounces behind him by sailing or bouncing or rolling one into the hole. All he had to do was forget that he was spooked and quit concentrating on the little things that didn't mean anything, like the fox running in front of the car or his history of losing to Beast. None of it would mean anything to Sandy's game as soon as it didn't mean anything to Sandy.

As he stepped onto the eighth tee, Sandy knew he had to win the hole or lose the match. He lofted a pinch of grass into the air to test the wind, and in the stillness of the coming midday, it fell straight down below his hand. Then he tossed aside one of the two clubs in his hand—I think it was the six-iron—and stepped up to the snowy-white hundred-compression Titleist he'd just taken out of a new sleeve of three.

In unison with Sandy, my right hand tightened gently, as if I too were gripping the club. To hide the involuntary action, I slipped my hand into my pocket and discovered something cool and hard and marvelous. It was March's moon rock. My fingers closed into a tight fist around the magic stone, and I could almost feel it begin to glow as I wished: "Go in! Go in!"

"Go in!" I silently and fervently urged as Sandy took the club back, turning then tilting his shoulders, reversing on the downswing, tilting then turning back, and carving across the lower inside corner of the ball so that it arced in a high-drawn trace of light to the green.

I never ceased to marvel at how Sandy could divide the back face of the ball into quarters, almost like slicing a cherry pie. He'd adjust his swing trajectory and move the clubhead into the quarter of his intention, hitting either a low-cut fade, a high fade, a high hook or a low draw to suit his needs. It was as if the land had been tailored to the swing rather than vice versa, golf mechanics and shotmaking at their finest, and Sandy used this skill at will. He used the high shots and the following breeze to stretch a seven-iron to a hundred and seventy yards, as he was doing here, or the easy-swinging low shots with a minimum of spin that could bore a hole into an onslaught of wind.

The greatest marvel of all was that he never knew how impossibly difficult these feats were. Sandy seemed to think that all good golfers understood and mastered such mechanics. And thus he underestimated his own abilities by half, shutting the door on the greatest tool of all: confidence.

"Don't move, hole," said Fromholz.

"Go in!" I silently begged the gods of golf, my hand squeezing the moon rock tightly. "Go in, go in!"

The ball hit two feet short of the hole and hopped directly into the cup. It was in the hole. There was no doubt about it, but still I kept wishing. "Go in. Go in." It had dived in there so hot, I figured it might be thinking about hopping out again.

There was a long silence, broken by March.

"I'll be damned! An ace in one!"

"With one hole to go," translated Fromholz. "This match is all even."

Before Sandy shook our offered hands of congratulation, he bent over to replace his divot, mopping the tears from his eyes so we wouldn't see them.

36

"Big girls don't cry," the school bullies taunted me as they twisted my spine. But I cried anyway. It took me a long time to learn there's no shame in yesterday's tears, only a salty aftertaste. That's part of what makes it possible to write about the way things were. But the meaning of this story that has so long haunted me is equally related to the way things are. And that is not so easy.

Freelance advertising writer. I dislike advertising in general but find that I'm pretty good at writing it, so instead of working for one firm and being assigned whatever stupid accounts please them, I basically work for no one. The only way I get on an account is to find a product I like, come up with a snappy way to sell it, and then pitch myself, and my idea, to the agency in charge. The agency then has three choices. Number one, they can kick me out on my ass because they think I'm an idiot. Number two, they can steal my idea because they think I'm a fool. Number three, they can buy my idea and hire me to see it through because they think I'm a genius. The infrequency of the latter leaves me a lot of time for golf.

Don't think this commercial independence in any way makes me an advertising elitist. My most successful gig to date has been boosting a marginal office products company into a hit regional chain, a feat accomplished through the oldest sham in the book: sex. I wrote a spot that featured a gorgeous long-legged secretary and a handsome upper-management male boss, both shopping and flirting at the office store where the beautiful people shop. And for a follow-up spot, I made the secretary a gentle but bluff young man and the boss a sexy business-suited woman. It's low rent, but it works.

That's why, when I got a chance to pitch to golf's classiest clubmaker—the Ben Hogan Company of Fort Worth, Texas—my mind immediately went to sex. This may sound like a leap of logic and a violation of faith, but sex has rarely been used to sell golf or golf clubs. Unable to come up with anything better, I was desperate enough to think it would work.

For once, the agency actually called me. They wanted a thirty-second spot and they wanted it to pop out of the screen. Something new and wonderful that would make people jump their lard butts up off their sofas and run out and buy a full set of Ben Hogan golf clubs for a sum of money roughly equal to the national debt of Argentina. Even though all golfers want to hit the ball farther, I knew we couldn't use that tack. Longer is the claim used to sell golf balls, not golf clubs.

Longer, no. Sexier, yes. Why sell only golf balls when you can make a commercial that will sell anything? The spot I pitched to the agency had a comely young woman watching a classically sculpted male golfer eyeing his target and grabbing a Hogan five-iron (in close-up, of course). Addressing the ball with his perfect stance, his fans in the background (including the babe) watch his fluid swing with long, arcing extension and a follow-through that slaps him on the ass in a manner with which we are all now familiar. We see the woman's little thrill at the slap on the ass and her disappointment as the ball lands ten feet past the pin. Then suddenly the ball spins furiously back toward the hole and drops in. The woman gasps with passion and, as the young stud kisses the club, we see the brand name again in close-up: "Hogan."

The agency sent me packing.

The next day I was riding Amtrak's Texas Eagle to Fort Worth. I had been given the opportunity to present the idea to the man himself, Mr. Ben Hogan, winner of four U.S. Opens, perhaps the greatest ball striker who ever lived, and the designer of the club with which Sandy had made that timely hole-in-one.

During the trip, I kept thinking about how Hogan was famed during his years on Tour for being a very quiet man. Several golfers reported that the only two words Hogan said during an entire round were while putting, and those of course were: "You're away."

Having been wined and dined the evening before by the potential producer and director of the commercial (both of whom needed the job as much as I did), I was convinced that my idea was flawless. "Nobel and Pulitzer prize material" was how they put it.

Still, the idea of meeting Hogan terrified me, and I walked into the Hogan complex with no more confidence than I had possessed at age thirteen when I walked into my first office building to see March. Again I was ushered down a hallway lined with golf photos—none featuring horses, I was disappointed to note—and steered through an imposing door to meet the man himself. If my mouth hadn't been so dry, I'd have peed my pants.

I sat down across from his desk, mesmerized by his lined face, reflective of a life's dedication to a single passion. I could see his eyes, flecked with the various victories and defeats of his life in golf. And it seemed to me that the darkness around them was just the shadow of the Greyhound bus that smashed head-on into his car on a lonely West Texas highway so many years before, mangling his body and threatening his ability either to play golf or to ever walk again. And the eyelids, blinking just a little more often than you'd expect, seemed no more than the constant memory of the failed nerve yips that had rendered him unable to putt even two-footers. And yet he had risen above it all, as a champion golfer, as one of the most respected names in the history of the game, and as the designer and manufacturer of a line of golf equipment that his customers have been known to take to their graves.

Suddenly I realized my idea was all wrong. I was a fool for thinking golf clubs were just another interchangeable product like underarm deodorant or Odor Eaters for shoes. Golf isn't sex. Golf is passion, the passion of graceful fools and awkward poets and those who refuse to lay down forever without first dreaming of fleeting perfection. I cleared my throat loudly and, failing to hack up any kind of alternate plan, said nothing.

Hogan looked me up and down, didn't seem too impressed by what he saw, and uttered two words: "You're away."

I think he was kidding me, but I gathered that it was my time to pitch. I bit my lip and told him that the idea I'd tossed at the agency was the infantile fantasy of a man overcome by temporary insanity, that it had absolutely nothing to do with his company, and could have been used to sell anything from pork rinds to porch swings. Then I hung my head in shame that I'd wasted his time.

This increased Mr. Hogan's word usage to three. "Good for you."

We spent the rest of the day touring his operation, watching the hand-lathing of persimmon clubheads, the hosels being readied for the insertion of high-tech shafts, and finally the finished clubs coming off the line. We passed the golden-lit hours of the early evening reviewing scrapbooks in the library that practically breathed of his many Tour wins, especially the near Grand Slam of 1953 when the British Open, U.S. Open, and Masters all fell to the attack of his relentless course management, and only the PGA escaped the grasp of his genius.

That night I awoke in a start, picked up a pen and paper from beside the hotel bed, and hurriedly scribbled down the dream that had been playing in a loop inside my head.

Traveling shot: The camera flies lovingly over the misty moors of Scotland. A bagpiper is seen in the distance. We hear the emotional lilting strains of "Amazing Grace." As the camera glides over a little hillock we see two men alone in an expanse of gorse and green. Close-up: A young Scotsman of the 1930s is dressed in the traditional golfing plus-fours of his day. He makes a breathtaking pass at his ball. Backlit by the shimmering waters of the Firth of Forth, the ball soars above the mist and bounds close to the hole on the seventh green at St. Andrews.

Near the Scottish golfer in the fairway is the young Ben Hogan, the initials BH on his sweater. He selects a club and swings crisply. The ball sails low and draws in on the flag, landing short and bounding tight inside his opponent's ball. Close-up: The young Scot extends a hand of congratulation to the young Texan. Both smile. Cut to: company logo: "Hogan—Timeless Perfection."

That's it. No babes, no bouncing breasts, no frenzied fans, no holes-in-one. We made the spot. It ran for sixty seconds instead of thirty, and sales went up sixteen percent in one month. I hoped Mr. Hogan would call to say "Good work," but he never did.

As Sandy strode down the eighth fairway to remove his ball from the hole, he might have been twenty-year-old amateur golfer and former caddie Francis Ouimet who defeated British pros Harry Vardon and Ted Ray in a play-off for the 1913 U.S. Open. Or Bobby Jones triumphantly strolling down the home hole at the Old

Course in St. Andrews, moments before being swarmed by thousands of Scottish fans upon winning his second British Open in 1927. He could even have been his own hero, Ben Hogan, winning the 1950 U.S. Open only a year after his bus accident, when the doctors said he'd never play again. Or he might have been a thousand other triumphant golfers on a thousand other splendorous days. For Sandy was living the supreme moment of the game—temporarily victorious before facing the next hole, or the next match, or the next tournament.

Had Sandy not been dressed as a golfer, I could just as easily have seen Babe Ruth rounding the bases in the 1926 World Series after pointing over the center-field wall, claiming in advance one of his 714 major league home runs. This one was for an eleven-year-old fan, the critically ill Johnny Sylvester, who despite the doctor's prognosis recovered and lived to return the favor years later by holding the great one's hand on Ruth's own deathbed. Or he might have been Jesse Owens climbing the steps of glory again and again, weighted by Olympic gold and lightened by the proof of his accomplishments in Nazi Berlin. But Sandy Bates was my friend and teacher and a hero who, like all heroes, would be remembered in some quarter of heaven for his fleeting but indelible moment of glory while tromping his own hallowed grounds.

Stepping across the green without putter or hesitation, Sandy removed the flag, bent so that his hand disappeared into the earth, and picked the magic ball out of the hole. We watched him silently: partners, opponents, spectator and judge, and deep in our own hearts, each of us was extremely jealous.

37

WHETHER YOU PLAY NINE, EIGHTEEN OR TWENTY-SEVEN HOLES, a golf course needs a tough finishing hole to weed out the losers. That's especially true for a nine-hole course where you may play the ninth from one to five times a day, depending on how die-hard a golfer you are. On a hot day, or when you're just sneaking in a little practice round before work, you may be quitting after playing only nine. If you've escaped more worldly worries, you may be passing number nine every couple of hours until it gets too dark to find your ball. You can play the first nine from the white tees, the second from the blues, and the third from the tips. If you're a big enough golf-nut to go for thirty-six or forty-five holes, you can always experiment with a nine-hole scramble or a one-club competition (a five-iron is a good choice).

Perhaps to discourage too much of this repetitive, course-crowding play, the Pedernales layout took the concept of a tough finishing hole one step further. So difficult was number nine that you'd be happy just to have survived the hole and delighted to put the clubs back in your trunk. From the back tees, it was four hundred and twenty-five yards long, with a big dogleg to the left, and a long iron from the fairway to a green elevated almost to heaven. The hole couldn't have been better suited for deciding a big match.

Pumped with adrenaline and covered with goose bumps at having just accomplished the ultimate feat in golf, Sandy stepped quickly to the tee. Taking the club back faster than usual, he snap-hooked his tee shot deep into the left rough. We were stunned. With the match even and the momentum in his favor, he'd choked like a rookie.

"Sorry, March," Sandy mumbled as he slunk back.

While Sandy hit, March had rested his hand—and most of his weight—somewhat affectionately on my shoulder. Though their team's outlook had recovered somewhat (till now), March hadn't recovered at all. His color had returned, but only in splotches, and he'd hit just one shot since the fisticuffs with Roscoe, and it hadn't been for beans. Now the pressure was weighing heavily on him. It took him a long time to get his tee into the ground, and as he prepared to swing, the ball fell off the tee. He bent to replace it, then backed away taking short, shallow breaths, as if he could cool himself like a panting hound.

"Roscoe," he gasped. "You hit. I got to catch my breath."

Roscoe didn't challenge the request, didn't call for a ruling about hitting in turn, didn't make a smart-ass remark. He just stepped up and hit his shot. It was the only nice thing I ever saw him do.

"Beast," Roscoe said to the big man. "Now you forget about that lucky hole-in-one thing and hit it good."

"Hole-in-one?" Beast asked as if he hadn't seen it. "Shit, that's old news, just like that birdie I made on seven. It don't matter anymore. The guys that win here take home the big bucks and everybody else sucks on the hind teat."

Why Beast had started with any woods at all was a mystery to me. He sure didn't need them. His one-iron shot was as certain as the day and just as long, sending the ball maybe two hundred and forty yards as the crow flies. What with cutting forty yards off the corner, his ball was soon nestled tight against the bottom of the hill, looking directly up at the green.

Now more than ever, it was up to March. Jewel gave him her blessing in the form of a kiss on his cheek. Then he looked at me for a long time, as if he was trying to memorize my face. With a final wink he stepped back onto the tee.

He had no energy for a practice swing or even for a simple waggle of the clubhead. Though he was saving all his available energy for the task at hand, it was easy to see that the well had gone dry. Shakily, he started the clubhead back, but already he was sinking, calling for his medicine as he hit the ground.

I ran to Roscoe's cart and reached for the pocket on March's bag where I'd put the medicine. The zipper was open partway but I didn't think anything of it; I just yanked it the rest of the way down and started pulling stuff out: a white handkerchief, an "Old Timer" pocket knife, rusted spare cleats, pencils . . . and nothing else. The medicine wasn't there.

"Billy!" called Jewel. "Hurry! Please hurry!"

Frantically I searched again through the stuff I'd dumped out, through the empty pocket, and through the other pockets too. There was no medicine.

"It's not here!" I cried. "It's not in the pocket where I put it!"

Sandy shoved me aside and began to search himself. That's when it dawned on me about the zipper being down. I wouldn't have done that, would I? Left the zipper down and let March's medicine bounce out?

God, please! Please don't tell me I've lost March's medicine.

I ran to him to see if he was better, but the fact was, he really didn't need the medicine at all. Not anymore. His head was in Jewel's lap and she was fanning his face, trying to give him a little air. He held up his hand toward me and I put mine in his. His palm felt tough and wonderful, but I knew that he was dying, and I began to cry.

"The pills aren't there," I told him, trying to hold back my sobs.

The last trump had been played and the look on March's face was wry. Lifting up his head, he gazed to the distant hills, then back to me.

"It's okay," he said. "It's a nice spot to die."

I remember he told me I shouldn't cry.

Roscoe hobbled over and looked down at his former partner.

"Looks like you drilled your last hole, March. Well, least you got clean living on your side."

March removed his right hand from mine and held it slowly out to Roscoe. They shook, despite everything, companions in the end. Then March pulled me toward him. He couldn't talk so well, but he had a big smile on his face because Jewel's tears were streaming off her cheeks and falling onto him like a small rainstorm. He pulled me down close, inches from his lips, and whispered something into my ear, whispered so softly that I couldn't even tell for certain what he said. It was two words, I thought: "Last green."

Just then Fromholz returned with some water and pulled me away.

I stepped back in shock. Last green? Of course it's the last green. What was that supposed to mean? *His* last green? *Our* last green? March was dying, Sandy was losing, and I was more confused than ever.

My hand was warm where March had held it. I thrust it into my pocket and found my magic moon rock waiting for me there. "All you have to do is wish," March had told me. I grasped the rock and squeezed with all my might, wishing my heart out: "Don't die! Don't die, March! Please don't die!"

March opened his eyes again and found the strength to speak.

"Jewel, you were the best thing in my life. I'm sorry I let you down."

Then his eyes closed slowly. Jewel looked up at us accusingly.

"Don't die!" I wished. "March, please don't die."

But it wasn't enough.

After a moment, Fromholz knelt down beside the lost lovers and very professionally put a finger to a vein behind March's ear.

"Well, fellas," he told us. "Ol' March here is just deader'n hell."

My breath left me in a single rush. Unable to think or even see, I took the moon rock out of my pocket and, through my tears, blindly tried to focus on it. The rock was a fraud, a phony, a false and hateful kind of worthless trickery that pretended responsibility for Sandy's ace, and then just as inertly, allowed March to die. It was fake magic, just like March was a fake father and an even bigger fake of a grandfather: now you see him; now you don't! I hurled the heavy rock off the hilltop as hard as I could. It sailed with a sudden breeze and far from my sight it struck the earth for the second time in a millennium.

Jewel was still kneeling at March's side, singing some little Mexican song for him. Roscoe leaned down and took her arm lightly.

"Come on, Jewel, let's go. There's nothing you can do now."

Jewel looked up at him coldly. "Roscoe Fowler, if I ever see you again," she hissed, "I'll cut out your heart with a rusty letter opener and serve it to you with a side of human decency! Now get away from me!"

Roscoe pulled back and walked toward his cart. "Crazy bitch!" he muttered.

I pulled the driver from March's hands, ready to plant it in the soft spot in the back of Roscoe's skull, but Sandy stopped me.

"Let's finish the match," he said. "That's what March would have wanted."

The driver was in my hands and March's ball was still on the tee as Roscoe, Beast and Sandy started down the fairway. I aimed over their heads and struck the ball a mighty blow. It soared into the sky, and as it started to fall, I thought I saw some glimmer of light, some essence of March's heart and soul, break away and fly up to heaven.

Like most boys, I once had a dog; the gentlest little half golden retriever-half Border collie you could ever imagine. She wasn't quite as dumb or stick crazy as most retrievers, and she'd missed out on some of her Border collie work ethic, but she loved to curl back her lips and nip at my heels as if I were a sheep out of line. She also loved to fetch my chip shots and drop them right where I could hit them again, without having to adjust my stance forward or back, and then she'd chase the ball again. A dedicated retriever of golf balls is one that doesn't mind if you blade it thin, shank it thick, or top it dumb, but brings them all back along with the occasional good shots.

One day the dreaded "S" word reared its ugly head and I shanked a little wedge shot that skidded across the practice green at Santa Fe Park and bounced out onto Beauregard Avenue. I yelled for her to stop, but a golden always gets her ball.

I don't remember the car that hit her or the driver who stopped to try to help. I just remember that sweet, beautiful dog as she came limping and dragging back toward me in horrid shock: screaming for me to make it better, crying for me to stop the pain, howling in lack of understanding of what had happened. How could life have been so wonderful one minute, chasing balls for her buddy, and so filled with pain the next?

It seemed to take her a long time to die. I buried her in the unkempt edges of the park, down by the river where she once caught a rabbit and carried it proudly back to show me. It was the only time I ever hit her—how dare she kill such a little creature! When I struck her she dropped the rabbit, and she'd been holding it so gently in her teeth that the bunny ran away unharmed. I've never quit regretting hitting that dog, not yet anyway. And the thing it taught me is that regret has the ability to change the past not one iota.

"A high rate of regret," March had told me.

What I gathered he meant was that his field was full, there was no more fertile imagination in which to sow weeds and stickers, only a field too overgrown to plow. And now March would have to plow no more. From here on in it would be nothing but smooth fairways and fast greens, and good bounces, an unbroken string of pars and birdies, and a very low rate of regret.

38

FROM THAT LAST, LONELY FAIRWAY I LOOKED BACK OVER MY SHOULDER
and saw that Jewel was still kneeling next to March. Her hair was in
disarray, the careful bun fallen and her tresses down about her face
like a veil. It was hot out in the sun and she had the two of them in
the shade of her little parasol.

She'll be okay, I thought. We'll leave her alone while we finish,
and then go back to help.

Between the tee and the fairway I'd almost cried out in despair
at the thought that my carelessness might have killed March. I remembered putting the medicine in the pocket of the bag and I
thought I remembered zipping it up, but there was no sound to go
with the memory of the zipper closing. We'd moved March's bag
to Roscoe's cart just after that. Maybe the medicine fell out when
the bag was tipped. . . .

And then it came to me. In a Texas flood of terrible understanding it washed my guilt away. Roscoe had been screwing around
with March's bag. I hadn't left the zipper down, Roscoe had.
Roscoe had stolen the medicine from March's bag, and either not

managed to close the zipper or left it down on purpose so that it would look like an accident.

Roscoe was climbing out of his cart nearby. Even in the heat he looked cool and composed.

Cold-blooded, I thought. Isn't that what it's called? Cold-blooded murder.

I was both lost and found; lost in a rage of hate and revenge, and newly discovered of the cynicism life imposes upon its suckers. Whether I might successfully enact the plan that was quickly taking hold in one side of my mind—to steal Roscoe's little gun and blow his head off—was beside the point. The other side of my mind had already concluded that whether or not I had the satisfaction of seeing his gushing blood flow deep into the cracked limestone, pumping out the last of his miserable life that seemed to have been conducted solely to confound my grandfather's happiness, whether I spat on Roscoe's grave or not, March was not coming back.

Jewel was once again alone and I was alone with her. The fishing trips on wild rivers, the backpack journeys into the high desert, all the things I would have done with my new father, grandfather, and friend, they were all just fodder for the conflagration burning hot inside me. Burning to a dry white ash that seared my tongue with the bitter taste of the way things really were and are and always will be: one big shit sandwich with just a little bit of bread and a whole lot of filling.

March had eaten his last, thanks to Roscoe; but Sandy still had to play out one more futile hole and the rest of his ill-advised life as if he had a chance. And that sorry son of a bitch Roscoe seemed to be enjoying every minute of it. That was the part that really pissed me off!

Roscoe was so confident now that he picked up his ball to allow

Beast to finish the hole solo. Scooping out another big wad of his poisonous tobacco, he shoved it into his cheek.

"Ith over!" he mouthed through all that crap. "I win! Beasth could three-putt and I'd thill win!"

He was right. Sandy's ball had veered into the left rough, the most inhospitable piece of terrain on the course, and he was searching there among knee-deep weeds, wildflowers and little white rocks for his one lonely pellet. A month farther into the summer and the whole hillside would be dry and barren, but today the remnants of the wet spring were still working against him.

Still uncertain just how I could help Sandy, I found myself dragging up next to Beast in the fairway.

"Well, ol' March died with his spikes on!" said Beast, laughing like the heartless prick that he was.

Determined to say nothing, I bit down on my lip until I tasted blood.

Beast couldn't have been more than an eight- or nine-iron from the green. I pulled out his eight-iron and began to work on the grooves with his little file, tilting my hand first to one side and then to the other in an effort to round off the edges and take some of the bite out of the big man's clubs. Beast was still laughing at his little joke when it dawned on him that he'd been had.

"Hey! That deadbeat back there owes me five hundred bucks! Son of a bitch! Well, I'm gonna get it back on this last green!"

"Last green!" That's what March had said to me. Or was it? No, March wouldn't have told me what I already knew. It wasn't "Last green!" that he'd whispered. It was "Fast green!" He had meant that this was another of the slick greens like number two and number five, and the putts would roll across it like ball lightning down a mountainside! That was the message: his last wish. March was gone but he wanted me to help Sandy win. He wanted me to keep Roscoe from getting his father's land.

Beast looked me in the eye.

"Nine-iron," he said.

I choked down a dry swallow and handed him the eight that I'd been filing smooth.

Beast took the club. Then he reached out, grabbed me by the front of my T-shirt, and lifted me toward him. I was caught, and knew that I would soon be dead.

"What the hell is this?" he demanded to know.

I stuttered, trying to tell him it was an accident, that I had meant to hand him the nine. But the words would not come out.

"I told you to hold that file square," he bellowed. "Not at an angle! You trying to screw me up?"

I couldn't believe my ears. He still hadn't seen the number on the club, no real surprise considering he was holding me completely off the ground.

I'm flying! I thought, grinning like a fool in the big dummy's face. My feet don't touch the ground and I'm flying!

"You want your buddy Sandy to win, don't you?" he said, shaking me for an answer. Suddenly the truth was out and I was no longer afraid of him.

"Yeah!" I told him. "I do. I wish he'd beat you. I wish he'd beat you every round and every hole and every day of your life!"

"Well, why don't you wish in one hand and shit in the other and see which one fills up first," Beast suggested as he set me down. "It don't matter, Skinny. I'm gonna win, square grooves or not. Especially with these woolly greens. I'm Beast, legendary golf monster. Your buddy Sandy, he's just a legendary choke. Now watch this."

Beast wrapped his big paws around the grip of the eight-iron, made a perfect nine-iron swing, and sailed the ball toward the elevated green. From below the hill all we could see was the flag, but it looked to me like the ball had gone way long.

"Where'd that end up?" he demanded to know as he handed me the club.

I shoved it into his bag.

"Perfect," I said. "Right at the flag."

"All *right!*" he said. "That's what I been talking about!"

Sandy's ball was another story. From the tee I'd seen his shot hit a rock or root and bound straight left. Now he was looking in the wrong place; thirty yards from where I'd last seen the ball. Fromholz was walking around doing his best to help, but he was no closer.

"Two minutes, Fromholz!" Roscoe yelled from his cart in the fairway. "He's only got two minutes left to look for that ball. And that's *noocular* time!"

Roscoe started laughing at his joke and laughing at March and Sandy and at me. He was right too. Sandy was running out of time and that was something I couldn't let happen. If he didn't find that ball, Sandy would have to go back to the tee, move March's limp body to one side, and hit another drive. There was no way he had that in him. Even if he did, he still wouldn't beat Beast.

I dropped Beast's bag and started up the hill to help Sandy.

"Hey! Where you going?" Beast yelled.

I kept walking.

"If you help him find that ball, you can forget about getting paid!"

He kept yelling but I tuned him out and hurried toward where I'd last seen Sandy's ball. When I found it half-hidden under a little bush, my heart sank.

Even without the bush, the ball was in a terrible lie: half dirt, half caliche, and what seemed like half a mile from the green. There were several cedars about twenty yards ahead of him, which meant jumping the ball up fast, and there was a larger cluster of live oaks near the green, which meant carrying the shot a long, long way. Not that I hadn't seen Sandy hit some amazing recoveries. I mean he had just made a hole-in-one with the pressure on full throttle. I had once seen him almost hole one from a creek at Colonial. The ball had been completely submerged in three inches of water, and Sandy had come out of there covered by the sheet of mud and moss that his swing had raised, but by God, he made par! This situation didn't look nearly so promising.

You could almost hear Sandy's heart racing when I yelled that I'd found the ball. He came running, but as soon as he saw the situation, his excitement was replaced by the seriousness of the matter at hand.

"Billy," he said. "Get my clubs."

I walked back to where he'd dropped his bag, hefted it on my shoulder, and brought it to him as if I were his caddie. Actually, I guess I was.

"Whadaya think I should do?" he asked me.

I handed him his five-iron.

"Hit it sweet," I told him.

Sandy smiled at me, then he took the club. As he stepped up to the ball and began to search for the proper angle that would accomplish the required miracle, I began to hear a buzz in the air, a slight electrical mumble that I couldn't quite identify until I looked at Sandy's lips, barely moving as he whispered to himself.

"Guldahl Nelson Hogan, Mangrum Thompson Trevino, Sanders Zaharias Rawls, Haynie Whitworth . . . March . . . Bates . . ."

His lips slowly stilled, the sound of the mantra faded away, and

Sandy took the clubhead back and up above his head. With the rest of his body almost motionless, his arms sliced the air and he picked the ball clean from the lie. It rocketed off his clubface, faded around the cedar trees and landed—I thought—somewhere near the green. Unfortunately, neither of us could see the target.

"Goddammit!" yelled Roscoe from the fairway, coughing on his chew for the second time that morning. "Goddammit, Beast! You better not let him beat you!"

39

I PICKED YOU 'CAUSE I WANTED SOMEONE WHO KNEW HOW TO carry a grudge!"

So March had spoken to Sandy earlier that morning. March would never know if he was right, but the rest of us soon would. After all the mighty drives, ripping irons, tender chips, and putts that "needed one more bean," after all the gamesmanship and trickery and spite, it had all come down to the flat blades: Sandy versus Beast, two quick rolls on a fast green for money and honor.

For Sandy, to make his twelve-foot putt and win the match would almost certainly mean redemption from the Beastly burden he'd borne on his shoulders for so many years. For Beast, the win literally meant salvation, the repaying of Benny Binion's Vegas loan sharks and a second chance at life, this time swearing only by the certain ball and club and never by the fickle dice. But instead of lining up his long putt from the back of the green, Beast was frantically searching through his bag for his last pack of butts, which I highly doubted he'd find, since they were in my pocket.

"What the heck?" I thought. "The guy smokes too much, anyway."

Finally he gave up the search, declined Roscoe's offer of a chew, and began to nervously examine the downhill putt from all sides. Since I was now Sandy's caddie, I tried to stay as far from Beast as possible. As you'd expect, he was pissed about my having found Sandy's ball, pissed that the ball I'd found was now well inside his own, and pissed that I'd been screwing up the grooves on his wonderful irons.

The word *pissed* would have been far insufficient to describe his mood if he'd known that the main reason he was so far past the hole was that I'd given him the wrong club. I prayed that I'd left no telltale grass stains on the eight-iron (certainly all the other clubs were spotless, cleaned after every shot). He was also annoyed that I'd abandoned his bag for Sandy's. Having to carry his own bag was an atrocious thing to Beast, and he no doubt blamed me for the missing cigs as well.

If this was bad for me, it was worse for Beast. What he needed to do was remember what he'd said about that other stuff not mattering anymore. It was all in the past, and a promising future lay in a good read of the slick downhill green and a sweet stroke right at the heart of the hole.

"Make sure it'll come up, asshole!" he told me as I tended the flag.

I pulled the pin from its seat, held it loosely in the center of the cup, and held my breath. It was a good stroke—not quite resembling his mechanical perfection on the putting green at dawn—but a smooth, steady roll, dead on line. If anything, the putt seemed a bit firm as the ball picked up speed moving down the slope. Growing larger as it came toward me, it began to gather momentum with the grain and the hill, refusing to break an inch in either direction.

I pulled the pin well clear and the speeding ball hit dead in the back of the cup, hopped into the air, and continued to roll about three feet past.

I stepped way back, close by the safety of Fromholz, as Beast silently marked his ball and turned his attention to Sandy. It wasn't over yet.

Sandy smiled to himself, even as he spoke to Beast. "Fast green, huh?"

Then, without even giving the putt another read, and certainly without consulting me, Sandy leaned gingerly over his ball and stroked it into the hole for a birdie and the victory. There was no pressure at all. It was almost as if he was winning dimes off his buddies at the practice green. The hollow rattle of the ball landing in the cup hung in the air a long time.

If March had only been there with us, Sandy's win would have been a jubilant and joyful occasion. As it was, no one spoke but Sandy.

"Shit!" he said, looking down at the putter in his hands. "I forgot to take off my glove! I *never* putt with a glove!"

40

MARCH'S CADILLAC, STILL SHINING IN THE GRASS BY THE FIRST tee, could have been a flashy hearse for an eastside funeral. It occurred to me that we the respectful living should load him up and take him back to the Devil's Sanctuary for a West Texas funeral there by his daddy's grave. He'd won that land back, and I felt certain he'd have wanted to make the long journey home.

These thoughts rose briefly above the oppressive pall of my grandfather's death; then I turned again to the explosive situation that surrounded me. There still existed the very real possibility that March might not go to his grave alone. Sandy was the sole living winner and was about to walk away with the cash. That did not, however, discount the chance that Fromholz would try to collect the Vegas debt that Beast still owed to a group of men as close to being a Texas version of the Mafia as anyone would ever get.

By this time I had full confidence in Fromholz's ability to handle the situation and that was precisely the problem. With Beast's history of violent outbursts, he was liable to get himself shot down like a rabid dog, and I was scared shitless that I would either be caught in the middle or just plain have to watch it happen.

Looking back on it now, the interesting part of what took place—all through the match perhaps, but certainly there in the parking lot—was not what happened, but why. On the golf course, I had witnessed the resolution of the past, the unraveling of a thirty-year-old mystery. In the parking lot, the final turn of the cards would reveal the future for more than one of our group.

The game hadn't been over five minutes, and already Roscoe and Beast were bickering as to whose shoulders should bear the burden of blame. Roscoe, of course, insisted that it was all Beast's fault for letting Sandy beat him. Beast alternated suggestions that the game was rigged with periods of brooding silence and a double dose of his usual profanities.

We arrived as a group at the three cars in the parking lot, Sandy's cheap Plymouth, Fromholz's black Chevy truck, and Roscoe's big Lincoln with the suicide doors.

"Okay," said Fromholz. "Ten grand of this belongs to Sandy."

Sandy took the cash.

"What about the rest?" Roscoe wanted to know. "What happens to March's wager? He's gone. I say we split it."

"It belongs to Billy," said Fromholz.

I could hardly believe it, and neither could Beast.

"No wonder that skinny piss-ant tried to screw me up all day!" complained Beast. "I protest the match!"

"Shut up!" Fromholz told him.

"No!" insisted Beast. "I ain't gonna shut up! That money's mine. I got screwed out of it and I want it."

I don't know how I could have been stupid enough to stray close to him, but as I peered into the bag of money that was being offered me, Beast reached out with one of his gigantic paws, grabbed me by my hair, and yanked me back toward him.

"The money's mine!" he repeated. In his other hand he brandished the jagged-edged shaft of his broken three-wood.

Fromholz shrugged as if this was either an inconvenience or a waste of time. Then he pulled out his big .357 Magnum and leveled it at the both of us, sighting down the barrel with his good eye.

"Beast," said Fromholz, "I'm gonna try my best to shoot your ear off. If I miss a little, I want you to know that it was my bad eye that made me do it."

There was a long and nervous pause as Beast considered his chances, which were slim and none. Then he released my hair, and I jumped away to safety.

"Crummy joke, huh?" Beast said feebly as he tossed down his broken weapon.

I knew I could count on Fromholz. I knew it. But then I noticed that in the distraction Roscoe had eased around to the back of his cart, opened the side pocket of his bag, and pulled out his little blue-steel automatic, which was now pointed at Fromholz.

"Okay, tough guy, Mr. Referee, bill collector, whoever you are: lose the gun."

What a hit man. Fromholz lets the guy get his gun out, lets him draw a bead on him, and then he does as Roscoe says. He lowers the .357 to his side.

"Now listen," said Roscoe. "March is dead. And as far as I'm concerned, I won. That's why I'm taking that cash. Blondie can keep his ten grand—he beat Beast—but the rest is mine. Now get out that deed and give it to me."

"There's a problem with the deed, Doc," said Fromholz as he passed it over. "March didn't sign it."

March wins again, I thought.

"*No problema*," said Roscoe with a laugh. "I been signing

March's name for thirty years. Matter of fact, I think I signed his name when we formed the company. I bet I can duplicate my own handwriting one more time. That land's gonna be worth a lot of money when the feds ram the new interstate through there. I don't believe March knew it, but with half of that land we were both wealthy men. Now I'm a real wealthy man."

"What about me?" Beast demanded. "Don't I get a share?"

"You don't get shit, big man!" answered Roscoe.

"That's right," said Fromholz. "But Roscoe, neither do you."

"Whadaya mean?" Roscoe demanded to know. "I got everything: the money, the land."

"You didn't get Jewel," I told him.

"Forget that bitch!" he told me right back.

Gun or no gun, there were some things I was not prepared to tolerate. March may have been my grandfather, but Jewel was my life, my family, my friend, my teacher, and my chef; I had no intention of letting Roscoe talk that way. I ran full bore at him, my arms flailing like a windmill. I didn't need Fromholz. The gun meant nothing. Roscoe was an old man. I was young. If I couldn't kill him with my hands, I'd kill him with one of his own golf clubs. Two steps from him I felt a yank on my neck, my feet ran right out from under my body, and I was on the ground flat on my back.

Beast again, I thought. He's got me now.

Leaning my head back for an upside-down view of my attacker, I discovered not Beast but Fromholz. He was holding me by my shirt, now ripped halfway down the back. They were all against me, everyone. I fought to hold back my tears.

"Sorry, kid," Fromholz told me. "That was a distinctly bad plan you had there. Besides, Roscoe's going to apologize for insulting your grandmother."

"The hell I am!" said Roscoe, thrusting the gun into Fromholz's face.

"Oh, you're gonna apologize all right, Pops."

"Why should I?" Roscoe asked.

"'Cause if you don't, I'll kill you."

Roscoe laughed. "You got balls, Ref, but if there's gonna be any killing done, looks like I'm the one to do it."

"Go ahead," Fromholz told him, slowly raising his gun back to level. "Pull the trigger. Kill me! Kill me while you got the chance."

"You're bluffing!" said Roscoe.

"Pull the trigger, Roscoe. It's empty anyway."

A panicked look crossed Roscoe's face. As Fromholz leveled the .357, Roscoe squeezed on his trigger and it snapped down loudly on an empty chamber.

My entire body jerked at the loud click. There was a frozen pause all around, then Fromholz shoved the barrel of his big pistol into Roscoe's gut. The older man let out a painful groan.

"Sorry, Doc. I tossed your bullets into the pond at number three. Somebody mighta got hurt."

"*You* mighta got hurt!" Sandy said to Fromholz. "He just tried to kill you."

"Nah! He didn't pull the trigger till I told him it was empty. Ol' Roscoe's not a killer. He's just a bad loser."

"He killed March," I heard myself say.

"That's crazy talk!" said Roscoe.

Sandy came over and put his arm on my shoulders. "March had a heart attack, Billy. You were there."

"Roscoe stole his medicine!" I told them. "I put it back in the bag, but Roscoe took it out."

"Don't listen to him!" Roscoe pleaded. "He's just a kid."

Sandy went over to Roscoe's bag and began to dig around. After a few moments he pulled out the missing prescription bottle with March's name on it.

"Shit!" said Sandy. "I'll settle this. Give *me* the gun."

Roscoe began stuttering excuses, which turned to confessions, and finally to a long list of apologies for which it was just too late.

"You got ten seconds," said Fromholz. "*Noocular* time, to get in that car and disappear forever."

"Wait for me!" begged Beast, pulling out his wallet and thrusting some bills at Fromholz.

"There's the fifty I won from March, and two hundred more. It's all I got, but take it. Tell Binion I'll pay the rest. I promise! He knows I'm good for it."

"Five seconds," said Fromholz.

Beast was still climbing head first in the window when the Lincoln roared off, the heat of the exhaust shimmering off the pavement as Roscoe's car disappeared beyond the hill that March's Cadillac had flown over at dawn.

Sandy and I were in shock. How could Fromholz have let a killer just drive away?

And that's when it happened. The trumpets sounded, the birds sang angelic symphonies, the gates of heaven swung open, and out popped the miracle of familiar speech.

"Morning, gents," came the voice. "Looks like you all got here early."

We wheeled around, and just behind us, standing arm in arm with Jewel, was William March: reprobate, poet, dreamer, and friend.

41

I CERTAINLY NEVER KNEW I WAS A PART OF ANYTHING SO GRAND or so well orchestrated. It was a con worthy of, and who knows, perhaps inspired by Titanic Thompson himself. I was not surprised to find that Fromholz was a part of the scheme, but Jewel's participation was almost more than I could fathom. Sandy, of course, knew even less about it than myself, and demanded to know why March had scared the shit out of us with that dying stunt.

"It was all your fault," said Fromholz. "After you shit-canned your drive on number nine, March was afraid you'd lose and he'd have to sign the deed for Roscoe."

"You're not a hit man?" I asked Fromholz.

Fromholz and March both had a good laugh over that one.

"Billy, the only thing I hit," Fromholz told me, "is golf balls. I'm the assistant pro at the Las Vegas Country Club. You'll have to come visit me sometime."

"Neat!" I told him. "Can you teach me to shoot craps?"

"Over my dead body," said Jewel. "One dishonest golf game is bad enough. We won't be visiting any casinos, thank you."

I glanced at March and he winked at me. I knew then that someday we'd have some fun together in Vegas.

After all these years, I still wonder how March could have
known that I would do my part to help carry the day. I suppose he
relied upon the fact that Jewel told him when the chips were down
I'd do the right thing. I hope I did. There was a time when I
thought I'd failed, but that was when I learned that the sky sometimes looks bluest from the bottom of a well.

I suppose the reason I've set all of this down is to testify that occasionally more saints are saved than sinners lost. That there are
moments of salvation and redemption and, yes, sweet revenge, moments when despair turns to hope, and darkness dawns to gold,
when absolutely all of life comes down to one final roll on a fast
green, and the player with the steadiest hands gets to make himself
a big fat sandwich with two thick slices of hot homemade bread
and not one single iota of shit.

For once, when all of the settling of scores was done, despite the
fact that I abandoned my employer to find Sandy's ball in a crucial
moment, the caddie walked away well paid. For in his haste, Beast
had left behind his square-groove clubs. And even though I learned
to spin the ball backwards with them, I never enjoyed them as much
as I enjoyed the thrill of handing Beast an eight-iron when he'd
asked for a nine.

But I was a little wheel in a big machine. It had been Jewel's idea
to bring Roscoe a bottle, Fromholz's four-wood had helped make
an eagle, and of course the most important piece of the puzzle was
our ace in the hole: Sandy Bates.

"I would have let you in on the con," March apologized to
Sandy. "But I wasn't sure you could play golf and act at the same
time."

"Play he did!" said Fromholz, adding the numbers on his scorecard. "Sandy was five under par for the nine: total of thirty-one."

"Thirty-one!" said Sandy. "Shoot, that's my lowest nine holes ever. I'd like to finish eighteen."

"The course record is sixty-three," I said. "You could beat that easy."

"Well," said March. "We've still got four sets of clubs."

"Me and Sandy against Fromholz and Grandpa!" I said, pulling off my torn shirt.

"Look out!" said Sandy. "It's the Wild Indian!"

The four of us were walking toward the number one tee, then March remembered Jewel and turned to her with his most beguiling smile.

"Jewel honey," he asked her. "Would you drive down to Mona's Restaurant to pick up some cheeseburgers for everyone?"

"Cheeseburgers?" she said in disbelief. "Cheeseburgers!"

I think for the first time in my life, my grandmother was totally flabbergasted.

Victorious, our foursome headed back onto the playing field with jewel calling after.

"Bill March!" she said. "You get back here this minute!"

Bill March, I thought. What a grand name!

I turned to March. "Is she talking to you or me?"

March put his arm around my shoulder.

"Both of us," he said.

We walked on, together.

EPILOGUE

A LOT OF HOOKS AND SLICES HAVE COME AND GONE SINCE THAT memorable match, and knowing that I'd never be able to forget its participants, I've done my best to keep up with them.

Fromholz, who I first thought was a bad man, turned out to be a good man to have around, and despite his lack of peripheral vision, quite handy with his six-shooter against snakes of all kinds.

"Just call me Dead Eye!" he told me.

Now he runs a private poker game in Vegas, where he personally deals the high-dollar games to rich suckers. The last time I visited him there I took in a few hands of cards and quit when I noticed that his longtime lady friend was winning most of the money.

In an ideal situation, I suppose Roscoe and Beast would have gone away wiser or more understanding, but if there's one thing I've learned, it's that nothing is ideal. Roscoe went on to the North Sea as head of the Glomar Explorer team and found a massive oil and gas field just where March's nose had indicated it would be. The last I heard of him, though, Roscoe had abandoned the cold and wet of Scotland for the sun and sand of Iraq. Soon after, war engulfed the country. Despite that, I can't help but think the old curmudgeon hasn't chewed—or swallowed—his last.

Carl "Beast" Larsen, I'm sorry to say, runs a driving range.

Sandy won the Texas State Amateur the year after our big match, and went on to qualify at the PGA school. Though he had toppled the giant and found the confidence his game was lacking, much to his disappointment, and my own, Sandy didn't make it when he went out on the Tour. He has, however, done just fine as a club pro these past twenty-some-odd years, and around the dinner table, carrots still become clubs and peas become balls as he tells his gaggle of blond-haired kids about his glory days competing against Arnie, Fat Jack, and Beast, the golf monster.

As always, he still has a breathtaking swing. His greatest claim to fame is a remarkable accuracy on par threes. Thus far Sandy has recorded twenty-seven holes-in-one.

March, Jewel and I, after moving to the Devil's Sanctuary, reclaimed the Dry Devil's Golf Club and operated it as a public course until—as Roscoe had predicted—the federal government sliced it in half with four silver ribbons of asphalt. It was just as well. The town of Sonora built a more civilized course, and I didn't have to mow the grass greens March was planning.

And March? A dead man, it seemed, before the game began (and even more so before it concluded), I saw him reborn or rejuvenated or reinvented of himself, and it was only the ghosts that had haunted him that went to an early grave.

We took our trips on horseback and our long drives to Mexico and Montana, but we were always happy to get back to Jewel and her little adobe house overlooking the Dry Devil's River. I still see him there, that wink, that smile, both indicating that he knew something the rest of the world had missed out on. He was my grandfather, he became my father; and in his last bedridden months, I suppose he became my son.

There's no doubt in my mind that March really is playing matches on that big golf course in the sky. My guess is he's managed to team up with Francis Ouimet, Bobby Jones, or Ti Thompson himself. Spotted one stroke too many, at the end of the round he collects the other team's halos or wings or golden putters, keeping them only long enough to polish them for another round tomorrow. Now that the Old Course at St. Andrews is open on Sundays, my guess is they sneak on for a little night golf.

Since March passed on a few years ago, my grandmother Jewel—whose unconditional love and patient wisdom held court over all—has assumed a respectable role in Sonora society where she continues to weave her charming magic to this very day. I drove out for the annual Wing Ding last summer, and there was a long line of wrinkled, leather-skinned old men waiting patiently to dance with her. Every one of them called her "Miss Jewel."

And me? With my hair already long, I became a part of the youth revolution of the sixties and abandoned golf for free love and Frisbees, both of which were a lot of fun. But the game of golf always knew that one day I'd come back. After an absence of almost ten years, one sunny afternoon I found myself parked by the side of a road, watching the foursomes come into the eighteenth green, and I knew it was time.

I've thought a lot about what's magic in the years since that fateful day: undying love, raising babies, playing eighteen holes without a three-putt. Now more than ever I wish that my lack of faith hadn't caused me to toss March's magic moon rock so deep into the woods. We could all use a little magic, even now, even those of us who are still able to count our friends as friends and our family as final.

As for my own son, Squirt—William March III—already he's surpassed me in getting out of sandtraps. I can only hope that my small fount of knowledge can keep up with his West Texas thirst for the unknown.

Sometimes we watch old westerns on TV, but we've yet to come across the one with the scene about what the white man and the red man know. Still, I've told him the story, and he has taken it to heart. We took a drive out into the Hill Country not long ago. I pulled over to enjoy the view, and he swept his hand across the horizon.

"See, Popi," he told me. "That's what neither of us know."

I haven't found him any moon rocks, but I am saving another even more important possession that March gave me. The inscription on the back of the photo is in the careful hand of a man who put his faith in salvation and sanctuary and the fact that no matter how far you wander, sooner or later, you will go home.

"Don't ever forget," it reads, "what an incredible journey we're on."

The photo may be old and worn, but it still shows two friends playing golf on horseback. March's was the Appaloosa.

HOME AND FOREIGN INVESTMENT
1870–1913

HOME AND FOREIGN INVESTMENT
1870-1913

Studies in Capital Accumulation

BY

A. K. CAIRNCROSS

*Professor of Applied Economics
in the University of Glasgow*

CAMBRIDGE
AT THE UNIVERSITY PRESS
1953

PUBLISHED BY
THE SYNDICS OF THE CAMBRIDGE UNIVERSITY PRESS

London Office: Bentley House, N.W. 1
American Branch: New York

Agents for Canada, India, and Pakistan: Macmillan

Printed in Great Britain at the University Press, Cambridge
(Brooke Crutchley, University Printer)

TO MY
MOTHER

CONTENTS

LIST OF FIGURES

LIST OF TABLES

PREFACE

The studies in this volume were drafted—and several of them published —in the five or six years before the war. They cover a wide range of subjects, but they have a common theme and can be traced to a common origin. The theme is capital accumulation and the fluctuations that accompany it; the origin was an undergraduate thesis on 'Capital Transfer and the Terms of Trade'. Reared on Keynes and Taussig, I thought that I detected both of the masters in confusion in their treatment of reparations and its consequences and was moved by so unaccustomed a spectacle to develop my own ideas on the subject. My interest in foreign investment and the dynamics of international trade gradually widened and eventually focused on two relationships: between foreign investment and home investment on the one hand, and between the migration of capital and of labour on the other. Not all the studies that follow deal specifically with these relationships; but all of them bear directly or indirectly upon them.

The central portion of this volume (Chapters V–IX) is a revised version of parts of the dissertation on 'Home and Foreign Investment in Great Britain, 1870–1913', which I submitted in 1935 for the degree of Ph.D. at Cambridge University. I cannot imagine that the theoretical section of the dissertation would be of much interest now, and I doubt whether it has been read by anyone since my examiners made their patient way through it. The statistical and historical sections, however, appear to have led a lively subterranean life in the footnotes of my colleagues, and I have been under pressure for some time to legitimize them in a printed text. I now do so with some hesitation.

My original intention was to use the dissertation as a kind of sketch and paint on a larger canvas in due course. In the introduction I confessed that I had 'simply written on a number of topics which interested me, without bothering very much how they could be made to fit together....I have thought it better to give a survey of the whole ground—at the risk of superficiality—rather than begin prematurely to dig some special patch. This dissertation, in other words, has been undertaken as a prolegomenon to research rather than as a piece of research itself.' Alas, the preliminary sketch had to be put away in the attic while I learned the trade of lecturer, was beguiled into writing on other subjects, and, with the war, turned to other trades and surrendered to other temptations.

It would, no doubt, have been possible for me to have published the dissertation without amendment immediately after its completion. But

I had too lively a sense of its deficiencies to have any wish to do so. It is one thing to try to satisfy a couple of examiners but quite another to waste the time of a large number of economists by letting loose on them a mass of supposititious statistics. I knew even in 1935 of the simple-minded who lie in wait for the man with the hardihood to speak in figures; who treat every statistical series, however ill-founded, with a sort of reverence; and who cannot see a statistical nut without itching to crack it under a mathematical steam-hammer. Publication would have been a *laissez-passer* for all so inclined; and the figures which I had marshalled for comparatively modest purposes would have been made to bear a weight of precision far beyond my intention.

How often, nevertheless, have I since come on some series of mine dressed in unfamiliar uniform and marching and counter-marching in an impossible campaign! It has been this sight that has convinced me of the need to publish. If I am to be honoured by quotation, I wish also to be honoured by criticism. The statistical material may be worth using, but only if its limitations are exposed to all who wish to do so.

When I was at last able to face the preparation of this volume for the press I had to decide what to do with the sketch in the attic. I easily concluded that it would be unwise to risk another long delay by starting afresh, and that I should limit myself to amendment. This proved a bigger undertaking than I had foreseen. All the working papers had gone; the basis of some of my estimates was highly obscure; and there were many features of my intellectual offspring that struck no parental chord in my memory. I was thus faced with the extremely distasteful task of undertaking research into my own research, and conducting a kind of post-mortem on myself. On the whole, the results were reassuring, and I even succeeded in conceiving some respect for the person in whose shoes I found myself standing.

An additional difficulty was to incorporate the results of later research into similar problems—notably the work of Hilgerdt, Hoffmann, Lenfant, Phelps Brown, Rostow, Rousseaux, Schlote, Tinbergen and Brinley Thomas. On the whole, I have made little use of this work because I felt that to do full justice to it would mean further delay and would oblige me to write a much longer book. I have preferred to confine myself to that part of my work which I judged to be still original and interesting, rather than to embark on a comprehensive analysis of the period.

Some important changes have been made in the chapter on 'The Statistics of Investment' and some less important changes in the succeeding chapter on 'Fluctuations in Home and Foreign Investment'. The main change is the addition of an analysis of savings and investment in 1907 based on the Census of Production. Another important change is the abandonment of my previous estimates of sales of machinery on the home-market—though I have included figures of iron and steel consumption and the conversion factors by which these were translated into engineering output. The estimates of residential building have also been completely revised; so have the estimates of shipping earnings.

Of the remaining chapters two (Chapters IV and X) are reprinted, substantially without amendment and two (Chapters II and III) have been largely rewritten. It would have been possible to expand any one of them into a separate book and at least one of them (Chapter IV) was originally written as a summary. I hope that the rather perfunctory treatment that such brevity enforces has not detracted from their readability.

There is still a great deal that could be done to improve the statistics of investment in the nineteenth century. The local authorities have more data on the history of building activity than I had previously supposed. It should be possible to construct more satisfactory series for the price of capital goods, whether the products of building or engineering. Very little has been written on profits (or dividends) in individual industries. The finance of railway building has not been adequately studied. No one has attempted to bring together indices of home investment—or even of industrial production—in all the principal countries so as to show how the national and international elements in the trade cycle interacted. I have drawn attention here and there to gaps in our knowledge that might readily be filled in the hope that someone may be encouraged to make the attempt.

When I first read a paper on 'Home and Foreign Investment' before the Keynes Club about twenty years ago, Keynes prefaced his comments on it by a reference to the origin of the Septuagint. He thought that the kind of history which I had presented to the Club should be submitted to a similar test before being accepted as holy writ. If seventy statisticians could be locked up, like the Hebrew scholars, in separate cells and each emerge with the same statistical series, it would be possible to accept their results without further question. Failing such proofs of inspiration and truth, one could only accept the plausible and reject the unplausible. This was a pronouncement from which I did not and do not dissent. The reader should look on what follows as one step to statistical exactitude and reflect on the sixty-nine steps that are most unlikely ever to be taken.

My obligations are heavy and not easily summarized. Most of the work was done as a Research Student of Trinity College. I am deeply grateful to the College for the opportunities afforded by the studentship and to Sir Dennis Robertson for constant help and advice during my tenure of it. I also benefited greatly from discussion with Mr Colin

Clark, and with a number of my fellow-students, particularly Mr R. B. Bryce. Among others in Cambridge who gave me encouragement and help were Professor Pigou and Lord Keynes.

In the revision of the manuscript I have had the assistance of Mr W. M. L. Murray and of Mr B. Weber, who has prepared the index. Miss Hatrick has worked wonders with an almost illegible text.

I am also indebted to Dr K. A. H. Buckley of the University of Saskatchewan for permission to use his figures of Canadian investment in Chapter III; to Dr Konrad Zweig for permission to reprint two charts from an article by him in *Weltwirtschaftliches Archiv*; to Sir Piers Debenham for permission to use some unpublished calculations of his in Chapter VII; to Sir Percy Mills for information on machinery prices; to Dr Horne and Miss Knox of the Corporation of Glasgow Health and Welfare Department; the staff of the Glasgow Dean of Guild Court; and to *The Manchester School*, *The Review of Economic Studies*, and *The Economic Journal* for permission to reprint Chapters IV, IX and X respectively. An earlier version of Chapter II appeared in *The Review of Economic Studies* in 1934 and Chapter III is based on a longer version published in *Weltwirtschaftliches Archiv* in 1937.

ALEC CAIRNCROSS

Department of Social and Economic Research
Glasgow University

CHAPTER I

CAPITAL ACCUMULATION IN THE VICTORIAN AGE

In the half-century that separated the death of Queen Victoria and the accession of Queen Elizabeth, the Victorian world began to come into focus. It was not, as Mr G. M. Young has insisted, a world that stood still, but one in which institutions, attitudes and ideas—the values as well as the apparatus of industrial society—were in rapid change. 'When I consider their assured morality, their confident acceptance of the social order, their ready undertaking of its obligations; I have a sense of solidity, tenacity, and uniformity, which all the time I know to be in large part an illusion of distance....If I place myself in 1900 and then look forward for thirty-six years, and backward for as many, I feel doubtful whether the changes made in the earlier time were not greater than anything I have seen since. I am speaking of changes in men's minds.'[1]

Behind these changes, dominating the intellectual and social development of the period, were a small number of powerful and continuously operating economic forces. Of these none was so important as the growth of capital. On the one hand, this resulted from the prodigious thrift of the Victorians. In a deeper sense, however, the faith and outlook that expressed themselves in thrift were born of economic expansion and the growth of capital, and the line of causation was from accumulation to thrift rather than the other way round. On the side of demand, the growth of capital responded primarily to the revolution in transport with the coming of steam. To cover the land with railways and the seas with steamships made tremendous demands on the limited savings of western European countries. But this was not the most important outcome. The new forms of transport enormously reinforced the pulling power of undeveloped countries overseas and set in motion a resettlement of population over the surface of the globe. Thereby they released a fresh demand for capital to provide, not the marginal additions that the emigrants would have needed in their own country, but the whole stock of a newly founded community.

It is this resettlement that governs economic development in the later Victorian period. It continued an earlier movement—and one, which, by widening the market, had played a major part alongside the cheapening of capital in the industrial revolution a century earlier. But the

[1] G. M. Young, *Victorian England: Portrait of an Age*, p. 149.

scale of resettlement was now altogether vaster. It was accelerated by the capital that Britain and other countries lent or invested, and represented the most effective investment in the production of foodstuffs and raw materials that Britain could have made. At its peak, in 1913, foreign investment took over half the total of British savings; at its peak, too, in the years between 1908 and 1913, foreign borrowing financed over half the total addition to the stock of capital in the largest borrower —Canada. It controlled the movement of import and export prices, and through these the cost of living and the standard of living. No other factor, whether technical ingenuity, greater capital, or better management, exercised so powerful an influence in raising real incomes. Not that the opening up of new countries was an unmixed advantage to Britain, nor that all British investment abroad was in such countries and assisted their development. But after 1870 the qualifications and exceptions dwindled in importance.

Resettlement was not altogether an affair of emigration of labour and investment of capital abroad. It took place also within Britain, the countryside losing millions to the towns and yet retaining a fairly steady population. Here, again, the readjustment in the balance was largely a response to the new forms of transport. The replacement of rural crafts by urban manufactures and of home-grown by imported food, the breaking down of rural isolation, and the greater ease of migration to other parts of the country or abroad, were all, in greater or less degree, traceable to railway-building and the introduction of the steamship. As with development abroad, it took the better part of a century for the transport revolution to exercise its full influence on the distribution of population—if, indeed, the effects have even now been exhausted.

In the middle of the nineteenth century the building of British railways and towns took nearly the whole of Britain's savings. A trickle of capital found its way abroad, partly to finance railway-building on the Continent, partly in commercial and banking ventures, and partly in speculative loans to foreign governments, generally in the Near East or in South America. It was not till after 1870 that the trickle began to assume really formidable proportions and the growth of capital came to centre on overseas development. Railways remained the favourite investment; but the railways that were financed were increasingly remote from London. With the railway-building went other investment: in docks, harbours and public utilities; in land, mines and forests; in primary commodities of all kinds. The frontier of natural resources was thrust back and the produce of the frontier found a ready market in Britain.

The process of development took place, like all biological development, in spasms. In the human embryo, hair will grow first in one place on the head, then in another. So in the development of the frontier, first one country came into the limelight, then another. Construction went forward with a rush and finance for a time was abundant. Then the momentum perished; and when the next spurt took place, it was likely to be in some quite different area of the world.

These fluctuations did not look to those who lived through them as they do to us fifty years further on. Where we discuss short and long cycles, they talked of panics and depressions in trade. The regularity with which trade recovered from every check, the unremitting accumulation of capital, the steady advance in standards of living, all convey the impression of ineluctable progress. It is easy to imagine that belief in progress was an article of faith with the Victorians. But is this not another illusion of distance? There were some pretty hard bumps from 1870 onwards, and to contemporaries it must often have seemed as if the peak had been passed. They saw foreign investment fall below zero in the seventies and began to query—for the first time—the social utility of capital accumulation. They felt themselves in the middle of an interminable depression in the eighties. By the nineties industrial leadership was passing to the United States and Germany. After the turn of the century they had to wrestle with a rising cost of living and increasing foreign competition. They were not conscious, as Macaulay was conscious, of a secure lead and a glorious destiny. Every cyclical check might mean a permanent loss of ground.

The forty or fifty years before 1914 were clearly an exceptional period in economic history. It was symptomatic of the period that western Europe had invested abroad almost as much as the entire national wealth of Great Britain, the leading industrial country, and a good deal more than the value of the capital physically located in Great Britain. It was also symptomatic that Britain herself had invested abroad about as much as her entire industrial and commercial capital, excluding land, and that one-tenth of her national income came to her as interest on foreign investments. These conditions can hardly recur. Translated into the circumstances of 1951, and applied to the United States, they would imply American investments overseas of no less than $600 billion and an annual return on those investments of some $30 billion (or the equivalent of the British national income). Private investment abroad, in recent years, has not exceeded $1 billion per annum, and even this total has only been sustained by very large investments undertaken by the American oil companies. But if the same proportion of American resources were devoted to foreign investment as Britain devoted (out of a far smaller national income) in 1913, the flow of investment would require to be thirty times as great. The entire Marshall Plan would have to be carried out twice a year. The very extravagance of such a hypothesis shows how little there is in common between the perspectives of the Victorian era and those of to-day.

Although the period was exceptional, it is full of interest from the point of view of economic theory. In the past it has been studied by economists mainly to gain an understanding of the trade cycle. But it is even more interesting for a study of the dynamics of continuous expansion. As has been suggested by a number of economists, the cyclical process was really subordinate to the process of growth and arose out of it. It is to the history of this period that one naturally turns to observe the interaction of long-period and short-period forces, the interplay of a few major variables, the magnitudes of the responses, the cumulative results. However guarded our interpretations, we are inevitably drawn to the Victorian age to verify those theorems in the study of capital and economic development which are beginning to find their way back into the text-books. I say 'back' because the classical economists gave their minds to this very problem of 'accumulation'. It plays a central part, for example, in the doctrines of Marx; but for a long time after Marx it practically disappears from the treatises.[1]

It may be of some help in the formulation of a satisfactory theory of economic development to summarize the experience of those years. In the forty years 1875–1914 capital at home (other than land) increased from about £5000 m. to about £9200 m., or by over 80%.[2] Foreign investment rose from £1100 m. to, say, £4000 m. in 1914, or by some 250%. Taking absolute figures, capital investment probably consisted of three parts home and two parts foreign investment. Of the investment at home, a large part was needed merely to maintain capital per head, for the number of employed persons rose by about 50% between the boom years 1873 and 1913. Out of a surplus of £4500 m. beyond what was necessary in order to keep domestic capital per head constant, not far short of £3000 m., or some 60–65%, was actually employed to increase Britain's foreign investments.

The cumulative rates of growth in population and in the national income and capital from 1875 to 1914, or from the peak of 1873 to the peak of 1913, were roughly as follows:

	%
Population	1
Income[3]	2
Capital[3]	$1\frac{3}{4}$

[1] R. L. Meek, 'Thomas Joplin and the Theory of Interest', *Rev. Econ. Stud.* no. 47.

[2] Using Stamp's estimate for 1914 and Giffen's (slightly amended) for 1875. The price level and the rate of interest were approximately equal at these dates.

[3] These are averages at compound interest. The simple averages would be $3\frac{1}{4}$ and $2\frac{1}{2}$% respectively.

Although income grew rather more rapidly than capital in real terms, the ratio between the two, in money terms, kept steady at just under $1:5\frac{1}{2}$. The reason for this lies in the slight fall in the cost of living and the slight rise in the price of capital goods over the period. In arriving at the rough percentages given above I have assumed a fall in the cost of living by 10 % between 1875 and 1914 and a rise in the price of capital goods (capital at home only) by 10 %.

Common experience suggests as normal, in a community at or near full employment, a rate of gross investment equal to 20 % of income; and a rate of net investment, or saving, equal to about half—generally a little over half—the rate of gross investment. If we apply these conditions to a population increasing at 1 % per annum, and with a total capital equal to about $5\frac{1}{2}$ years' income, we obtain the following results:

(i) Capital will grow at a rate that can be expressed as

$$\frac{\text{Savings}}{\text{Income}} \div \frac{\text{Capital}}{\text{Income}},$$

and this will work out at $\frac{1}{55}$ or, say, 2 % per annum.

(ii) Maintenance and depreciation will be of the same order of magnitude, i.e. 2 % per annum. Since the stock of capital will be growing, however, this does not necessarily mean renewal of capital assets every fifty years. On the one hand, depreciation of stocks and consumers' goods (other than houses) are excluded from gross investment as usually measured; on the other hand, major repairs are usually included as well as renewals.

(iii) Capital per head will be rising at 1 % per annum.

It is usual to treat capital accumulation as the chief source and cause of economic progress; and much of what has already been said lends support to this view of things. But for some purposes it is preferable to turn the relationship round and examine the growth of capital as a function of the increase in income. As the nation becomes richer it needs more capital, not to produce new goods or to improve technique, but to provide the same things in greater abundance. A large slice of current savings is needed to 'widen' capital rather than to 'deepen' it. The most obvious illustration is the growth of stocks and work in progress, which must generally keep pace with output. If stocks and work in progress come to half a year's income—the evidence suggests something rather less—they will form $\frac{1}{2} \div 5\frac{1}{2}$ or 9 % of the national capital; and if income and capital rise at approximately the same rate, the proportion of current savings needed to maintain stocks at an adequate level will also be 9 %.

A second illustration is residential building. Suppose that the capital required to house the population is equal to about one year's income.

(This assumption seems to be broadly applicable to the late nineteenth century.) Then if this situation holds—that is, if standards of housing do not move ahead faster than the general standard of living—dwelling-houses will form $1 \div 5\frac{1}{2}$ or 18 % of the national capital. Allowing for household equipment, furniture, and so on, the proportion will be even higher. Moreover, the proportion of current savings needed to house the population will also be 18 % if capital and income, in money terms, increase at the same rate.

Even to build houses similar to those already standing, so as to provide house-room for the natural increase in population, will absorb 1 % of a year's income or 10 % of current savings. It will also be necessary to provide many other services—shopping facilities, schools, water supply, and so on, as population increases. A large proportion of current savings, therefore, will be hypothecated to providing for the growth in population. It is arguable from the foregoing analysis that the proportion is of the order of 50 %; and that, if the rate of population growth doubles, so that the rate of increase, both of population and of capital, is 2 % per annum, capital per head will cease to grow. This would be perfectly consistent with a continuing rise in capital per head in industry. For there are many fixed assets—the railways, for example —which could be stretched to cover a larger population without comparable additional outlay on capital account. The real issue is whether the rate of savings is independent of population growth. If it is—as seems likely—and if it is a simple function of income, the rate of capital accumulation, given full employment, will tend to vary inversely with the rate of population growth.

If, next, we take account of foreign investment, it is at once apparent why capital at home per head of population rose so slowly. If total capital per head was rising at only 1 % per annum, the use of as much as half the nation's savings for investment abroad would automatically arrest any rise in domestic capital per head. Foreign investment was never as high as domestic (net) investment (except in 1913), but it was frequently half as large. In other words, domestic capital per head was often growing at as little as half of 1 % per annum; and at least half of this was needed for capital 'widening'—for example, to allow stocks and residential building to keep pace with population and income. Home investment did little to promote a growth of national income at the rate of 2 % per annum; indeed, the sources of this growth lay far less within the United Kingdom than abroad.[1] It was not the growth of capital *in*

[1] Even with a marginal productivity of 10 %, a growth of capital by $\frac{1}{2}$ % per annum would not by itself add more than about $\frac{1}{4}$ % to the national income unless it facilitated some simultaneous advance in technique, yielding a return to the consumer in lower prices, not to the investor in additional dividends.

British industry that transformed the standard of living, but the reduction in the price of British imports.

There has been a great deal of argument amongst economists about the apparent inflexibility of the distribution of income in the years 1880–1914. But would one expect any great change under nineteenth-century conditions? If capital earned, say, 6 % (i.e. if it was valued, like house property, at an average of 17 years' purchase of net income) and amounted to 5½ years' income, it would receive 33 % of the national income. For this to vary it would be necessary for the ratio of capital to income or the yield on capital to vary.

Now, on the whole, capital and income tend to maintain a fairly steady ratio to one another. One might expect income to increase rather more rapidly, especially with the opening-up of new countries, but against this, building costs show a slower rate of decline than other costs so that an increasing proportion of the national income is needed in order to maintain a constant rate of growth of real capital. The difference between the two rates of growth could rarely exceed 1 % per annum and would normally be much lower. In fact, measured in money, it was negligible. But even if it had been as high as 1 % per annum—if, say, capital had risen by 2 % and income by 3 % per annum—this would in forty years have done no more than reduce capital from 5½ to 3¾ years' income.

At the same time a large reduction in the return on capital was most unlikely. The yield on British capital was settled not by the outlets for it in British industry but by the opportunities of investment in other continents. The proportion of savings flowing abroad was too large for the two capital markets, home and foreign, to be independent of one another, even if the rates of return offered were not identical. The pace of overseas development did not slacken, for there were always large tracts of fertile land, new mineral resources, and so on, to be opened up. As soon as one settlement appeared to be yielding diminishing returns, another could be begun in a different area, while investment in the first was shaken down in preparation for yet another advance. Thus there was little need for any large-scale readjustments in yields because savings were excessive or because a faster rate of accumulation had become desirable and practicable. In 1914 the return on capital was what it had been forty years previously; and so, too, therefore, was the share of capital in the national income. It was impossible to foresee that that would be so; but in the circumstances it can hardly be thought surprising. In real terms domestic capital per head rose only by some 10 %, so that there was little change in the balance between capital and labour at home; and overseas, large loans were made without outrunning the quite exceptional opportunities of investment that happened to exist.

In the argument set out above no account has been taken of land as an element in the national capital. But there was a time when land was more than half the national capital, and even in 1875 it formed about a quarter. If either of the two 'determinants' of the share of capital (excluding land) were to increase, the share of capital (including land) might remain constant because of a gradual fall in land rent. In practice, land rent was too small an element in the situation for even the substantial reductions that took place from the late seventies onwards to have much effect.

Shares were not constant throughout the forty years. It is well known that at first capital lost ground and later regained it. It is also well known that the first period (from 1873 to 1896) was one of falling prices and the second (from 1896 to 1913) was one of rising prices. Again, it is hardly very surprising to find that inflation and deflation had the effects commonly attributed to them. The rate of interest, for example, behaved in the way that Irving Fisher would have predicted—rose when money was losing value, and fell when money was gaining value. Profits (including the return on overseas investments) were undoubtedly higher in the second period than the first. Rents, though they moved down and then up, probably showed smaller fluctuations than the cost of living. Finally, the national income itself rose less steeply after 1896 because of the movement of the terms of trade against Britain and perhaps also (though I am a little sceptical of this) because real costs ceased to fall or fell more slowly. Wage-earners gained most from the favourable movement in the terms of trade in the seventies and eighties and lost most from the subsequent reversal. On the other hand, capital lost through the damper that falling prices put on development, and gained from the very change in the terms of trade that cut into real wages in Britain, but made the primary producing countries more attractive and more profitable outlets for British capital.

Although the share of capital was the same at the beginning and end of the period, the share of capital invested in Britain was not. It formed a diminishing proportion of total capital and the return to it a diminishing proportion of the national income. Looking back, this would appear to have resulted from two circumstances. The first was the falling-off, after the middle seventies, in railway-building. For over thirty years the main investment effort in Britain had been concentrated on railways, but by 1875 most of the main-line railways were already in being, and from then on railway-building normally absorbed smaller amounts of capital and, what was more important, a smaller proportion of new capital. The second circumstance was that industrial capital was still relatively small. Fixed capital in manufacturing industry was less in 1875 than the capital of the railways. It was transport and commerce that used large amounts of capital, not industry. In cotton, for example, the amount of capital employed was about £100 m. Yet at that time the cotton textile industry employed half a million workers, provided one-third of British exports, and was much the largest manufacturing industry. Even a rapid rate of growth in industrial capital, therefore, could not, starting from so narrow a base, readily take up the slack, when railway-building eased off.

The period of forty years that I have concentrated on witnessed some interesting see-saws about which much is said in later chapters. There was the price see-saw, down and up, already discussed. There was the home/foreign investment see-saw, one alternating with the other. There was an emigration see-saw, with periodic bursts followed by periodic lulls.

One such see-saw is in many ways the prototype of the others. In alternate decades (we have no yearly figures) the building industry expanded, then stood still or even contracted. In alternate decades, the cotton textile industry paused on its upward course and resumed it. The figures of employment in England and Wales are as follows:

Year	Employment in		Change in employment	
	Cotton textiles[a]	Building[b]	Cotton textiles	Building
1871	458	567	—	—
1881	488	690	+30	+123
1891	546	706	+58	+ 16
1901	529	953	−17	+247
1911	605	887	+76	− 66

[a] For 1871–91 from H. of C. 468 (1895); for 1891–1911 from the *17th Abstract of Labour Statistics*. The figure for 1871 is partly estimated.

[b] See below, p. 146.

This counterpoint, on examination, turns out to be a variation on an earlier theme, the see-saw of home and foreign investment. The building industry carried out a large proportion of home investment, and the cotton industry played a corresponding part in earning the foreign exchange out of which investments abroad were made. Thus the process of capital accumulation, now at home, now abroad, meant changes in the distribution of effort within Britain between capital goods and exports. When, as in engineering, both home and foreign markets were supplied, this shift of effort did not necessarily mean any large displacement of labour. But the building industry had no foreign market; the cotton industry had only a limited home market. Those industries, therefore, were peculiarly exposed to the winds of investment as they blew, now off-shore, now on-shore. The cotton industry, being highly localized, was to all appearances the more vulnerable. But the appearance only became reality after the first World War. There were other export industries to share the impact; there were alternative employments in Lancashire to ease the blow. It is perhaps significant, however, that when foreign investment fell off, it was the employment of men in cotton textiles that reflected the changed circumstances, while the employment of women continued to increase. There may well have been some direct movement between cotton and building in the textile manufacturing areas of the country.

It would be a serious error to study investment fifty years ago as if we knew, or ever could know, all the facts. We are ignorant enough in 1952 of many of the most elementary facts about *current* investment, for all that our curiosity on the subject is so much sharper and our statistical dossier so much bulkier. We do not know, for example, whether the national capital is greater or less than before the war.[1] We do not know with any precision the magnitude of the fluctuations that are occurring in stocks and work in progress. Our knowledge of a period nearly two generations back is inevitably even more patchy. We can use a telescope as often as we like and swivel it down the century in search of this or that 'law' of development. But our observations are uncertain and blurred. What one man professes to see another may see differently.

This is particularly true of those cycles, long and short, which economic astronomers have reported in the Victorian skies. The figures of fixed capital investment reveal cyclical fluctuations of considerable amplitude and are at least not inconsistent with the theory that it was investment that dominated industrial fluctuations. But the evidence is insufficient to rule out any other hypothesis. For the trade cycle a more minute analysis, using monthly data, would be necessary. There are no reliable statistics of investment in machinery and plant—the element in fixed capital investment most sensitive to cyclical influences. We know little or nothing of the fluctuations in stocks. Yet a change in the level of stocks and working capital by 10% in one year was capable of producing as large a reduction in effective demand as a cut in gross fixed capital formation by 25%, or an increase in net savings by 50%.

[1] *A priori*, I should guess that capital has been accumulating at about 2% per annum, and that, if the national capital fell by 25% during the war, it must now be some 10% below the total in 1939. This would imply some growth in domestic capital, but not enough to offset the heavy loss of foreign assets.

An *attempt* to reduce stocks by 10 % would have as large an effect even if, in the end, the reduction were much smaller because of an involuntary accumulation of unsold goods. Nothing that is adduced in later chapters would disprove a theory of the trade cycle before 1914 in terms of alternate stock-building and running down of stocks, with the various forms of fixed capital formation being pulled out of their long-term courses into a new orbit under the erratic visitations of a change in stocks.

Long waves have been less frequently the subject of theory. That fluctuations occur in various economic phenomena with peaks many years apart is beyond dispute. But there is rarely any constancy in the periodicity or any concentration on a standard period. The building cycle and the horse cycle show certain regularities that might be described as long waves. But there is no interdependence between them. The building cycle varies from town to town and country to country; in periodicity, amplitude and timing. If we are to speak of long waves, therefore, we must limit ourselves to a local fluctuation. Long waves that are not local are revolutions rather than cycles.

The chapters which follow do not attempt to derive a theory either of short or long fluctuations from Victorian experience. They do, however, analyse that experience in order to show what part capital accumulation played in the economic system; how it responded to influences at home and abroad, and how it in turn affected economic development. The starting-point is generally Britain; but wherever one begins—in a new country like Canada or an old one like France—the argument runs along the same paths. Britain is simply the most convenient point of vantage from which to look out over the Victorian world.

CHAPTER II

FLUCTUATIONS IN THE GLASGOW BUILDING INDUSTRY, 1856–1914

In the last twenty years fluctuations in building activity have attracted an increasing amount of attention. This has been so for three reasons: first, because of the violence of the fluctuations that have occurred; secondly, because of the impact of those fluctuations on the general level of economic activity; and thirdly, because although building has been one of the main strategic factors in the trade cycle, there has nevertheless been a difference of rhythm between cycles in building and cycles in trade.

It is not difficult to understand why building activity should be so unstable. The demand for durable goods is generally more variable than the demand for goods that have a short life and are in need of constant replacement; and no goods are so durable as buildings. It is also apparent why building activity should exercise a strong influence over the general level of employment and trade. Building is one of the largest and most widespread of all industries. It ramifies from the brick-making, timber, cement, steel and other building-material industries at one end into the plastering, plumbing and painting trades at the other; and it sets the pace for a wide range of industries, such as furniture-making, electrical engineering, and the making of office equipment, that contribute to the fitting-out of the empty structure. The impact of building on employment and trade is not governed, however, solely by the size of the industry. It depends also on the role of fixed capital investment, of which building is the major part, as one of the main determinants of the level of industrial activity.

It is on the phasing of cycles in building, rather than on their amplitude or importance, that recent studies have dwelt. Attention has been concentrated on residential building construction because, while commercial and industrial building has generally fluctuated more or less in phase with the trade cycle, the building of dwelling-houses has often shown a marked divergence. The two components of new building activity are of roughly equal magnitude. Both respond to a number of common influences, such as the general economic situation, and each reacts in various ways on the other. There is, however, no identity between the influences governing factory-building and those governing the erection of new dwelling-houses; each requires separate analysis.

In seeking an explanation of fluctuations in residential building, some economists have laid stress on forces on the side of demand, and some on forces on the side of supply.[1] The first explanation may run either in terms of money incomes or in terms of demographic factors. It may, for example, correlate the number of new houses built with the rate of increase of population or with a more refined index of changes in the number of potential households. The second explanation generally runs in terms of the cost of new building in relation to the return to be expected on house-property. This return is measured by an index number expressing the movement of house rents relatively to long-term rates of interest, the latter being taken either as a measure of the cost of the necessary finance or of the return that could be obtained by investing the same capital in other ways. It is worth reflecting a little on these two lines of approach before looking at the available statistics for corroboration.

Building need is frequently identified with demographic factors. It is assumed that if the population increases in a given ratio the number of houses required will increase in the same ratio, unless there is a simultaneous change in the age-distribution, the marriage-rate, or some other demographic factor. Now it is no doubt true that the most powerful influence on the side of demand has generally been population growth; and that, in the long run, if the size of the population shows a steady trend upwards or downwards the level of building activity will be affected in the corresponding direction. But it is far from true that population growth, however measured, is the only important influence on the side of demand; or that the number of houses built, assuming freedom of enterprise and no rent restrictions, need conform at all quickly to the trend in population. The demand for houses depends upon the level of rents; if rents fall in relation to other elements in the cost of living, as recent experience has shown, many new households will come into existence, and the pattern into which the population will group itself will not be decided by some predetermined formula such as the number of married couples, plus a fixed proportion of the number of single persons in given age-groups. The demand for houses also depends upon the level of income in relation to house rents; if people are better off, they will spend some part of the increase in their income on an improvement in the accommodation that they enjoy. It is only if rent and other elements in the cost of living keep step with one another, and if real income per head remains constant, that rent and income can be left out of account.

Moreover, standards of housing change: people may decide to spend

[1] For an analysis of the recent literature, see C. E. V. Leser, 'Building Activity and Housing Demand', *Yorkshire Bull. Econ. Soc. Res.* (July 1951).

a bigger proportion of their income on house-room or to occupy larger or smaller houses at the same level of rent. New houses may offer amenities not available in existing houses or be located in places more convenient to existing householders. Since only a small number of new houses are erected annually in relation to the existing stock, the result of any rapid change in amenities (for example, the introduction of bathrooms after 1880) or in facilities (for example, the development of suburban transport through tramways and electric railways) may be a marked acceleration in new residential construction. The demand for new houses may also be powerfully affected by decisions to speed up the demolition of existing property. This is not just a question of slum clearance. The coming of the railways, for example, made it worth while to clear large areas in the centre of the bigger towns. There is a steady process of conversion of older house property, some-times into offices or commercial premises, sometimes into boarding-houses, private hotels, service flats and the like, so that the existing stock of buildings may house a diminishing or increasing number of persons. The demand for new houses, therefore, depends upon what is happening to existing houses as well as upon any net change in the demand for house-room.

It follows from this that the building of new houses does not neces-sarily respond promptly to changes in the demand for house-room, still less to any demographic changes underlying them. The demand for new houses might remain high even when an increasing number of older houses were standing empty. Similarly, there might be very little new building in a period of increasing demand if a large number of houses stood empty at the beginning of the period. The number of empty houses, however, could not increase very far without putting a damper on new building; and if the number of empty houses fell progressively in response to an increase in demand, builders would eventually feel the benefit as a growing proportion of the fresh demand was deflected to new houses.

In the long run, therefore—and how long a run remains to be assessed by statistical analysis—we should expect fluctuations in residential building to reflect changes in the demand for house-room (subject to any simultaneous changes affecting existing dwelling-houses either by way of demolition, improvement, or conversion to other purposes). We might also find that in the circumstances examined, the dominant influence on demand was population growth; but this conclusion would lack general application and apply only in those circumstances.

If we turn now from demand to supply, we are faced with an ap-parently quite different set of factors governing new building. The speculative builder of pre-1914 days was concerned to make a profit on the sale of the houses that he constructed. There does not appear, however, to be any annual data relating the price that new houses fetched to the cost of their construction or showing the fluctuations from year to year in the profit-margin of the average builder. The best that can be done is to construct an index compounded of the various elements that may be presumed to have determined this profit-margin: the cost of construction, the level of house rents, and the long-term rate of interest. This index is sometimes spoken of as the 'investment incentive'. It is, however, an *ersatz* measure of incentive to the builder, and is defective in various ways. First, there is rarely any accurate index of building costs, particularly if it is local building costs that are in question; secondly, the level of rent on existing property does not necessarily correspond to the level of rent on new property; thirdly, the long-term rate of interest on government securities may not show the same fluctuations as the rate on mortgage bonds, by which the purchase of house property is commonly financed. Apart from this, the use of an index of this kind presupposes a perfect market when the market was often imperfect; the builder might have been glad to build if he could have raised additional capital at the current rates. It is indeed quite probable that the impulse to a building boom came at times as much from a more ample supply of funds or from a more active market for house property as from any movement in interest rates and rents.

How are the two lines of approach, one from the side of demand and one from the side of supply, to be reconciled? How could the level of building be governed by two apparently independent sets of forces? The answer might appear to lie in the ordinary theory of value. If a building boom was initiated from the side of demand, by, say, a spurt in population, property would fetch higher prices, rents would move up, and the index of investment incentive would also rise; a fall in the demand for house-room would exercise a corresponding check on rents and depress this index. If the boom originated on the side of supply, presumably because of a fall in costs or interest rates, the construction of additional houses would eventually drive down rents, and this would simultaneously secure additional tenants and restore the investment index to its equilibrium level.

In fact, however, rents do not show the plasticity that this presupposes; they are notoriously sticky. They may even go on rising when the demand for house-room is falling.[1] Changes either on the side of demand or of supply are free, therefore, to exercise a direct influence on building without any intermediate change in rents.

It is a safe rule that, when prices are sticky, stocks become the controlling factor in balancing supply and demand. Houses are no exception;

[1] See below, p. 32.

Table 1. *Residential building in Glasgow, 1862–1914*

Year[a]	No. of houses for which plans were passed	Average rooms per house	Average cost per room (£)	Mason's wages per hour (d.)	Empty houses at Whitsun (%)	Average rent[b] of	
						Occupied houses (£)	Unoccupied houses (£)
1863[c]	(1114)	2·07	—	5	7·13	—	—
1864	448	2·53	—	5	5·21	—	—
1865	778	2·15	—	6	3·51	—	—
1866	772	1·98	—	6½	1·89	—	—
1867	1195	2·05	—	6¾	(1·80)	—	—
1868	2204	2·29	—	6¾	1·69	—	—
1869	3184	2·24	—	6½	1·65	—	—
1870	3325	2·14	—	6½	2·14	10·18	10·90
1871	3841	2·06	—	6½	2·09	10·14	11·12
1872[d]	(2735)	1·91	—	7	2·12	10·24	11·69
1873[e]	4463	1·95	68	7½	2·54	10·49	9·90
1874	4392	2·15	68	8	3·99	10·87	10·03
1875	5582	2·24	89	8½	4·37	11·16	11·65
1876	5746	2·40	81	9½	4·91	11·41	12·64
1877	3963	2·16	100	9½	6·48	11·72	12·99
1878	1033	2·33	84	6½	7·94	11·93	11·99
1879[e]	501	2·65	65	6	10·25	11·72	11·40
1880	492	3·02	69	6	11·22	11·33	10·61
1881	419	2·22	78	6½	9·86	11·14	10·06
1882	512	2·54	69	7	7·84	11·00	10·63
1883	391	2·59	84	7½	5·96	11·02	9·81
1884	587	2·29	72	7	5·17	11·05	9·31
1885	764	2·19	74	7	6·14	11·05	9·10
1886	1262	2·46	65	7	6·56	11·00	9·40
1887	1021	2·37	68	7	7·30	11·00	9·33
1888	1202	2·11	72	7	6·72	11·04	9·00
1889	1545	2·26	69	7¼	6·05	10·99	9·18
1890	1253	2·03	67	7½	4·69	11·03	9·19
1891	1561	2·28	77	7¾	—	—	—
1892[e]	2051	2·58	83	8¼	—	All houses	Unoccupied houses
1893	2573	2·54	79	8½	—		
1894	3466	2·62	84	8½	—		
1895	3497	2·46	77	8¾	—	13·19	12·86
1896	3370	2·39	82	9	2·92	—	—
1897	4870	2·24	88	9	—	—	—
1898	5618	2·34	90	9½	—	—	—
1899	3730	2·32	103	9½	—	—	—
1900[e]	2536	2·47	98	9½	2·97	—	—
1901	2446	2·65	101	9½	2·66	13·79	9·91
1902	5349	2·69	98	9½	2·97	13·95	11·09
1903	4837	2·60	110	9½	3·82	14·13	13·25
1904	2894	2·43	85	9½	5·88	14·24	13·45
1905	2085	2·62	98	9	7·51	14·17	12·79
1906[e]	2863	2·32	91	9	7·77	14·16	12·94
1907	1442	2·62	96	9	8·28	14·11	12·62
1908	1028	2·57	96	9	9·34	14·09	12·15
1909	1167	3·01	93	8½	9·48	—	—
1910	1283	2·81	88	8½	10·71	14·09	12·34
1911	284	2·26	86	8½	10·72	13·95	12·10
1912	200	2·50	91	9	10·35	14·26	—
1913[e]	461	3·49	99	10	9·25	14·22	—
1914	373	3·62	102	10	6·94	14·33	—
Total 1873–1914	95,112	2·41	88	—	—	—	—

[a] Calendar year from 1862 to 1872; from 1 September to 31 August thereafter.
[b] For the years 1870–79 houses in the Parliamentary burgh only. In 1880 the corresponding figures were £11·48 and £10·85.
[c] 1 September 1862 to 31 December 1863.
[d] 1 January to 31 August 1872.
[e] Boundary extension. The extensions in 1891 and 1912 were the only important ones.

Table 2. *Occupied and unoccupied houses in Glasgow, 1870–1914*

Year (1 June)	Total no.[a] of houses	No. of occupied houses	No. of unoccupied houses	Annual increase in col. 1	Annual increase in col. 2	Annual increase in col. 3
1870	101,405	99,234	2,171	—	—	—
1871	103,030	100,876	2,154	1,625	1,642	−17
1872	104,978	102,748	2,230	1,948	1,872	76
1873	107,787	105,043[b]	2,744	2,809	2,295	514
1874	111,357	106,906[b]	4,451	3,570	1,863	1,707
1875	112,401	107,483	4,918	1,044	576	467
1876	114,350	108,731	5,619	1,949	1,248	691
1877	117,071	109,490	7,581	2,721	759	1,972
1878[c]	118,332	108,936	9,396	1,229	−585	1,814
1879	119,105	106,889	12,216	773	−2,047	2,821
1880	119,421	106,014	13,407	316	−875	1,191
1881	119,727	107,923	11,804	306	1,909	−1,603
1882	120,157	110,736	9,421	430	2,813	−2,383
1883	119,648	112,524	7,124	−509	1,788	−2,297
1884	119,538	113,352	6,186	−110	828	−938
1885	120,458	113,062	7,396	920	−290	1,210
1886	120,907	112,978	7,929	449	−84	533
1887	121,815	112,924	8,891	908	−54	962
1888	122,703	114,457	8,245	888	1,533	−646
1889	123,351	115,888	7,463	648	1,431	−782
1890	123,951	118,135	5,816	600	2,247	−1,647
1891[c]	—	137,858	—	—	1,558	—
1892	—	138,837[b]	—	—	979	—
1893	—	140,245[b]	—	—	1,408	—
1894	—	142,293[b]	—	—	2,048	—
1895	—	144,152	—	—	1,859	—
1896	—	146,281[b]	—	—	2,129	—
1897	—	148,957	—	—	2,676	—
1898	—	152,173	—	—	3,216	—
1899	—	155,496	—	—	3,323	—
1900[c]	162,207	157,379	4,828	—	1,883	—
1901	164,363	159,988	4,375	2,156	2,609	−453
1902	166,190	161,247	4,943	1,827	1,259	568
1903	168,881	162,443	6,438	2,691	1,196	1,495
1904	173,197	163,002	10,195	4,316	559	3,757
1905[c]	179,261	165,766	13,495	3,186	−114	3,300
1906	180,331	166,306	14,025	1,070	540	530
1907	181,968	166,894	15,074	1,637	588	1,049
1908	182,852	165,762	17,090	884	−1,132	2,016
1909	182,501	165,215	17,286	−351	−547	196
1910	184,112	164,397	19,715	1,611	−818	2,429
1911	183,283	163,630	19,653	−829	−767	−62
1912	182,511	163,624	18,887	−772	−6	−766
1913	181,302	164,528	16,774	−1,209	904	−2,113
1914	179,048	166,612	12,436	−2,254	2,084	−4,338

[a] The figures for 1881 and later years include a small number of hotels and lodging-houses (approximately 100).

[b] Approximations. Complete figures for the nineties are unfortunately lacking.

[c] Extension of boundaries; the extensions in 1878 and 1900 were negligible.

the number of empty houses is at least as important as the level of rents. Suppose, for example, that building costs, rents and interest charges never altered. Building booms might still occur; but it would be the number of empty houses that would act as an index of changes in demand or supply and take the brunt of an increase or decrease.

Table 3. *Houses in the Parliamentary burgh of Glasgow, 1856–80*

Year	Total	Occupied	Un-occupied	Increase col. 1	Increase col. 2	Increase col. 3
1856	75,931	—	—	—	—	—
1857	77,794	—	—	1,863	—	—
1858	80,519	—	—	2,725	—	—
1859	83,229	—	—	2,710	—	—
1860	85,203	—	—	1,974	—	—
1861	87,579	82,493	5,086	2,376	—	—
1862	89,588	82,885	6,703	2,009	392	+1,617
1863	91,699	85,163	6,536	2,111	2,278	−167
1864	92,595	87,767	4,828	896	2,604	−1,708
1865	93,288	90,008	3,280	693	2,241	−1,548
1866	93,386	91,623	1,763	98	1,615	−1,517
1867	(93,706)	92,021	(1,685)	(320)	398	(−78)
1868	95,002	93,393	1,609	(1,296)	1,372	(−76)
1869	97,118	95,516	1,602	2,116	2,123	−7
1870	99,120	96,995	2,125	2,002	1,479	+523
1871	100,504	98,414	2,090	1,384	1,419	−35
1872	102,286	100,177	2,109	1,782	1,763	+19
1873	104,504	101,902	2,602	2,218	1,725	+493
1874	107,520	103,423	4,097	3,016	1,521	+1,495
1875	108,182	103,696	4,486	662	273	+389
1876	109,621	104,530	5,091	1,439	834	+605
1877	112,141	105,062	7,079	2,520	532	+1,988
1878	113,105	104,496	8,609	964	−566	+1,530
1879	113,881	102,448	11,433	776	−2,048	+2,824
1880	114,147	101,575	12,572	266	−873	+1,139

Source: Reports of W. West Watson and John Strang (City Chamberlains of Glasgow).

No figures of empty houses have ever been collected officially in the United Kingdom (except in the decennial census; and even then the figures are for unoccupied, not empty, houses). It happens, however, that a continuous series exists for Glasgow from the 1860's. It happens also that, not altogether accidentally, there is an abundance of statistical data on other aspects of housing and building in Glasgow over nearly a century. It is possible to assemble a more complete statistical dossier on building fluctuations in Glasgow than for perhaps any other town in the world. The figures for Glasgow might be expected, therefore, to be of peculiar value in analysing building fluctuations and the inter-connexions of the main factors that give rise to them.

The available statistics for Glasgow include details of plans passed annually since 1862 by the Dean of Guild Court ('linings'), and of occupied and unoccupied houses within the city limits back to 1860. The data on plans passed include the number of houses by size of house, the number of shops, and the value of plans for each of the following groups: houses and shops; public buildings; churches, halls and schools; warehouses, stores and workshops; and alterations and additions.

Plans passed are not an exact index of work done, but the divergence between the two, making allowance for the time-lag, is not likely to be great. A fee was charged for all 'linings' granted, and these 'linings' expired one year after the original grant; that is, work must have been commenced, but not necessarily completed, within the year. The Guild Court officials estimate that not more than, say, 3–4 % of plans passed are abandoned, and this accords with experience elsewhere.[1] On the other hand, some work did not require the sanction of the Dean of Guild Court. The railway companies, for example, carried out building operations by private Act of Parliament; and the erection of dwelling-houses formed part, albeit a small part, of such operations. The activities of the railways were mainly of importance in the seventies when they demolished a thousand houses in Glasgow and no doubt also built a large number.

The lag between the issue of a lining and the carrying out of the work varied greatly, as a lining might cover a single house or several hundreds. It has been assumed that plans passed during the calendar years 1862–72 were carried out with an average lag of six months, and that, when the Dean of Guild's year became 1 September to 31 August in 1872 the lag to the completion of the work became ten months. The convenience of this assumption is that it permits of comparison between the figures of residential building and the figures of occupied and empty houses (which are for June of each year).

Since the plans passed are given both by value and quantity it is possible to extract from them a rough index of building costs. The value figures represent surveyors' first cost, at so much per cubic foot of building, checked from the cost of work done for the Corporation, and

---

[1] Mr C. D. Long, for example, found that only 2 or 3 % of American building permits were allowed to lapse (*Building Cycles and the Theory of Investment*, p. 98). He also found that most building is finished in the calendar year in which the permit is taken out.

revised in the light of actual cost. The quantity figures relate to houses in the sense of structurally separate dwellings with independent access from street, lobby, or outside staircase. It would obviously be extremely misleading to treat the average cost per house as an index of building costs in view of the changes that took place from year to year and over the period in the size-distribution of the houses under construction. But it is perhaps not altogether misleading to make use of the average cost per room without trusting it too far and checking it against figures of masons' wages and the cost of materials.

The data on occupied and empty houses are unfortunately not altogether complete; but I have hazarded a few guesses to fill in the

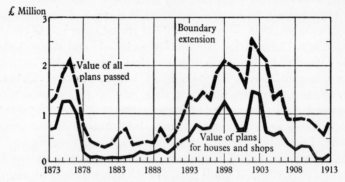

Fig. 1. Fluctuations in building plans passed, 1873–1913.

blanks. Taken in conjunction with the valuation roll, these data make it possible to calculate the average rent of occupied and unoccupied houses in successive years. The figures of occupied and empty houses are available not only for the city as a whole, but from 1903 onwards by individual ward and by size of house.

The extraordinary violence of the fluctuations in the Glasgow building trade is brought out clearly in Fig. 1. A building boom starting about 1867 continued until 1877, gathering momentum almost every year. With the failure of the City of Glasgow Bank in 1878 a period of severe depression set in, the value of new houses and shops falling from over a million and a quarter in 1875–6 to a comparatively negligible amount three years later. In the early nineties building at last began to show signs of revival, and Glasgow, like the rest of the country, experienced a dozen years of uninterrupted boom. Between September 1901 and August 1903 (when a Municipal Commission was beginning an inquiry into the housing shortage), plans for houses and shops to the value of close on £3,000,000 were passed by the Dean of Guild Court.

In the following three years the demand for occupied houses declined sharply and building, though still active, tapered off. In 1907 the boom finally broke, and from then until the twenties few houses were erected.

The demand for house-room, as measured by the number of houses occupied, naturally fluctuated within more modest limits. As measured by the annual increment in houses occupied, however, it showed remarkable instability both in the short run and from decade to decade (Fig. 2).

First of all, there was a marked cyclical rhythm. The increment in houses occupied reached a maximum in the booms of 1873, 1882, 1890,

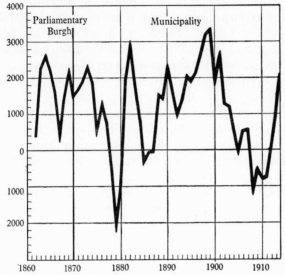

Fig. 2. Annual increment in occupied houses, 1860–1914.

1899, 1907 and 1914, and was at a minimum in the depressions of 1879, 1885–6, 1892, 1904–5 and 1908. The more sudden the depression, the more violent the change in trend. In 1908, for example, demand jumped from a progressively increasing number to a large negative quantity. It is possible that this rhythm was more marked in Glasgow than in other British towns because of the large proportion of the population that was employed in the capital goods industries. There is, for example, fairly close agreement between shipbuilding activity and the demand for house-room, and the violence of the fluctuations in the one can be read in the other.

The pressure of unemployment and wage-cuts was sufficient in nearly every slump to cause an actual fall in the number of houses occupied. In the seventies and eighties the unemployed crowded together with their relatives, or in lodging-houses, or even under haystacks and hedges; the one-apartment houses (or 'single-ends') emptied and filled regularly with the coming and going of depressions. A fall in marriages had a similar result. Between 1877 and 1879, for example, the number of marriages fell from 4943 to 4180; enough to exert a substantial influence on the demand for houses when the number occupied was growing at only 1000 per annum. A further cyclical influence—and perhaps the most important, if the experience of other countries is any guide—was an inflow of workers from other parts of Scotland in times of boom and a falling-off or reversal of this flow in times of depression.

The cyclical fluctuations in demand find little or no echo in supply. Close inspection of the figures of plans passed, whether in terms of value or of number of rooms, suggests that, if anything, residential building fell off at the peak of a boom. There is evidence of this in 1890, in 1899 and again in 1907. In 1882 and 1913 building activity was so low already that the evidence is obscure. Plans for houses of one room, however, do show a distinct cyclical pattern, with peaks in 1873, 1881, 1889, 1899 and 1906.

The second feature of the fluctuations in demand is the alternation of long periods of growth and stagnation. The short cyclical fluctuations were superimposed on a couple of long waves: one rising to a peak in 1873 and subsiding finally after 1877; a second reaching a double-headed peak in 1899 and 1901 and dying away in the next two or three years. These long waves in demand coincided with the so-called long building cycle, the two peaks in this cycle occurring in 1876 and in 1902 (with a subsidiary peak in 1898). The successive upswings and downswings are shown below:

Period	Increase in number of houses occupied[a]	Number of houses for which plans were passed[b]
1864–1877	+ (17,295)[c]	+ 42,330
1877–1887	+ 3,304	+ 6,982
1887–1903	+ 31,554	+ 49,904
1903–1912	− 1,697	+ 13,246

[a] To 1 June.   [b] To 1 September.   [c] Parliamentary burgh only.

The long cycles in demand had a twofold origin. They reflected the influence of migration; and they reflected the rate of demolition and conversion of house property. There are no figures to show the flow of population into, and out of, Glasgow year by year, but census data provide a measure of the balance of migration in each decade. The growth of population was irregular, not because of any fluctuation in the rate of natural increase, but because of the sharp reversals, between one decade and another, in the balance of migration. In the sixties and nineties there was a large net inflow, while in the intervening period, and still more after the turn of the century, there was a large net outflow. If it were possible to locate the turning-points more precisely, it is almost certain that the first would lie some years after 1871 and the second some years after 1901; that is, they would tend to approach, if not coincide with, the turning-points in the building cycle.

Period	Net increase in population	Balance of births and deaths	Balance of migration to Glasgow	Increase in houses occupied
1861–1871	+87,532	+46,522	+41,010	+15,921 [a]
1871–1881	+19,674	+57,650	−37,976	+7,016
1881–1891	+54,295	+65,321	−11,026	+11,770
1891–1901 [b]	+103,639	+75,295	+28,344	+22,130
1901–1911 [b]	+22,787	+105,425	−82,638	+764

[a] Parliamentary burgh only.   [b] Greater Glasgow.

The figures given above show the growth of population within the city limits. There was, however, a simultaneous fluctuation in the rate of development of suburban Glasgow. This fluctuation not only had direct repercussions on building activity within the municipality but was also to some extent the counterpart and explanation of the ebb and flow of migrants into or out of Glasgow. If we take the larger area into which Glasgow eventually grew by extension of its boundaries,[1] the figures become:

Year	Net increase in population (000's)	Excess of births over deaths (000's)	Balance of migration (000's)	Migration to Glasgow (000's)	Migration to suburbs (000's)
1861–1871	119·6	55·0	+64·6	+41·0	+23·6
1871–1881	102·9	79·1	+23·8	−38·0	+61·8
1881–1891	103·8	93·1	+10·7	−11·0	+21·7
1891–1901	140·1	102·6	+37·6	+28·3	+9·3
1901–1911	27·8	118·8	−91·0	−82·6	−7·4

Migration into the larger area fluctuated less than into Glasgow proper, and the growth of population was also at a more even pace. The main

[1] To be precise, Registration Districts 622, 644 and 646, including Maryhill, Partick and Govan.

reversal that took place was after 1901 when a large inflow gave way to an even larger outflow. This corresponded to a general change in the flow of migration throughout Britain, the current setting, a little after the turn of the century, away from the towns and in the direction of North America. In earlier decades the correspondence between a large flow of emigrants and a reduced flow of migrants into Glasgow was less close:

Year	Net loss by migration from Scotland (000's)	Net gain by migration into Glasgow and suburbs (000's)
1861–1871	117·0	64·6
1871–1881	93·3	23·8
1881–1891	217·4	10·7
1891–1901	53·4	37·6
1901–1911	254·0	−91·0

Although net emigration from Scotland fell in the seventies, Glasgow did not feel the effects in a larger inflow; and in the eighties and nineties, the changes in the flow of emigrants were on a much larger scale than the simultaneous changes in migration into Glasgow. It would seem, therefore, that Glasgow's experience was somewhat in contrast with the general experience of large English towns over those three decades, the general tendency being for population to migrate to the towns in the seventies and nineties and away from them in the eighties.[1]

The figures for Glasgow and suburbs are much more in line with the general experience, however, than the figures for the municipality proper. In the sixties the boom in shipbuilding brought great prosperity, and may have influenced migration to Glasgow. But Partick and Govan, where some of the new yards were located, were outside the city limits. These areas grew rapidly, particularly in the seventies. In that decade the great clearances effectively prevented a large growth of population within the city, and the building industry had its hands full with reconstruction on the one hand and the housing of close on an extra 100,000 persons in the suburbs on the other. It is not altogether surprising, therefore, that no *greater* movement of population into Glasgow occurred in that decade. For some part at least of the period there must have been an acute housing shortage within the town. In the eighties the development of the suburbs was more gradual. The apparent falling-off in the nineties—contrary to what could be confidently expected—is partly due to the extension of the city boundaries in 1891

---

[1] See chapter IV.

and to the consequent reduction in the area treated above as 'suburban'. It is difficult to be certain, however, that it is not simply the reflexion of some lack of comparability in the figures.

If we leave suburban development on one side and analyse the figures for Glasgow proper, it is plain that the inflow and outflow of population was large enough to dominate the demand for house-room. Between the sixties and seventies the change in the balance of migration was equivalent to an average of 8000 per annum, while the natural increase of population was only about half as great. Thus, if building activity in 1860 had been in line with the rate of natural increase, migration would first have doubled the demand and subsequently cut it to vanishing point. The actual fluctuations were far larger; but so, no doubt, were the annual (as distinct from the decennial) fluctuations in migration. It takes time for a building boom to get under way—indeed, this is one of the main reasons why it develops the characteristics of a boom—and it is the initiating impulse that needs explanation rather than the dimensions of the subsequent oscillation. Migration was powerful enough to serve as such an impulse, whether as accelerator or as brake.

The outflow that started in the middle seventies brought the first major boom to an end. The reversal of this flow in the nineties gave the second most of its impetus. When the outflow started again, on such a scale as to arrest the growth of population almost completely, the second boom, too, petered out. The building cycle was little more than a migration cycle in disguise.

But what, then, caused the migration cycle? The introduction of tramways, electric light, and other new-fangled, urban conveniences were not unimportant. The ups and downs of local industries may have played a part. But there was also a deeper influence at work. The drift to and away from Glasgow was part of a larger drift, discussed elsewhere in this volume (Chapter VIII), now to the cities, now to foreign countries. As a rule, when emigration from Scotland was low, Glasgow grew fast; when emigration was high, Glasgow houses stood empty and the building industry was idle. It was the prosperity of the Dakotas, so to speak, that brought building to a standstill in Dalmarnock.

The emigration that took place was chiefly to countries to which British capital was flowing; it was active when foreign investment was active, depressed when foreign investment was depressed. In the intervals of depression capital and labour alike waited until the products of the exploited countries came into more urgent demand, or offered scope for new methods, or until (for whatever reason) prospects of settlement or investment appeared to have improved. During these pauses there was simultaneously pressure on house accommodation and a surfeit of cheap money; when the game began again, the need for houses and the funds for their construction vanished together. Moreover, the very cessation of foreign investment, by bringing to this country distress sales of raw materials and foodstuffs, drove more and more of the agricultural workers to the towns and increased the purchasing power of the industrial population; the building industry prospered at the expense of colonial development.

The second important influence at work was demolition and conversion. There are no figures of either; but by deducting the net increase in houses from the total approved for construction it is possible to obtain a rough indication of the 'disappearance' of houses either through demolition or conversion to business and other uses. No importance attaches to the magnitude in any one year of the figures obtained in this way; they are much too rough and ready. The lag in plans passed cannot have been exactly and consistently ten months; the two sets of figures may make use of slightly different definitions of a house; and some plans were never carried into effect. Taken over a period of several years, however, the divergence between 'gross' and 'net' new building ought to be a reliable guide to fluctuations in demolition and conversion.

Table 4. *Rate of 'demolition' at Glasgow, 1873–1913*

Year[a]	Number of houses built annually	Annual increase in houses occupied or unoccupied	Rate of 'demolition'
1873–1877	4829	2109	2720
1878–1882	591	263	328
1883–1889	967	615	352
1890–1899	3199	1940	1259
1900–1907	3056	2581	475
1908–1913	737	−634	1371

[a] 1 September to 31 August from houses built and from June to June in the year following for houses occupied and unoccupied.

The result is shown in Table 4. Two conclusions may be hazarded. The first, for which there is good supplementary evidence, is that the rate of demolition in the middle seventies was extraordinarily high. For five years nearly 3000 houses a year were demolished in a city where the number of inhabited houses was rising at not much above 1000 a year, and where nearly twenty years were to pass before 3000 houses were again erected in any single year. Over a sixth of the town was pulled down between 1870 and 1878. Even in the great reconstruction boom in the nineties, when, all over the country, house property was being reconditioned and rebuilt, the rate of demolition was only half as rapid. The extensive clearances of the seventies were due in large measure to the City Improvement Trust, which was set up in 1866 to pull down the pestilential 'Frying Pan Alleys' of the city and expended £1·6 m. between 1870 and 1883, displacing over 30,000 people in the course of its operations. The railway companies were also active.

The second, more tentative, conclusion is that the highest rates of demolition tended to succeed periods of housing shortage rather than to coincide with them. In the seventies it was only after the steepest climb in the number of inhabited houses was over that demolitions reached such tremendous proportions; there seems even to have been a dip in the rate of demolition, while the demand for additional house-room was at its peak. After 1878 the shock of the City of Glasgow Bank crash was as paralysing to those who contemplated pulling buildings down as to those whose business it was to put them up. In the nineties both took courage again; and the last years of the century were probably the only period when a peak in the demand for additional house-room coincided with a peak in the rate of demolition. A second peak in the one prolonged the building boom until 1903–4; but the other did not recover again until 1907, when the population was on the point of falling and the housing shortage was already over.

The evidence for the second conclusion is too uncertain for any theory of the matter to be worth elaborating. It is, however, obvious that so far as demolition arose from the activities of the local authorities they had greater scope and less reluctance in demolishing house property when there was a margin of empty houses available and when the building industry was already in high gear. In the years immediately before 1914, the very large amount of empty property must have provided a special incentive to private owners to demolish their property.

Over the whole period from 1871 to 1914 the total number of houses for which plans were passed was 105,000, or about 2400 per year. This total exceeded the net addition to the number of houses standing (excluding those added by boundary changes) by some 46,700. If 3 % of the houses for which plans were passed were never built, and if, say, 3000 houses were converted to business uses, this would mean that for every ten houses built, four were demolished; and that of every ten houses standing in 1870, four had been pulled down by 1914.

Equilibrium between the rate of demolition, the demand for house-room, and the rate of new construction depends largely upon the number of empty houses. They are both a residue and an initiating force; they are the stocks whose accumulation spoils the market and whose de-cumulation provides a buffer until builders see a profit again. But they are not necessarily an *exact* index of surplus or shortage. Many empty houses will be old-fashioned or lacking in modern conveniences; too large or too small; in areas from which the population is removing; or in an almost uninhabitable condition. And there will, of course, be the usual residuum: the counter and shop-window stock, so to speak.

The competition of empty and newly erected houses, therefore, may be very imperfect; empty houses in the centre of the city may be *proof* of a demand for houses in the suburbs, and empty single-roomed houses may be evidence of a desire to spend more in rent. Figures bearing on the location and size of unoccupied houses in Glasgow are very scanty. But it can be said with fair certainty that abrupt changes in the amount of unoccupied property were never merely local, and that they damped down or accelerated new building over a wide area. The dispersion of empty property was largely a matter of secular change or of the varying pace of recession or revival in different groups of industry rather than of annual, or even cyclical, movements of taste or in the activities of building contractors. In Glasgow, at any rate, fluctuations in empty property were a fair index of housing scarcity.

The number of empty houses rose and fell over longish periods without much apparent response to cyclical influences (Fig. 3). If the figures are analysed in terms of annual increments, however, they reveal a strong cyclical pattern not unlike that shown by the annual increment in houses occupied. If the total number of houses, occupied and empty, had remained constant, the two sets of figures would have been identical in magnitude and opposite in sign. If, on the other hand, residential building had followed the trade cycle closely, the number of empty houses might have shown no variation from a steady trend throughout the cycle, more houses being built and occupied in the boom and fewer in the slump. It is significant that, of the three sets of increments in the total number of houses, in occupied houses and in empty houses, it was in the last two that the cyclical pattern was marked and that the first showed little or no correlation with the trade cycle.

The turning-points were not quite the same, however, for empty as for occupied houses. The rise in occupied houses was at its maximum in 1873, while the fall in empty houses was at its maximum much earlier. In 1879, 1882, 1885 and 1890 the turning-points coincide. After the nineties, for which no figures are available, the turning-points again coincide in 1901 and 1908, but the change in empty houses is a year ahead in 1904 and 1906.

Since the number of empty houses is the difference between the number of houses available and the number of houses occupied, these cyclical variations do not correspond to some independent influence operating on the building industry. They merely witness the comparative insensitiveness of residential building to the trade cycle; cyclical fluctuations in demand were taken up, over the period of the cycle, predominantly by opposite fluctuations in the stock of empty houses.

It required more than a cyclical movement in empties to alter the trend in residential building. An extra thousand empty houses or so might do no more than raise the proportion standing empty from 3 to 4%. The position was different if the movement in empties persisted

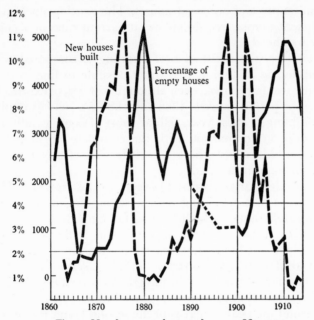

Fig. 3. New houses and empty houses, 1860–1914.

for a series of years. The upswings would generally continue for some time after empties had begun to increase and come to an end when they were some 2% above normal; the downswings would last until empties had reached their maximum and filled up again to, or beyond, normal. The boom of the sixties and seventies began with 2% of all houses unoccupied, the boom of the nineties with about 4%. The first boom broke in 1877, when the proportion of empty houses was not much over 6%, the second in 1903–4 when the proportion was still no more than about 4%. It was no accident that on both occasions the proportion subsequently climbed to a much higher figure. Builders were able to read the signs. In 1876–7 the number of empty houses suddenly rose by nearly 2000, and the number of extra houses occupied amounted to only 750; in addition, the proportion of empty houses had risen in each of the past six years. In 1902–3 the number of empty houses rose by 1500 and the following year by 3750, the largest increase ever recorded in a single year. At the same time, there must have been increasing difficulty in selling new houses, for the total number of houses occupied rose in 1903–4 by only 500, equivalent to one-tenth of the current rate of construction. Thus it was not so much the absolute number of empty houses that broke both booms, not even the upward trend, but the alarming jump, and still more, the changed relationship between the movement in empty and occupied houses. The existing stock suddenly became sufficient to meet requirements, at current rates of occupation, for many years ahead.

When, therefore, the curve of new building is compared with the curve of empties, as in Fig. 3, it is quite possible to find years when house-building was fairly brisk, even although 6 or 7 % of existing houses were empty. The period between 1886 and 1889 is a good example. But the rate of building in those years fell far short of boom conditions and was 'brisk' only in comparison with the complete stagnation of the previous slump. Moreover, there was little sign of any marked and abrupt deterioration in demand.

There is an interesting contrast between the last stages of the two major booms, the first exploding with a resounding crash, while the other slid gracefully and gradually down, taking eight years to expire. The explanation is partly to be found in the collapse of financial facilities in 1878; partly in the greater momentum behind the first boom—the rate of expansion was faster and the peak rate of building was greater; but probably most of all in the greater severity of the check in demand—the proportion of empty houses climbed to 10 % in the first two years beyond the peak, whereas in the second boom the proportion of empty houses did not reach 10 % until eight years beyond the peak.

The logistics of the building cycle depend a good deal upon the magnitude of the swing in empty houses that builders are prepared to treat as normal. Clearly if they are prepared to go on building until one house in ten is empty, the cycle might be a very long and very severe one. In a stable population the rate of house-building would probably average about 1 % per annum of the standing stock of houses. If population were growing at 1 % per annum, the rate might be 2 % per annum. The normal proportion of empty houses might be 2 %. To allow this proportion to grow to 10 % in such circumstances would be tantamount to anticipating the next four years' requirements. No doubt if builders knew for certain the trend of population and expected no more than average luck, they would not get themselves into such a fix. No doubt also the trend is a lot easier to work out after the event than to predict before it. But the fact remains that it often takes more than a 10 % vacancy rate to reduce house-building to a trickle. To work off the surplus with the industry working at half the normal rate would take eight years, and to accumulate it again with the industry working at twice the normal rate would take another four. A swing in empties between 2 and 10 %, therefore, could easily be transmitted into a cycle of, say, twelve years, *without any change in demand whatever.*

This is no more than a hypothesis. But the hypothesis is framed round the recorded experience of Glasgow. In some respects Glasgow's experience was exceptional. The proportion of empty houses in London from 1871 onwards never rose above 8%; in Hamburg the maximum was 9 %. In the suburbs of Glasgow, however, the proportion touched 17 % in 1880; in Clydebank it fell from 15·5 % in 1911 to 0·4 % three years later.

Thus the explanation of the building cycle instead of centring round the demand for houses, may gravitate towards the building industry and the supply of houses. It would be easy to show that output cannot be expanded quickly in an industry made up almost entirely of small men, each taking large risks in relation to his financial resources, and each building only a few new houses a year. It takes time for them to enlarge the scale of their work and speed up the rhythm of house-building. They have men to train, capital to borrow, organization to learn and buyers to find. Thus the build-up is slow; a shortage of houses has time to develop quite a long way before it can be overtaken; by the time it is overtaken the industry is likely to be swollen to excess and rolling along a great deal too fast. The inevitable shock to which the industry is ultimately submitted spells bankruptcy and disorganization on a large scale. After a prolonged setback it is necessary to start the next build-up under the same difficulties as before.

This is, of course, the ordinary cyclical process that can be observed in almost any industry whether the trade cycle is operating or not. It helps to account for the length and severity of the building cycle. But it is doubtful whether, if it were not fed by fluctuations in demand, it would give rise by itself to cycles so pronounced as those observable in building. In the case of Glasgow, at all events, it was not so much the characteristics of the building industry as the migratory habits of the population that dominated the cycle.

One would expect to find the stock of empty house-room reacting on its price. There is no completely satisfactory index of house prices nor of house rents. But a fair substitute for the latter can be arrived at by dividing, each year, the aggregate rental of dwelling-houses by their number at the same date. This procedure suffers from the disadvantage of treating all houses on the same footing and makes no allowance for any difference between new houses just built, old houses just demolished and the existing stock of houses. A gradual rise in housing standards and in the size of houses built would raise the rental even when rents were quite steady. The real trend in rents, therefore, was less steeply upwards than is implied in Table 1. But the figures in Table 1 probably give a faithful enough picture of the changes from year to year, allowing something for the influence of new building on the average in times of boom.

It is obvious from Table 1 that rents were more than sticky. They were apt to rise quite rapidly just when the number of empty houses was rising rapidly. This happened in 1875–8 and again in 1901–4. In the eighties, average rents fell while the number of empty houses was falling, and then remained comparatively steady while empties rose and fell again. It was generally years before a reversal in the trend of empties was reflected in a reversal in the trend of the rent at which they were offered.

Rents climbed fastest in the seventies and nineties. In the first of those two periods there was surprisingly little real basis for an inflation of rents. The number of empty houses rose steadily from 1871 onwards. The number of occupied houses rose rapidly and consistently up to 1874, but the rate of increase changed little after 1868 and yet rents did not rise markedly until 1873. When they did rise it was speculation that sent them up. The speculators bought property, raised rents and then tried to sell out at a profit.[1] Their confidence in the continuance of the rise induced them to hold property unlet for a longer period until tenants offered the higher rent demanded. The high building costs resulting from the boom contributed to their initial success. At the height of the boom, in 1876, speculative confidence that rents would go on rising was demonstrated in the offer of an average of seventeen years' purchase for house property when only four years previously 14·3 was the average and five years later pessimism was to bring it down again to 13·5.[2]

The fall in rents which followed was particularly severe for unoccupied property and for the larger type of house. At the height of the boom it

---

[1] Nicol, *Vital Economic and Social Statistics of Glasgow, 1881–85*, p. 49.

[2] W. Fraser, 'Fluctuations of the building trade and Glasgow's house accommodation', *Proc. Roy. Phil. Soc. Glasgow*, 1908, p. 27. Fraser also gives the following figures for later years:

| 1886 | 12·8 | 1896 | 14·1 | 1906 | 13·0 |
| 1891 | 13·0 | 1901 | 14·9 | 1907 | 12·1 |

had been the unoccupied houses that had been the more highly rented, but after 1879 this ceased to be true; even in the nineties, so far as can be seen, the rent of unoccupied houses remained the lower. The fall in the rents of 'larger' houses in 1879 and 1880 may be gauged from the decline in the number of houses rented at more than £10 by a full 10%.

After the bank crash of 1878, rents fell steadily till 1890, when the first signs of improvement became apparent. Closer inspection of available figures shows that the fall came to an end as early as 1886 for houses rented at less than £10—chiefly of one and two apartments, although a good many three-roomed houses at this period were let for less than £10 per annum.[1] Some reflexion of this situation can be seen in the high percentage of plans for houses of one and two apartments passed in the years 1886–9. From 1881 to 1885 the percentage had been 66, in the next four years it averaged 70, and in the period 1892–6 it fell again to 62.[2]

In the nineties came a sharp rise in rents which was not, however, quite so great as might appear from Table 1. The average rent for a dwelling-house in the district annexed was much higher than within the city limits, and the amalgamation pulled up average rents there by about 21s. A further part of the rise can be traced to the extensive reconstruction and rebuilding of the period and to the stricter sanitary requirements of the local administration. In all, the rise in rents in the nineties was probably about 10%. The rise came to an end about 1904 and was succeeded by a gradual fall, which lasted almost until the outbreak of war.

Rents of empty property followed a similar but more erratic course, although events confined to a few districts or a single class of house sometimes obscure the general trend. In 1882, for instance, the apparent recovery in rents is the consequence of a sharp fall in the number of houses at low rentals vacant in the Barony parish. And in 1873–4 the fall in rents was largely confined to unoccupied houses rented at more than £10 per annum.[3]

The information on fluctuations in cost is relatively meagre. The valuation of new buildings by the liners of the Dean of Guild Court is on

---

[1] In 1891 (after annexations which raised average rentals) the average rent of houses of one apartment was £5. 5s., of two apartments £8. 10s., and of three apartments £14 per annum. In the course of ten years these figures became £6, £9, and £15 respectively. (*Evidence of City Assessor before Municipal Commission on the Housing of the Poor* (1904), p. 3.)

[2] See also Table 1, which brings out the fall in the average size of house built in those years.

[3] The figures of plans passed show a depression in the building of houses of four to six apartments in 1871–3. Though the average rent of occupied houses rose in 1873 the larger houses did not participate.

the same basis from year to year and may be regarded as reliable.[1] The value of sites and of fittings (e.g. plumbing work) is not included. As the number of houses of one to five apartments is specified separately and houses of more than five apartments seldom exceed 3 % of the total, the aggregate number of apartments, and hence the cost per apartment,[2] can be calculated with fair accuracy. The results are given in Table 1. In the same table are given some statistics of masons' wages in Glasgow during the period. An increase of a penny an hour in wages raised the cost per room by about £10.

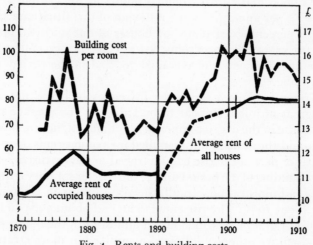

Fig. 4. Rents and building costs.

Perhaps the most interesting deduction to be made from these calculations is the frequency with which a maximum in the cost per apartment succeeds a maximum in house-building, as if the final *coup de grâce* to building booms came from the side of cost rather than of demand. In 1877, 1899 and 1903 there are clear maxima in building costs and the bursting of a speculative bubble; in 1883 there is another maximum that may have checked an incipient revival.[3] Moreover, the rise in costs in these years was apparently not due to a rise in the price of building materials. We are left, therefore, with wages as the element in cost which rose in the closing stages of the boom; whatever happened to materials, there is no doubt that wage concessions were made first when plans for house-building were beginning to decline. On the other

[1] For seventy-three tenement properties erected in 1906–7 the average cost per apartment worked out at £92 which is very close to the average of the Dean of Guild Court linings for those years (Fraser, loc. cit. p. 37).

[2] One-roomed houses cost more proportionately to build, but the final figures would not be greatly altered if account could be taken of this fact.

[3] 1883 was a year of wage advances and strikes.

hand, wage and cost reductions seem to have had little effect on output. When demand was low, building was perhaps a little more active in years of low than of high cost; but these were mere spurts—bargain-hunts. 1886, for instance, was probably a year of this kind, and so also were 1906 and 1909–10. Similarly, there were years when temporary *increases* in cost reduced output. Something of this description took place in 1881, 1883, 1905 and 1907–8. But all this is a matter of the distribution of a small, occasionally a normal, output over a period of depression; the real stimulus to revival came invariably from the side of demand.

On the finance of building in Glasgow there is space only for the very briefest comments. Capital for building was required by the master builder and by the landlords who were his chief customers. The former was seldom himself a man of capital, many building contractors being ex-workmen. They borrowed from building societies,[1] from banks, and from dealers in raw material,[2] and economized capital by the sale of ground rents. In 1888 the rate of interest on second mortgages, such as builders entered into with timber dealers, was usually 6%,[3] but of changes before and after 1888 little is known.

The rate of interest is a much more important element in the calculations of the house-owner than of the builder, and it is the former who fixes the tempo of house construction. It was usual in Glasgow, as elsewhere, for the landlord to raise two-thirds of the value of his property on mortgage and hope for some 6 or 7% as a minimum on the remaining third after covering all risks, ground burdens, and cost of repairs and management.[4] A slight rise in the rate of interest on bonds necessarily brought down the return on the landlord's capital more than proportionately. Thus if 'bond rate' was 4% and the gross rent from a tenement costing £2100 was £150, the landlord would be obtaining a net return of some £44 on a margin of £700, i.e. $6\frac{2}{7}$%. A rise in bond rate of one-eighth (i.e. to $4\frac{1}{8}$%) would lower the net yield to $5\frac{2}{7}$%, i.e. by almost one-sixth.

On the progress of bond rate and the return on the landlord's margin a few scraps of information are available. The rate on first mortgages was generally about 1% above the rate on Consols. In 1850–5 it was $3\frac{2}{3}$%, from 1855 to 1870 4%, in 1877 $4\frac{1}{2}$%, in 1890 4%; then it fell

---

[1] Binnie, Evidence before Municipal Commission (1904), Q. 6962.
[2] *Digest of Evidence on Town Holdings* (Cassell, 1888), p. 142.
[3] Ibid.
[4] On small houses the deduction from gross rental to cover such costs would be about a third (Binnie, Evidence before Presbytery Commission on Housing (1891), p. 152; Committee on Artisans' and Labourers' Dwellings (1881), VII, Q. 4909).

to as low as 3 % or even $2\frac{3}{4}$ % in 1896; by 1904 it had risen again to $3\frac{1}{4}$ %, by 1908 to $3\frac{3}{4}$ % and by 1912 to 4 %.[1] Property-owners were earning 7 % on their 'margin' in 1890 and in 1900. In 1904 a case in which the landlord was earning $6\frac{5}{8}$ % net was cited as typical,[2] and in 1914 it was stated to be no more than $3\frac{1}{2}$–$4\frac{1}{2}$ %.[3] The landlord was caught between rising interest rates and falling demand.

These movements in interest rates help to explain the boom in house-building in the nineties and the depression after 1906; the fall in interest rates reinforced the rise in rents in the first period just as the rise in interest rates reinforced the fall in rents in the second. But neither interest rates nor rents were the primary forces at work. Both were governed by the ebb and flow of capital and labour between Britain and countries overseas. Foreign investment and emigration were low in the nineties and high from 1904 onwards; and when the tide turned, carrying with it cheap money and a throng of tenants, the building industry all over Britain was left on the rocks.

[1] Binnie (1891), p. 152; Cd. 8111 (1915), pp. 3 *et seq.*; T. J. Millar, *Building Society Statistics and Finance*; Evidence before Municipal Commission (1904), p. 344.
[2] Fraser, loc. cit. p. 36.
[3] Cd. 9235 (1919), p. 5. Cf. also Cd. 8154, Appendix 18.

CHAPTER III

INVESTMENT IN CANADA, 1900–13

This essay starts from a very simple point, but one which, in previous discussions of investment in Canada, has hardly received the attention which it deserves. Investment by one country in another means a transfer, not of purchasing power in the sense either of cash or of income, but of capital. Changes in the money supply and in incomes may accompany a transfer of capital: but they are plainly not the same thing. A transfer of capital (at any rate where capital is being borrowed for productive investment) means that one country's stock of instruments of production is enlarged out of the savings of another country. It means, as a rule, that certain changes take place in employment and constructional activity in both countries; that, for example, the borrowing country experiences a building boom while the building trade in the lending country is depressed. These are the fundamental changes. And we must never be led to neglect them by concentration on monetary changes and banking policies.

I. *The Background to investment*

Investment in Canada after 1900 took place against a background of scarcity and expansion. First, and above all, there was an almost continual scarcity of labour. Complaints of labour shortage came from all lines of business. In manufacturing, employers reported that they were ready and anxious to employ many more hands if suitable men could be found. Railway construction was repeatedly held up while contractors searched for men; sometimes horses stood idle in the stables because teamsters were unobtainable. At harvest time the shortage was acute; the railway companies undertook the transport of labour from the east, and special arrangements were made to bring labourers from abroad with a view to settlement of the immigrants out of their harvest earnings. In mines and lumber camps, in building, domestic service and transportation, the same scarcity of labour was everywhere felt.

There was a shortage, secondly, of concrete capital. The rapid growth of population and the immigration of large numbers of young workers strained the limited supply of house-room to the point of famine. Between 1901 and 1911 the number of occupied dwelling-houses increased by 387,000; in the same period the number of families increased by 447,000.[1] The shortage was greatest in the western provinces. At Calgary, for example, 'scores of citizens' had to keep their families in the east because there were no houses to be had. In British Columbia, more than a quarter of the married men had left their wives in some other province or country, presumably for the same reason.

Congestion on the railways was almost equally great. After every abundant harvest there was a shortage of cars. In the summer, the companies were hard put to it at times to arrange for the transport of settlers and their effects. New track and equipment were constantly required for homesteads, mines and lumber camps off the existing railway routes; and the additional traffic carried on these new branch lines made it necessary to provide larger terminals and repair shops.

The scarcity of these and other forms of concrete capital expressed itself in a corresponding scarcity of money capital. If the country was to be opened up rapidly, an enormous outlay on the purchase or construction of capital instruments was essential. To meet this outlay the savings of Canadians were altogether inadequate. There was not enough capital inside Canada. Canadian savings had to be supplemented, therefore, by borrowings from abroad. The size of the borrowings which Canada succeeded in making is some measure of the scarcity of capital after 1900.

Scarcity in all these forms led not unnaturally to higher costs. Weekly wages, to deal first with labour, rose by nearly 50 %, and hourly rates in an even higher ratio.[2] The rise varied enormously between localities and industries, so that we cannot speak of average changes with much confidence. Some broad conclusions would appear, however, to be warranted by the evidence. First of all, there was a rise in real wages as well as in money wages. The cost of living increased by from 40 to 45 %, while weekly wage-rates increased by nearly 50 %.[3] Secondly, the rise in wages was greatest in the sheltered industries and least in those which had to face competition from imports. In building, domestic service, printing, transportation and municipal service, the average increase was 58 %;[4]

[1] In the previous decade both increased by only 150,000. The number of persons per dwelling rose from 5·2 in 1901 to 5·9 in 1911, although the average size of family fell simultaneously.

[2] The reduction in hours between 1900 and 1913 was probably about 5 % on the average (cf. the data in the *Cost of Living Report*, vol. II, p. 431).

[3] Up to 1910 weekly wage-rates and the cost of living kept pace with one another, and even in 1912 the indices given in Table 9 (below p. 59) show only a 1 % difference. The index of weekly wages used by Viner (*Canada's Balance of International Indebtedness*, 1900–13, p. 243), and taken from the *Cost of Living Report*, shows a slightly faster rise in money wages up to 1912 and a gradual rise in real wages.

[4] Calculated from data in the *Cost of Living Report*, vol. II, pp. 428–30. The weights given by Coats (building, 14; domestic service, 20; printing, 2; transportation, 8; municipal service, ½) have been used.

in mining, brewing, and the leather, textile and metal industries the average increase was 31·5 %, or, if the clothing trades (including tailoring, etc.) are included, by 37 %.[1] In agriculture the rise was intermediate—just over 50 %.[2] Thirdly, the changes in wages and prices in different provinces were such as to raise real wages faster in the west than in the east. Generally speaking, the further west the province the higher, both in 1900 and in 1913, were money wages and the cost of living. But between 1900 and 1913 there was a levelling up in wages and prices, both rising faster in the east than in the west. As the levelling-up process was carried further in prices than in wages, the result was a relative improvement in real wages in the provinces west of Ontario. But the change in favour of the west—especially when rents are taken into account—was not great.

Scarcity of concrete capital did not lead everywhere to a rise in the price which its services fetched. The rent of dwelling-houses, it is true, increased by from 60 to 70 %, and business rents increased twice as rapidly. But railway charges remained practically constant, freight rates moving down and passenger rates up. Public utility charges, too, were for the most part lower. The failure of these prices to rise can be explained in part by the large measure of public control exercised over them. Prices were regulated by statute, charter, or public commission, and were not determined solely by considerations of profit.[3] Nevertheless, the fact that public utilities continued to make large profits at the low prices is an indication that other factors were at work. Of these, one was obviously the coming into play of economies of scale. Whereas the provision of more house-room became progressively more expensive the faster the population grew, the provision of water, gas, electricity and transport became progressively cheaper. Moreover, the fact that houses required to be built by Canadian labour, whereas rails, locomotives, generating equipment, tubes, boilers and so on could be manufactured by foreign labour whose wages rose less rapidly, kept down costs in public utilities relatively to building costs.

The changes in the price structure are illustrated in Fig. 5. They were not all by any means in the direction normal to inflation: wholesale prices lagged behind the cost of living, and the cost of living lagged

[1] Calculated from data cited above. The weights used were: mining, 5; brewing and distilling, ½; leather, 1; textiles, 3; metals, 8; clothing, 7.

[2] These figures are for weekly earnings. They are based upon quotations that did not remain constant in number, and to which the chain method appears not to have been applied. No serious error, however, is involved. In the building industry, where hours were reduced by about 9 %, the rise in hourly rates of wages varied from 52 % (bricklayers) to 90 % (rough carpenters), and averaged 70 %. In no other industry did hours fall so heavily.

[3] Viner, op. cit. p. 245.

slightly behind money wages. The fan opening out between import prices, export prices and domestic prices, each progressively more free to cut loose from the movement of world prices, does, however, exhibit the normal outcome of inflation in a country running up an adverse balance of payments.

Finally, scarcity of money capital sent up the rate of interest. The return both on Dominion and on Provincial government bonds rose by

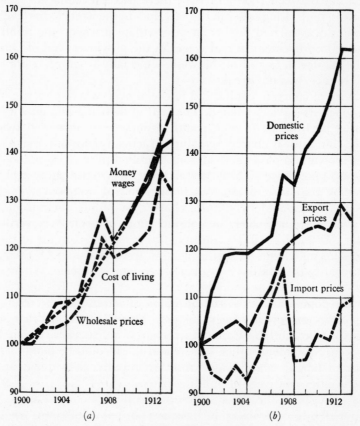

Fig. 5. (a) Wages and prices, 1900-13; (b) Import, export and domestic prices, 1900-13.

20 %, on first mortgages on city house property in the same proportion, and on the bonds of cities, counties and townships by upwards of 40 %. The terms on which Canada was able to borrow in London and New York grew steadily more onerous.

With scarcity and rising prices went expansion. In every year except 1908 and 1909, the labour supply was augmented by immigrants from Europe and the United States. On balance, about 650,000 persons, a large proportion of whom were young men in the prime of life, settled in Canada in the decade 1901–11. In the next three years, the net immigration was nearly 500,000, more than the natural increase of population in the same period.[1] On the average, for every two Canadians entering the labour market for the first time, three immigrants offered their services simultaneously.[2] Not only did immigration dominate the labour market in terms of magnitude; it dominated it also in sensitivity. So long as there was a shortage of labour, immigrants poured in;

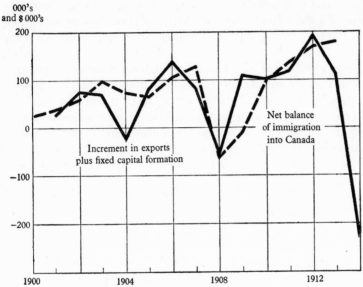

Fig. 6. Immigration into Canada and economic expansion, 1900–13.

wherever the demand for labour was deficient and no jobs were to be had, intending immigrants stayed where they were, while workers in Canada moved to countries less depressed or more congenial. The burden of adjustment to changing demands for labour was borne largely by migrants.

With expansion of the labour supply went investment in capital of all kinds. Roughly $2500 m. was borrowed abroad—not far short of

[1] These figures are almost certainly underestimates. There is reason to believe that net immigration in the decade 1901–11 was at least 1 million (see p. 63).

[2] The number of immigrant arrivals was 2,850,000, or 200,000 per annum. A small proportion, about 15 %, of these were children. On the average, therefore, about 170,000 persons entered the Canadian labour market annually; if we omit married women, perhaps 150,000 persons. At the same time, about 110,000 Canadian-born children reached the age of 15 in each year between 1905 and 1910. Of course, large numbers of immigrants and Canadians migrated later to the United States and other countries. But we are dealing here only with *entrance* to Canadian industry.

Canada's own savings during the period—and out of the proceeds, railway tracks and towns were built, and lands, forests and mines were developed, often with immigrant labour. The capital equipment (and the debt) of the country enormously increased.

The driving force behind Canadian development in those years was the rise in agricultural prices all over the world. From the mid-nineties onwards, Canadian exports were fetching higher and higher prices, while interest rates and construction costs remained comparatively low. Thus the scarcity of labour and of capital equipment in Canada were symptoms of a more fundamental scarcity of Canadian export goods on world markets.[1] Investment and immigration kept step with export prices.[2]

The large stretches of fertile prairie which the railways kept opening up enabled Canada to take increasing advantage of high prices without immediate risk of an equal rise in costs. High prices operated in conjunction with an elastic supply of virgin land; development was profitable and there was plenty of room for development. But it would be a mistake to lay stress exclusively on agricultural development. The rise in export prices was not the sole factor at work. Between 1900 and 1913 rich deposits of mineral ores were found and developed in the Cobalt, Porcupine and other districts. Canada became the leading nickel producer in the world, and copper, silver and gold were exported in large quantities. These minerals sold at low prices, but mining costs were also low and production was highly profitable. In other industries, improved methods of production were favourable to an expansion in Canadian output.[3]

The process of expansion was thrice interrupted. About the autumn of 1903 there began a transient depression which lasted till the end of 1904 and was felt mainly in the east. A second and much more severe depression spread from the western provinces in the early summer of 1907 and continued all through 1908. The third and last depression, that of 1913–14, also began in the west.

---

[1] The price of grains and fodders at wholesale in Canada rose by 37·1 % between the triennial periods 1901–3 and 1911–13; animals and meats rose by 38·9 %; and dairy produce by 33·8 %. By contrast, the average rise in wholesale prices in Canada was only 21·6 %. (These estimates are based on the indices in the *Cost of Living Report*, vol. II, p. 20.)

[2] It may be suggested that Canadian export prices had little to do with the decisions about railway-building taken by the Canadian Government (or even by the companies). But these decisions were taken in a boom atmosphere which was largely the product of high export prices; and the railway-building would have been much more costly (and probably much less rapid) had it not been for the confidence of the British investor in the healthy prospects of the primary Canadian industries.

[3] Cf. Viner, op. cit. pp. 264–7.

II. *Investment and the balance of payments*

We may now return to the thesis with which this essay began and analyse the connexion between a transfer of capital to Canada and the volume of investment in Canada: that is, between investment and the balance of payments.

An increase in investment, unaccompanied by any change in thrift, tends to raise money incomes. An increase in exports generally has the same effect. The rise in incomes, initiated from the side of investment or of exports, tends to be cumulative. At first there may be some disinvestment in stocks, or some increase in short-term funds abroad. Later, as incomes continue to expand, savings are made and there is an increased outlay on imports. The original adjustments give place to others once the settled preferences of consumers find time to express themselves. But at each stage along the path of expansion one fundamental equation will be satisfied. We have:[1]

Investment in Canada ('Home Investment')

= Borrowings from abroad + Canadian investment in Canada

= Debit balance of payments on current account + Canadian investment abroad + Canadian investment in Canada

= Imports – Exports + Canadian savings.

Hence

'Home Investment' + Exports = Canadian Savings + Imports.

This equation may be interpreted causally to mean that any increase in the joint total of home investment and exports will drive up income to a level at which Canadians seek to make an exactly equal addition to their savings and expenditure on imports. Such an interpretation, however, is possible only with important qualifications.

First of all, a *net* increase in home investment or in exports—and still more in the sum of the two—is frequently the balance of an initial increase at one point over the resultant decrease at another. A rise in railway-building may force up interest rates and check house-building; a rise in wheat exports may be achieved by creating a scarcity of labour in the lumber camps. Again, exports may go up because investment is falling; for instance, when credit restriction forces merchants to dispose of stocks abroad, or when unemployment and reduced buying power are freeing goods for export which, in better times, would find a market at home. Or exports may fall off because of an expansion in investment

---

[1] I abstain from precise definition in the hope that these terms are sufficiently intelligible without further explanation.

and home demand. A primary change in investment or in exports works through other forms of investment and other exports as well as through incomes, savings and imports.

Secondly, savings and imports are not passive factors depending solely on income as determined by the current level of investment and export. A change in thrift may be of some importance, especially when prices alter so as to redistribute income in favour of the thrifty. A rise in import prices, by raising the cost of living, can also affect the demand for Canadian goods and so depress Canadian incomes. The public may seek to buy imports in preference to home-produced goods. And so on. Nevertheless, there is overwhelming evidence that, so long as incomes remain constant, outlay on consumable goods (home-produced and imported) is remarkably constant also, and that, in the short run, it is fluctuations in income which, more than anything else, alter savings and imports.[1] It is to home investment and exports, therefore, that we must look for an explanation of the changes that took place in the Canadian balance of payments.

It is not easy to test this reasoning against the facts. There are no statistical series for investment and savings, carefully defined. In 1937 I made a number of hazardous calculations in an article published in *Weltwirtschaftliches Archiv* (on which the present essay is based) and emerged with estimates which I labelled 'Canadian Home Investment' for the years 1900–13. It is unnecessary to reproduce these calculations here as they have now been superseded by the much more thorough investigations undertaken by Dr K. A. H. Buckley of the University of Saskatchewan.[2] Dr Buckley has been kind enough to allow me to make use of his estimates, which are given in Table 5.

Dr Buckley's estimates are partly on an annual, partly on a quinquennial basis. The annual figures cover constructional activity (including repair work), and investment in machinery and equipment, but not changes in stocks. The quinquennial figures show new construction and repair separately and include estimates of the net change in stocks. Since the data do not permit of the estimation of annual changes in stocks, the best that can be done is to use fixed capital formation (gross of repairs) as an index of changes in home investment. Unfortunately, this makes it impossible to attach any precise meaning to the corresponding concept on the side of savings. I shall make use of the term 'Gross Canadian Savings', conscious that it will diverge from actual savings whenever the level of stocks is in course of change, and that it

[1] Cf., for example, C. Bresciani-Turroni, 'Egypt's balance of payments', *J. Polit. Econ.* 1934; and J. H. Williams, *Argentine's International Balance of Indebtedness.*

[2] 'Real Investment in Canada, 1900 to 1930' (unpublished dissertation available in the London School of Economics Library).

Table 5. *Fixed capital formation in Canada, 1900–15*

Year	Value of total con-struction[a] ($m.)	Gross investment in machinery and equip-ment[b] ($m.)	Total fixed capital formation ($m.)	Net increase in inventories[c] ($m.)	Cost of con-struction[d] (1900–4 = 100)
1900	127	52	179		95·9
1901	127	60	187 ⎫		94·8
1902	156	73	229 ⎪		99·4
1903	194	90	284 ⎬	222	103·8
1904	213	75	288 ⎪		106·0
1905	247	82	329 ⎭		109·1
1906	307	100	407 ⎫		116·6
1907	351	125	476 ⎪		123·3
1908	316	108	424 ⎬	262	123·0
1909	383	117	500 ⎪		121·6
1910	440	136	576 ⎭		126·1
1911	519	167	686 ⎫		129·4
1912	586	224	810 ⎪		133·9
1913	580	249	829 ⎬	360	141·8
1914	471	170	641 ⎪		137·9
1915	355	102	457 ⎭		135·7

[a] K. A. H. Buckley, op. cit. p. 49. These figures include repairs estimated by Dr Buckley at $255 m. for 1901–5, $403 m. for 1906–10, and $523 m. for 1911–15. The figures for 1912 have been amended by Dr Buckley.

[b] Ibid. pp. 90–3. I have added an allowance for freight and mark-ups on the basis of quinquennial estimates given by Dr Buckley.

[c] Ibid. p. 116.

[d] Ibid. p. 49. I have converted from a 1913 to a 1900–4 base.

will exceed net savings by including both sums expended on repairs and sums required for the replacement of capital assets.

The most important constituent of gross home investment in Canada was undoubtedly railway-building. A further large item was the construction of highways, bridges, canals and harbours. These two items together accounted in 1913 for nearly $300 m. out of a total of just over $800 m. Dr Buckley's estimates for this group—which falls a little short of total investment in transport—is shown in Table 6. This table also shows the gross earnings of the main-line railways as an indication of the resiliency of their revenues; a threefold expansion in ten years provided strong encouragement to investors to finance more railway-building in Canada. The final column, showing the rapid growth in

Table 6. *Investment in transport, 1900–14*

Year	Gross investment[a]		Gross earnings of main line railways[b] ($m.)	Value of wheat crop ($m.)
	Steam railways ($m.)	Highways, bridges, canals, harbours ($m.)		
1900	34·1	(6·0)	70·7	55·6
1901	38·9	6·9	72·9	85·3
1902	44·6	8·3	83·7	93·6
1903	55·9	9·9	96·1	78·5
1904	61·3	11·0	100·2	69·0
1905	75·2	12·0	106·5	106·1
1906	94·1	10·6	125·3	125·5
1907	136·5	17·5	146·7	93·1
1908	135·0	20·8	146·9	112·4
1909	131·0	22·5	145·1	166·7
1910	151·6	31·9	174·0	132·1
1911	170·7	42·1	188·7	230·9
1912	210·2	53·5	219·4	224·2
1913	232·4	65·1	256·7	231·7
1914	177·0	64·7	243·1	—

[a] Including replacement and repair (Buckley, op. cit. pp. 153–4).

[b] Year ending 30 June. Excludes government-owned railways and electric railways.

value of the wheat crop, provides a measure both of the pace of agricultural development and of the need for additional transport facilities.

Adding together fixed capital formation and exports and deducting imports (inclusive of invisibles as well as of commodity trade), we obtain (in Table 7) what I have called above 'Gross Canadian Savings'.

The sum of exports and home investment increased in every year except 1904 and 1908; the same is true of imports. The changes in both totals (as shown in columns 4 and 5) kept step very closely, indicating (as we should expect) that savings maintained a relatively steady trend.

An inflationary impulse, then, coming from investment and exports raised money incomes in Canada at a rate dictated by the public's thrift and by its demand for imports. In real terms, what this meant was that the rising export and constructional industries—notably agriculture and building—were bidding successfully in the labour market for immigrant and mobile labour, while the industries exposed to foreign competition in the Canadian market found it increasingly difficult, in

Table 7. *Investment, savings and trade, 1900-14*[a]

Year	Exports plus fixed capital formation ($m.)	Imports ($m.)	'Gross savings' ($m.)	Increase in col. 1 ($m.)	Increase in col. 2 ($m.)
1900	361	234	127	—	—
1901	386	245	141	25	11
1902	462	276	186	76	31
1903	532	329	193	70	53
1904	511	328	187	−21	−1
1905	591	363	228	80	35
1906	728	429	299	137	66
1907	800	495	305	82	66
1908	743	440	303	−57	−55
1909	852	509	343	109	69
1910	954	623	331	102	114
1911	1071	729	342	117	106
1912	1265	889	347	194	160
1913	1376	951	425	111	78
1914	1135	805	330	−239	−146

[a] The figures for exports and imports in this table are those given by Professor F. A. Knox in 'Dominion Monetary Policy' (Appendix to the Report of the Royal Commission on Dominion Provincial Relations). They are revisions of estimates by Viner and include all current items, visible and invisible, except gold.

the face of the resulting scarcity of labour and rising costs of production, to hold their own, even in an expanding market. There was a reorientation of the labour force away from consumption goods (which could be imported cheaply) and towards the constructional industries (which, backed by foreign loans, could afford to pay high wages); there was a further reorientation of labour away from foreign trade goods and towards domestic, non-traded goods.[1] These two changes were not

[1] Cf. Viner, op. cit. pp. 262-3: 'It is difficult to explain the decline in the percentage of exports to total commodity production, without reference to the capital borrowings from abroad. Some of the relative decline in exports was undoubtedly due to the increasing extent to which Canadian raw materials were being manufactured in Canada for Canadian consumption, instead of being exported in their crude form in exchange for imported manufactured goods. But this increase in manufactures would not have been possible in nearly the same degree had it not been for the foreign investments of capital in Canadian manufacturing enterprises. The expansion of manufacturing not only absorbed an increased proportion of the Canadian production of raw materials, but it withdrew labour, from the production of raw materials which otherwise would have been exported, to the construction of plant and equipment and the fabrication, from imported raw materials, of manufactured commodities for

distinct. They arose from the fact that many of the capital goods which Canada was in the process of acquiring had to be constructed on the spot. Canada could not import railway track, bridges and houses. She could, and did, import men to do the work. The men were clothed with imported textiles, equipped with imported tools, and fed on agricultural produce which would otherwise have gone to supply foreign markets. But had Canada wanted ships and locomotives only, they might have stayed at home and supplied their wants from much the same sources.

Symptomatic of the changed state of the labour market when investment was at its peak were the changes that took place in wages and in prices. We have seen that wages rose most in the 'domestic' industries and least in industries competing with imports. That this was true also of prices is well known from Professor Viner's work. The rise in domestic (wholesale) commodity prices between 1900 and 1913 was 61·7 %;[1] the rise in Coats's weighted index for all commodities was 31·9 %.[2] The explanation of this change is, I believe, twofold. First, the urgent demand for labour from the constructional trades put pressure on all industries either to raise wages or let labour go. The domestic industries were in a position to meet this pressure by raising wages. They had no foreign competition to face, and could raise prices without fear of a shrinkage in demand. The rapid increase in population, indeed, coupled with a rising standard of living, brought about a quite unprecedented expansion in the demand for domestic goods and services, in terms both of money and of real resources. On the side of supply, however, these goods could only be provided at increasing cost.[3] Manufactures and imports, on the other hand, were supplied for the most part under conditions of decreasing cost. This divergent trend in (real) costs, like the divergent trend in wages, operated to widen the margin between domestic and other prices.[4]

domestic consumption. The development of roads, towns, and railroads, made possible by the borrowings abroad, absorbed a large part of the immigration of labour, and these consumed considerable quantities of Canadian commodities which would otherwise have been available for export.'

[1] Viner, op cit. p. 230.

[2] *Cost of Living Report*, vol. II, p. 23.

[3] Two out of three of Viner's twenty-three 'domestic' commodities are agricultural products (op. cit. p. 230, n. 2).

[4] Cf. A. G. Silverman, 'The international trade of Great Britain, 1880–1913' (unpublished Ph.D. thesis in Harvard University Library), pp. 201–2: 'Because of perishability or large transportation costs, the sources of local supply are limited and apt to be subject to increasing costs. There is little incentive or opportunity for technical advance and improved organisation under such conditions. Competitive opportunities in other industries, in which the advantage is greater, means higher wages all round: and this further increases costs in the production of domestic commodities such as are included in [Viner's] index.'

There were, of course, other factors at work. The great rise in the earnings of domestic servants, for example, is probably to be associated with the comparative scarcity of women immigrants. The scarcity of wives and of domestic servants both arose from this, and each no doubt reinforced the other; where wives were scarce, domestic servants were in demand, and where servants were scarce, wives were in demand.

III. *The forces governing home investment and exports*

(a) *Agriculture*

We have now to examine the forces which, in their turn, controlled home investment and exports. Over the period as a whole, the most important were the rise in agricultural prices in world markets and the opening-up of low-cost farming land and mineral deposits.[1] Even in the short period agriculture exercised a powerful influence alike on domestic purchasing power, borrowings abroad and credit policy. A good harvest made it easy and profitable to borrow abroad, while the banks were less exacting in granting advances, and had larger resources out of which to lend. A harvest failure left people poorer and without the money or inclination to make capital extensions, while the banks, finding their reserves depleted because of an unfavourable balance of payments, pursued a policy of caution. The excellent harvest of 1901 and 1902 sent up exports and investment in those years and (even more) in 1903.[2] The comparatively disappointing harvest of 1903, followed by the still shorter crop of 1904, brought about a minor recession of business, which lasted until the beginning of 1905. In that year, crops and business activity moved up together, the arable area being greatly extended in the meantime to take advantage of the high prices offered for grain.[3] In 1906 and 1907 harvests were poor and investment fell off. In 1908 the crops, with the exception of wheat and pastures, were rather better, and as prices rose far above normal, agricultural exports fetched higher values than in 1907 and investment began to recover.[4] The succeeding years, with the outstanding exception of 1910, saw a series of bountiful harvests which came to an end only in 1914. Investment, financed largely from abroad, was on a correspondingly ample scale, and, supported by the government's expansionist policy of railway-building, and by the encouraging steadiness of grain prices, was able to surmount the harvest failure of 1910 without difficulty.

[1] Viner, op. cit. pp. 261 et seq.; above, p. 42.

[2] It should be remembered that the export statistics of any calendar year reflect the state of the crops both in that year *and* in the preceding one.

[3] Wheat prices in Canada rose sharply in 1904 under the influence of two successive short crops in the United States.

[4] 1908 was a year of famine in India.

(b) Foreign borrowing and banking policy

We come at last to investment by foreigners and banking policy. What part did they play?

Investment by foreigners sustained 'home investment' at a level beyond the savings of Canadian citizens. Had foreigners been less willing to embark their capital in Canadian enterprises, 'home investment' would have been undertaken on a less ambitious scale, the pressure on the labour market would have been reduced, and Canadians would have been able to supply more of their own requirements instead of importing goods from abroad. Any reduction in investment in Canada tended to make the balance of payments more favourable: directly, by curtailing imports of capital goods; and indirectly, by freeing labour for the production of traded goods. It also reduced the volume of employment by checking the inflow of migrants, and, in the short period, by throwing men out of work. In this way the demand for traded goods fell, while the supply tended to increase; a reduction in investment led first to a reduction in imports of all kinds, and later— although this was not a *necessary* consequence—to a rise in exports. Home investment—as determined largely by foreign borrowing— governed the balance of payments.

There was, however, no guarantee that the balance of payments and foreign borrowings would move evenly up or down, or that the transfer of capital would take place smoothly. Equilibrium was, in point of fact, preserved by the Canadian banks. Banking policy was important in two ways. First, in the absence of any organized bill market in Canada, the proceeds of loans issued abroad were transferred to Canada through the agency of the Canadian banks. The banks held large reserves in foreign centres (mainly in New York), and the primary effect of an increase in foreign borrowing and a bigger loan transfer than usual was to add to these reserves. The Canadian banks lent abroad what foreigners lent to Canada. The balance of payments remained unchanged and the real transfer was postponed. In short, the Canadian banks, being practically the sole dealers in foreign exchange, maintained a steady price for it by adding to their stock or allowing it to run down according as there was a surplus or shortage arising from commercial and loan transactions. Their secondary reserves[1] took the place of gold as the residual item in the balance of payments.[2]

[1] That is, call loans elsewhere than in Canada and net balances due from banks outside Canada. The proportion of *cash* reserves to demand liabilities was kept relatively steady.

[2] Although *loans* on short-term were not made abroad by other Canadian bodies, there was some *borrowing* on short-term by Canadian governments and private corporations—especially in 1912–13. This borrowing—and the arranging of short-

In the second place, the Canadian banks pursued a loan policy calculated to keep fluctuations in their secondary reserves within limits. It has been suggested that the banks played a purely passive role, and refused 'no deserving request for an extension of credit'.[1] This is as hard to believe of a group of banks as it is of a single bank. No bank can maintain an inflexible conception of what is 'deserving' when its reserves are slipping away. There would be no sense in the repeated complaints of monetary stringency in 1907 and 1913 if 'deserving' borrowers were not finding it difficult to arrange credits. The builders who were reported in 1913 to be using their own savings to pay for work on dwelling-houses in the suburbs of Montreal[2] were hardly less credit-worthy than those who had no difficulty in raising money six months earlier. Nevertheless, it is clear that circumstances might give an *appearance* of passiveness to the behaviour of the banks. Since a favourable balance was normally accompanied by a rise in investment, the demand for credit and the secondary reserves of the banks tended to move upwards together; so that it becomes difficult to disentangle changes in credit policy from changes in the demand for loans in the recorded statistics of bank advances.

Banking policy exerted a double influence on the money supply. First, the banks did not offset an increase in their foreign assets (such as was brought about by an increase in foreign borrowing) by a decrease in their domestic assets. Any acquisition of funds for transfer to Canada, therefore, increased the banks' foreign assets and domestic liabilities simultaneously. An increase in investment financed from abroad meant an automatic expansion in the money supply in Canada. The increase in investment, reinforced by the expansion in the money supply, drove up money incomes and prices and helped to turn the balance of payments against Canada, causing the secondary reserves of the banks to return towards their former level. This was the first way in which fluctuations in the secondary reserves of the banks were kept within limits.

Secondly, the banks were able to affect investment and the balance

term credits with British financial institutions or manufacturing companies—can also be regarded as an equilibrating factor in the balance of payments. But it was never, so far as I am aware, of more than minor importance (cf. Viner, op. cit. p. 122). It should also be noted that call loans in New York made directly from the Canadian head offices of banks without agencies in New York are reported as call loans in Canada and are not included, therefore, in secondary reserves (Viner, *Studies in the Theory of International Trade*, p. 432).

[1] 'There is abundant evidence...that (the banks) neither contracted nor expanded their current loans primarily because of the state of their cash reserves' (Viner, op. cit. p. 176).

[2] Canadian *Labour Gazette*, May 1913, p. 1182.

of payments in a more direct manner by extending credit more freely whenever their secondary reserves increased.[1] Fig. 7 shows fairly conclusively that changes in bank advances responded to the changes in secondary reserves at a rather earlier date. The most important exception is the year 1910, when the banks, out of the abundance of their secondary reserves, maintained easy terms of credit and helped to keep up home investment when poor crop conditions might have caused a setback.[2]

The control of credit by the banks gave them power to check or encourage home investment. Whenever foreign borrowings were not

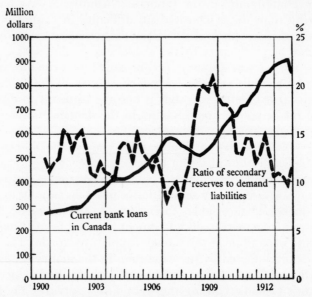

Fig. 7. Current bank loans in Canada and secondary reserves, 1900–13.

inflating home investment fast enough to bring about a real transfer, the banks were forced at first to take up the difference in foreign lending or in gold imports. They could then use their power over home investment, relaxing the terms of credit until their secondary reserves were at a lower, more satisfactory level, and the original increase in foreign lending had passed over into home investment. The more complaisant they were in large swings in their secondary reserves, the less violently did they require to modify the terms of credit. Had they sought to keep secondary reserves constant, they would have forced correspondingly wide fluctuations on Canadian investment and money incomes. The

---

[1] The assets of the banks in Canada other than advances rose comparatively smoothly throughout.   [2] Cf. above, p. 49.

fact that secondary reserves were allowed to swing between less than 8 and over 20 % of demand liabilities in Canada suggests that, on the whole, credit policy operated to dampen rather than to aggravate those fluctuations.

Whatever the mechanism by which foreign borrowing was translated into investment in Canada, it was governed both by the domestic circumstances that made investment attractive and by the circumstances abroad that made the raising of capital there a practicable operation. Within Canada circumstances remained favourable throughout nearly the whole of the period. The opening up of the west offered a good return to the farmer if he had adequate transport and labour; it offered a good return to the railways if they could raise capital at low rates of interest and hire the men to build the permanent way; it offered a good return to the immigrant, discontented with a low and apparently stationary standard of living; and it had the backing of the government, which was anxious to accelerate the whole operation. The expenditure of borrowed funds itself generated an inflation that made investment still more

Table 8. *Foreign borrowing and trade, 1900–14*[a]

Year	Net long-term capital movement into Canada ($m.)	Debit balance on current account ($m.)	Commodity exports ($m.)	Commodity imports ($m.)	Terms of trade (1900–4 = 100)
1900	29·8	36·6	156·0	176·5	92·4
1901	35·1	23·1	170·2	182·6	99·9
1902	40·3	32·0	190·4	203·4	103·5
1903	51·7	74·1	201·9	251·8	101·5
1904	58·9	97·5	176·1	249·2	102·7
1905	109·5	87·3	205·2	263·6	102·2
1906	102·3	102·0	254·0	312·3	95·3
1907	91·1	166·9	253·8	363·0	95·9
1908	218·1	134·4	249·3	282·6	116·6
1909	249·4	158·3	269·0	339·6	118·0
1910	308·2	251·3	280·8	429·0	112·8
1911	343·4	363·7	284·1	506·3	113·2
1912	316·1	421·3	351·7	626·0	110·7
1913	541·7	408·2	442·9	654·9	106·1
1914	320·6	288·2	369·1	470·8	—

(a) The estimates in cols. 1–4 are taken from F. A. Knox, *Dominion Monetary Policy*, and are based on those of Viner. The debit balance on current account includes the balance of trade in gold. The estimates in col. 5 are calculated from the indices of export and import prices in Table 10 (below, p. 61).

profitable and attractive; the arrival of immigrants in need of housing gave an additional impulse to construction. But everything rested on two props: the continued inflow of foreign capital and the continuance of market conditions favourable to Canadian exports. With the London capital market strained to the uttermost, it was inevitable that one of the props should wobble a little now and then; and with the double risk of short crops and a setback in agricultural prices the other, in a community so dependent on the export of primary produce, was not altogether secure.

The magnitudes involved in foreign investment in Canada are shown in Table 8. These are of interest mainly as showing how little the process of expansion was interrupted even by the external factors. But they also put in a rather clearer light the connexion between foreign investment and the terms of trade. There was a time when the causal connexion was traced from the first of these to the second. But the evidence points in the reverse direction. It was *after* the terms of trade moved to Canada's advantage that the main bursts of investment in Canada occurred. If it had been impossible to borrow abroad, these improvements might not have been sustained; the changes in investment and in the terms of trade were wrapped up together in the whole process of expansion. But it is certainly misleading, if the two things have to be isolated and a causal sequence established between them, to argue as if the experience of Canada showed that capital transfer *provoked* a favourable change in the terms of trade.

IV. *The fluctuations in investment*

We can now give a brief sketch of the fluctuations that did take place between 1900 and 1913—the 'interruptions' of which we spoke above.[1]

The expansion in Canadian trade and investment that began in 1900 received no check until late in 1903. The depression which set in towards the end of that year can be traced to a combination of circumstances of which the chief were a comparatively poor harvest, a severe winter, and a slump in the United States. In 1904 exports fell off, the rise in investment slackened, and imports marked time. In the labour market there were reports of unemployment amongst unskilled workers in nearly all the provinces,[2] and immigration was less active. Wages ceased to rise. On the capital market, interest rates were higher,[3] and although

---

[1] P. 42.

[2] Canadian *Labour Gazette*, January 1905.

[3] Cf. the yield on city mortgages (Table 12, below). The rise in interest rates reflected the restriction of credit by the banks.

the building industry was very busy in the west, there was a reduction in building in Montreal, Quebec, Hamilton and other towns in the east.[1] The banks, whose secondary reserves had been falling since August 1902,[2] began to lend less freely in the second quarter of 1904. Between April 1904 and February 1905, advances rose only $5 m. as compared with an increase of $36 m. between April 1903 and February 1904. After April 1904, however, secondary reserves rose very quickly, partly, no doubt, because of credit restriction, but partly also because of heavy borrowings abroad. In 1905 investment, exports, immigration, wages, bank advances, etc., all resumed their upward course.

The depression of 1904 was a brief affair—little more than a spell of dull trade. It originated in the export industries and had no serious repercussions on investment. The slump of 1907–8 was more complicated in origin. Exports in 1907 were up to the level of the preceding year; but they failed to increase, in spite of fetching higher prices. At the same time, foreign borrowing was becoming more difficult because of the tightness of money in London and Wall Street. Thus home investment, which continued to increase in 1907, began to outrun foreign borrowings and to deplete the secondary reserves of the Canadian banks. This forced on the banks a deflationary policy which reacted seriously on investment and proved only too successful in restoring equilibrium to the balance of payments.

The net foreign assets of the banks began to decline in the last quarter of 1906;[3] in the first quarter of 1907 the decline was carried further, and secondary reserves fell below 8 % of demand liabilities in Canada (compared with a previous minimum of 10 % in June 1904). After April, bank advances ceased to expand, and by the end of the year had fallen by $30 m. In June it was reported that money was tight 'owing to delayed deliveries of the western crop of 1906'.[4] But in July and later months, when the 1906 crop had long been delivered, complaints

[1] In the spring of 1904 it was reported from Winnipeg that 'employment agencies were literally besieged with applicants for employment. Large contributions to the ranks of the unemployed came from the camps, and there was a very observable influx from the United States' (Canadian *Labour Gazette*, April 1904, p. 1114). But by the summer, there were boom conditions here and at Calgary, Edmonton and Vancouver.

[2] Secondary reserves fell from a high point of $70·8 m. in August 1902 to $42·2 m. in April 1903; from this low level they recovered to $55·4 m. in September 1903, but by April 1904 were down again to $40·7 m. These movements were partly seasonal.

[3] This is not shown in the statistics of secondary reserves (for quarterly data, see Viner, op. cit. pp. 166–7). There was a sharp increase in 'deposits elsewhere than in Canada' (which are not included in secondary reserves) and no compensating increase in foreign assets.

[4] Canadian *Labour Gazette*, June 1907, p. 1321.

continued to be made. Tight money was holding up building in the west as early as July.[1] By October, the east felt the same influence.[2]

The harvest of 1907 happened to be rather a poor one. Exports of lumber and raw materials, moreover, were hit by the slump in the two chief markets for Canadian exports—Great Britain and the United States. No relief to the stringency of credit could be expected, therefore, from the favourable repercussions of an increase in exports. Instead, the export situation created an atmosphere still more unfavourable to investment. There was less traffic on the railways, operating expenses were as high as ever, and net earnings were falling. The fall in building construction, therefore, tended to be reinforced by a fall in railway construction.[3] Immigration, wages and imports all fell in sympathy.

By the middle of 1908, prospects were much better. Secondary reserves had been rising gradually for some months; in the second half of the year they nearly doubled. Foreign borrowing was on a larger scale than ever, and whereas imports fell heavily to meet the reduction in investment and employment, exports remained steady. Interest rates and costs were both lower, and harvest reports were favourable. Bank advances, however, continued to fall until February 1909, and apart from railway construction in the west (e.g. on the Grand Trunk Pacific)[4] investment was also on the decline.

The first signs of recovery were observable in the autumn of 1908. The building permits passed at Winnipeg, for example, were well up on the 1907 figures in the second half of 1908.[5] In the east, manufacturing industry was reported to be showing an improvement towards the end of the year. By 1909 recovery was well under way.

The final depression had little connexion with exports. Export prices, it is true, fell—and fell heavily—in 1913. But export *values* were well up on 1912. Again we must look to the 'financial stringency', of which the west was complaining in February and the east a few months later, for

---

[1] Canadian *Labour Gazette*, July 1907, p. 9; August 1907, p. 115; September 1907, p. 283.

[2] Canadian *Labour Gazette*, October 1907, p. 354. High building costs were also blamed. For mortgage rates, see Table 12.

[3] The part played by high building costs was also important.

[4] This line had the backing of government guarantees; the decision to proceed with construction was not governed simply by economic considerations.

[5] The value of building permits in each half-year was (in $m.):

	1st half-year	2nd half-year
1906	7·1	5·7
1907	4·4	2·0
1908	2·2	3·3
1909	5·5	3·8
1910	9·9	5·2

See Canadian *Labour Gazette*, August 1910, p. 177.

an explanation of the depression. The financial stringency followed a great reduction in secondary reserves in the second half of 1912.[1] Home investment was again outrunning foreign borrowing, and forcing the banking system to restrict credit. Advances did not actually fall until the last two months of 1913; but the brake seems to have been put on as early as October 1912. In the year from October 1912 to October 1913, the increase in advances was no more than $25 m., compared with an increase of over $110 m. in the preceding year.

As in the slump of 1907–8, it was building activity which proved most sensitive to rising interest rates and credit control. The builders who, in Montreal, were predicting a record year in April were being forced in May to abandon plans for the construction of 'several large buildings', mainly because of dear money.[2] The fall in building activity and in other forms of investment operated to reduce imports and maintain the secondary reserves of the banks. By 1914 the course of events in 1908 was being repeated on a bigger scale than before. But the autumn of that year, unlike the autumn of 1908, brought no promise that the slump would reach a normal end.

V. *The 'smoothness' of the capital transfer*

There is one final point which I should like to discuss. It is often said that the transfer of capital to Canada took place 'smoothly'. What this means is not too easy to understand. If it means: without an excessive rise in prices, who is to say what is excessive and what is not? If it means: without large movements of gold, the explanation of the smoothness of the transfer is that the Canadian banks preferred to vary their holdings of more profitable assets—loans at call to the New York money market; and that they were willing to allow these 'secondary' reserves to vary within wide limits. If it means, finally: without causing disturbance to trade and employment, the answer is that there was in fact a good deal of disturbance and unemployment.

Nevertheless, it may be admitted that, in comparison with the transfer of capital in the inter-war years, investment in Canada took place with surprising smoothness in all of these senses. Why was this?

First, it was accompanied by a *labour* transfer on an equally enormous scale. Immigration and investment fluctuated closely with one another; so that, for example, whenever a railway was being built, foreign countries furnished the men as well as the capital. They also furnished much of the railway material. The result was to limit the pressure on Canadian labour to adapt itself to the new situation; much as the

[1] There was a fall from $170·4 m. in June to $123·3 m. in December.
[2] Canadian *Labour Gazette*, April 1913, p. 1052; May 1913, p. 1182.

migration of Scottish workers to England to help in the construction of Scottish-owned railways would facilitate the transfer of capital.

Secondly, the transfer was smoothed out by the credit policy of the Canadian banks. Sudden changes in foreign borrowings were offset by equal changes in the loans of the banks in foreign money markets. The banks thus acted as a buffer and steadied the real transfer of capital.

Thirdly, it must not be overlooked that the whole period was one of rapid expansion with an undercurrent of optimistic expectations. It was easy for a country to make adjustments so long as prices kept rising and the demand for labour was keen. Those who could not make a profit or find a job in one trade had no difficulty in moving to a more hopeful line of business. Recessions in business activity were short, and due more to rashness and over-hastiness than to any deficiency of profitable opportunities for investment. All this was true not only of Canada but of all other countries. The stresses and strains of capital transfer were far more readily borne in an adaptable world of rising prices and rising profits than in one with a background of falling prices, business losses and chronic unemployment.

Put rather differently, the adjustments that Canada had to make were to a steadily expanding volume of foreign borrowing. There were no abrupt transitions from a debit to a credit balance of payments; in 1907–8, for example, foreign investment in Canada was not lower than in earlier years, but far higher. But, as everyone knows, it is impossible to go on indefinitely making all the adjustments in one direction; there comes a day of reckoning to the confirmed debtor when the source of funds dries up or when—still worse—repayment is demanded, more often than not at a most inconvenient moment. It is the shudder of an economy under *that* tremendous impact which makes capital transfer so stormy a passage, not the tackings this way and that under a fair inflationary wind.

Finally, investment before the first world war *was* investment, and not just a swop of one kind of money or security for another. When Canada borrowed, she did so with a view to increasing her stock of capital instruments, and of hiring labour or buying equipment to assist in the work of construction. She invested what she borrowed. And, as we have seen, an increase in investment has a powerful effect on the balance of payments. The two cannot readily move far out of line with one another. Thus the fact that it was a genuine capital transfer (as defined in the opening paragraph of this essay), and not a new-fangled pseudo-capital transfer, contributed as much as anything to make the transfer take place so smoothly.

STATISTICAL APPENDIX

Wages

I have used a wage index which differs considerably from the index of weekly wages constructed by Coats[1] and used by Viner. In Britain, net increases or decreases in weekly wages, as reported by the Board of Trade,[2] moved in close correspondence with available indices of money wages. It is reasonable to apply the same principle to Canada, where, between 1903 and 1913, the Department of Labour published statistics of increases and decreases in weekly earnings in a large number of trades.

Table 9. *Wages and the cost of living, 1900–13*

Year	Wages in all industries [a]	Wages in all industries [b]	Cost of living [c]	Wholesale prices [d]
1900	100·0	100·0	100	100·0
1901	101·6	101·6	—	100·2
1902	103·8	103·8	—	103·6
1903	108·4	106·5	—	103·7
1904	108·8	109·3	—	104·5
1905	109·9	113·1	110	107·6
1906	119·5	116·5	—	113·5
1907	127·0	122·6	—	122·1
1908	121·6	124·8	—	118·2
1909	125·6	129·0	125	119·4
1910	130·2	134·0	129·9	121·0
1911	135·8	137·9	133·8	123·9
1912	142·5	145·0	140·9	136·0
1913	148·9	148·9	142·9	131·9

[a] Figures for 1900–2 and for 1913 taken from *Cost of Living Report*, vol. II, p. 431. Others interpolated on basis of net changes in weekly earnings of which the Department of Labour had record.

[b] Alternative estimate from *Cost of Living Report*, vol. II, p. 431.

[c] *Cost of Living Report*, vol. II, p. 435. Cost of living in December of each year for a working class family of five, spending 20 % of its budget on house rent.

[d] *Cost of Living Report*, vol. II, p. 22. Converted to a 1900 base by Viner, op. cit. p. 220.

Accordingly, I have adopted Coats's weighted index number of weekly wages for the years 1900–2 and 1913 and interpolated on the basis of the Department of Labour's statistics.[3] The same procedure has been repeated for the wages of unskilled labour and of building workers.

[1] *Cost of Living Report*, vol. II, p. 427.
[2] In its *Annual Reports on Changes in Wages and Hours of Labour*.
[3] As given in the *Cost of Living Report*, vol. II, p. 424.

The indices obtained in this way are in agreement with the reports published from time to time in the Canadian *Labour Gazette* on the state of the labour market,[1] with the fluctuations that took place in the note issue, and so on.

On the other hand, they diverge in some years, e.g. 1904 and 1908, from Coats's index of weekly wages. It is quite clear that these were bad years in which some setback in money wages is likely to have taken place. Coats's index, however, shows an almost uninterrupted rise. It is also difficult to reconcile the figures for wage-cuts and wage-advances with the figures for average weekly wage-rates. One set of figures shows a large reduction in wages in lumbering in 1908; the other a rise. One shows wages in the building industry rising sharply in 1903, the other in 1904. I think the figures of wage-cuts and wage-advances the more plausible of the two.

Cost of living

I have used Coats's estimate of the increase in the weekly expenditure on foodstuffs, fuel and rent of a family of five with an income of $872 in 1900. This shows a rise in the cost of living between 1900 and 1913 of 42·9%. For the retail cost of foodstuffs Coats estimates the increase at 41·5%, for fuel at 25·4%, and for working-class rents at 61·7%. The index for foodstuffs is unsatisfactory and may slightly understate the rise. The rise in rents may also be a little on the low side. On the other hand, Coats omits some items such as imported manufactures (including clothing) and services like railway transport, electric lighting, water supply and so on, which either rose comparatively little, or fell in price (electric light fell by nearly 30%).

Wholesale prices

Viner's index of domestic commodity prices is an unweighted average for twenty-three products, of which two out of three are agricultural products such as potatoes, milk, hay and strawberries (op. cit. p. 230, note 2). Since these products are liable to erratic fluctuations in supply and price, the index is not altogether satisfactory; but it probably reflects with fair accuracy the changes which we know to have taken place. It agrees closely, for example, with Coats's index of house rents, which usually reflect the trend in domestic commodity prices. I have, therefore, used Viner's index without change. For most purposes, however, it is preferable to use a 1900–4 rather than a 1900 base (cf. Silverman, op. cit. p. 258) as the fluctuations in prices between 1900 and 1902 were peculiarly erratic.

[1] As summarized in the *Cost of Living Report*, vol. II, pp. 418 et seq.

For export prices, Viner gives three different indices (op. cit. p. 233). In the first, exports are weighted according to importance in 1900–4; in the second, according to importance in 1913; the third is unweighted. In the first index, the twenty-one most important commodities of export in 1900–4 are weighted by (1) dividing them into three groups of two, four and fifteen commodities, so that each group represents an approximately equal value of exports; (2) constructing a price-index for each group; and (3) taking an average of the three price-indices. The second index is constructed on similar lines for the twenty-two most important articles of export in 1913.

These three methods of weighting yield results between which there is surprisingly little agreement. No one method, moreover, can claim superiority over the others. I have been driven to use yet a fourth method—one which is rather complicated but which offers a common-sense way out of the difficulty.

Table 10. *Export and import prices, 1900–13*

Year	Domestic prices	Export prices (weighted according to importance in 1900–5)	Export prices (weighted according to importance in 1908–11)	Index of export prices [a]	Index of import prices [b]
1900	100·0	100·0	—	100·0	100·0
1901	111·5	101·6	—	101·6	94·0
1902	118·5	103·3	—	103·3	92·2
1903	119·1	105·0	—	105·0	95·7
1904	119·1	103·0	—	103·0	92·7
1905	120·9	108·2	86·3	108·2	97·8
1906	122·8	114·0	88·2	112·1	108·7
1907	135·6	120·5	96·1	119·9	115·6
1908	133·6	121·2	98·7	122·2	96·8
1909	141·0	122·5	100·2	124·0	97·1
1910	145·7	—	100·9	124·9	102·3
1911	151·4	—	100·1	123·9	101·1
1912	161·8	—	104·5	129·4	108·0
1913	161·7	—	101·8	126·0	109·7

[a] In calculating this index each of the price indices for the subgroups of exports has been converted to a base of 1908–11 = 100. It is assumed that the weighting assigned to the commodities in each subgroup did not alter greatly between 1900 and 1908–11.

[b] Using the following weights: textiles 2, iron and steel manufactures 4, raw materials 2, foodstuffs 1.

I have started from the weighted price-indices for groups of export commodities given by Viner in a later chapter (op. cit. pp. 265, 270). By inspection, the main changes in weights took place very quickly between 1906 and 1908; a second rapid change took place in 1912–13. That is, in the periods 1900–5 and 1908–11 weights did not change greatly. First, therefore, I have weighted exports according to the importance of each of Viner's groups in 1900–5 and calculated an index of export prices for the period 1900–8. Next, I have used the weights appropriate to the years 1908–11 to construct an index for the period 1905–13. For the years where these two indices overlap I have taken the average of the proportionate changes. The final index represents a fair compromise between the indices constructed by Professor Viner.

The calculation of an index number of import prices is a more difficult proposition. The index used by Viner takes no account of imports of manufactured goods, although these formed nearly two-thirds of total imports. In particular, Viner uses no indices of the price of textile manufactures. As textiles were imported almost exclusively from Great Britain we can cover this group of imports by using Silverman's index of the price of British textile exports.[1] For manufactures of iron and steel I have used an index of metal prices in the U.S.A., which supplied Canada with practically all of its iron and steel imports.[2] In addition, I have used the indices of the prices of imported foodstuffs and raw materials calculated by Viner (op. cit. p. 236). The heavy weighting— two-thirds—given to metals and raw materials may exaggerate the violence of the fluctuations that took place in import prices.

The index number which this calculation yields does not differ greatly from the one constructed by Viner. It shows a rise of less than 10 % between 1900 and 1913, compared with a rise of 14 % in Viner's index.

Migration

In Fig. 6 I have used the official statistics of immigration and Viner's estimates of emigration.

That these figures underestimate the balance of immigration into Canada is readily demonstrated. The population of Canada increased between 1 June 1901 and 1 June 1911 by 1,835,000. The birth-rate in 1901 was approximately 27 per 1000 (at the time of the census there were

[1] A. G. Silverman, 'Monthly index numbers of British export and import prices, 1880–1913', *Rev. Econ. Statist.* 1930.

[2] This index is an unweighted average for forty-four iron and steel products published in *Bulletin* no. 181 of the Bureau of Labor Statistics, U.S. Department of Labor.

24·5 children of under 1 year per 1000 of the population). The death-rate in 1911 was approximately 14 per 1000 (Viner, op. cit. p. 48), and in 1901 was at least as great (e.g. the proportion of the population over 60 was much higher). The natural increase was thus at most 13 per 1000, or 70,000 in 1901 and 93,700 in 1911. The aggregate natural increase was, say, 800,000 over the ten-year period; and the net gain by immigration must, therefore, have been at least 1 million as compared with about 650,000 in the estimates which I have used above.

Table 11. *Immigration into Canada, 1900–13*

Year	Immigrant arrivals [a]	Saloon immigrants [b]	Total	Emigration from Canada [c]	Net balance of migration
1900	41,681	2,537	44,218	20,937	23,281
1901	55,747	3,338	59,085	21,196	37,889
1902	89,102	3,660	92,762	34,279	58,483
1903	138,660	4,397	143,057	45,101	97,956
1904	131,252	4,414	135,666	61,807	73,859
1905	141,465	4,882	146,347	82,376	63,971
1906	211,653	5,977	217,630	113,731	103,899
1907	272,409	7,436	279,845	152,467	127,378
1908	143,326	5,164	148,490	209,752	−61,262
1909	173,694	4,174	177,868	187,400	−9,532
1910	286,839	3,311	290,150	190,286	99,864
1911	331,288	3,715	335,003	198,537	136,466
1912	375,756	3,526	379,282	209,458	169,824
1913	400,870	3,614	404,484	225,392	179,092

[a] *Canada Year Book*, 1936, p. 186.
[b] Viner, op. cit. p. 46.
[c] Viner, op. cit. p. 57.

An alternative estimate of the natural increase is obtained by deducting the estimated number of deaths, plus the number of children entering Canada as immigrants, from the total number of children less than 10 years of age in Canada at 1 June 1911. This also points to a figure of rather less than 800,000 for the ten-year period.

Finance

In Table 12 are reproduced some of the more important statistics relevant to a discussion of monetary policy over the period. The annual increase in the note issue throws light on changes in wage incomes. The annual increase in the 'secondary' reserves of the banks helps to explain their inflationary or deflationary bias. The state of the balance of payments is shown in the changes taking place in the net foreign assets of the bank. The annual change in bank advances is a measure of the rate at which the banking system was expanding or contracting credit. The yield on city mortgages is an index both of the cost of raising capital in the building industry, and of the ease or difficulty with which a mortgage could be arranged at the current rate.

Table 12. *Money and credit in Canada, 1900–13*

Year	Increase in cash in hands of public [a] ($m.)	Increase in secondary reserves of banks [b] ($m.)	Increase in net foreign assets of the banks [c] ($m.)	Increase in bank advances [d] ($m.)	Yield on city mortgages [e] (1900 = 100)
1900	5·9	—	—	—	100·0
1901	4·6	19·4	20·5	13·6	100·5
1902	5·7	0·9	−3·0	33·7	100·3
1903	6·0	−7·5	−20·2	61·5	100·8
1904	1·9	22·8	17·1	29·4	102·0
1905	2·7	3·0	11·4	44·6	99·7
1906	8·2	−5·6	−20·2	90·3	102·5
1907	6·5	−21·6	−24·3	−7·9	108·6
1908	−5·1	90·8	84·7	−44·8	106·1
1909	3·1	22·7	24·2	80·9	107·2
1910	10·2	−41·2	−36·4	84·4	109·8
1911	9·8	5·6	−28·4	97·8	111·0
1912	13·3	−5·4	−9·0	106·4	114·7
1913	11·0	6·5	12·6	−25·3	121·2

[a] Increase in average monthly circulation of the notes of the Chartered Banks and of Dominion Notes of $1, $2, $4 and $5.

[b] Increase in call loans elsewhere than in Canada and net balances due from banks outside Canada.

[c] Net foreign assets are taken to be net balances due from abroad plus current and call loans elsewhere than in Canada, less deposits elsewhere than in Canada.

[d] Increase in current loans in Canada of Canadian Chartered Banks between 31 December and 31 December. Current loans in Canada and elsewhere were not separately distinguished before July 1900. The increase in advances in 1900 may have been about $15 m.

[e] Index number (weighted by population of cities) of interest on loans secured by first mortgages on city house property (*Cost of Living Report*, vol. II, p. 724).

CHAPTER IV

INTERNAL MIGRATION IN VICTORIAN ENGLAND

There are few better quarries for the theory of economic development than Victorian England. Under the influence of a few compelling forces, operating steadily over the greater part of a century, society was gradually transformed in scale and structure, in custom and belief, in the work that had to be done and the livelihood that the work afforded. The balance was altered, for example, between town and country, industry and agriculture, home and overseas investment, births and deaths. Railways were built, towns grew, trade expanded; and these things happened, not as isolated events, but each in association with the others as part of a common response to persistent pressures; as continuous and interconnected adjustments, free from any revolutionary break, to the disturbing forces of technical change, the opening up of new countries, the accumulation of capital, and so on.

Such a process of adjustment can be studied from many angles. It can be traced, but only partly traced, in the statistics with which the period, unlike earlier periods, abounds; in the curves of growth that rocket upwards one after another until the Victorian Age, seen graphically, begins to look like a fireworks display. These curves should not be allowed to conceal but should rather illumine the other non-measurable adjustments, in outlook and institutions, that went on simultaneously.

Yet the statistics of Victorian England, for all their fascination and all their abundance, have not been turned to the service of economic dynamics at all adequately. This is true, for example, of the statistics of the labour market whether in terms of mobility between occupations and industries or in terms of migration from place to place. There is no study of the broad pattern of change over the period, or of the parameters of change within it. The following pages are intended as a contribution to such a study. They relate to internal migration— to those marginal shifts in population in which the forces making for a redistribution of population can be detected and measured.

Estimates of internal migration over ten-yearly intervals can be arrived at from the census returns of population and the returns of births and deaths in each of the registration districts in England and Wales. By setting the actual increase in population against the excess of births over deaths, it is possible to calculate without much difficulty the balance of gain or loss by migration in each decade for all registration districts. The only difficulties are that the registration of births before 1875 was incomplete to an extent not known with accuracy; and that the boundaries of the registration districts were changed from time to time. Some new registration districts were created and some old ones disappeared; for example, the 623 registration districts that existed in 1850 had increased to 630 in 1891, and to 634 in 1911.

The registration districts can be grouped together into towns, coalfields and rural residues, so as to reduce the total to 160, and the towns can then be classified as 'Large', 'Residential', 'Old', 'Industrial', 'Textile', and 'Military'. The grouping adopted here is roughly the same as that evolved by Mr T. A. Welton in his *England's Recent Progress* after something like 50 years' work on population statistics. The large towns are taken to include an area on the periphery that had not been built up in 1841, and which was beginning to be insufficient for urban expansion in 1911. London, for example, stretches from Barnet and Edmonton in the north to Croydon in the south, and from Romford and Dartford in the east to Chertsey in the west. Similarly, outlying suburbs are included in Manchester, Liverpool and the other big northern towns. The main change from Welton's classification is the division of the country into north and south, the dividing line being drawn roughly between the Severn and the Humber. This division leaves all the major industrial and mining areas (apart from London) in the north. Welton's classification of large towns includes Bristol, but as this leaves only two large towns in the south, one London and the other Bristol, it has seemed preferable to classify Bristol with old towns in the south so as to isolate the growth of London and facilitate comparison with eight large northern towns.

This grouping (the details are given in Table 13) may seem a rather arbitrary one from the point of view of trends in population and migration. The older towns, for example, have little in common but their age; Coventry and Northampton might more suitably be classed with Wolverhampton and Kettering than with Maidstone and Worcester. There is no sharp line of division between 'old' and 'residential', between 'military' and 'residential', or between any of these groups and 'industrial'. In the 'rural residues' there are towns of some size like Grantham, Llanelly and Shrewsbury as well as villages and rural areas. Yet Welton's classification, which was devised for very different purposes, is by no means inappropriate to an analysis of general trends; *any* classification of towns by industrial affiliation would be extremely difficult and might yield results no more instructive.

Table 13. *Registration districts in England and Wales grouped into towns (excluding colliery districts and rural residues)*

Large towns:
1 Southern
  London
8 Northern
  Birmingham
  Hull
  Leeds
  Leicester
  Liverpool
  Manchester
  Nottingham
  Sheffield

Textile towns:
22 Northern
  Ashton-under-Lyme
  Blackburn
  Bolton
  Bradford
  Burnley
  Bury
  Dewsbury
  Glossop
  Halifax
  Haslingden
  Huddersfield
  Keighley
  Kidderminster
  Leek
  Macclesfield
  Oldham
  Preston
  Rochdale
  Saddleworth
  Stockport
  Todmorden
  Wharfedale

Industrial towns:
14 Northern
  Barrow
  Burton
  Cockermouth
  Crewe
  Doncaster
  Middlesbrough
  Millam
  Potteris
  Rotherham
  Rugby
  Stafford
  Walsall
  Whitehaven
  Wolverhampton

Industrial towns (*cont.*)
11 Southern
  Falmouth
  Grimsby
  Helston
  Kettering
  Luton
  Penzance
  Redruth
  Southampton
  Swindon
  Tilbury
  Wellingborough

Old towns:
7 Northern
  Carlisle
  Chester
  Coventry
  Derby
  Northampton
  Wakefield
  York
13 Southern
  Bristol
  Cambridge
  Exeter
  Gloucester
  Ipswich
  King's Lynn
  Lincoln
  Maidstone
  Norwich
  Oxford
  Reading
  Worcester
  Yarmouth

Residential towns:
9 Northern
  Blackpool
  Harrogate
  Leamington
  Llandudno
  Malvern
  Morecambe
  Rhyl
  Scarborough
  Southport

Residential towns (*cont.*)
26 Southern
  Bath
  Bedford
  Bournemouth
  Brentwood
  Brighton
  Cheltenham
  Clacton
  Cromer
  Eastbourne
  Easthamstead
  Guildford
  Hastings
  Herne Bay
  Isle of Wight
  Maidenhead
  Poole
  Reigate
  Southend
  Staines
  Thanet
  Torquay
  Tunbridge
  Watford
  Weston-super-Mare
  Worthing
  Uxbridge

Military towns:
16 Southern
  Aldershot
  Canterbury
  Chatham
  Colchester
  Deal
  Dover
  Farnham
  Folkestone
  Godstone
  Plymouth
  Portsmouth
  Salisbury
  Sheerness
  St Germans
  Weymouth
  Windsor

The statistics in the tables for the two decades 1881-1901 are calculated from Welton's book and can be taken to be completely accurate, but as we go forward from 1901 and backward from 1881, changes in the boundaries of registration districts diminish the accuracy of the calculations. These changes are not of such an order of magnitude, however, as to upset the conclusions drawn below. They are rarely large, and large changes can generally be taken into special account. Two such changes, for example, are associated with the growth of Barrow and Middlesbrough, and tentative calculations have been made for these two towns.

The calculations cannot unfortunately be continued up to 1951. Since 1911, returns of births and deaths have ceased to be made for the old registration districts, which have been superseded by urban and rural districts. It is not possible, therefore, to compare inter-war and pre-1914 experience on the basis of the statistics given here.

The statistics do not refer to the total volume of movement between districts, but only to the balance of movement. This is important for two reasons. First, there is generally a surprising amount of migration into areas which, on balance, are losing population. Especially if a district lies, so to speak, between areas of high and low potential, the current of migration will bring to it migrants from the area of low potential to set against the still larger outflow from it to the area of high potential. Secondly, each district is far from homogeneous. In the towns there is a centrifugal thrust of population to the suburbs from the centre, so that one part of the town gains while another loses. In the colliery districts there is often a displacement of population from one part of the coalfield to another. In districts like Burnley, which include several different towns (e.g. Nelson, Colne and Padiham) and a rural fringe (Pendle), there may be a large amount of internal movement, which, if the boundaries of the district were redrawn, would automatically increase the total balance of movement.

Fig. 8 summarizes the changes in migration from one decade to another. The steady drift from the countryside to the towns was unbroken, both in the north and in the south, from the forties to the seventies. In the eighties this movement was checked, especially in the north, by heavy emigration; in the following decade the drift to the towns was resumed on its former scale as emigration fell off; but after the turn of the century town-building received a second check, and this time it seems to have been the towns which supplied most of the emigrants.

Migration to the towns was at its peak in the forties when the inflow of Irish immigrants supplemented the movement from the English countryside and may, indeed, have been on a comparable scale. London, Liverpool and Manchester grew particularly rapidly, the two last-named gaining more by migration than ever before or since. The textile towns also showed heavy net gains in comparison with the following decades.

Irish immigration died away after 1851 and the inflow to the towns fell slightly. For the next thirty years the pattern of internal migration was extraordinarily stable. Movement to the towns remained high, with a rather faint upward tendency. The fortunes of individual towns, of course, varied greatly: some, like the textile and most of the northern

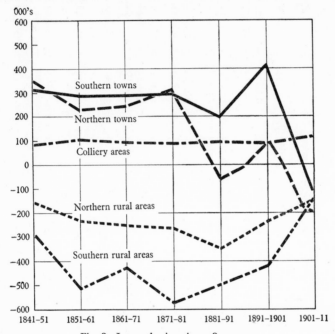

Fig. 8. Internal migration, 1841–1911.

towns, shared the general experience; others, like the military towns in the south, were less and less successful in attracting migrants from one decade to the next. Birmingham's peak in net immigration came in the fifties; for Leicester, Hull and Nottingham it came in the seventies. But these variations were relatively unimportant; the outstanding conclusion from Fig. 8 (and the further details given in Table 14) is that up to 1881 the movements of population were along channels that seemed fixed and deep, and that it was not until the eighties that they overflowed into unfamiliar courses.

The change in the eighties fell with particular vehemence on the northern towns. From gaining over 300,000 by migration in the seventies

Table 14. *Gain (+) or loss (−) by migration from towns, rural residues and colliery districts, 1841–1911*

	1841–1851	1851–1861	1861–1871	1871–1881	1881–1891	1891–1901	1901–1911	Total
1. Towns:								
(a) Large:								
London	+273,649	+244,473	+261,595	+307,260	+168,945	+226,476	−231,887	+1,250,511
8 Northern	+249,334	+195,522	+185,751	+187,800	+21,381	+143,598	−90,049	+893,337
(b) Textile:								
22 Northern	+57,944	−4,179	+31,915	+92,856	+3,734	−40,612	−51,725	+89,933
(c) Industrial:								
14 Northern	+28,494	+34,076	+11,527	−5,997	−88,601	−51,429	−81,069	−152,994
11 Southern	−7,230	−4,592	+18,668	−11,362	−5,916	+25,377	+6,712	−15,679
(d) Old:								
7 Northern	+17,503	−435	+3,515	+6,793	−17,109	+311	+5,366	+15,944
13 Southern	+19,605	−17,738	+19,327	+14,340	−24,308	+1,461	−34,691	−22,004
(e) Residential:								
9 Northern	−5,409	+4,939	+11,159	+29,752	+21,739	+59,675	+18,375	+140,230
26 Southern	+2,053	−2,142	+42,595	+27,247	+44,773	+83,441	+129,395	+327,362
(f) Military:								
16 Southern	+24,077	+66,862	−16,101	−44,009	+13,122	+72,519	+8,478	+124,948
Northern towns	+347,866	+229,933	+243,867	+311,204	−58,856	+111,548	−199,102	+986,450
Southern towns	+312,154	+286,863	+288,748	+293,476	+196,616	+409,274	−121,993	+1,665,138
	+660,020	+516,789	+532,615	+604,680	+137,760	+520,822	−321,095	+2,651,588
2. Colliery districts:								
9 Northern	+82,287	+103,467	+90,860	+84,474	+90,303	+85,158	+113,999	+650,548
3. Rural residues:								
12 Northern	−158,770	−229,368	−253,510	−263,029	−349,124	−237,423	−152,522	−1,643,770
12 Southern	−284,400	−513,205	−429,521	−574,423	−496,320	−423,017	−142,380	−2,863,266
	−443,170	−742,573	−683,031	−837,452	−845,444	−660,440	−294,902	−4,507,036
Total (net emigration):								
North of England	+271,383	+104,022	+81,127	+132,649	−317,677	−49,717	−237,625	−6,748
South of England	+27,754	−226,342	−140,773	−280,947	−299,704	−13,743	−264,373	−1,198,128
	+294,121	−122,320	−59,556	−148,298	−617,381	−54,460	−501,998	−1,209,892

they lost nearly 60,000 in the eighties. The transformation can be traced in all but one (Leeds) of the large towns in the north, and in each of the subgroups of northern towns, rather faintly in the residential, but very obviously in the textile and industrial. The southern towns, apart from London, show no such transformation, and most of the subgroups, indeed, attracted more migrants (or lost fewer) in the eighties than in the seventies. Some explanation can be offered from the particular circumstances of individual towns like Tilbury and Swindon. But the contrast is too great to be explained away so easily. The most obvious hypothesis—that the rural residues adjoining the northern towns lost less of their population than in the seventies while migration from the rural residues in the south was greater—proves to be the reverse of the truth. We can only suppose that the north took most of the shock of the great wave of emigration in the eighties. For the north of England as a whole a net gain by migration of 130,000 in the seventies changed to a net loss of 300,000 in the eighties; in the south there was only a minor difference in the net loss of population between one decade and the other. Naturally this does not mean that all the extra emigrants came from the north of England: those who, in the previous decade, would have moved in from the south of England or from Ireland presumably emigrated instead; there was some continental immigration, mostly to London; and there may also, to judge from the growth of the residential towns, have been some disposition on the part of returning emigrants to settle in the south rather than in the north.

The experience of the following years confirmed the tilt in the geographical balance in favour of the south. In the nineties, when emigration was temporarily checked, the north continued to lose population while the outflow from the south almost ceased. This was in contrast to the long period in the middle of the century when the north was gaining, and the south losing, population. The southern towns now took much the larger share of the migrants from the rural residues. The increase in migration into London was not large; but the military and residential towns in the south showed a conspicuous gain by migration.

In the nineties there was little emigration. But after the turn of the century emigration recommenced on an increasing scale. For the first time the towns now lost through an *outflow* of population, although not so heavily that their growth was arrested. London lost as many of her citizens by migration as she had acquired by migration in the nineties; her population continued to grow, but at a rate 30 % lower than before. Of the large northern towns, only Manchester and Hull showed a net gain by migration. Nearly every group of towns showed a diminished increase by migration or an actual loss; the principal exception was the group of south coast resorts which had been growing at an accelerating pace ever since the sixties, largely by migration.

The colliery districts, defined within wide boundaries so as to include a population that amounted in 1911 to over 5 million inhabitants, did not share the fluctuations of the towns. The net inward movement into the group hardly varied at all from an average of about 100,000 per decade. But individual coalfields showed no such constancy of growth. In South Wales, for example, there was a large, consistent, but unsteady, gain by migration throughout the period; in Durham (which includes Newcastle, Sunderland, South Shields, and other towns) there was a net gain in every decade but the last; but in Wrexham, Cannock and Ashby-de-la-Zouch there was an almost consistent loss. The Lancashire coalfield provided evidence of increasing costs of operation in the gradual transition from a large net inflow in the seventies into an even larger net outflow after 1900. The Yorkshire and Derbyshire coalfields, as one might expect, showed exactly the opposite trend.

It is unnecessary to comment in detail on the fluctuations in each group of towns; it is also extremely difficult, because all the working sheets were stolen in transit during the war. A full analysis, including a study of migration by age and sex, will be found in Welton's *England's Recent Progress*, which covers the eighties and nineties and can be supplemented by a subsequent article for the following decade.[1]

The most noticeable feature of the migration into London is the net loss in the final decade—a loss that is partly to be accounted for by the improvement in transport facilities and the consequent growth of outlying suburbs and dormitory towns. In the previous sixty years, London enjoyed an uninterrupted gain of population, large enough, until the nineties, to dominate urban development in the south. In the nineties, the other southern towns attracted almost as many migrants as London; and in the following decade they continued to show net gains while London was losing migrants (although continuing to grow).

The pattern for the large northern towns closely resembles that for London except that the check in the eighties was more marked and in the years after 1901 less marked. Some of the towns attracted migrants at a fairly steady rate throughout (Manchester and Hull, for example). Few diverged much from the general pattern, although the peak in net immigration occurred in different decades for different towns.

The textile towns have not, unfortunately, been analysed so as to separate cotton and wool, spinning and weaving, men and women. The general outline is of a heavy net gain in the forties, a small net loss in the fifties, increasing net immigration in the sixties and seventies, giving

[1] *Journal of the Royal Statistical Society*, 1913, p. 304.

way to an increasing outflow thereafter. This reflects the diminishing importance of textiles in the national economy (the actual growth of population in the textile towns follows the same trend) rather than the more general forces governing migration to the larger towns. The net inflow seems to have been predominantly of women. In the eighties, for example, there was a net gain of 17,000 women and a net loss of 13,000 men; in the nineties the net loss of 40,000 consisted almost wholly of men. Not all the textile towns followed the general trend; when the

Fig. 9. Migration to the towns, 1841–1911.

tide of migrants began to turn in the eighties, Bolton, Burnley, Oldham and Stockport between them still showed a net gain of over 50,000; and in the nineties of nearly 20,000.

For the northern industrial towns (including, for example, Middlesbrough, Wolverhampton, the Potteries, Rotherham and railway centres such as Rugby, Crewe and Doncaster), the pattern is not unlike that for the larger towns, with a steep downward trend from initial gains to later heavy losses. The fifties were the period of maximum inflow and the eighties of maximum outflow. The southern industrial towns include four small Cornish towns as well as Southampton, Swindon, Luton, Tilbury and others. The constant outflow in the earlier decades came mainly from the Cornish towns; the gains after 1891 were due largely to the growth of Southampton.

The fluctuations in the remaining groups were erratic, sometimes in conformity with the general pattern, sometimes entirely contrary to it. The old towns in the south, except in the fifties, followed the pattern of London closely; the military towns did not. The residential towns in the north kept in step with the larger towns, but on a rising trend; but the residential towns in the south showed nothing of the general see-saw in migration after 1881. The inflow into these towns mounted with the growth of the south coast resorts, some of which, like Hastings, Eastbourne, Bournemouth and Poole, gained more migrants in the eighties than in the nineties, unlike almost every other town in England.

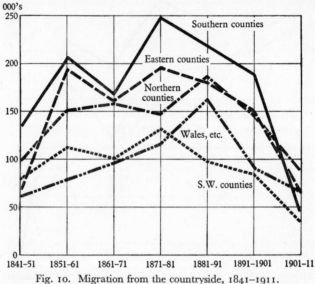

Fig. 10. Migration from the countryside, 1841–1911.

In the twentieth century, internal migration is chiefly between one industrial area and another; in the nineteenth century it was chiefly between the countryside and the towns. This meant that the centres of outflow—the depressed areas of the period—were in close juxtaposition with the centres of attraction. The towns, swelling with the growth of a railway system and of urban industry, drew on the natural increase of their rural hinterland. At the same time, centres of attraction in America and the Colonies competed for migrants, and as this competition was intermittent, urban expansion and colonization tended to alternate with one another in successive decades.

The most striking features of the rural outflow (as will be seen from Fig. 10) are its comparative steadiness and its magnitude. In the south the outflow at the beginning of the century appears to have been very small, but it rose rapidly to a peak in the fifties, was checked in the sixties, reached a new peak in the seventies, and then began to fall steadily until in the final decade after 1900 a sharp fall brought it below the level of any previous decade since the thirties. In the north, the steadiness of the outflow is even more remarkable. There was a gradual rise to a peak in the eighties, and a rather more rapid fall in the two following decades.

Both in north and south the rise and fall in the movement of population from the rural areas had little to do with agricultural prosperity and depression. The crescendo between the thirties and the seventies coincided, not with the worst years of agricultural depression, but with the so-called 'Golden Age of English Farming'. A second period of agricultural prosperity after 1900 coincided with a spectacular falling-off in rural depopulation. In the intervening years of prolonged depression, the outflow reached its peak and began to subside. Depression and prosperity, therefore, were each compatible with an increasing or diminishing outflow.

The main cause of rural depopulation was the building of railways and the consequent revolution in transport. Railway-building provided employment, and stimulated employment; it put the towns in need of more metal workers, engineers, and so on. Railway-building also increased mobility, both by taking men long distances to assist in the work of construction, and by making journeys to town easier and cheaper. It provided a vent for the surplus population of the countryside. Finally, the railways, by improving communications, immensely reinforced the competitive power of large-scale, urban enterprise and brought about the displacement of rural crafts and small country industries to the towns. Simultaneously with these changes, the chief rural industry, farming, was adapting itself to foreign competition and rising wages by economizing labour, partly through mechanization and partly through conversion of arable to pasture. The displaced labour in the countryside, ousted by urban or American competition, found a cure for unemployment by moving to the towns and to America.

The subsidence of the outflow after 1890 appears to have been due mainly to the fall in fertility that followed inevitably on the heavy migration of previous decades. In a single decade, as many as 40% of the young men aged 20–30 might migrate from some rural districts, and the final loss from one generation might come to nearly 2 out of 3. In the south-western rural districts, total births fell by 40% in forty years, although the fall in population was no more than 13%. Fewer potential migrants were being born, because the parents who might have reared them had already migrated.

Other forces co-operated to check the outflow—the revival in British agriculture after 1900, the suburbanization of the countryside, the

Table 15. *Losses by migration from rural residues of England and Wales, 1841–1911*

	1841–1851	1851–1861	1861–1871	1871–1881	1881–1891	1891–1901	1901–1911
1. Gloucester and Somerset	45,675	61,558	54,229	75,782	65,692	58,009	39,702
2. Hants. and Berks.	18,737	36,043	27,984	37,838	33,550	33,414	+9,905
3. Herts. and Essex	15,286	39,338	31,336	54,201	39,418	32,443	485
4. Bucks. and Oxford	19,543	30,351	29,340	43,687	29,524	30,994	5,229
5. Kent and Surrey	13,836	15,315	12,860	18,601	26,173	20,907	17,962
6. Sussex	19,904	22,893	11,687	17,291	22,913	12,088	+2,179
	132,891	205,498	167,436	247,400	217,270	187,854	42,294
7. Wilts. and Dorset	33,583	45,579	37,897	55,194	43,778	40,818	16,316
8. Devon	30,162	42,668	35,771	42,724	31,046	30,035	13,667
9. Cornwall	15,930	24,801	27,377	33,440	22,992	13,995	5,367
	79,675	113,048	101,045	131,358	97,816	84,848	35,350
10. Suffolk, Norfolk	42,770	83,208	70,112	77,656	79,495	71,812	33,601
11. Lincs., Rutland	11,668	50,932	40,754	43,496	54,687	36,814	9,730
12. Northants, Cambs., Hunts., Bedford	17,306	60,432	50,174	74,513	56,052	41,689	20,894
	71,744	194,572	161,040	195,665	181,234	150,315	64,225
13. Hereford, Salop	16,578	15,061	37,203	51,201	56,192	34,220	27,782
14. Carmarthen, Pemb., Cardig.	20,590	24,884	32,217	26,158	35,180	22,949	+1,445
15. Merioneth, Montg., Radnor	15,564	13,004	8,053	16,423	29,812	12,795	19,653
16. Monmouth, Brecon	2,787	8,059	8,225	13,104	13,016	9,401	6,291
17. Carnarvon, Anglesey	1,100	10,275	6,633	3,398	15,784	5,835	11,155
18. Denbigh and Flint	4,290	7,100	3,839	5,563	12,295	6,433	2,255
	60,909	78,383	96,170	115,847	162,279	91,633	65,691
19. Cumberland, Westmorland	9,926	13,346	13,886	18,548	16,875	18,117	12,280
20. Durham, Northumberland	5,670	21,284	20,427	19,825	22,614	12,410	12,128
21. Lancs. and Cheshire	7,755	16,058	11,320	9,552	17,434	29,159	15,804
22. Stafford, Warwick, Worcs.	14,436	18,127	20,108	22,054	35,282	24,834	14,509
23. Leics., Notts., Derby	25,904	34,319	44,954	28,178	29,417	19,570	14,187
24. Yorks.	34,170	47,851	46,645	49,025	65,223	41,700	17,923
	97,861	150,985	157,340	147,182	186,845	145,790	86,831
Total:	443,170	742,573	683,031	837,452	845,444	660,440	294,641

exhaustion of work suitable for transfer to the towns. It is probable, too, that the law of diminishing returns was operating to protect what was left of rural industry just as it was operating to protect agriculture. Changes in the structure of agriculture were temporarily arrested because the limits of known technique had been reached.

One feature of rural depopulation merits special attention. Fig. 10 shows clearly that the rural districts in the north did not react from decade to decade in the same way as rural districts in the south. Especially in the later decades, the rural districts fall into two separate groups, coinciding with the division into north and south, and exhibiting distinct patterns of variation. In the north the pattern is one of steadily increasing emigration up to 1890 with a temporary check in the seventies; in the south there is a rise up to 1880 with a temporary check in the sixties. These patterns are characteristic not only of the totals for north and south but to a surprising extent of constituent counties also. It is only in some of the smaller northern counties that there is any marked divergence from the general movement. No satisfactory explanation of this difference between northern and southern rural districts has so far suggested itself.

In spite of the heavy outflow from the countryside—a net outflow equal to nearly three-quarters of the starting population and to one-third of the total births over the period—there was no depopulation in the strict sense; in 1911 the population of the rural areas was higher, both in the north and in the south, than in 1841. In one decade only—the eighties—was there an actual reduction in the population of the group as a whole. Some individual rural areas, especially those in the south, suffered a heavier loss and an absolute decline in population. But on the average the rural districts marked time while the population of other areas was increasing rapidly. In 1841 the population of rural districts formed 39% of the total for the country; by 1911 it formed no more than 19% (i.e. less than half the proportion seventy years previously).

If the rural areas grew least, the colliery districts grew most. In seventy years their population multiplied fourfold. This rapid increase was due in only limited measure to migration. Out of a total increase of just over 4 millions, five-sixths was due to the excess of births over deaths and only the remaining one-sixth to the gain by migration. The large northern towns, with a population rather greater in 1841 and a net gain by migration fully one-third larger, nevertheless had a smaller population than the colliery districts in 1911 because of their lower rate of natural increase. The difference in natural increase existed throughout: in the earlier decades, the colliery districts more than made

Table 16. *Growth of population in England and Wales, 1841–1911*

	Population in 1841	Population in 1911	Natural increase 1841–1911	Net gain (+) or loss (−) by migration 1841–1911	Ratio of gain or loss to natural increase %	Population in 1911 as proportion of population in 1841 %
1. Towns:						
(a) Large:						
London	2,261,525	7,314,738	3,802,252	+ 1,250,511	+ 32·9	323·7
8 Northern	1,551,126	5,191,768	2,747,306	+ 893,337	+ 32·5	334·7
(b) Textile:						
22 Northern	1,386,670	3,182,382	1,705,779	+ 89,933	+ 5·3	229·5
(c) Industrial:						
14 Northern	603,214	1,812,219	1,361,999	− 152,994	− 11·2	300·4
11 Southern	296,009	708,693	428,363	− 15,679	− 3·7	239·4
(d) Old:						
7 Northern	289,819	648,769	343,006	+ 15,944	+ 4·6	223·9
13 Southern	664,682	1,375,651	732,973	− 22,004	− 3·0	207·0
(e) Residential:						
9 Northern	206,897	559,022	211,895	+ 140,230	+ 66·2	270·2
26 Southern	692,185	1,770,030	750,483	+ 327,362	+ 43·6	255·7
(f) Military:						
16 Southern	470,821	1,212,413	616,644	+ 124,948	+ 20·3	257·5
Northern towns	4,037,726	11,394,161	6,369,985	+ 986,450	+ 15·5	282·2
Southern towns	4,385,222	12,381,525	6,331,165	+ 1,665,138	+ 26·3	282·3
	8,422,948	23,775,686	12,701,150	+ 2,651,588	+ 20·9	282·3
2. Colliery districts:						
9 Northern	1,320,342	5,334,002	3,363,112	+ 650,548	+ 19·3	404·0
3. Rural residues:						
12 Northern	2,425,614	2,875,113	2,093,257	− 1,643,770	− 78·6	118·5
12 Southern	3,749,228	4,085,691	3,208,729	− 2,863,266	− 89·2	109·2
	6,165,842	6,960,804	5,301,986	− 4,507,036	− 85·0	112·9
Total:						
North of England	7,783,682	19,602,876	11,825,942	− 6,748	− 0·1	251·8
South of England	8,125,450	16,467,616	9,540,294	− 1,198,128	− 12·6	202·7
	15,914,148 (a)	36,070,492	21,366,236	− 1,209,892	− 5·7	226·6

(a) Including 5106 persons travelling by train on the night of the Census of 1841.

up in lower mortality rates for their comparatively low fertility; later, the advantage in mortality rates was reinforced when fertility in the towns began to decline.

The large towns owed more of their growth to migration than the colliery districts. Over the full stretch of seventy years, migration added about one-third as much to the population of London and the large northern towns as the excess of births over deaths. But this understates the importance of migration in the Victorian Age. If the final decade after 1901 is omitted, the ratio of net gain by migration to natural increase rises to one-half. Moreover, as is well known, short-distance migration greatly preponderates over long-distance migration; the wide boundaries drawn round London and the other large towns, therefore, may exclude, in the earlier years, a large centripetal movement from the rural periphery to the urban core.

Although most other towns of any size sucked in migrants in the early stages of growth, the aggregates for each group reveal no consistent pressure of migration, except towards the residential and military towns. The residential towns, with a low natural increase, were more dependent for their growth on the attraction of migrants than any other group. The northern residential towns, for example, added 70 % to their starting population by migration alone; even so, however, they grew no more rapidly than the average for other groups of towns. The textile towns, after attracting immigrants in large numbers for many years, parted in the last two decades with half as many as they had gained, and the influence of migration in their growth is disguised in the final totals. Similarly with the industrial and old towns: the heavy immigration that promoted the expansion of towns like Barrow and Coventry was counterbalanced by a movement from other towns in the same group in a later phase of growth.

The outcome of the migrations of those years, together with differences in the rate of natural increase, was a pronounced change in the distribution of population. The rural residues sank from 38·8 to 19·3 %; the colliery districts rose from 8·3 to 14·8 %; the towns from 52·9 to 66·0 %. The north of England triumphed over the south, mainly by superior fertility (and not, as we used to be taught, by attracting migrants). In seventy years the north gained three more inhabitants for every two added to the population of the south.

Although designed to illuminate migration, these statistics throw an incidental light also on the balance of births and deaths in the Victorian era.[1] The curve of births mounted steadily until the seventies, and from

[1] See Table 19. The other tables upon which this section is based have not been reproduced.

Table 17. *Net gain* (+) *or loss* (−) *by migration to or from eight large towns*

	1841–1850	1851–1860	1861–1870	1871–1880	1881–1890	1891–1900	1901–1910
Manchester	+ 73,033	+ 33,755	+ 35,453	+ 51,434	+ 17,258	+ 31,568	+ 4,671
Liverpool	+ 107,184	+ 68,703	+ 56,907	+ 49,017	− 15,057	+ 22,788	− 11,754
Birmingham	+ 37,791	+ 46,861	+ 14,996	+ 19,785	− 10,248	+ 42,588	− 23,484
Leeds	+ 4,336	+ 11,090	+ 20,734	+ 6,763	+ 15,489	+ 13,766	− 29,489
Sheffield	+ 8,798	+ 26,101	+ 26,647	+ 4,389	+ 2,170	+ 15,337	− 18,996
Leicester	+ 372	− 5,345	+ 12,585	+ 17,578	+ 10,147	+ 9,948	− 10,528
Hull	+ 14,460	+ 3,058	+ 13,328	+ 16,839	+ 7,156	+ 9,595	+ 4,041
Nottingham	+ 3,360	+ 11,299	+ 5,101	+ 21,995	− 5,534	− 1,992	− 4,510
Total	+ 249,334	+ 195,522	+ 185,751	+ 187,800	+ 21,381	+ 143,598	− 99,049

Table 18. *Net gain* (+) *or loss* (−) *by migration to or from nine colliery districts*

	1841–50	1851–1860	1861–1870	1871–1880	1881–1890	1891–1900	1901–1910
Durham group	+ 49,939	+ 63,393	+ 84,260	+ 31,635	+ 8,221	+ 23,386	− 23,845
Glamorgan group	+ 52,076	+ 39,627	+ 11,033	+ 12,213	+ 87,225	+ 40,326	+ 129,295
Wigan group	+ 3,203	+ 9,038	+ 2,949	+ 15,679	+ 5,071	− 12,639	− 29,796
Chesterfield group	− 8,826	− 5,404	+ 122	+ 15,914	− 1,326	+ 22,233	+ 26,881
Barnsley group	− 6,649	+ 1,960	+ 2,197	+ 11,222	+ 1,037	+ 5,717	+ 11,257
Wrexham	− 235	+ 2,661	− 1,984	− 1,907	− 1,122	− 618	− 2,875
Nuneaton	+ 438	− 3,602	− 7,327	− 1,996	+ 36	+ 7,682	+ 8,402
Cannock	− 820	+ 271	+ 1,992	+ 5,744	− 3,293	− 1,285	− 2,837
Ashby-de-la-Zouch	− 2,206	+ 1,652	− 2,382	− 4,030	− 3,272	+ 356	− 2,483
Total	+ 82,287	+ 103,467	+ 90,860	+ 84,474	+ 90,303	+ 85,158	+ 113,999

then on at a diminishing rate until the peak in 1903. The curve of deaths rose fastest in the sixties, and in the following decade was not far short of the eventual peak reached in the nineties. The outcome of these similar, but not altogether congruent, fluctuations was a natural increase of population that was rather less in the sixties and a good deal more in the seventies than accorded with the trend, a fall in the natural increase in the nineties, and a surprisingly sharp rise thereafter to figures never since approached. These fluctuations should be interpreted in the light of the very high proportion of deaths occurring in infancy—over 40 % of deaths in the mid-Victorian period were of children under 5. This alone tended to produce sympathetic changes in births and deaths. When the two got out of phase it was because of a sudden drop in infant mortality (as after 1900), or (as in the seventies) because of improvements in public health, slum clearance, and the growth to maturity of a generation born in times more prosperous than those that followed the Napoleonic wars.

The first group of districts to show a declining number of births was that of the southern rural residues. This reflected heavy emigration in previous decades; and the really astonishing thing is that births should have continued to rise up to the sixties in spite of the loss of perhaps half of each generation. In the northern rural areas, the peak in births came later, in the seventies. It is also noticeable how much steeper was the fall in births in the southern residues; at the end of the period, births in the northern rural areas were almost as large as at the beginning, while in the southern areas they were 25 % less; less than half the difference was due to the greater growth of population in the north.

The changes in rural births and deaths can be analysed in terms of the average birth- and death-rates in each decade. In both north and south the peak in the birth-rate came in the sixties and by that time fertility (measured by this crude index) had risen in the north slightly above the south. The fall in the birth-rate was not perceptible until the eighties, but by the beginning of this century the birth-rate was nearly 30 % down on the peak. Except in the earliest years (when the figures of births are not altogether reliable) the birth-rate in the rural areas, in spite of the drain of young migrants, remained higher than in the residential towns but below the level of the other areas. The death-rate showed a similar trend; it was steady or actually rising in the mid-Victorian decades and showed no large reduction until the eighties; and the south, which at first had the higher rate, overtook the north in the eighties and ended with a perceptibly lower death-rate. Throughout the entire period, the rural areas had the lowest death-rates in the country with the exception of the 'residential' towns in the south, which had death-rates close to those for the southern rural residues.

Table 19. Birth- and death-rates in England and Wales, 1841–1911

	1841–1851		1851–1861		1861–1871		1871–1881		1881–1891		1891–1901		1901–1911	
	Birth-rate	Death-rate	Birth-rate	Death-rate	Birth-rate	Death-rate	Birth-rate	Death-rate	Birth-rate	Death rate	Birth-rate	Death-rate	Birth-rate	Death-rate
1. Towns:														
Large:														
London	30·8	23·8	33·0	23·0	34·8	23·5	34·7	21·4	32·9	19·3	29·8	17·9	27·5	14·6
8 Northern	36·4	28·1	37·6	26·1	38·3	26·9	38·7	24·6	34·6	21·8	31·9	20·4	29·8	17·3
Textile:														
22 Northern	36·6	24·0	37·5	24·6	36·7	24·7	36·9	23·8	31·5	20·8	27·8	19·4	23·5	16·2
Residential														
9 Northern	32·5	22·3	31·0	20·5	31·9	21·6	30·6	20·7	27·7	18·5	25·3	17·9	22·0	15·4
26 Southern	30·0	20·2	29·4	19·6	30·4	19·5	29·4	18·2	27·3	16·4	24·5	15·6	21·2	13·4
2. Colliery districts:														
9 Northern	35·4	23·4	39·0	23·6	39·6	23·5	41·9	23·1	36·9	19·8	35·9	19·2	32·9	19·5
3. Rural residues:														
12 Northern	29·4	19·3	31·0	19·7	32·5	20·1	32·0	19·4	29·5	17·5	27·6	17·1	24·5	14·6
12 Southern	31·5	19·7	32·1	19·7	32·3	19·2	31·3	18·2	29·3	16·7	26·0	15·8	22·7	13·4

The textile towns followed closely behind the rural areas. Starting with the highest birth-rate of any group, they ended with one of the lowest, the fall in the last three decades being no less than 36 %. The death-rate, which was also very high initially, rose to a peak in the seventies, and thereafter fell to about the average for the country. Among the larger towns, London had a much lower birth- and death-rate than the towns in the north; in both groups the sixties emerge as a period of particularly high rates, both for births and deaths, with the seventies ushering in lower death-rates and the eighties lower birth-rates. The subsequent fall in the death-rate was much greater than the fall in the birth-rate; so much so that by the end of the period the birth-rate was nearly twice the death-rate—a ratio well above that for other areas at that or any earlier time.

The colliery districts depended for their growth on a high natural increase and, in fact, on a high birth-rate. At the start, the birth-rate does not appear to have been much above the average, but by the seventies it had climbed to 42 % above the average, and even the reaction to 33 % in the first decade of the century left a large margin over the next highest group, the large northern towns. The death-rate of the colliery districts varied less than anywhere else; it started not much above the average for the 'residential' districts, changed only insignificantly when the birth-rate increased, and fell surprisingly little after the general improvement in public health from the eighties onwards. It is striking to find that the death-rate for the colliery districts moved from one-sixth *below* the average for the large towns in the north at the beginning of the period to one-eighth *above* at the end. Yet for all this high death-rate, the colliery districts still had the highest rate of natural increase—as they had had ever since the fifties.

CHAPTER V

THE VICTORIAN CAPITAL MARKET

I. THE INVESTOR

In the nineteenth century, the leading investors were landed proprietors, merchants and industrialists. Until the rise of the Joint Stock Company, there was a distinct cleavage between the industrialists and the other groups. Industrial enterprises tended to finance their expansion out of their own earnings and were founded out of private savings or the advances of local banks. There were few industrial issues to which 'outsiders' could subscribe. Landlords, professional men, and middlemen were forced to invest in 'The Funds', or in mortgages, or simply to make deposits with their banks.

The cleavage, however, was more apparent than real. The manufacturers were sometimes themselves landowners or ex-merchants; their rent-roll or their profits might well provide the capital with which to start their business. They owned only their *fixed* capital, which at that time was a much smaller proportion than now of industrial capital. Their working capital, which was advanced to them by their banks, was generally furnished, by devious routes, by the gentry of East Anglia and Devon. The commercial paper of the Lancashire millowners, remitted to the London money market, was purchased by billbrokers acting as agents for the country banks of the agricultural districts.[1]

With the growth of railway finance in the forties, the openings for private investment widened. The Stock Exchange, at that time dominated by the Consols market, and offering opportunities for a flutter only in foreign bonds and mines, became transformed into an agency for the provision of capital to British industry. The growth of fixed capital ceased to depend entirely upon the profits which industrialists were able to earn, and reflected more and more the willingness of shareholders to subscribe to new issues. The importance of land rent as a source of capital steadily dwindled, at first because of the rise of industry and commerce, and later because of the long depression in agriculture after 1874. The landowners were replaced by a 'stock-and-bondholding aristocracy' as the chief owners of wealth and the chief accumulators of capital.

The typical private investor was always a man of wealth. In the time of Hume the whole of the National Debt was in the hands of 17,000 persons: in 1888 this number had increased tenfold, but the average

---

[1] Bagehot, *Lombard Street*, p. 287.

holding was still above £4000.[1] In Indian Guaranteed Railway Securities there were, in 1870, just over 50,000 English investors holding on an average nearly £1800.[2] Colonial stocks were never issued in London in denominations of less than £100 before 1909.[3] Clearly, the bondholders cannot have been a very numerous class.[4]

Their numbers were, however, increasing. A growing middle class was being enriched by industrial progress and familiarized with the Stock Exchange by the financial press. Improvements in communications, the development of Joint-Stock finance, compulsory education, the Married Woman's Property Act, and a rising standard of living were bringing about a striking change in the personnel of the investing public. Retailers, professional men, skilled workers and women were all being attracted to the Stock Exchange. In 1864 the average shareholding in Alamillos's (a company with a paid-up capital of £70,000 formed in 1863 to work lead mines in Spain) was two hundred shares (nominal value £2 each), and the largest shareholders were three gentlemen, a vice-admiral, a copper-smelter, a solicitor, and a wharfinger; while among the smallest holders were a lady of title, a professor of chemistry, a clergyman, and a banker's clerk.[5] Compare with this the list of shareholders in Selfridge's in 1914. There is a marked change both in the social status of the holders and in the size of their holdings. The list includes several different sorts of retailer and domestic servant—for example, a dressmaker, a valet, a governess, a housekeeper, a caretaker, and a grocer—owning from two up to forty shares (nominal value £1). The small capitalist had advanced beyond the savings' bank stage. He was beginning to displace the gentleman of means and the inevitable clergyman as a centre of disturbance at stormy shareholders' meetings. But he was still a far from preponderant influence. The wealthy share-holders still owned the bulk of the capital and directed the flow of investment.[6]

---

[1] E. T. Powell, *Evolution of the Money Market*, p. 643. The omission of institutional investors would bring down the average.

[2] Report on the Working of the Indian Railways, 1870–1.

[3] T. Schilling, *London als Anleihemarkt der englischen Kolonien*, p. 51.

[4] Shareholders, particularly in home rails, were probably more numerous. In 1902 there were nearly 800,000 holders of railway shares (less an allowance for duplication, many capitalists owning shares in different companies). Of this number, about 40% were holders of ordinary shares (H. of C. no. 400, 1902). The average holding of debenture stock was about £2000, and the average holding of ordinary stock not much over £1000. In 1912 a third of the shareholders in the Midland held less than £500 stock (*Railway News*, Jubilee volume, 1914). For earlier years see H. of C. no. 219 of 1886 and H. of C. nos. 317 and 625 of 1845; and the discussion of the latter in L. H. Jenks, *Migration of British Capital*, p. 374.

[5] E. T. Powell, *Mechanism of the City*, pp. 126–7.

[6] In Britain in 1912, there were under 200,000 persons owning property worth £5000; the total value of their property came to over two-thirds of the national

The Estate Duty statistics suggest that in 1913 only about 2 % of the value of stocks, shares, and other securities dealt in on the Stock Exchange belonged to those whose property was worth less than £1000, and only 10 % to those whose property did not exceed £5000. Tables 20 and 21 will give some idea of the distribution of property between rich and poor, and of the class of property in which investors at different levels of wealth tended to specialize.[1]

Table 20. *Distribution of property as shown by estate duty statistics (average of 1911–12, 1912–13, and 1913–14). Proportion in which various classes of property were distributed between estates liable to duty*

Class	Stocks, funds, shares, etc.	House property and business premises	Other property	Money lent on mortgage, bonds, bills, etc.	Cash in hand and at bank	Agri-cultural land	Policies of in-surance	Total
Gross								
Below £300	0·2	1·9	1·3	0·5	6·8	0·7	5·7	1·3
£300–£500	0·3	2·7	1·4	1·0	5·2	0·6	3·5	1·4
Net								
£100–£500	0·2	5·4	1·6	0·5	1·8	1·8	4·8	1·7
£500–£1,000	1·1	9·0	3·9	3·5	9·0	2·8	8·2	3·9
£1,000–£5,000	8·2	28·6	16·3	19·2	23·0	13·4	23·4	15·1
£5,000–£10,000	8·1	13·3	11·2	13·2	10·0	9·1	11·2	9·8
£10,000–£20,000	11·2	11·1	13·0	13·9	9·7	10·4	11·0	11·3
£20,000–£25,000	4·0	2·6	4·3	4·1	2·7	3·8	3·2	3·6
£25,000–£40,000	8·7	6·1	9·3	9·4	5·2	8·1	6·6	7·9
£40,000–£50,000	4·1	2·6	4·0	4·2	2·4	3·9	2·8	3·6
£0·1 m.–£0·15 m.	6·6	3·5	7·0	4·6	3·6	7·9	2·1	5·7
£0·4 m.–£0·5 m.	2·2	0·8	3·3	1·9	1·7	1·1	0·7	1·9
£0·8 m.–£1 m.	1·8	0·3	4·3	0·7	1·6	1·5	2·1	1·6
Total	100·0	100·0	100·0	100·0	100·0	100·0	100·0	100·0

Some broad conclusions can be drawn from these tables. In the first place, although capitalists owning less than £1000 worth of property were of little importance in the capital market, those who were worth between £1000 and £25,000 owned nearly 40 % of the national wealth. The chief form in which this class of more than half a million persons held its wealth was in stocks and shares, the proportion varying from about a quarter in the £1000–£5000 group to nearly a half in the

wealth. Capitalists owning more than £500 net formed 7 % of all income-earners and owned seven-eighths of the national wealth. (Clay, *Problem of Industrial Relations*, p. 291.)

[1] The samples above £100,000 are too small to be altogether reliable.

£20,000–£25,000 group. The assets in which it *specialized*, however, in comparison with other classes, were house property and insurance policies of which it held 56 and 49 % respectively. Stock Exchange Securities, indeed, were the assets of which it held the *smallest* proportion of the total—31·5 %.

Table 21. *Composition of each class of estate (by percentage)*[a]

Class	Stocks, funds, shares, etc.	House property and business premises	Other property	Money lent on mortgage, bills, etc.	Cash in hand and at bank	Agricultural land	Policies of insurance	All other
Gross								
Below £300	6·7	20·0	9·4	2·6	32·0	2·7	14·3	13·3
£300–£500	10·4	28·0	9·8	5·0	24·3	2·3	8·7	11·5
Net								
£100–£500	5·9	45·7	9·2	2·0	6·8	5·8	9·3	15·3
£500–£1,000	13·1	34·4	10·0	6·1	14·7	4·1	7·2	10·4
£1,000–£5,000	24·3	27·4	10·7	8·5	9·7	4·9	5·3	9·2
£5,000–£10,000	36·5	19·5	11·3	9·1	6·5	5·1	3·9	8·1
£10,000–£20,000	44·4	14·2	11·4	8·3	5·5	5·3	3·3	7·6
£20,000–£25,000	49·3	10·2	11·8	7·6	4·6	5·9	3·1	7·5
£25,000–£40,000	49·4	11·0	11·6	7·9	4·2	5·7	2·8	7·4
£40,000–£50,000	50·6	10·6	11·0	7·7	4·2	6·1	2·7	7·1
£0·1 m.–£0·15 m.	51·9	8·8	12·0	5·4	4·0	7·7	1·3	8·9
£0·4 m.–0·5 m.	52·0	(4·8)	17·4	6·6	5·5	3·0	1·2	9·5
£0·8 m.–£1 m.	49·0	3·2	26·6	2·7	6·3	5·2	4·5	2·5
Total (£m.)	140·1	45·2	31·0	21·1	19·9	17·5	10·6	313·8

[a] Trade assets (i.e. book debts, stock, goodwill, etc.) averaging £16·1 m., household goods averaging £8·4 m., and ground rents averaging £3·8 m. have been omitted from the table. They are included in the grand total of £313·8 m.

In the second place, there seems to have been a fair constancy in the proportions in which estates of over £20,000 were distributed between different types of asset. Apart from a tendency for the proportion in house property to fall, and for the proportion in 'other property' (including, no doubt, industrial enterprises privately owned) to increase, these large estates are of much the same pattern. Stocks and shares form about half, agricultural land about 6 %, and cash in hand and at bank about 5 %. The pattern of small estates, on the other hand, gradually changes as the average size increases. There is a large, and, at first, growing proportion of the wealth of small capitalists invested in house property, shops, etc., and an equally large, but falling, proportion held in the form of cash. The proportions formed by other assets show equally well-defined trends. Capitalists with less than £1000 owned nearly 20 %

of the total value of house property and over 20 % of the total value of insurance policies. They were thus in a position to make their influence felt here and there in the capital market while remaining of quite minor importance in the market as a whole.

The influence of the working-class investor was also small. His saving was generally done through institutions—Friendly Societies (£67 m. by 1912), Post Office Savings Banks (£182 m.), Trustee Savings Banks (£54 m.), voluntary or compulsory insurance agencies, and so on. Or he might buy government securities, or lend his savings to his town council on mortgage or deposit. In all, working-class savings are unlikely to have exceeded £500 m. in 1913.[1]

Investors had marked preferences not simply for different types of asset but also for the assets of particular countries. They might be familiar, or imagine themselves to be familiar, with the circumstances of some country through having relatives domiciled in it, or through trade connexions with it, or through having bought some of its bonds at a previous date. Or they might rate its credit highly for sentimental reasons, or in the belief that repudiation would induce their government to intervene, or because default had been rare. British investors had a preference for the securities of empire countries and no great liking—partly because of political distrust—for the bonds of European governments. They lent large sums to America and—at one time—to the Near East—in the one case, in the expectation that a rapid growth of wealth would prove the best security against default, and in the other, in the belief that national honour was too deeply involved for the government to be indifferent to the insolvency of our debtors. The preferences of investors were to a large extent quite arbitrary, and the price of a security in the London market was by no means a reliable guide to its probable yield. In the American Rails market, for instance, although it was the largest and best organized of all markets in foreign securities, the investor repeatedly showed a lack of discrimination which can only be explained in terms of laziness, ignorance, and prejudice.[2]

[1] Clay, op. cit. p. 288.

[2] See, for instance, Giffen's *American Railways as Investments* (1873), pp. 54, 67, etc.; *American Municipal Bonds as Investments* (1873), p. 38; and S. F. Van Oss, *American Railroads as Investments* (1893), p. 175 et seq. Van Oss remarks: 'There are at the time of writing 39 descriptions of American bonds paying between 4 and 4½ % upon net outlay, which as a safe investment, find no parallel among any other stock quoted at corresponding prices.... Yet they are classed with a miscellaneous lot of second-class foreign railway stock—Turkish, Argentine, Central American and so forth—which can no more rank with St Paul, North Western, or Burlington bonds than can the dilapidated Ottoman Empire or a turbulent Central American Republic with the United States.... The most cursory comparison with other classes of securities must clearly show that the credit of American bonds is, as a rule, from ½ to 1 % below the point to which they are fairly entitled' (op. cit. pp. 180–1).

There is some evidence that there was greater readiness to lend abroad in Scotland than in England. The Colonial Banks were often under the control of Scotsmen and had agencies for collecting deposits all over Scotland. In the eighties, *The Scotsman* had more than a dozen advertisements for money on debenture and deposit by Australian Land and Investment Companies alone. Edinburgh was reported to be honeycombed with agencies for collecting money for use in all countries and for all purposes, generally on the security of land mortgages.[1] Private investment on a large scale also took place through the building up of mercantile establishments, in South America and the Colonies, in Scottish ownership.[2] Finally, Scottish trust funds seem to have been placed more freely than English in colonial securities.

The preferences of investors were influenced to some extent by legislative measures such as the series of Acts regulating the investment of Trust Funds. The great majority of Trust Deeds generally specified the investments which were permissible under them,[3] but when no directions were given, the Trustee was authorized by Statute to invest only in a limited range of securities. Up till 1889 these securities consisted of Consols, Bank and East India Stock, and mortgages of freehold and copyright estates in England and Wales. The Trustee Acts of 1889 and 1893 extended the list to include the stock of English Corporations and of Guaranteed Indian Railways, the debentures of British and Guaranteed Indian Railways, and a number of other securities. In 1900, the Colonial Stock Act made a further extension in favour of the registered and inscribed stocks of colonial governments.

It is doubtful, however, how far the force of law or of custom was successful in reducing the yield on favoured securities. The prestige of inclusion in the Trustee List seems to have become more ineffectual as the list grew longer. In 1866, three out of every seven proprietors of Bank of England Stock were trustees.[4] Consols also owed their esteem in large measure to the narrowness of the Trustee market. But by the time colonial government loans were included, it would appear that their added prestige brought no tangible benefit and merely set the seal upon a position already won.[5]

---

[1] *Banking in Australasia* (Anonymous, 1883), p. 80.

[2] For South America see M. G. Mulhall, *The English in South America* (1877), pp. 328, 403, etc.

[3] *Economist*, 1886, p. 1046: 'Corporation stocks..., Colonial bonds, English railway debenture and guaranteed stocks, Indian guaranteed railway stocks, and even the bonds of the better American railways, appear to be the securities most in demand for the investment of trust moneys.'

[4] E. T. Powell, *Evolution of the Money Market*, p. 84, n.

[5] A. S. J. Baster, 'The Colonial Stock Acts', *Econ. Hist.* 1933, p. 602.

2. THE FOREIGN CAPITAL MARKET

The London money market specialized almost entirely in the issue of foreign securities, and in the financing of trade and commerce. The large issuing houses like Rothschild's, Baring's, Schröder's, Hambro's and so on, were nearly all founded by foreign families which settled in England as merchant bankers and developed a large acceptance business. They did not possess the apparatus of investigation necessary for home industrial flotations, but were admirably placed for the handling of loans to foreign governments and corporations. They had excellent sources of information and indispensable remittance facilities. The prestige which they lent to an issue was paid on the same principle as an acceptance guarantee; and it was generally well paid. They were under no temptation to dabble in home industrial issues (except the very largest).

Competition between issuing houses was generally limited to business with new borrowers. The older houses could afford to look with indifference on the competition of less reputable houses like Bischoffsheim's for the loans of impecunious governments; and with repugnance on the efforts of 'syndicates' to promote both borrowers and loans.[1] The effect of competition was very often to 'augment the risks of marketing the loan in the face of the efforts of the unsuccessful banker to cry it down'.[2] Countries which, like the Argentine, had no fixed agent in London, had usually to put up with worse terms and less disinterested advice than those which had.[3] Brazil, all of whose loans were handled by the Rothschild's, had a standing in the London market little worse than Holland's. Monopoly was not without its advantages.

Foreign borrowers, who had discovered the convenience of dealing with a single agent, hesitated to transfer their custom. It was damaging to their credit, and to their chances of accommodation in times of crisis. For it created suspicion in the mind of the public, and destroyed the goodwill of long association with the issuing house. Yet transfers did take place. Between 1860 and 1876, Russia had dealings with Baring's, Rothschild's, Hope's, Hambro's, Schröder's, Raphael's, and Thomson, Bonar & Co.; Peru with Heywood, Kennard & Co., Thomson, Bonar & Co., Schröder's, and Stern's; Egypt with Frühling and Goschen's, the Anglo-Egyptian Bank, the Ottoman Bank, and Bischoffsheim's.[4]

[1] H. Drummond-Wolff, *Rambling Recollections*, vol. II, pp. 63 et seq.
[2] Jenks, op. cit. p. 273.
[3] H. E. Peters, *Foreign Debt of the Argentine Republic*, pp. 37–40.
[4] See Jenks, op. cit. pp. 421 et seq. Some of these houses co-operated in the issue of a single loan. For an unsuccessful attempt by South Australia to break away from Nivison's and the Bank of Adelaide in 1908, see Schilling, op. cit. p. 58, and the *Economist*, 12 September 1908, p. 486.

As time went on, there was increased competition from other financial centres, and through the rise of the foreign and colonial banks and the greater independence of former borrowers. The importance of the merchant bankers declined, and though they continued to make issues on behalf of many foreign governments, they devoted more attention to the business of underwriting.[1] A colonial bank, for example, might arrange an issue for its government and secure the assistance of Baring's in floating it. It was not always publicly known whether one of the private banking houses was behind a particular loan.

The expenses of issue varied enormously. On high-class issues they were seldom more than 2–3 %. According to Dr Schilling, the customary rate for the underwriting of colonial loans was 1 %, while the issuing bank received a commission of $\frac{1}{4}$–1 %. In addition, the official broker was paid $\frac{1}{4}$ % for arranging the underwriting, and there was a further payment of $\frac{1}{4}$ % on applications bearing a broker's stamp.[2]

Much higher rates were quite common. The underwriting commission on foreign loans was often as high as 5 %.[3] South American countries sometimes paid over 20 %,[4] or sold a loan outright to a contractor leaving the terms of issue to his discretion.[5] Even Argentine paid 10 % on some of its loans: on the Public Works loans of 1886 and 1887 the costs of issue were 5 and $7\frac{3}{4}$ %, although the credit of the country was steadily improving.[6] Reliable data for other countries are difficult to obtain as the loan contract was generally kept secret.

The system of issue also varied. The issuing house might simply receive subscriptions to a loan on behalf of a foreign borrower, and shoulder no part of the risk of failure. It would lend its reputation and influence with the brokers, offer its advice on the state of the market, prepare the prospectus and do all the necessary clerical work. Thus it would act more or less as an issuing broker with a valuable reputation and some useful facilities of issue. This system, which made no provision for underwriting, gradually lost popularity. When there was a miscalculation of

---

[1] E. Jaffé, *Das Englische Bankwesen*, p. 55. In Paris there was a similar decline in the importance of the private banking houses.

[2] Schilling, op. cit. pp. 42, 52. J. Burn, *Stock Exchange Investments* (1909), p. 215, also gives 1 % as the usual underwriting commission. At an earlier date (1875), Rothschild's took a New Zealand loan of £4 m. 'firm' on a commission of 2 % (*The Economist*, 2 October 1875, p. 1166). This commission probably included all expenses of issue. [3] Schilling, op. cit. p. 44 n.

[4] The Paraguay Loan of 1871, issued at 80, was bought by the 'contractors' at 64.

[5] In the case of the Santo Domingo loan of 1869, the loan undertaking involved the acceptance of a principal of £320,000 and the payment of interest and sinking fund of £1,472,500 in twenty-five years (i.e. 18 %). The contractor floated a loan for £757,700 at 70 (i.e. to raise £530,000) and claimed the balance over £320,000. Only £38,000 was ever remitted to the Santo Domingo Government, which ultimately repudiated the loan. [6] Peters, op. cit. p. 41.

the market, the applications for the loan were often totally inadequate and the borrowers were forced either to make a second issue on more favourable terms[1] or to unload the unallotted portion on the market over a series of years.

The issue was generally made at a fixed price. Colonial governments, however, up to about 1900, were in the habit of setting a minimum price, and floating their loans by tender. At times this was extremely successful and the whole loan was allotted at an average price well above the minimum.[2] But the system was unpopular with the market, and now and then there were ignominious failures. In 1891, for example, Queensland floated a loan, under the auspices of the Bank of England, at a net price of 92. Only 10 % was applied for, and the remainder had to be placed with a syndicate, after negotiation, at 89¾.[3] It is clear that in practice, issues on tender were 'stagged' by syndicates which gradually unloaded on the public, exactly as if the loan had been underwritten at a price equal to or greater than the minimum advertised.[4]

A second system was for the issuing house to buy the loan outright. This was known as the 'contracting' system. It was commonly used where the borrower's credit was not in the first class, or where the need for money was urgent. It was never used where the amount of the loan was large, but it *was* used by the smaller and less scrupulous issuing houses. After the seventies, the increased amount of business and the improved credit of the surviving borrowers caused the system to lose much of its popularity. But until the end of the century it was still used extensively. Baring's, for example, never underwrote a single issue. It was this refusal to underwrite, in fact, that brought about the crisis of 1890.[5]

A third system of issue involved underwriting. This developed, apparently, in the sixties and seventies. Up till that time, issuing houses acted independently, making no attempt to insure their loans against a poor response, and sharing with the borrower the whole risks of

[1] This did not always involve the withdrawal of the first issue.

[2] For instance, a Queensland loan of 1895, issued at a minimum price of 97½, was allotted at an average price of £102. 0s. 6d.

[3] The fiasco was due, according to *The Economist* (30 May 1891) to the 'inability of already overloaded syndicates, which have previously supported these issues to do so now, and the indisposition of the general public to adopt the "tender" form of application'. After the failure, the Bank of England had to put up with a certain amount of recrimination from the Queensland Finance Minister (*The Economist*, 1891, p. 707).

[4] In actual fact some of the loans were underwritten at the minimum price (Schilling, op. cit. pp. 42, 53 n.).

[5] H. Osborne O'Hagan, *Leaves from my Life*, vol. I, pp. 378–9.

failure. In the Egyptian loan of 1868 and the Turkish loan of 1869—both for large amounts—it was found necessary to make use of 'syndicates' in placing the loans. The loans appear to have met with success, and the system of underwriting by 'syndicate' spread rapidly. From early accounts it seems that at first the practice was for part only of the issue to be underwritten,[1] but in course of time it became customary to have the whole of the issue underwritten. The underwriters included wealthy individuals, insurance companies, banks, trust and finance companies, brokers, and—when the issue was an industrial one—the customers, or probable customers, of the company making the issue. The majority of the underwriters acted purely as insurance agents, with no intention of taking up stock unless called upon to do so. If an issue 'missed fire', they generally financed themselves by pledging their stock with the banks, such advances to the new issue market coming, in times of boom, to a fairly large amount.[2] On the other hand, there were many underwriters, particularly the insurance companies, whose intention was to take up stock whatever the fate of the issue, and who, in effect, were given a rebate for being firm holders.

The arrangement of terms and the issue of the prospectus were only the first stage in the marketing of the loan. It was usual for the issuing house to arrange with the jobbers at what quotations dealings should commence, and to create an appearance of market activity by what were known in America as 'Wash Sales'. One broker might be sent in to buy, and another to sell, simultaneously, or the jobbers might be given the right to buy from, or sell to, the underwriters at a certain price, so that they could rig the market without fear of being landed with stock. Dealings began before allotment, usually at a premium; the

---

[1] Cf. the 'Sketch History of Foreign Loans', *Bankers' Magazine*, 1876: 'The Syndicate guaranteed the placing or disposal of a certain portion of the whole loan, perhaps 1/3 or even $\frac{1}{2}$....Each member...agreed to take so much stock at a certain price, perhaps 5 or even 10 per cent below the price of issue in the prospectus....In some cases in addition to taking stock firm, the Syndicate had an option to take a further amount up to a certain date. Options of this kind would be exercised when there appeared a fair prospect of the stock being worked off through the market, at prices leaving a profit above the Syndicate price. This frequently happened, although the amount taken firm by the Syndicate was not much more than covered by the subscriptions for the loan, the wide margin between the price of issue and the Syndicate price enabling sales of stock to be made at a profit to the Syndicate, although at prices below the issue figure.' Cf. also *S.C. on Loans to Foreign States* (1875), p. xlvi; and (on the subject of options) D. C. Blaisdell, *European Financial Control in the Ottoman Empire*, p. 39.

[2] E. Sykes, *Banking and Currency* (7th ed. p. 255) states that loans to the London Stock Exchange at the outbreak of war in 1914 totalled £80 m. A substantial part of this must have consisted of loans to underwriters. It was stated in 1913 that the public also was buying new issues on overdraft (*The Economist*, 19 July 1913, p. 108).

premium indicating either a genuine public demand for a new loan, or an attempt on the part of the promoters to create the impression that there was such a demand. This gambit, which was very widely used, was called the 'Premium Dodge'.[1] It probably originated in attempts to defend the loan against bear attacks.[2] Once adopted by some, however, it came to be the almost universal practice, even of houses of the very highest standing. The representative of Baring's was the only witness before the Committee on Foreign Loans of 1875 who denied its use.[3] He had apparently forgotten the Argentine Loan of 1866, when, before subscriptions were finally closed, Baring's repurchased £200,000 of Argentine bonds in order to keep the market price above the issue price.[4]

The Premium Dodge appears, on the whole, to have been of secondary importance compared with the practice of 'making a market' by Wash Sales. Giffen was emphatic that the practice of premium quotations had been discredited even before 1870. 'The advertising agents and promoters with whom I came in contact', he declared, 'universally accepted as a fact that the interest of the public in new issues was most difficult to excite, and that it was not excited by the quotation of premiums.' He admitted, however, that 'the impression was very general that [promoters] were bound to make a market, and they allowed for this expense'.[5] It is difficult to resist the conclusion that, having decided to make a market, promoters generally preferred to rig it, however unsuccessful they might pretend to be in their efforts.[6]

The object of these manœuvres was either to ensure the success of the issue or to get rid of unallotted stock. An appearance of marketability was useful both in attracting the hesitant investor and in securing a quotation on the Official List. The premium also was bait to new subscribers—'stags' who expected the premium to be maintained after allotment, and who might cancel their applications if they heard that the loan had been badly subscribed for. The system, in short, made costly provision for the sale of the loan to gullible investors, and for the nursing of unsuccessful issues, besides offering excellent scope for specu-

---

[1] H. Lowenfeld, *All About Investment* (1909), p. 178. It was not used in the issue of loans to first-class foreign governments (*R.C. on the London Stock Exchange*, Q. 3183).

[2] 'Speculative selling from pique or jealousy.' *R.C. on the London Stock Exchange* (1877), Q. 3158, 3166.

[3] Jenks, op. cit. p. 278.

[4] Peters, op. cit. p. 23.

[5] *R.C. on the London Stock Exchange*, Q. 7464, 7480.

[6] Giffen pointed out that the high-class dailies in London and the provinces did not quote premiums on new issues (Q. 7470); but (*a*) there was a large number of investors in close touch with the Stock Exchange, to say nothing of the brokers themselves; and (*b*) the rig often continued long after the grant of a special settlement.

lative manipulation. There was nothing necessarily reprehensible about it, provided the issue was a bona fide one, made by a responsible issuing house and honestly underwritten.

There is reason to believe that these conditions were normally satisfied. There were always, of course, unscrupulous promoters who made new issues chiefly because of the superior opportunities for market-rigging which these offered. It was easy to corner the market through a refusal to allot to those who had sold heavily (at a premium) before allotment, and to speculate with the funds raised by the issue itself.

On the whole, however, the underwriter who was left with stock on his hands behaved more or less like any large owner of stock who wished to sell out with the least possible loss. As for dealings before allotment, their chief evil was probably the enhancement of the cost of company flotation rather than the duping of the investor.[1]

3. THE HOME CAPITAL MARKET

The capital market for home investment was a much more complicated affair. The London Stock Exchange was of quite minor importance, except for issues by the British government, corporations and existing companies, particularly the railways. The business of London was almost entirely the financing of governments and foreign enterprises. The local authorities and the railway companies, while raising most of their capital in London, could also borrow in the provinces, the local authorities on mortgage or by private negotiation, the railway companies on debenture or by the issue of shares. The gradual amalgamation of the railways increased their dependence upon London, since there was neither the same incentive to enlist the support of local capitalists, nor the degree of imperfection of the capital market which made borrowing in the provinces worth while. The local authorities came more freely to London as their borrowing powers were extended, and as the decrease in the National Debt created a demand for corporation stocks, which in 1888 became a Trustee Investment. Short term issues of bills were also made during, and after, the nineties; and there was a good deal of borrowing, especially when money was dear, through the Public Works Loan Commissioners.[2]

Companies already in possession of their capital (other than railways) seem to have been responsible for more than half of the issues of home

---

[1] They have been prohibited under rule 159 (2) of the Stock Exchange since 1920. An earlier rule prohibiting them was made in 1864 but was repealed a year later. (*R.C. on the London Stock Exchange*, Q. 1520–4 and p. 368.)

[2] See G. Biddell, *Loans of Local Authorities*, p. 69 etc.

industrials on the London market in the years immediately before the first world war.[1] By *value*, the importance of issues by old companies was very much greater. In the three years 1911–13, the value of issues made by new companies (i.e. companies registered within one year previous to the date of issue) averaged £8 m., while the value of issues by old companies (i.e. companies registered at an earlier date) averaged £22·5 m.[2] These figures include issues by railway companies, investment trusts, etc., payments to vendors in cash, payments made for the purchase of land, the acquisition of other concerns, or for repayment of outstanding loans, and finally cash not fully subscribed. In 1907 the total value of issues for investment at home, excluding issues by railways, financial concerns and housing and estate businesses, and correcting for cash payments to vendors was no more than £13·8 m.[3] It is clear that even in times of booms not more than about 10 % of real investment at home was financed through new issues on the London Stock Exchange by industrial concerns and that of this 10 % the proportion raised by new companies averaged under a third.

The raising of capital for new companies operating in Britain was done largely in the provinces, sometimes by private negotiation between business associates or with members of some wealthy family, and generally by the investment of their own capital by the directors or owners and their friends. Public subscription on the Provincial Stock Exchanges was of quite subsidiary importance. It is true that only 165 out of 378 public companies formed with a prospectus and registered in England and Wales—taking an average of the years 1911–13—applied for a special settlement on the London Stock Exchange.[4] But the companies not making application were apparently the smallest, and may have included some which intended to operate in foreign countries. The face value of the shares bought by the public in these 378 companies amounted to no more than £9·5 m. Of this £9·5 m. probably half was subscribed for companies intending to operate abroad (including certain

[1] F. Lavington, *The English Capital Market*, p. 208.

[2] G. L. Ayres, 'Fluctuations in New Capital Issues in the London Money Market, 1899–1913' (unpublished M.Sc. thesis in London University Library), Table 9. *The Economist* average for the years 1911–13 is £36 m. per year, including issues by public bodies: Ayres gives £32 m. His average for all issues, including issues offered in London and other centres, is in almost exact agreement with the similar total of *The Economist*, viz. £66·6 m.

[3] Ayres, op. cit. pp. 201–2. It would appear from the paper on 'Recent Capital Issues', published in *Studies in Capital and Investment*, that the correction to be applied for expenditure on existing assets may have been much larger than Ayres's figures indicate. The objects for which new capital is raised are not always made particularly clear.

[4] Lavington, op. cit. p. 203.

mortgage companies and investment trusts),[1] and possibly a further quarter by companies floated in London. The provinces, therefore, cannot have supplied more than £2–3 m. to companies formed with a prospectus and employing their capital at home.[2] And even this total is in excess of the amount expended in the creation of new capital assets.

A rather larger total was raised by public companies formed without a prospectus, the shares being placed privately and sometimes unloaded gradually on the Stock Exchange, or disposed of by an Offer of Sale. In the years 1911–13 about a sixth of such companies applied for a Special Settlement on the London Stock Exchange. Probably they raised about £12 m. in the provinces for purposes of home investment.[3]

To this total, and to the total of capital raised by public companies formed with a prospectus, an addition should be made for unsold shares placed after allotment and for sales in the provinces of the debentures and securities of undertakings not formed under the Companies Acts (e.g. Public Utilities). This addition is put by Lavington at £9 m., but it cannot, of course, be estimated with accuracy.

Adding together London and Provincial issues we get a total of approximately £54 m. as subscriptions to home issues other than those of railways and public bodies in the years 1911–13. This total includes cash payments to vendors, and purchases of land and existing assets.[4] It is not easy to determine what proportion of the total is formed by such transfers. Lavington makes a deduction of one-sixth, and this is almost certainly much too conservative. £45 m., therefore, is to be regarded as the maximum, rather than as a rough estimate, of the average amount of capital supplied by the stock markets of England and Wales[5] for real home investment in the years 1911–13. It will be remembered that these were years of exceptionally active business on the Stock Exchange.

The importance of private companies must be emphasized at this point. In 1913 they numbered almost 80 % of all companies, and in the years 1911–13 they formed five-sixths of all new companies registered.[6] Private companies were usually small, and details of their capital are difficult to obtain. They were not allowed to make any appeal—except

---

[1] In 1912, for example, 60 % of the capital of companies registered in Edinburgh with a prospectus was for 'foreign' companies. In England the proportion was probably lower, but more companies would make issues in London.

[2] Lavington's estimate is £4 m. (op. cit. p. 204).

[3] This is Lavington's estimate (p. 204); I should be inclined to put the figure lower.

[4] And also, of course, all preliminary expenses. These are not, however, a capital transfer.

[5] Capital raised on the Scottish exchanges probably averaged well below £5 m.— perhaps no more than £2–3 m.   [6] Returns of Joint Stock Companies, 1914.

through the issue of debentures—to the investing public; they published neither a prospectus, nor a statement in lieu, nor an annual balance-sheet.[1] It is certain, however, that a large amount of capital was invested in them annually, and likely that they had a greater incentive than public companies to re-invest their profits whenever possible. In addition to private companies, there were also, of course, private firms—partnerships and so on—into which a small amount of new capital flowed each year.

It is probable that at least half of the additions to capital of industrial concerns operating in Britain came from undistributed profits. The Colwyn Committee supplied interesting details of a sample inquiry for 1912. Out of trading profits amounting to £312 m., companies put to reserve (either for capital extensions or for liquid balances) £102 m., or, deducting income tax, £96 m.[2] This total excludes the undistributed profits of private firms not registered as limited liability companies, and it includes the undistributed profits of some companies whose main assets were abroad. It also includes additions to reserves in the form of cash or securities—both by manufacturing concerns, and by insurance companies, banks, and so forth. The total of £96 m. is thus an under-statement of profits put to reserve, but an overstatement of real capital investment undertaken out of profits. The distribution of the £96 m. between different producers was as follows:

	£m.	£m.
Manufacturers:		
Mining, Iron and Steel	22	
Textiles	8·1	48·8
Others	18·7	
Transport (including shipping)		10·8
Distribution (wholesale, retail,		
finance, insurance, etc.)		36·5
		96·1

What is true of 1911–13 is even more true of earlier years. Few companies relied upon the Stock Exchange when setting up in business, or when making capital extensions. In the Coal, Iron and Steel group, for instance, the paid-up capital of all companies whose shares were quoted on any British exchange was no more than £29 m. in 1882 and most of the shares were listed only in the provinces.[3] The Sheepbridge Coal and Iron Company, the Staveley Coal Company, and Vickers'

[1] Lavington, op. cit. p. 202.

[2] *Report of Committee on National Debt* (1927), para. 45 et seq. The proportion of net profits carried to reserve was thus 31 %. *The Economist* sample for 1912 shows a proportion of only 25·3 % (Hobson, *The Export of Capital*, p. 40).

[3] Calculated from Burdett's *Official Intelligence* which was first issued in 1882.

were quoted (officially) only at Sheffield, and Pearson and Knowles' only at Manchester. But there were, of course, dealings in London, and some of the largest companies like Bolckow, Vaughan's and Ebbw Vale were included in the London Official List.

Similarly, industries like building, textiles, chemicals, engineering and agriculture were almost entirely independent of the stock market. Either the unit was small, or the standing of the borrower was little known outside a limited area. Businesses of this kind might be sold to the public either for family reasons or in moments of speculative enthusiasm on the Stock Exchange.[1] But the bulk of the firms in these industries remained in private hands. The cotton industry raised fairly large sums on debenture (for instance, on the Oldham exchange), and placed shares (without the issue of a prospectus) by private negotiation among local people.[2] It also raised money from the deposits of its employees. But very little of the industry was under the control of joint-stock companies.

It was the public utilities, financial institutions, transport industries, and public bodies which drew most heavily on the Stock Exchange. Middlemen of all kinds, wholesalers, retailers, importers and exporters, were also large borrowers: and the light industries (especially tobacco) and the providers of services and amusements formed another important group.

It is clear, then, to sum up, that 'the vast majority of joint-stock companies coming into being each year were either already in possession of their capital or obtained it by way of private negotiation';[3] that the borrowings of old companies much exceeded the borrowings of new; and that re-invested profits were a more important source of accumulation than either. It is clear, also, that private companies and firms, even in 1913, were absorbing a considerable proportion of total savings without the aid of any organized capital market. And, finally, it is clear that no very large amount of capital went into *manufacturing*, and that of the capital which did, a comparatively small proportion was raised by public issue on the Stock Exchange.

When we turn to the marketing of home issues, the chief points requiring explanation are the development of underwriting and the reluctance of companies to have resort to the Stock Exchange for their capital.

Until 1900 the payment of brokerage and underwriting commissions out of capital was, in the view of the courts, illegal.[4] It was regarded as

---

[1] The most notable case of this was the conversions of the large breweries into public companies in the nineties.

[2] Lavington, op. cit. p. 208.

[3] Ibid. p. 202.

[4] D. Finnie, *Capital Underwriting*, p. 47. See also O'Hagan, op. cit. vol. I, p. 154.

7-2

equivalent to the issue of shares at a discount, and it was a cardinal principle of the Act of 1862 that the nominal amount of the shares of a limited company was payable in full.[1] Obviously, therefore, the advantages of underwriting could only be secured if the law was evaded. That the law was in fact evaded was admitted on all hands.

The chief devices were the offer to the underwriters of a call at par on unissued shares; the issue of shares at a premium, and the use of the premium to pay the expenses of promotion; the payment of a high nominal sum to the vendor, the vendor paying the underwriters out of the surplus; and finally the issue of founders' shares.[2]

The Companies Act of 1900 legalized underwriting, but appeared also to make illegal some of these devices. Companies were empowered, for the first time, to contract directly with the underwriters before the offer of shares for public subscription, if the underwriting commission was fully disclosed in the prospectus. But the payment of commissions by vendors and promoters was apparently made illegal, although the House of Lords overruled this view.[3] And the Act in effect precluded the payment of commission for underwriting on the reconstruction of companies.[4] In the Consolidating Act of 1908 the arrangement of underwriting by third parties was again sanctioned.

The commissions actually paid were usually from 5 to 6 %, although payments of over 50 % or less than 3 % were not unknown. There was no legal limit. Since publication of commissions paid did not take place before 1900, it is impossible to judge how costly company promotion was in earlier years. That it was costly there is, however, no doubt, small companies being particularly expensive to float. In 1909 Mr Lowenfeld put the minimum expenses of flotation at £2000, which included advertising and printing expenses, the fees of the bank, brokers, solicitors and accountants whose names appeared on the prospectus, and the underwriting commission. It was easy to spend much more. Some firms of brokers and solicitors considered themselves 'but poorly re-

---

[1] *Report of Company Law Amendment Committee* (1906), chapter 25. This did not apply to debentures or to issues by companies registered abroad.

[2] *J. Inst. Bankers*, 1896, p. 161; Finnie, op. cit. p. 47.

[3] For instance, it decided that the Act did not deprive companies of the right of giving a call on shares as a consideration for underwriting (*Report of Company Law Amendment Committee*, chapter 16.)

[4] Ibid. The effects of the Act can be clearly traced in the statistics of new companies formed after 1900. Companies with less than £5000 nominal capital, or even £20,000, showed practically no decline. Companies with a higher nominal capital fell off, the ratio of diminution being greater, the larger the capital. The larger the company, the greater the probability that it would be floated on the Stock Exchange, and hence the greater the proportion which held back. Most of the larger companies were being formed simply in order to take over private firms.

munerated by a fee of 1000 guineas for merely giving the promoters the right to print their name on a prospectus, their work and out-of-pocket expenses being paid extra'.[1] Outlay on advertising and on underwriting might each run into five figures. These heavy expenses afford one very obvious reason for the reluctance of firms—particularly *small* firms—to make use of the Stock Exchange.

The work of company flotation was done largely by individuals like O'Hagan and by ephemeral promoting groups, to a limited extent by trust and financial companies, and only in exceptional circumstances by the large issuing houses: by the banks, practically never. There were practically no permanent intermediate organizations which made it their business to investigate profitable new ventures and capitalize their prospects by the sale of securities to the public, staking their reputation on the success, not simply of the issue, but of the company. There was, in fact, no investment banking in the usual sense. The financiers who did act as intermediaries were moved by the prospect of a purely financial profit and were under a strong temptation to over-value or 'overload' their issues without regard to the ultimate earning power of the new company. It was not unnatural, therefore, that new companies, dominated by industrial interest, should be formed independently of the Stock Exchange. It was generally cheaper to raise money privately.

Old companies wishing to sell out to the public or to raise additional capital were offered rather better facilities. They had already some reputation with their customers, their shareholders, and investors generally, had an established record to offer for scrutiny, and had often some past experience of company finance. But except for companies of the very highest standing, the machinery of issue was quite inadequate.

The comparative unimportance of the Stock Exchange in the provision of new capital for British industry was thus, to sum up, a consequence of four main influences. First, the preoccupation of the issuing houses with foreign loans. This was partly a matter of historical development, of the training and personnel of the merchant bankers. But it was also a matter of the larger size of foreign issues. English industry was still organized in small-scale units; there was a wealth of entrepreneurial ability and of would-be entrepreneurs, and there were not the same opportunities of standardized mass production as in other countries. As a result, the average issue of home industrials was too small to attract the wealthy issuing houses from an already profitable business with foreign governments and foreign enterprises. Nor, secondly, were the commercial banks willing to perform the function of intermediary. Their passion for liquidity—born of long experience of financial panics—made them hesitate to dabble in the long-term financing of industry,

[1] H. Lowenfeld, *All About Investment* (1909), p. 175.

although they had no objection—as we have seen—to making advances to underwriters. A third and most important influence was the absence of any urgent need or desire on the part of business men for Stock Exchange facilities. It was possible to raise money through friends or relatives (the concentration of capital in the hands of the few making this easier), or to make extensions of existing undertakings out of current profits. And where business men could retain full control with the help of such borrowings and of bank overdrafts, their strong individualist bias kept them clear of the Stock Exchange. These three influences combined to reduce the demand for the services of intermediaries and to make such intermediaries as did offer their services either expensive, or incompetent, or unacceptable. It must also be borne in mind, finally, that Britain was already tolerably well supplied with capital, that housing, transport, and public utilities required far more capital than industry, and that the Stock Exchange was generally taken up with financing two at least of these groups.

CHAPTER VI

THE STATISTICS OF INVESTMENT, 1870–1913

I. INVESTMENT AND SAVINGS IN 1907

In this and the next two sections my main object will be to devise an index of gross home investment from 1870 to 1914 and to improve on C. K. Hobson's estimates of foreign investment for the same period.[1] No index of investment can hope to represent with any great accuracy the changes that took place from year to year or over the period; but even an imperfect index may convey a much less blurred, and by no means more misleading, impression than any other summary or tabulation of events could give.

The index of gross investment which ultimately emerges does not correspond to any precise definition. The supply of data exercises a far more powerful influence on the measurement of investment before 1914 than the requirements of economic analysis. It is enough to say that gross investment is taken to include foreign investment (the balance of payments on income account) and gross fixed capital formation (as measured by the output of certain capital goods—ships, dwelling-houses, railway track and the like—built for use in Britain or for British owners). Stocks are excluded because no estimate of any value can be made of the changes that occurred. Repairs are also excluded, although some estimates are given. On the other hand, renewals are included unless a net figure for capital expenditure happens to be available.

There should be no need to emphasize the tentativeness of the calculations. The available material is fragmentary and often unreliable or difficult to interpret with certainty. When the Whitehall bloodhounds, following the stronger scents of post-war national income statistics, still lose the quarry now and again, it is hardly to be expected that the trail of Victorian investment can be easily and confidently followed.

The statistics of Victorian investment start inevitably from the Census of Production of 1907. This provides by far the most secure base for the construction of estimates both of total fixed capital formation and of its constituents. It also provides some important clues to the rate of saving.

In the General Report, prefixed to the Final Report on the Census,

---

[1] C. K. Hobson, *The Export of Capital*, p. 204.

Mr A. W. Flux made a number of estimates, of which the following are of most immediate interest:[1]

	£m.
National income	1918–2158
Net investment (or savings)	320– 350
Maintenance of existing capital	170– 180
Net investment at home (excluding consumers' goods)	170– 190
Net investment abroad	100

The details of these estimates are not given. The estimate of net investment does not include anything for additions to stocks in the hands of merchants and traders, but does include additions to work in progress in some industries (e.g. shipbuilding and engineering) and to stocks of durable goods in the hands of consumers. Consumption in 1907 of durable consumers' goods (including 'furniture, musical instruments, carriages, motors, cycles, plate, jewellery, hardware, hollow-ware, china, earthenware, etc.') was £65 m.[2] This figure appears to be the value at works or port of landing and so to include no allowance for carriage, merchants' profits, etc. Flux puts *net* investment in consumers' durable goods (no doubt at retail value) at £50–60 m.

The estimate of net home investment is arrived at by deducting an allowance of £170–180 m. for wear and tear and depreciation from a total of £350–360 m. for gross fixed capital formation. All that is said about the latter figure is as follows:

'It is possible, by an examination of the Returns made to the Census of Production Office, to separate the various classes of output into such as are adapted for the personal use of consumers, and such as, by their nature, must be employed in making or repairing machinery, plant or buildings. Making a corresponding analysis of the Trade Accounts, it is found that the value at works or port of landing of the goods made or imported for use in the United Kingdom in making or repairing plant and machinery, together with the value of buildings and other works of construction, maintenance and repair carried out by private firms and companies, public utility companies, and Government Departments and Local Authorities, was about £320–325 m., and additions for carriage, merchants' profits, etc., may have raised the total value of those products, as placed at the disposal of their users, to about £350–360 m.'[3]

I have been unable to reconstruct the total of £320–325 m. from the census details and strongly suspect that it includes some element of duplication.[4] I am also inclined to regard the addition of £30–35 m.

---

[1] *Final Report on the First Census of Production of the United Kingdom* (1907) [Cd. 6320], pp. 32–3.

[2] Ibid. p. 31.   [3] Ibid. p. 30.   [4] See below, p. 120.

for carriage and merchants' profits as excessive, particularly as about half the total consists of building and construction work (i.e. structures which are not subsequently moved or merchanted), and much of the remainder represents work done by firms or public authorities on their own account (i.e. at cost).

Details are provided of the estimate for wear and tear and depreciation. First of all, it is said that some £130–135 m. can be identified in the census returns as the cost of repair or maintenance work.[1] Again, I have found it impossible from the published data to arrive at so large a total.[2] Secondly, figures are given, partly for actual outlay on repairs, partly for depreciation, showing a total of £170–180 m.:[3]

	£m.
Railways	21
Local authorities	17·5
Ships	8·5
Houses	33
Agriculture	15
Manufacturing industry	75– 85
	170–180

Of these figures, the first is said to represent the actual expenditure by the railway companies (as shown in the Annual Railway Returns) on maintenance of way, works, etc., and on repairs and renewals of engines, carriages and wagons. The second represents the total returned to the Census of Production Office by local authorities, tramway, canal and harbour authorities. The third is the total repair work carried out in 1907 by private shipbuilders. The next figure is the allowance made by the Commissioners of Inland Revenue for repairs to houses in the year 1907–8. The estimate for agriculture represents the annual depreciation on permanent improvements (£12–13 m.) and on tenants' fixtures, implements, etc. (£3·5 m.). Finally, the total of £75–85 m. is arrived at by estimating manufacturing capital at £1500 m. (of which mining and quarrying account for £150 m. and gas, water and electricity for £350 m.), taking two-thirds of this total for buildings and plant, and depreciating over a ten-year period at 4%.

Of the main estimates given by Flux, the first has been confirmed by subsequent research, and a figure of approximately £2000 m. for the net national income in 1907 appears to be near the mark.[4] The last, on

---

[1] Census, p. 31.
[2] See below, p. 122.   [3] Census, pp. 35–6.
[4] A. R. Prest ('National income of the United Kingdom, 1870–1946', *Econ. J.* March 1948, p. 57) gives an estimate of £1035 m.

the other hand—that for foreign investment—appears to be too low; instead of £100 m., the total was more probably about £135 m.[1] Net investment, or savings, was put at £350–400 m. for 1913 by the Colwyn Committee in 1927, and most other estimates lie within that range.[2] This seems consistent with Flux's estimate of £320–350 m. for 1907, although savings may not include quite the same items in the two estimates.

Before suggesting any amendments to Flux's totals, I should like to set out the main items composing gross capital formation in 1907. In doing so, I shall abide by the census distinction between work done on buildings, plant and machinery and work done on consumer goods[3] —in effect, treating the building and engineering industries as the industries adding to or maintaining capital at home and all other industries, with qualifications, as making goods for consumers or for exports. I shall include work done on buildings and plant by firms' own staffs, and exclude work done for the Army and Navy. I shall, however, give figures for naval shipbuilding, in order to provide a basis for analysing changes in the shipbuilding industry as a whole.

(a) Building work

The census distinguishes building work, nearly all of which is done by firms in the building industry, and construction, which is undertaken mainly by firms outside the building industry, and includes highways and bridges, railway construction, harbours, waterworks and public utilities of all kinds. Output in 1907, free of duplication, came to £129 m., of which about £74·5 m. represented building work, and £54·5 m. construction other than building.[4] Details of the latter figure are given, no allowance being made for any duplication arising out of subcontracting.[5] The figure for building work is arrived at after adding in building work done in the timber trades (£1·0 m.), in other trades (£0·1 m.), and by 'employees of public authorities, gas, water and electricity undertakings, railway companies, tramway companies, canals, harbour, dock and other public utility companies'

---

[1] See below, p. 180.

[2] *Report of the Committee on National Debt and Taxation,* 1927, p. 16. See also F. Lavington, *The English Capital Market,* p. 205 (where an estimate of £400 m. is given for 1913); *The Economist,* 10 October 1925, p. 365 (where a lower estimate of £380 m. is used); A. L. Bowley and J. C. Stamp, *The National Income, 1924,* pp. 56–7 (where the total for 1911 is put at £403 m.). These references are taken from J. H. Lenfant, 'Investment in the United Kingdom, 1865–1914', *Economica,* May 1951, p. 162.

[3] Cf. above, p. 104.

[4] Census, p. 744.   [5] Ibid. p. 764.

(£6·3 m.).[1] An allowance of £6½ m. is then made for duplication. The census states that 'by far the greater part of [sub-contracting] was in respect of building work',[2] and, in fact, it assigns the whole of the duplication to building.

To the total of £129 m., four additions fall to be made. First, iron and steel and engineering firms undertook structural work on buildings amounting to £8·1 m. Secondly, manufacturing firms carried out construction, alteration and repair work with their own employees, the total cost of the work being £5 m. Thirdly, the returns made by a large number (18,000) of small firms were not tabulated, and jobbing men working on their own account or on materials provided by their employers were not required to make returns. The allowance to be made to cover such work might be about £5 m. Fourthly, some building work may have been done by the employees of commercial enterprises not covered by the census (e.g. warehouses, department stores, and the like). Allowing for this item, we may put the grand total for all building and construction in 1907 at £150 ± 5 m.[3]

It is necessary, in order to avoid duplication under other headings, to split this total into its main constituents. The first, and perhaps the most difficult, item to estimate consists of dwelling-houses. These are included under private premises (which include shops, factories and warehouses). The *maximum* outlay on new 'private premises', assuming no duplication, and including all the items not separately distinguished, would come to £40 m. The figures (in £m.) are given in the table on p. 108. The total does not include building work, costing £7½ m., done by

---

[1] Ibid. p. 763. It may assist any future wanderer in the Census labyrinth if I give what I take to be the constituent items included in the total of £6·3 m. They are:

	£m.
Railway companies	2·050
Gas works	2·441
Local authorities	1·286
Naval establishments	0·313
Electricity undertakings	0·142
Waterworks, tramways and canals	0·088
	6·320

[2] Ibid.

[3] An estimate of £150 m. implies that the building work done under the last three headings came to £13 m. The total can hardly have been much less. An outlay of £13 m. would involve the use of building materials costing about £6 m. Now the value of building materials produced and not embodied in the work totalling £129 m. was approximately £14 m. (Census, p. 744; £143 m. minus £129 m.). Exports and imports of building materials were approximately equal, so that building materials worth £14 m. were either used or put into stock. This figure, however, includes manufactures of glass, engine packings, etc., and materials bought by private persons. These are unlikely to have accounted for more than about half the total of £14 m.

the employees of local authorities, railway companies, and so on,[1] but does include about £6 m. for work subcontracted to other builders and so duplicated in the total.[2] Very little of the £7½ m. went on new dwelling-houses—at most about £200,000. On the other hand, a great deal of the subcontracting must have arisen in the building of new dwelling-houses. Assuming that the element of duplication due to this factor was

	New construction	Alteration and repair	Not separately distinguished	Total
Private premises	32·01	23·80	6·81	62·62
Public premises	5·72	1·32	0·47	7·51
Churches	1·54	0·54	0·19	2·27
Not separately distinguished	0·12	0·06	0·89	1·06
	39·38	25·71	8·36	73·45

no greater and no less than in the rest of the building work done, and that the work not separately distinguished can be divided in the known proportions for work that was so distinguished, new construction of 'private premises' amounted to some £33½ m. The further deduction to be made from this total for new factories, warehouses and shops can hardly have been less than 10 % in a boom year like 1907 and may have been substantially greater.[3] This indicates that the value of new dwelling-houses erected may have been between £25 m. and £30 m.

An independent check on this calculation is possible. In 1907 the number of new houses built was approximately 120,000.[4] The average cost of a new house built in Glasgow in that year was £250 (excluding site value), and this figure is also used by contemporary writers in relation to the country as a whole. Thus the new houses built in 1907 are likely to have cost some £30 m., certainly not much less and quite probably more. The Inhabited House Duty statistics offer a further check. In 1907 they showed a net increase in the gross annual value of all houses, except those used solely for trade, of £2·3 m. Taking 14 years' purchase of this (the average for house property included in estates, passing at death in 1907), we obtain a total of over £32 m., inclusive

---

[1] See above, p. 106.

[2] This is slightly less than the figure of £6½ m. given on p. 107 because some of the work subcontracted was to firms in the timber trade whose output is not included in the total of £73·4 m. Such work is not duplicated in this total, although it is, of course, in the larger total covering all building work.

[3] Part of the £8·1 m. for iron and steel structural work was likely to be in respect of factories and warehouses; public utilities and railways are also included elsewhere.

[4] See below, p. 155.

of site values.[1] At that time, the construction of new dwelling-houses was falling, and the corresponding figure for 1908 was only £24·8 m. The work done in 1907 was probably intermediate between these two figures.

These various calculations point towards a total lying between £25 m. and £30 m. I propose to use a figure of £28 ± 2 m., including new houses erected by local authorities.

The next step is to analyse other building work and to obtain separate totals for new construction and repair. The figures of building work given in the table above, when redistributed so as to allocate what is not separately distinguished between the various headings, but without eliminating duplication, appear as follows (in £m.):

	New construction	Alteration and repair	Total
Private premises	36·5	27·0	63·5
Public premises and churches	8·0	2·0	10·0
	44·5	29·0	73·5

Starting from this point, eliminating duplication, and adding in the building work done by manufacturing, commercial and other concerns, by firms in the timber trades, by local authorities and naval establishments, and by jobbing workers and small builders whose work was not tabulated, it is possible to make a very rough analysis of the total. The main assumptions that I have made are that the jobbing workers and small builders were engaged almost entirely in house repairs; that of the work done by the firms in the timber trades about half was on public premises and half on shops, warehouses, etc.; that of the work done by the employees of manufacturing and other concerns about £1 m. out of £8 m. was on 'public premises'; and that the bulk of all these additions should be made to repairs rather than new construction. The resulting totals, shown on p. 110 (in £m.), exclude iron and steel structural work, work done by the employees of railway companies, and public utilities, and all construction work other than building.

These figures are not much more than elaborate guesses; but they do not seem altogether unreasonable. It is possible to check the estimate for alterations and repairs against the allowance for repairs made under Schedule A, which amounted in 1907 to £33 m. This figure included

[1] This leaves out of account the 'drag' due to rent reductions given effect to between revaluation years and the site value of the new properties (see Stamp, *British Incomes and Property*, pp. 31–2). The first of these cannot have been large in 1907 when the general trend in rents was upwards; the second might amount to 10–15% of the value of the properties.

hotels, shops, warehouses, offices, factories, hospitals, schools, and so on, as well as private dwelling-houses, so that it is comparable in scope with the items included above totalling £38·5 m. The Schedule A allowance does not relate to repairs actually executed but is intended to cover

	New construction	Alteration and repair	Total
Dwelling-houses	28·0	25·0	53·0
Shops, offices, warehouses, etc.	8·0	10·0	18·0
Public premises, including churches	8·5	3·5	12·0
	44·5	38·5	83·0

normal wear and tear, together with provision for the eventual replacement of the premises.[1] It is probable that the allowance (one-sixth of the gross rent) was adequate for private dwelling-houses but too low for commercial property.[2] As 1907 was a prosperous year, it would not be surprising if the Schedule A allowance fell somewhat short of the actual outlay on repairs and alterations in that year, particularly if some of the alterations were of a character properly debited to obsolescence (which is not covered by the allowance for repairs).

Some check is also possible on the distribution of repairs between dwelling-houses and other property. In the table given above, repairs to dwelling-houses form 65 % of the total. In the Inhabited House Duty statistics, the proportion by gross annual value was about 60 %, although one would have expected a higher proportion by gross annual value than by actual expenditure on repairs.

Finally, the value of new construction can be checked against the increase in the gross annual value of houses and messuages under Schedule A. For England and Wales in 1907 this came to £2·83 m., for Scotland to £0·26 m., and for Ireland to £0·06 m., making an aggregate of £3·15 m. Neglecting any reductions in rent made during the year, and taking 14 years' purchase, this yields a total of just over £44 m., inclusive of sites.[3] This is rather less than would accord with the total of £44·5 m., exclusive of sites, given above. Moreover, some allowance is necessary for the cost of iron and steel structural work not so far included and amounting, perhaps, to about half of the total of such work, i.e. to £4 m. If this were added to the value of new commercial and public buildings, the total for new building would be raised to £48·5 m.

While these checks do not yield complete agreement, they do not

---

[1] Cf. Stamp, op. cit. p. 62.   [2] Ibid. pp. 195–6.

[3] See above, p. 108. In Scotland, both increases and decreases of rent are ignored.

suggest that there is anything radically wrong with the estimates given above. They certainly provide no evidence that the estimates are too low.

(b) General engineering

The output of the engineering trades is dealt with in the census under various headings. Structural iron and steel work has already been included under building and construction. Shipbuilding and marine engineering work, work done by the railway companies, local authorities and public utilities, road vehicles and aircraft, tools and implements, and electrical engineering are dealt with separately. The output of the general engineering trades, excluding railway locomotives, railway and tramway equipment, ordnance, and iron and steel structural work, was £63·5 m.[1] In this total there is an unknown element of duplication, consisting partly of work given out (e.g. for the installation of engines and machinery), partly of machinery accessories and parts (including parts returned with machinery and sold, e.g. to repairers). Most of the work given out was probably to building firms in connexion with iron and steel structural work, and has already been included under building and construction; the rest is duplicated in the returns of other engineering firms. Hence the full amount, £3·6 m., should be deducted. Since the total value of materials used by repairers was £3 m., it is unlikely that parts returned and sold to repairers were large in value. Machinery accessories and parts, to the value of £3·7 m., are best omitted altogether, since they must have been used either for export, for embodiment in new or repaired machinery, or for sale to manufacturers for the maintenance of their plant. Whatever use they were put to, it would involve duplication to enter them separately. In addition, the total of £63·5 m. includes £1¼ m. for marine engines sold to shipbuilders.[2] Making the necessary deductions we are left with a total of about £55 m.[3] From this a further small deduction should be made, say £½ m., for work on locomotives, ordnance, etc., appearing under the headings 'Work in progress' and 'Repair and jobbing work'.

In 1907 exports of machinery, excluding locomotives, but including accessories, some railway equipment, and marine engines exported as such, amounted to approximately £30·5 m. and net imports to £3·3 m.

---

[1] Census, pp. 125 et seq.   [2] Ibid. pp. 130, 134.

[3] Mr Colin Clark (*Investment in Fixed Capital in Great Britain*, Royal Economic Society Memorandum, no. 49, October 1934, p. 7), in reaching a total of £75 m., has included ordnance (£2·8 m.), the output of public utility companies and government departments (which he puts at £1·6 m.) and only £9·6 m. for repairs executed by firms' own staffs (instead of the Census total of £16 m.), and has deducted only £2·5 m. for duplication. He has made no deduction for the marine engines included under other headings.

Allowing 6 % for transport and other charges,[1] and, say, £1·5 m. for exports of accessories, railway signals, etc., we have to deduct some £24 m. to obtain the balance retained for home use. This balance, amounting to £30·5 m., was made up as follows:

	£m.
New machinery	18·0
Work in progress	6·0
Repairs	6·5
	30·5

Of the new machinery the largest item was textile machinery; investment in textile machinery in 1907 amounted to £5½–6 m. Agricultural machinery seems to have been comparatively unimportant, almost the entire output being exported. For the general engineering trades as a group, the output of new machinery was approximately £44 m. and exports £30·5 m., so that exports on the average formed about 70 % of output. This proportion cannot be applied, however, to the value of the work done by firms in the general engineering trades, since these firms sold various accessories and parts, forgings and semi-manufactured goods, marine engines, and so on, to British firms; undertook repair work; and, in 1907, made large additions to work in progress.

(c) Shipbuilding and marine engineering

The value of work done in 1907 in private yards, eliminating all duplication, amounted in 1907 to £40–41 m., exclusive of general engineering work and other goods, but inclusive of marine engines made by engineering firms and fitted by shipbuilding firms.[2] From this there falls to be deducted some £4 m. for war vessels (including a small allowance for engines returned separately by the marine engineering firms that built them). On the other hand, about £0·5 m. of repair work undertaken by lighthouse authorities, railway, canal and harbour authorities has to be added. The total of some £37 m. was distributed as follows:

	£m.
New ships	18·5
Repairs	9·0
	27·5
Exports	9·5
	37·0

[1] The Census assumes a much higher allowance, but I can see no justification for exceeding 6 % on capital goods, most of which are likely to have been exported without the use of an intermediary.

[2] Census, p. 135. Mr Colin Clark's figures for 1907 (loc. cit. p. 8) omit engines valued at £3·5–4 m. that were returned separately from the hulls to which they were fitted.

Some of the repairs were for foreign owners; and similarly some repairs to British vessels took place abroad. Of the output of new ships, some were in replacement of existing vessels, and only the remainder represented an increment in British shipping capital. The capital value of the British mercantile marine was about £150 m.,[1] and the normal allowance for depreciation was 5 % per annum. In addition, 230,000 gross tons of old shipping was sold to foreigners. Thus net investment in shipping in 1907 fell far below £18·5 m. It was probably not more than £10 m.

For war vessels the output in 1907 can be summarized as follows:

	£m.
New vessels from Royal dockyards	3·4
New vessels from private dockyards	4·0 [a]
Repairs and other work in naval dockyards	2·5
	9·9

[a] Including £½ m. for engines fitted by marine engineering firms.

The total of just under £10 m. is somewhat lower than the Admiralty's return of expenditure on naval construction in 1907 amounting to £11·1 m. The difference may represent repair work carried out by private yards and already included above; but part no doubt represents work carried out abroad.

(d) Electrical engineering

The work done by the electrical engineering trades has to be entered net of any equipment, such as insulated cables, batteries, etc., that are used by building, contracting and engineering firms and included in the value of their output. In particular, all telegraphic and telephonic equipment is included under construction work, other than building.[2] Some electrical equipment is included in the value of electric lines and works constructed or repaired (amounting to £1·8 m.); and some electrical goods were no doubt used by manufacturing firms in work of construction and repair carried out by their employees, by shipbuilding firms, railway companies, etc.

It is difficult to say how much should be deducted from the output of the electrical engineering trades on this account. The gross total, excluding telegraph and telephone cables and accessories, and deducting net exports and all work subcontracted, was £11·2 m. This can be reduced to £10 m. after deduction of electrical equipment used in the

---

[1] See below, p. 171.

[2] The value of such work in 1907 was £4·7 m. The materials used amounted to about £3 m., and this was well in excess of the value of telegraph and telephone cables and accessories consumed in the United Kingdom.

c

8

work on electric lines and works referred to above. The lowest figure that can be taken is the value of electrical machinery and parts (less exports), contract work executed in the United Kingdom, and repair work for customers, together with some allowance for materials used in carrying out contract work. The first three of these items totalled £5·6 m., and the last cannot have been less than £1 m. The total for this group, therefore, lies between £6·6 m. and £10 m. I propose to use a figure of £7·5 m.

(e) Railway companies

The work of construction, repair and maintenance undertaken by employees of the British railway companies is given in the 1907 Census as £34·7 m.[1] Part of this total—£2·1 m.—is made up of miscellaneous goods such as tarpaulins, lamps and so on, or of gas and electricity manufactured by the railway companies for their own use. On the other hand, the total excludes work to the value of £2·3 m. carried out by the building industry on the permanent way and other structures of the railways and light railways;[2] and by the engineering industry in manufacturing locomotives to the value of about £1·5 m. for sale to the railway companies.[3] In addition, engineering firms in the carriage and wagon trades made or repaired railway carriages and wagons to the value of about £2 m., mainly for private wagon-owners.[4] This gives a total of £38·4 m. for construction and maintenance work on the railway system. The total can be divided roughly as follows:

	£m.
Constructional work on permanent way, bridges, docks, etc.	17·4
Locomotives	9·4
Carriages and wagons	10·2
Other work (telephones, steamboats, road vehicles, hoists and cranes)	1·4
	38·4

[1] Census, p. 165.

[2] Ibid. p. 763. How much of the total was work done on light railways is not stated.

[3] Ibid. pp. 128, 130. The output of locomotives from the engineering trade was £4·5 m., while exports (including road locomotives and valued at port of shipment) came to £3·4 m.

[4] The output of railway carriages, wagons and parts from the carriage and wagon trades came to £7·7 m. A large proportion of this output was exported, but no figures are available for exports of all-steel wagons and trucks. Exports of other wagons and of carriages came to £4·3 m. out of a total output (including an element of duplication) of £5·3 m. Allowing for some duplication (of parts and accessories) and for the margin between value at works and free on board ship, we may put domestic sales at £1–1½ m. In addition, repairs to the value of £0·7 m. were carried out, so that, in round figures, the work done on rolling stock for use on the British railways was approximately £2 m.

Of this total, perhaps about £1·7 m. was financed by private wagon-owners, so that the outlay of the railway companies was approximately £36·7 m. This figure is not easily reconciled with the figures given in the railway companies' accounts. Expenditure on repairs and renewals was about £23·3 m., *excluding* the value of locomotives purchased by the companies.[1] This total consists of three items: maintenance of way, works and stations, repair and renewals of carriages and wagons, and repair and renewals of locomotives. It is not clear under what heading the work done on telephones, steamboats, road vehicles, hoists and cranes, amounting to £1·4 m., is classed. Assuming that such work is not included in *any* of the three items, we obtain the following picture (in £m.):

	Total construction and repair	Repair and renewals	Difference
Permanent way, etc.	17·4	11·1	6·3
Locomotives	9·4	6·0	3·4
Carriages and wagons	8·5	6·2	2·3
	35·3	23·3	12·0

The total of £12 m., representing the margin between total construction and repairs and renewals is substantially in excess of the expenditure of the railway companies on capital account, which is estimated below at just under £10 m.[2] If it were possible to allocate the miscellaneous items, such as telephones and road vehicles, between new construction and repair the difference would increase. On the other hand, if the railway companies debited their purchases of locomotives to repairs and renewals, a large part of the unexplained difference would disappear. Whatever the explanation, the census provides evidence that my estimates for the railways—£23·3 m. for repairs and maintenance and £9·8 m. for capital expenditure in 1907—are too low by some 10 %. The underestimate is likely to be due to the exclusion of some fairly large items from repairs and renewals.[3]

[1] See below, p. 137.
[2] Ibid.
[3] My estimates differ at various points from those of Mr Colin Clark (loc. cit. p. 10). He has included construction and repairs to hoists and cranes (£0·3 m.) under work done on permanent way, stations, etc. Work done on rolling stock and locomotives by the companies should be £16·1 m., not £15·9 m. as given by him. Finally, I have put private wagon construction and repairs (and carriages built for the railways—for example, for the London Underground railways) at £2·0 m. compared with his £0·9 m.

A substantial part of the total for railway companies given above is included under building and construction. The engineering work done by or for the railway companies[1] consisted of:

	£m.
Locomotives, carriages and wagons (made or repaired)	16·04
Locomotives, carriages and wagons (purchased)	1·80
Locomotives, carriages and wagons (private owners)	1·70
Hoists and cranes: repairs	0·30
Road vehicles: construction and repair	0·27
	20·11

(f) Local authorities and public utilities

The work of construction and repair undertaken by local authorities in 1907, excluding work done by their gas, water and electricity undertakings, came to a total of £19·7 m. This total included the following items:

	£m.
Highways and bridges	11·2
Sewers and sewage disposal works	2·1
Tramways and light railways	2·0
Harbours, docks and canals	1·7
Buildings	1·3
Other works	1·4
	19·7

The building industry carried out work to the value of £11·3 m. on highways, sewers, waterworks, etc., and a large proportion of this must have been on behalf of local authorities.[2] In addition, work done by the staffs of gas, water and electricity undertakings in public ownership amounted to £4·5 m. Thus the aggregate value of work of construction or repair financed by local authorities and by gas, water and electricity undertakings owned by local authorities lay between £24·2 m. and £35·5 m., together with any purchases of machinery and plant made during the year.

The total outlays on construction and repair of gas, water and electricity undertakings was £8·2 m., and a further £2·85 m. was spent on similar work done on contract by builders. The total was divided as shown in the first table on p. 117 (in £m.).

Work done by the employees of canal, dock and harbour companies on construction and repair (mainly the latter) amounted to £850,000.

---

[1] Work done on steamboats and telephones to the value of £0·80 m. is included elsewhere.

[2] Census, p. 762. Total for construction, omitting railways.

Tramways and light railways not operated by local authorities carried out work valued at £600,000. The work done on telegraph and telephone lines and in the manufacture of telegraphic and telephone apparatus by the G.P.O. and the National Telephone Company amounted to £4¼ m., of which about £3 m. represented new construction and the balance of £1¼ m. repairs and alterations.

	New construction [a]	Repairs [a]	Total
Gas	1·1	2·8	3·9
Water	2·8	1·4	4·2
Electricity	1·9	1·1	3·0
	5·8	5·3	11·1

[a] The division between new construction and repair is approximate.

Taking all these various items together, we obtain an aggregate for local authorities and public utilities (excluding nearly all work done on contract by the building industry) of £36·5 m. made up roughly as follows (in £m.):

	New construction	Repair	Total
Local authorities	3·4	16·3	19·7
Gas, water and electricity undertakings (including public undertakings)	5·8	5·3	11·1 [a]
Canal, dock and harbour companies	0·15	0·7	0·85
Tramways and light railways	(0·15)	(0·45)	0·6
Telegraph and telephone lines	3·0	1·25	4·25
	12·5	24·0	36·5 [a]

[a] Including £2·85 m. for work done on contract by building firms.

Nearly the whole of this amount, however, is already included in the total for building and construction. The only items not so included are:

	£m.
Electrical equipment	1·15
Trams	1·05
Telephone accessories	0·25
Waterworks and canals	0·15
	2·60

(g) Miscellaneous items

There remain a large number of miscellaneous items, some of which are perhaps not true constituents of gross capital formation but are rather of the nature of running repairs while others cannot be estimated with any precision.

(i) Repairs by manufacturers to their own plant

In 1907 manufacturers spent £16 m. on repairs to plant carried out by their own employees.[1] Of this total, £2·1 m. was spent by engineering firms[2] and £7·25 m. by firms in the iron and steel group as a whole.[3] About £5 m. out of the total of £16 m. represented materials bought from other firms,[4] but it is unlikely that there can be much duplication between this £5 m. and the amounts already included for engineering output.

(ii) Tools and implements

The output of tools and implements in 1907 was £5¼ m. and net exports came to £1·8 m. While some part of the output consists of consumer goods, the bulk does not. I propose to take a figure of £3 m. for inclusion in gross capital formation.

(iii) Trams, horse-drawn vehicles, colliery wagons, etc.

Trams made or repaired by the companies operating them have already been included. In addition, there was an output of £0·5 m. from the carriage and wagon trades, partly for export. The carriage and wagon trades also produced colliery wagons to the value of £180,000. At the same time, the output of horse-drawn vehicles from the carriage, cart and wagon trades came to £0·9 m.,[5] and these trades also executed repairs to the value of about £2½ m. Making allowance for exports, for other work done by these trades, and for similar work done by other firms and not already included, I should be inclined to put new construction (excluding consumers' goods) at £1 m. and repairs at £2 m.

(iv) Motor vehicles

The output of commercial motor vehicles in 1907 was probably negligible, and the cycle and motor trades can be regarded, therefore, as engaged almost exclusively in the production of consumers' durable

---

[1] Census, p. 98.   [2] Ibid. p. 129.   [3] Ibid. p. 98.
[4] Ibid. p. 129.   [5] Ibid. p. 709.

goods. The total output, divided about equally between cycles and motors, lay between £10·9 m. and £12·9 m.,[1] and home consumption, after adding the excess of imports over exports, was some £2 m. higher, say £14 m. in all. Of this total £1·7 m. represented repairs.

(h) Other work

In various trades, work is done that should be included if gross capital formation is defined broadly. For example, the new shops, offices and factories that were built in 1907 needed equipment and furnishing. There is some shop-fitting undertaken by the timber trades (and included under the heading of manufactured joinery), some general jobbing work done by blacksmiths, galvanized sheet repairs, and so on. Other items not included so far are brass goods (such as gas meters and various builders' and engineers' goods), ships' nets, machinery brushes and belting, casks, iron and steel pipes, and tyres. Some of these are large items (for example, the value of finished brass goods retained for home use was £5·9 m.), but they are partly duplicated elsewhere. It is probable, too, that some of the various accessories, castings, forgings, etc., that are produced are used by firms not covered above (e.g. coal-mines,[2] warehouses and schools), and that an item for engineering work should be included in parallel with the addition of £3 m. made for building and construction.[3] I have taken a round figure of £10 m. to cover all these miscellaneous headings.

The figures of gross fixed capital formation can now be added up:

		Total (£m.)
Building and construction		150
Engineering work:		
By general engineering firms	30·5	
By shipbuilding firms	27·5	
By or for railway companies	20·0	
By manufacturing firms on their own plant	16·0	
By electrical engineering firms	7·5	
By public utilities, local authorities, etc.	2·5	
Tools and implements	3·0	
Trams, horse-drawn vehicles, etc.	3·0	
	110·0	110
Other work		10
Total		270

[1] Census, p. 140.

[2] It is not clear whether coal-mines are included in the 'manufacturing firms' that spent £16 m. on work of construction and repair undertaken by their own staff.

[3] Cf. above, p. 107.

This total is obviously far short of Flux's. Even if naval shipbuilding (£10 m.) and guns and gun-mountings (about £3 m.) were added, the resulting total of £283 m. would be some £40 m. below Flux's estimate of £320–325 m. Moreover, I see no reason to add anything like 10 % for costs of merchanting, freight and installation. The installation costs are already included in the output of the building industry; most of the output is either not moved at all, but built or assembled where it is required, or made at the point at which delivery is taken (like ships and locomotives); and few capital goods in their finished state are handled by intermediaries.

Making a nominal addition of £5 m. to cover costs of this kind I should be disposed to allow a margin of error in the estimates of engineering output of £10 m. The final totals would thus read:

	£m.
Building and construction	150 ± 5
Engineering and other work	125 ± 10
Total fixed capital formation	275 ± 15

In order to arrive at an estimate of savings in 1907 from this figure it is necessary to deduct repairs and renewals and to add additions to stocks (including, on a wide definition of savings, stocks in the hands of consumers) and net foreign investment. I shall give presently a rough estimate of repairs, but not for the additional allowance for obsolescence and depreciation that has to be added. For this it is simpler to proceed along the lines followed by Flux. His calculations are obviously open to criticism, since at some points they rest on actual repairs and at others on the provision for repairs and renewals that is necessary in order to maintain capital intact. The figure for ships, for example, is for repairs actually carried out and neglects replacement requirements altogether. Nevertheless, the total of £170–180 m. seems to me, in the light of the calculations that have been made for other countries, to be about right. It represents 8½–9 % of the national income. This is less than the 10–11 % for the United States that Professor Kuznets arrives at, but since a large proportion of British capital was overseas and less capital per head was used at home, there are good reasons for expecting a rather lower percentage.

Additions to stock in 1907 were probably slightly greater than normal. Stocks were probably equal to about 5 months' income (i.e. to about £400 m.), and the increase over the year may have been of the order of 5–10 % (i.e. rather faster than the increase in the national income). We may take a figure of £30 m. as the best guess on very little data. Part of this £30 m. is already included in the form of additions to work in progress by general engineering firms (£6·7 m.), and in one form or another under some of the other headings. It might be sufficient, therefore, to put the addition to be made for stocks (including working capital) at £20 m.

The savings made by consumers in the form of goods in their own possession consist mainly of furniture, jewellery, carriages, cycles and motor vehicles. The high figure of £65 m. put forward by Flux is a gross total including, for example, china and pots and pans. The net addition was obviously far smaller. For the items listed above, the gross value of home consumption was about £30 m. at works.[1] From this, and from a comparison with the value of the new houses built in 1907, it would seem reasonable to credit consumers with an addition (at retail value) of about £30 m. These estimates may now be compared with Flux's:

	Cairncross (£m.)	Flux (£m.)
Gross fixed capital formation	275	350–360
Addition to stocks	20	—
Addition to consumers' durable goods	30	(50– 60)
Gross capital formation	325	(400–420)
Less repairs, renewals, etc.	175	170–180
Net home investment	150	(220–250)
Net foreign investment	135	100
Net savings	285	320–350

The main difference is in the first item, the second and third items more or less counterbalancing one another. No less than £30 m. of the difference under this heading is due to the addition made by Flux for transport and merchanting. The omission of naval shipbuilding, and guns and gun-mountings accounts for another £13 m. It would obviously be possible to accumulate the remaining £35 m. from the census schedules. But the real difficulty is to know whether this would not be mere duplication. Work appearing as engineering output reappears as materials used by building contractors; work done by the timber trades is duplicated in the value of ships, offices, etc. Although I am loath to set aside figures that were obviously compiled with great care, I do not feel disposed to make an addition of a third to my total for engineering work (the total for building and construction is not in dispute) merely because the total of £320–325 m. appears in the census, without supporting detail.[2]

[1] Some disinvestment in horses and carriages should be taken into account.

[2] Mr Colin Clark (op. cit.) reaches a total rather lower than mine and pro tanto lower than Flux's. He puts fixed capital investment in 1907 at £247 m. and repairs

The estimates given above indicate a roughly equal division between the increments in capital at home and overseas. They also imply that net savings were about 14 % of the net national income; that gross fixed capital formation plus foreign investment came to 20·5 % of the net national income; and that gross investment (including additions to stocks and to consumers' durable goods) was as high as 23 %. Using Flux's estimates, those figures would become 16–17·5, 22·5–23 and 25–26 %. On quite general grounds I should be doubtful of such high percentages.

We may now turn back to regroup the data and make a rough division between new construction and repair.

The figures given in Table 22 continue the division between building and construction work and engineering work. Details are given for the more important public utilities, and the work done by the railway companies and local authorities is assigned to its appropriate heading. The census data on repairs are used but are not always sufficient to allow the total work done on construction and repair to be divided between the two. For example, the work done by manufacturing firms to their own plant totalled £16 m., but it is not known how much of this was new construction, and I have made a quite arbitrary estimate of £2 m. The aggregate omits all 'Other work' estimated above at £10 m. and the allowance of £5 m. for merchanting and transport costs.

Table 22 shows a slight excess of new building over repair work, and a larger excess of new engineering work over repairs. The total of £120 m. for repairs is below the census figure of £130–135 m., but the difference could be largely accounted for out of the £10 m. of 'Other work' omitted (much of it being repair work), and the naval and ordnance repairs that have been excluded. I should be disinclined, however, to raise the total for repair work above £125 m. out of the total of £275 m. for gross fixed capital formation. New construction (including fittings of all kinds) would then amount to £150 m.

Adding the increment in stocks and work in progress and in consumers' durable goods we have a gross figure of £200 m. On the basis of the estimates made so far, this was divided as follows:

	£m.
Net increment in fixed capital (including building, engineering and shipbuilding work in progress)	100
Renewal of fixed capital	50
Increment in consumers' durable goods	30
Increment in stocks	20
	200

at £103 m., compared with £260 m. for building and engineering output (above, p. 119) and £125 m. for repairs (below, p. 122).

Table 22. *New construction and repairs, 1907 (in £m.)*

	New construction	Repairs and alterations	Total
Building:			
Dwelling-houses	28·0	25·0	53·0
Shops, warehouses, offices, factories	8·0	10·0	18·0
Public premises	8·5	3·5	12·0
	44·5	38·5	83·0
Construction:			
Structural work to:			
Buildings, bridges, etc.	8·0	—	8·0
Highways and bridges	2·4	10·9	13·3
Railway companies [a]	5·8	10·6	16·4
Light railways and trams	1·6	0·8	2·4
Gas, water and electricity	5·1	5·0	10·1
Harbours, docks, canals	3·8	1·9	5·7
Salvage and sewage disposal	2·2	1·6	3·8
Telegraph and telephone lines	3·3	1·4	4·7
Other work (mainly by local authorities)	1·2	1·6	2·8
	33·4	33·8	67·2
Engineering:			
General engineering	24·0	6·5	30·5
Electrical engineering	6·5	1·0	7·5
Shipbuilding	18·5	9·0	27·5
Work done by manufacturing firms to their own plant	2·0	14·0	16·0
Railway companies:			
Rolling stock	5·7	12·2	17·9
Other [a]	0·1	0·5	0·6
Private wagons	1·0	0·7	1·7
Trams, horse-drawn vehicles, etc.	1·1	2·9	4·0
Tools and implements	3·0	—	3·0
Public utilities (not already included)	0·8	0·8	1·6
	62·7	47·6	110·3
Total of all work	140·6	119·9	260·5

[a] Construction work done by the railways to the value of £1 m. appears under 'gas, water and electricity' and 'harbours, docks, canals'. Repairs to hoists and cranes and road vehicles are included under 'Other' in engineering work. Other railway work is included under 'Shipbuilding' and 'Telegraph and telephone lines'.

It is almost impossible to check the figure of £50 m. for renewals. For shipping alone an allowance of £9 m. might be required to cover depreciation and sales of old ships. The gross annual value of houses and messuages coming under Schedule A in 1907–8 was £213 m. and the capital value about £3000 m.,[1] so that a sum of, say, £10 m. might be necessary to cover obsolescence and depreciation in addition to current repairs. This would leave the bulk of the £50 m. to be accounted for by other items.

The most difficult point of reconciliation is between the estimate of £75–80 m. for depreciation and repairs in manufacturing industry and the much lower figures for repairs in Table 22. These show only £10 m. for repairs to industrial and commercial premises and a maximum of £33 m. for engineering repairs (excluding railway companies and public utilities).

2. THE STATISTICS OF HOME INVESTMENT

For the period before 1914 it is possible to obtain annual series indicative of investment in ships, railways and dwelling-houses. The loan expenditure of local authorities provides some measure of investment in public buildings and public utilities. For general engineering a crude index of iron and steel consumption must do service in the present state of knowledge. These five items allow of the calculation of a rough index of gross fixed capital formation. The proportion which they formed of the total in 1907 is shown below:

	New construction	Repairs	Total
Ships	18·5	9·0	27·5
Railway companies	(13·4)	(23·3)	36·7
Local authorities	(7·0)	(18·0)	(25·0)
Dwelling houses	28·0	25·0	53·0
Machinery	24·0	6·5	30·5
Total	90·9	81·8	172·7
Proportion of total	64·6	68·2	66·3

The work done on contract for local authorities is not known, so that all that has been attempted above has been to add the work done by the employees of local authorities, the work done by publicly owned gas, water and electricity undertakings, and an estimate of the work done on contract for those undertakings. This yields a total of only £7·0 m. for

[1] Stamp, op. cit. p. 404.

new construction, whereas the loan expenditure of local authorities, including all the work done by the building industry on public buildings, highways, sewers, etc., was £23·6 m. On the other hand, the £13·4 m. shown above for new construction by or for the railway companies is neither the total of new construction nor the expenditure charged to capital account. It is simply the difference between the total of £36·7 m. estimated in the previous section as the total value of work of construction and repair and the total of £23·3 m. that can be traced as renewals and repairs in the Annual Railway Returns. Expenditure on capital account in 1907 appears to have been about £9·8 m., and this is the figure that will be included in what follows for 'new construction' by the railway companies.

These two amendments make the total for new construction £105·1 m., or nearly three-quarters of the aggregate for all new construction in 1907. Thus the five items listed are likely to reflect fairly accurately the movement of total new construction. For some of the items (railways and—very crudely—ships and dwelling-houses) it would be possible to make annual estimates of repairs. On reflexion, however, I have preferred to limit my estimates to new construction, both because it is more easily measured and because it is more highly variable. Thus the estimates which follow are not of gross fixed capital formation in the usual sense since they omit repairs, nor are they of net investment since they include renewals (except railway renewals), but are intermediate between the two.

(a) Shipbuilding

I have taken the net tonnage of merchant vessels launched for home and colonies as an index of new merchant construction. It happens that the only available price index relates to dead-weight carrying capacity, and I have therefore converted from net to dead-weight tons on the basis of estimates made by Sir Norman Hill.[1] Since sailing vessels generally sold for about three-fifths of the price of steamships, I have reduced the figures for sailing vessels by two-fifths. The resulting index of new

[1] See Crammond, *The British Shipping Industry*, p. 13. The ratio of dead-weight to net tons has been made to rise as follows:

(i) For *steamships*: from 1·75 (1870) by 0·025 annually to 2·25 (1890), and thereafter by 0·020 annually to 2·73 (1914).

(ii) For *sailing vessels* (wood and iron): from 1·30 (1870) by 0·015 annually to 1·60 (1890); then by 0·010 annually to 1·70 (1900); then no change until 1914.

Mr J. Williamson, in the *Annual Reports of the Chamber of Shipping* (e.g. 1889, p. 39), used to take 1·75 as the ratio for all steamships afloat, and 1·33 as the ratio for sailing vessels. See also the *Report of the Commission on Measurement of Tonnage* (1881), pp. 17, 39, 782–4, etc.

mercantile construction, expressed in equivalent dead-weight tons of steamships, is shown in Table 23.

The volume of mercantile construction fluctuates with the tonnage launched but is not necessarily measured accurately by it. The fitting-out of completed hulls generally lags behind the launching of new vessels, which in turn lags behind the commencement of new vessels. On the whole, therefore, one would expect figures of launchings to provide a better index of the volume of activity in shipbuilding than either tonnage completed and added to the register or tonnage commenced. In 1907, when shipbuilding activity was declining fairly rapidly, the gross tonnage of all merchant vessels launched came to about 1·66 m. gross tons, while the tonnage constructed, according to the Census of Production Report, was 1·60 m. gross tons or some 3 % less.[1] So close a measure of agreement between tonnage launched and work done, however, particularly in a year of falling output, is probably unusual.

A price index of new ships is less readily calculated. The best that can be done at present is to take the quotations given by Giffen from the *Circulars* of C. W. Kellock,[2] and supplement them from the well-known quarterly estimates of the price of a new 7500 ton steamer given in *Fairplay*. These are available from 1898, when Giffen's figures stop. A comparison of the Census of Production figures for 1912 with those of 1907 shows a rise in building costs (including machinery) from £17·0 to £20·8 per gross ton, i.e. by 22 %. The rise in selling price as estimated in *Fairplay* was 27 %. It is fairly clear both from this example and from inspection that the price index fluctuates rather too violently. It is also probable that the astonishingly rapid fall in the seventies and eighties is exaggerated, although isolated estimates by contemporary experts offer some confirmation. The index relates to the price of fairly small vessels. It is a rough guide to market quotations but not necessarily to average realized prices.

The index shows the price of steamships per dead-weight ton. Multiplying by the volume of new construction, also expressed in dead-weight tons, we have an index of the value of mercantile construction. In 1907 the value of ships built for British owners was £18·5 m., and using this as a base it is possible to work out estimates for the other years.

About half the total tonnage in the years immediately after 1870 was launched on the Clyde. It happens that contemporary estimates are

---

[1] The tonnage constructed was 'a figure calculated to represent the actual amount of shipbuilding work done', whether the vessels were completed or only partly built in 1907 (Census, p. 133).

[2] *Report of the Commission on Trade Depression*, vol. I, p. 169 (for 1870–82); and *J. R. Statist. Soc.*, March 1899, p. 48 (for 1882–98).

Table 23. *Home investment in shipbuilding, 1870–1914*

Year	Volume of new construction (dwt. tons 000's)	Price of new steamships (1907 = 100)	Value of new mercantile construction (uncorrected) (£m.)	Value of new mercantile construction (corrected) (£m.)	Value of repair work (£m.)	Value of naval building and repairs (£m.)
1870	462	227	10·3	8·6	4·4	2·0
1871	575	280	15·8	13·3	6·2	1·7
1872	654	280	18·0	15·3	6·4	1·4
1873	586	305	17·6	15·0	7·1	2·1
1874	772	296	22·5	19·3	7·1	2·5
1875	536	239	11·4	9·8	7·4	2·6
1876	435	229	9·8	8·5	6·2	2·9
1877	605	215	13·8	12·0	4·9	2·5
1878	681	198	13·3	11·6	5·7	2·6
1879	640	173	10·9	9·6	5·5	2·2
1880	744	202	14·8	13·0	7·1	2·3
1881	910	218	19·5	17·2	8·1	2·4
1882	1210	214	25·5	22·7	8·3	2·7
1883	1423	148	20·7	18·5	6·3	2·9
1884	849	132	11·0	9·9	5·7	3·3
1885	608	127	8·1	7·3	4·5	5·4
1886	461	114	5·2	4·8	5·1	4·4
1887	566	127	7·4	6·7	5·6	3·7
1888	967	132	12·6	11·5	6·5	3·3
1889	1346	148	19·6	18·0	7·6	4·5
1890	1308	148	19·1	17·6	7·9	6·5
1891	1273	115	14·4	13·4	6·1	6·5
1892	1245	115	14·1	13·1	6·2	5·3
1893	990	99	9·7	9·1	5·2	4·3
1894	1222	99	11·9	11·2	5·8	5·6
1895	1148	99	11·2	10·6	5·8	7·1
1896	1156	94	10·7	10·1	5·8	8·6
1897	1051	106	10·9	10·4	6·7	6·6
1898	1619	118	18·8	18·0	7·4	8·4
1899	1759	129	22·3	21·4	8·5	9·5
1900	1748	135	23·2	22·4	8·7	11·2
1901	1808	122	21·7	21·0	7·5	11·3
1902	1851	112	20·4	19·8	7·7	11·6
1903	1518	108	16·1	15·7	7·9	15·2
1904	1811	95	16·9	16·6	7·2	14·4
1905	2130	99	20·8	20·6	7·7	12·9
1906	2322	104	23·8	23·7	8·8	11·7
1907	1882	100	18·5	18·5	9·0	11·1
1908	1035	88	9·1	9·1	7·5	11·0
1909	1301	88	11·4	11·5	7·7	12·9
1910	1559	91	13·9	14·1	8·2	16·4
1911	2396	100	23·5	23·9	9·3	16·1
1912	2346	127	28·8	29·4	12·0	17·3
1913	2601	133	34·6	35·5	13·0	18·2
1914	2243	118	26·2	27·0	9·6	19·1

available of the value of the ships launched on the Clyde for several years before and after 1870 (including, however, the value of warships and vessels built for foreigners). These estimates, which are likely to be reliable, are given in Table 24.[1] They indicate that the estimates for those years in Table 23 are too high. In 1874, for example, the value of 260,000 net tons of new shipping launched on the Clyde (nearly all iron steamers) was under £6·5 m., while the value of 520,000 tons launched for British owners in that year (including nearly 200,000 tons of sailing vessels) is put at £22·5 m. in Table 23. If the Clyde figures are scaled up, they yield a total for the United Kingdom which compares as follows with the figures already calculated:

| Year | Value of new ships launched | |
	Estimate in Table 23 (£m.)	Estimate based on Table 24 (£m.)
1870	10·3	7·0
1871	15·8	9·25
1872	18·0	14·0
1873	17·6	—
1874	22·5	13·0
1875	11·4	9·0
1876	9·8	8·0
1877	13·8	8·25

The sets of figures move in much the same way, but the one set is consistently above the other. The reason for this is presumably that by 1907, which provides the base for Table 23, a higher proportion of the tonnage built consisted of the more expensive vessels, and that there was a growing divergence between the price and average value per ton of shipping. In 1907 the average value per dead-weight ton of all ships built for British owners was about £10, while the price of a small steamer was just over £5 per ton. There was thus a considerable margin between the price of a tramp and the price of the average vessel, and this margin was almost certainly a good deal wider in 1907 than in 1870.

I have therefore applied a correction, similar to the correction applied below to dwelling-houses, for the increasing 'complexity' of the average ship. The effect of this correction, at the rate of ½ % per annum, is to reduce the figures in the early seventies by about 20 % and bring them

[1] They were made by Mr W. West Watson in his Annual Reports on *Vital Social and Economic Statistics of Glasgow* on the basis of figures supplied to him by most of the local shipbuilders.

Table 24. *Shipbuilding on the Clyde, 1860–80*

Year	Net tonnage launched on Clyde (000's)	Net tonnage launched in U.K. for home owners [a] (000's)	Value of shipping launched on Clyde (£m.)	Net tonnage building or under contract on Clyde at end of year (000's)
1860	47·8	212·0	—	—
1861	66·8	200·8	—	—
1862	70·0	241·4	—	—
1863	123·3	361·0	—	106·0
1864	178·5	431·9	Nearly 5	140·0
1865	153·9	415·2	Over 4	109·4
1866	124·5	341·2	—	71·9
1867	108·0	269·1	—	124·1
1868	169·6	316·2	Over 3¾	134·8
1869	192·3	354·3	Over 4	141·0
1870	180·4	342·7	3½	180·2
1871	196·2	354·4	Over 4½	301·8
1872	230·3	393·0	Nearly 7	247·4
1873	232·9	370·7	—	192·6
1874	262·4	521·2	Nearly 6½	182·3
1875	211·5	420·6	Over 4½	137·5
1876	174·8	360·4	Nearly 4	161·4
1877	169·4	433·7	Over 3	140·2
1878	212·0	428·2	—	83·0
1879	157·6	356·8	—	149·2
1880	248·7	403·8	Nearly 13	314·7

[a] Prior to 1871 the figures relate to new tonnage registered in the U.K.

Source: Annual Reports of Glasgow City Chamberlain (*Vital, Social and Economic Statistics of Glasgow*).

more into line with the estimates given above based on the data for Glasgow.

I have made a tentative estimate of the repair work carried out on merchant vessels in British yards, and although I have no great faith in it, I reproduce it in Table 23. It is based on the value of repair work done in 1907 and fluctuates with clearings from British ports of British vessels with cargo. Thus it complies with at least three known requirements of an index of the volume of repair work: it rises in good times and falls when trade is bad; it is comparatively steady; and it varies with the activity of British shipping. Clearings of sailing vessels have been given equal weight with clearings of steamships, since sailing

c

vessels were slower, and repairs in relation to carrying capacity at least as great.[1]

Table 23 also shows, for completeness, the value of naval work. Complete, and presumably reliable figures of this exist and bring the total for 1907 up to £38·5 m. No account is taken of the construction of ships for export to foreign countries or of trade in ships, new or old.

The figures of shipbuilding output can be related to other information about the industry: for example, figures of wages, dividends, unemployment, and so on. I have given in Table 25 some of these figures. The unemployment statistics, while a useful indication of the timing of changes in shipbuilding activity, are a less satisfactory guide to the amplitude of these changes.[2] The greatest fluctuation in unemployment was from 7·6 % in 1906 to 23·2 % in 1908. If there was no change in the number of workers in the industry—and there may have been some emigration—employment must have fallen by a sixth. Amongst unskilled workers a fall in employment of a quarter or a third seems quite probable. The price of steamships fell by 15 %. Thus we should expect a fall in the value of all shipbuilding work done by at least a third, and cannot regard a fall of 40 % in work done for home owners as in any way unreasonable.[3]

The course of dividends is also in keeping with our figures. The range of fluctuations is very great—more than in any other industry in the same period—and affords some corroboration of the sharp movements in the price of steamships. The successive peaks in dividends in 1900, 1905 and 1913 are, however, on a falling curve while the peaks in

---

[1] In converting from volume to value the index has been given a more distinctly upward trend by raising the figures for each year in the ratio of dead-weight to net tons assumed to be appropriate for new steamships built in that year. This simplifies the calculation, since the price index is in terms of dead-weight tonnage. But some such correction for trend would also seem necessary to allow for the fact that improvements in shipbuilding technique which lowered the price of new ships were unlikely to be fully shared in by the repairing section of the industry.

The estimates of repair work in Table 23 are equivalent to about 10s. 6d. per dead-weight ton of British shipping in 1870 and to about 6s. per ton in 1907; giving a ratio of about 175 to 100 against a fall in the cost of new steamships from 227 to 100.

The 1912 Census of Production showed an outlay on ship-repairing of £9·9 m. The estimate in Table 23 is £12 m. It is possible to account for most of this discrepancy by supposing that repairing costs lagged behind ship prices; but the main point is that such a large discrepancy is possible.

[2] They are based on returns from the shipbuilding unions and refer, therefore, to the more skilled, and less frequently unemployed, workers in the industry. The number employed in shipbuilding in 1911 was over 150,000, while the membership of Trade Unions making returns of employment in that year was 58,000.

[3] The output of vessels built for *foreign* owners (including war vessels) was almost as great in 1908 as in 1906.

Table 25. *Shipping and shipbuilding, 1870–1914*

Year	Value of all shipbuilding work for U.K. owners or Government (£m.)	Unemployment[a] (%)	Gross tonnage commenced[b] (000's)	Net profit per gross ton of White Star Line[c] (1900=100 =£4·36)	Earnings per dwt. ton of Nitrate Producers' Co. (1900=100 =£2·4)	Dividends declared by Shipping companies[d] (1899–1913=100)	Shipbuilding companies[d] (1899–1913=100)
1870	15·0	—	—	—	—	—	—
1871	21·2	—	—	—	—	—	—
1872	23·1	1·0	—	—	—	—	—
1873	24·2	1·2	—	—	—	—	—
1874	28·9	2·5	—	—	—	—	—
1875	19·8	5·9	—	—	—	—	—
1876	16·6	8·5	—	—	—	—	—
1877	19·4	8·3	—	—	—	—	—
1878	19·9	9·4	—	—	—	—	—
1879	17·3	9·5	—	—	—	—	—
1880	22·4	8·0	—	—	—	—	—
1881	27·7	1·8	—	—	—	—	—
1882	33·7	0·7	—	—	—	—	—
1883	27·7	2·1	—	—	—	—	—
1884	18·9	20·8	—	—	—	—	—
1885	17·2	22·2	—	56·7	—	—	—
1886	14·3	21·6	—	67·2	—	—	—
1887	16·0	16·7	—	77·8	—	—	—
1888	21·3	7·3	1075	96·9	—	—	—
1889	30·1	2·0	1187	101·9	—	—	—
1890	32·0	3·4	1021	109·4	—	—	—
1891	26·0	5·7	1148	81·5	—	—	—
1892	24·6	10·9	854	76·8	—	—	—
1893	18·6	17·0	904	71·8	—	—	—
1894	22·6	16·2	975	64·7	—	—	—
1895	23·5	13·0	1041	67·1	—	—	—
1896	24·5	9·5	1116	94·1	—	—	—
1897	23·7	7·6	1121	97·1	47·6	—	—
1898	33·8	4·7	1590	96·7	66·4	—	—
1899	39·4	2·3	1341	51·1	53·2	94	127
1900	42·3	2·5	1421	100·0	100·0	100	139
1901	39·8	3·7	1579	46·1	56·2	69	133
1902	39·1	8·2	1067	53·3	38·3	49	124
1903	38·8	12·0	1055	47·9	25·3	46	110
1904	38·2	14·0	1376	34·6	29·8	42	116
1905	41·2	11·9	1803	49·7	25·2	51	132
1906	44·2	7·6	1617	57·7	22·8	58	122
1907	38·6	9·2	1433	57·8	24·8	58	107
1908	27·6	23·2	796	18·4	21·0	43	58
1909	32·1	22·1	1182	37·6	25·3	49	51
1910	38·7	13·2	1360	64·8	30·0	65	51
1911	49·3	4·3	1923	58·6	36·7	82	59
1912	58·7	3·9	2115	48·1	78·8	117	82
1913	66·7	3·1	1866	57·6	62·4	118	88
1914	55·7	3·9	1427	45·3	70·0	—	—

[a] Up to and including 1896 percentage of unemployment in the United Society of Boiler-makers and Iron and Steel Ship Builders; thereafter as given in the *Annual Abstracts of Labour Statistics*. In 1897 the unemployment percentage in the first series was 8·6.

[b] *Lloyd's Register.*   [c] *Fairplay*, 1 January 1920, p. 103.

[d] G. L. Ayres, 'Fluctuations in new capital issues on the London Money Market, 1899–1913' (unpublished M.Sc. Thesis available in London School of Economics Library).

construction in 1900, 1906 and 1913 are on a rising curve. This reflects the failure of steamships to hold the high level of prices reached in the first of these peaks, in the middle of the South African war.

The course of the shipbuilding trade before the war was dominated by the fluctuations in shipping freights, the influence of costs of construction and operation being subordinate. Freights in turn depended very largely on the state of the wheat crop in the United States and in Europe, partly because a very high proportion of British shipping was

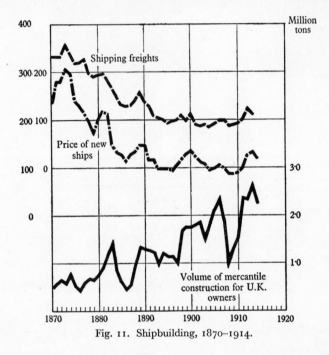

Fig. 11. Shipbuilding, 1870–1914.

engaged in the transport of wheat, partly because the imperfections of the freight market gave North Atlantic freights a disproportionate influence on new construction.[1]

Harvest fluctuations provide the explanation of a rather puzzling dip in the output of steamships at the top of many pre-war booms. In 1873, for instance, there was a temporary drop in the number of tons launched, and a rise in the following year. This rise followed a similar revival in the freight market, consequent upon the failure of European crops in 1873 and heavy exports from the United States where the harvest was abundant. Similarly, the lateness of the decline in ship-

[1] See the discussion in Professor D. H. Robertson's *Study of Industrial Fluctuation*, pp. 24, 78–83, etc. (especially note 1 to p. 81).

building in 1883[1] was partly due to the good United States crop of 1882. In 1891, at the commencement of the next slump, there was a rise of over 10 % in tonnage commenced, and the increase was reflected in the comparatively slight fall in launchings in 1892. Again the explanation is to be found in the conjunction of crop failures in Europe and good harvests in the United States; there was a rise in home freights in 1891, and this, in spite of a heavy fall in outward freights, encouraged the placing of new orders.[2] Another dip in tonnage commenced took place at the height of the next boom, in 1899–1900, and there was then a rise until the autumn of 1901. The same sort of thing seems to have happened in 1906–8, and in 1913 tonnage commenced again fell before the boom was at its height. These fluctuations followed the course of shipping freights fairly closely, and agricultural influences can be clearly traced in the changes in the freight market.

Whether crop fluctuations are a sufficient explanation of the course of shipbuilding may, however, be doubted. It would be surprising if, at the beginning of every pre-war slump, the United States had good crops and Europe had poor ones. Some weight should be attached to the circumstance that working-class purchasing power (and hence imports of food) did not reach its maximum until the end of the boom; and to the fact that imports of timber tended to be high when shipbuilding was active.[3]

Costs of construction were an important factor in early years, but more as a secular than a cyclical force.[4] When improvements in materials and carrying power were taking place rapidly there was naturally more temptation to scrap obsolete vessels. Moreover, the heavy fall in building costs in Britain from 1874 to 1886 put her in a favourable position for competition with the vessels of other countries. In the short

[1] Tonnage under construction did not fall until the first quarter of 1884, when the depression was already severe.

[2] It should be observed here that even an accurate index of *average* freights (which is very difficult to construct) is a treacherous guide to the incentive to build more ships. Freights on all routes do not move together, and a special type of ship is often necessary for particular products. The monopolescent opportunities of particular companies are also of some importance. It is worth pointing out that the trade of the British Possessions with the United Kingdom (which is underweighted in C. K. Hobson's index) rose in 1874, in 1882 (very markedly), in 1891, in 1901 and in 1909. Our ships had something of a monopoly in this trade, and must have benefited when it increased.

[3] Reference to Fig. 16 (p. 198) will show that shipping freights and imports of foodstuffs moved in close correspondence with one another between 1885 and 1913. But imports of foodstuffs depended upon working-class purchasing power, not simply on harvest fluctuations.

[4] 'If the men were to offer to-day to work for 2d. an hour, the employers would not lay out a lot of money in building vessels' (Mr R. Knight before the Royal Commission on Trade Depression in 1886; Q. 14, 964).

period, costs rose sharply in the boom and fell—the fall in constructional costs being often very heavy—at the beginning of the depression. But during the freight boom shipowners would not be deterred from placing more orders by the rise in building and operating costs; freights rose by at least as much. There were higher profits (from which, if necessary, new construction could be financed), more cargoes, more ships in use and in need of replacement, more up-to-date vessels on the seas to excite the envy of shipowners. On the other hand, there was more uncertainty—uncertainty whether to hold off from placing orders until ships could be obtained more cheaply, uncertainty whether a rise in wage costs and the price of coal might not wipe out the paper profit on new ships, uncertainty about the continuance of the boom in freights and the competition of other companies.

Finally, there was the influence of finance. Cheap money was often available to the industry when other openings for investment were closing up. Professor Robertson has suggested, for example, that 'a considerable share of the cheap money of the nineties, when the doors of foreign investment were closed, drifted for want of something better to do into the hands of [speculative and inexperienced] shipowners'.[1] It is not unlikely, too, that the high volume of construction in the late seventies and early eighties was aided by credit facilities associated with the low level of foreign investment in those years.

By contrast with total shipbuilding output (and also with the construction of steamships) launchings of sailing vessels were always at their minimum well on in the boom and at their maximum in the middle of the depression. This peculiarity can be explained on the assumption that changes in the popularity of sailing vessels were correlated with changes in the price of coal, since outlay on coal is an important part of the running costs of steamships, and since changes in the cost of other items affected both types of vessels more or less equally. In fact, however, there appears to have been a considerable lag between changes in the export price of coal and fluctuations in the construction of sailing vessels. The ratio of sail to steamship launchings did not rise until a late stage in the boom—often two years after shipbuilding output had begun to improve. Taking into account the length of the period of construction, however, this lag is not altogether surprising. In the first years of depression coal prices were high relatively to pre-boom experience; and the current return on different types of vessel may have impressed itself less forcibly on shipowners than their recollections of the boom. It is also possible that the increase in the construction of sailing vessels during the depression was associated with the customary expansion in our

[1] D. H. Robertson, op. cit. p. 26.

imports of foodstuffs after employment had reached (or even passed) its peak, foodstuffs—and particularly wheat—being the chief cargo of sailing ships.

(b) Railways

The estimation of the capital expenditure of British railways before 1914 is surprisingly troublesome. Although returns were made, under Abstract A of the Railway Returns, they do not appear, so far as I am aware, in any Parliamentary publication, with the single exception of the year 1913, when a new form of return was adopted. Rather than go through the companies' accounts, which would be extremely laborious and not, so far as I can judge, appreciably more accurate, I have made use of the figures for the leading railways published by a number of technical journals. *Herapath's Railway Journal* gave statistics of capital expenditure for thirty-seven British railways during the twenty years 1874–93. These statistics, however, sometimes include large items for subscriptions to other lines, and outlay on canals, steam-boats, docks, etc., which either do not represent acts of investment at all or are not, strictly speaking, railway investment. Where it is obvious that some large purchase has been included in capital outlay, I have made a rough interpolation; otherwise I have left the figures as they stood. Partly to save trouble—no aggregate for the thirty-seven companies being given —partly to check the reliability of the figures, I have taken the total for three groups of four companies during each half-year from 1874 to 1893.[1] To the aggregate for the sample I have added 10%, and have treated the resulting total as capital expenditure on rolling stock or lines open for traffic or in course of construction by all British railways in the twenty years 1874–93. For the years 1870–3 I have used the companies' accounts as given in *Bradshaw's Shareholders' Guide*. The figures given there are unfortunately not for the calendar year but for 30 June–30 June, so that my estimates are distinctly tentative.

After 1893 I have made use of the excellent statistical supplements to the *Railway News*. I have been able to distinguish railway investment from subscriptions to other lines, expenditure on steamboats, etc., and have taken a rather larger sample—sixteen companies instead of twelve.[2] Details are given for the leading thirty companies, and from these it

---

[1] The three groups were: Midland, London and North Western, Great Western, North Eastern; Great Northern, Great Eastern, North British, Caledonian; Lancashire and Yorkshire, Manchester, Sheffield and Lincoln, London and South Western, and London, Chatham and Dover. The totals for these groups do not by any means move together, but there is nothing incredible about the divergences.

[2] The four additional companies were: South Eastern; London, Brighton and South Coast; Metropolitan; and Metropolitan District.

has been possible to estimate total capital expenditure for 1894 and 1895 and make a comparison with figures in continuance of those calculated from *Herapath's Railway Journal*. I have added a sixth to the total for the sample of sixteen companies, and this makes a satisfactory splice with the figures for the earlier years.

The *Railway News* ceased to include statistics of capital expenditure in its supplements in 1902, and from that year until 1909 I have used the totals for twenty-one leading companies published in the *Railway Times*,[1] checked by figures for sixteen companies for the years 1900–6 published in the *Financial News*.[2] As the *Railway Times* totals for 1900–1 are approximately equal to my estimates of capital expenditure by all British railways, I have left the figures for the later years as they stand, on the assumption that subscriptions to other lines, etc., by the twenty-one companies which are included in the *Railway Times* total cancel out with capital expenditure by companies not included.

Finally, for 1910–12 I have treated the proposed expenditure on capital account by fifteen English railways as given in *The Economist* as an index of actual capital expenditure by all companies in these years. The figure for 1913 is the total of railway capital outlay given in the Railway Returns for that year, excluding outlay on steamboats, land and similar items. I have no means of judging whether it fits in with my other estimates, as *The Economist* ceased to publish details of proposed capital expenditure in the middle of 1913.

Railway expenditure on repairs and renewals is also not too easy to calculate. The Railway Returns give figures for expenditure on maintenance of way, works, etc., and on renewals of carriages and wagons, but not for expenditure on repairs to, and renewals of, locomotives. It is possible, however, to form a rough estimate of this expenditure from the figures of outlay on materials and wages for the repair and renewal of engines by the fifteen leading companies. These figures are not given before 1889, so that it has been necessary to suppose that in earlier years the proportion of expenditure on engines to total expenditure on upkeep remained constant. Purchases of locomotives from engineering firms are omitted from the Board of Trade figures, but do not appear to have come to more than £1–1½ m.[3] I have made no

---

[1] *Railway Times*, 9 July 1910.

[2] Quoted in *Railway Times*, 2 March 1907.

[3] In 1907, according to the Census of Production, engineering firms sold locomotives to the value of £1½ m. to British railway companies. In 1913 the expenditure on upkeep of all British railways came to £26·4 m., compared with an estimate of £25 m. reached by the method described above; but the excess of £1·4 m. was not all in respect of locomotives (comparison is made difficult by the change in the form of return introduced in 1913).

Table 26. *Railway investment, 1870–1913*

Year	Capital expenditure of a number of companies during		Estimated capital expenditure of all British companies (£m.)	Estimate of total expenditure on repairs, renewals, etc. (£m.)	Gross investment of British railway companies (£m.)
	1st half year (£m.)	2nd half year (£m.)			
1870	4·75	4·75	10·5	7·6	18·1
1871	5·25	5·50	11·8	8·5	20·3
1872	5·75	5·00	11·8	9·1	20·9
1873	6·00	6·83	14·1	10·7	24·8
1874	7·41	7·87	16·8	11·8	28·6
1875	7·56	8·29	17·4	12·1	29·5
1876	7·58	7·34	16·4	12·3	28·7
1877	7·22	6·92	15·6	12·6	28·2
1878	6·55	5·46	13·2	12·1	25·3
1879	4·71	4·46	10·1	11·4	21·5
1880	3·89	5·14	9·9	11·9	21·8
1881	4·57	5·60	11·3	12·4	23·7
1882	5·01	5·75	11·8	12·8	24·6
1883	6·19	6·82	14·1	13·1	27·2
1884	5·87	6·19	13·3	13·2	26·5
1885	4·79	4·12	9·8	12·7	22·5
1886	3·63	3·66	8·0	12·3	20·3
1887	3·11	3·33	7·1	12·6	19·7
1888	3·25	3·32	7·2	12·8	20·0
1889	3·68	4·37	8·9	13·6	22·5
1890	4·00	5·46	10·4	14·3	24·7
1891	5·54	6·16	12·8	14·7	27·5
1892	5·27	5·83	12·2	14·9	27·1
1893	4·56	4·45	10·5	14·7	25·2
1894	3·89	4·42	9·7	15·0	24·7
1895	5·05	4·70	11·4	15·1	26·5
1896	5·27	5·54	12·6	16·0	28·6
1897	5·02	6·96	14·0	16·8	30·8
1898	6·34	7·66	16·3	17·7	34·0
1899	6·85	8·98	18·5	18·7	37·2
1900	8·17	9·49	20·6	19·5	40·1
1901	7·99	(7·25)	17·3	20·2	37·5
1902	6·63	6·11	14·5	20·8	35·3
1903	6·48	5·99	14·4	21·3	35·7
1904	5·54	4·72	12·4	21·3	33·7
1905	4·71	4·82	11·6	21·5	33·1
1906	4·54	4·02	10·2	22·5	32·7
1907	4·52	4·48	9·8	23·3	33·1
1908	4·34	3·53	6·9	23·1	30·0
1909	2·96	2·60	5·6	23·1	28·7
1910	2·50	2·45	5·0	23·9	28·9
1911	2·97	2·62	5·6	24·6	30·2
1912	3·09	3·48	6·6	24·7	31·3
1913	—	—	(8·3)	(25·0)	33·3

Table 27. *Factors influencing fluctuations in railway investment,*
1870–1913

Year	Profits of all British railways [a] (£m.)	Mean price of four railway common stocks [b]	Price of five pref. and debenture railway stocks [c]	Number of passengers on British railways [d] (millions)	Increase in number of passenger carriages [d] (000's)
1870	23·1	—	—	336·5	—
1871	25·4	—	—	375·2	2·15
1872	26·0	145	100	422·9	1·20
1873	26·2	142	100	455·3	1·07
1874	26·1	143	102	477·8	0·81
1875	27·8	143	104	507·0	0·76
1876	28·3	137	106	534·5	0·99
1877	29·0	131	106	549·5	0·54
1878	29·4	126	105	565·0	0·37
1879	29·1	128	107	562·7	0·61
1880	31·9	145	110	603·9	0·85
1881	32·1	150	112	623·0	0·92
1882	33·1	156	112	654·8	0·76
1883	33·3	155	112	683·7	1·05
1884	33·0	151	116	695·0	0·73
1885	32·4	144	116	697·2	0·63
1886	32·7	143	118	725·6	0·56
1887	33·5	145	119	733·7	0·81
1888	34·6	150	127	742·5	0·53
1889	36·4	164	130	775·2	0·59
1890	36·2	165	128	817·7	0·93
1891	36·3	162	128	845·5	2·05
1892	35·8	163	132	864·4	0·96
1893	34·4	160	135	873·2	0·98
1894	36·5	161	138	911·4	0·44
1895	37·5	165	147	929·8	0·73
1896	39·7	177	155	980·3	0·05
1897	40·0	184	151	1030·4	1·77
1898	39·4	181	146	1062·9	1·07
1899	40·7	179	140	1106·7	1·05
1900	38·7	166	134	1142·3	1·50
1901	38·1	153	130	1172·4	1·42
1902	40·6	150	130	1188·2	0·76
1903	41·2	144	126	1195·3	0·65
1904	41·2	140	121	1198·8	0·23
1905	42·1	143	123	1199·0	0·46
1906	42·7	141	117	1240·3	0·66
1907	43·4	—	114	1259·5	0·93
1908	41·8	—	113	1278·1	0·12
1909	43·4	—	111	1265·1	0·02
1910	46·1	—	108	1306·7	−0·19
1911	47·6	—	—	1326·3	0·22
1912	45·7	—	—	1294·3	−0·06
1913	48·0	—	—	—	—

[a] Inland Revenue figures as given by Stamp, op cit. pp. 220–1. The 'net receipts' of the railway companies, as given in the Railway Returns, show very similar fluctuations.
[b] Average of highest and lowest during the year of Midland, London and North Western, Great Western, and North Eastern ordinary stocks (P. L. Newman in *J. Inst. Act.*, July 1908, p. 318). The figures for 1872–3 are 12-monthly averages taken from a monthly index (for 1872–88) which I have calculated on the basis of data put at my disposal by Mr P. K. (now Sir Piers) Debenham.
[c] Twelve-monthly average calculated by Mr Debenham for three railway debenture stocks (Great Western, Midland and North Eastern) and two preference stocks (Midland and North Eastern).
[d] Railway Returns.

addition to provide for these purchases, some of which must have been on capital account. How much of railway maintenance expenditure might properly have been charged to capital account as 'betterment' is not easy to say, but the amount seems generally to have been small.[1]

The results of all these calculations are shown in Table 26. I have added in Table 27 some figures which may help towards an understanding of the fluctuations in railway investment—figures of profits, of security prices, of passenger traffic, and of rolling stock.

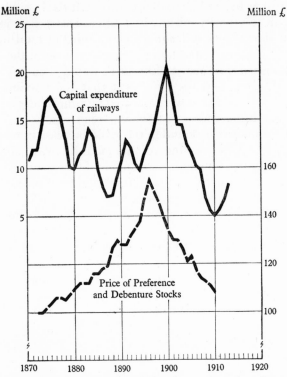

Fig. 12. Capital expenditure of British railway companies, 1870–1914.

The periods of most active railway investment were apparently the middle seventies and the years 1896–1904. Both of these were periods in which the yield on railway capital was either stationary or declining, but they succeeded periods in which profits were abnormally high, and the first at any rate was a period in which the yield on other investments was falling relatively to the yield on railway capital. The railway companies had the encouragement of past profits, expanding revenue, and

---

[1] Cf. *The Economist*, 19 February 1898 ('The permanence of English railway capital'), and 23 February 1901 ('Railway capital expenditure'); on the other hand cf. post, p. 141, n. 1.

a favourable stock market. They took the opportunity to raise new capital and expend it on the construction of new mileage, on station extensions, widenings of existing lines, additions to rolling stock and so on. Indeed, they continued to invest even when capital was no longer so cheap. Railway stock was at its highest in 1897–8 and had fallen at least 20 % below the peak by 1903; yet railway investment was higher in 1903 than in 1897. Similarly, although railway stock reached its maximum in 1875, capital expenditure remained very high in the next two years, and in 1878 was almost at the boom level of 1873.

It is difficult to say why railway investment was so slow in tailing-off. The construction of new mileage—about a third of total investment— was probably a rather 'intractable' item; once begun, the work would have to be finished, and new rolling stock would then have to be built or purchased. It is perhaps significant that the maxima in railway investment in 1883 and 1891 were followed by abnormally large increases in new mileage in operation in 1885 and 1893.

A second reason is to be found in the rapid increase in receipts during the two periods. An increasing volume of traffic was being carried at fixed prices, although congestion was no doubt causing average costs to increase. Investment in rolling stock, track and terminal facilities would offer good prospects of reducing working costs and would be pushed on so long as this prospective reduction was greater than the interest charges on the new capital.

It must also be remembered that the rise in security prices up to 1875 and to 1897 was very great, and was some years in being wiped out. The following table shows the movements in price of the leading railway stocks between 1870 and 1879:

Price of ordinary stock of five leading railways[1]

At the beginning of		At the beginning of	
1870	100	1875	124
1871	108½	1876	137
1872	140	1877	126
1873	134½	1878	122
1874	133½	1879	112½

In the nineties the increase was chiefly in debenture stocks, the yield on which fell from about 3½ % in 1888 to 2¾ % in 1896. It was 1904 before the yield again rose to 3½ %. Even on a falling market, therefore, the terms on which capital could be raised were comparatively favourable.

In addition there were influences special to both periods. In the

[1] Average of £100 ordinary stock in each of the following railways: London and North Western, Midland, Great Western, Lancs and Yorks, and Caledonian.

seventies there was a heavy outlay on the relaying of track with steel rails. This outlay was partly financed out of revenue,[1] but part also was probably charged to capital account. The relaying—and also the widening and extension—of track was made particularly attractive to the railway companies after 1873 by a heavy fall in the cost of steel rails, which, after fetching £15. 10s. per ton in 1873 fell to less than £10 in the second half of 1874, and to about £5 at the beginning of 1879.[2] After 1900, a good deal of the capital expenditure of the railways was incurred for electrification and for the building of underground railways.

Finally, attention may be drawn to the rapid increase in passenger traffic in the seventies and in the nineties, and to the comparatively slow rate of increase in the eighties and in the first decade of this century. Population, and particularly urban population, was increasing faster in the first two periods than in the second. The growth of population and of suburbs brought increased revenue and offered increased scope for investment. Changes in emigration affected the railways as they affected the rest of home investment.[3]

[1] Compare, for instance, expenditure on maintenance of way, works, etc., with expenditure on repairs and renewals of carriages and wagons (both per mile of open railway):

Year	Main-tenance of way, works, etc. (£)	Repairs and renewals (£)	Year	Main-tenance of way, works, etc. (£)	Repairs and renewals (£)
1870	260	119	1876	397	161
1871	289	129	1877	404	166
1872	308	136	1878	373	163
1873	366	149	1879	339	155
1874	398	155	1880–4	353	174
1875	393	165	1885–9	318	184

The more or less steady fall in expenditure on maintenance of way, works, etc., after 1877, compared with the steady rise in other upkeep costs, strongly suggests that relaying of track was going on at an abnormal pace in the years 1873–8. Such an abnormal outlay can hardly have been offset by equally rapid depreciation.

[2] *Reports of British Iron Trade Association*, 1878, p. 63; 1879, p. 37.

[3] It would be interesting to see a thorough study of the capital expenditure of one or two railway companies. Averages for the whole industry are not a reliable guide to the complex of incentives to investment. I have not had time, however, to supplement the general comments given above by a detailed study of the history of particular companies.

(c) Local authorities

Estimates of the loan expenditure of British local authorities have no greater claim to reliability than those just given for railways. For England and Wales, the Local Taxation Returns give figures from 1883 onwards; for Scotland, loan expenditure is known since 1893;[1] and for Ireland, since 1907. It has been necessary, therefore, to assume that before these dates loan expenditure did not differ much from receipts from loans. But even receipts from loans can only be traced with great difficulty in the years before 1883.[2]

The loan expenditure of local authorities, as estimated in this way, is shown in Table 28. The purposes for which loans were raised were not stated in full before 1884–5, but the rate at which the outstanding debt of different types of local authority was increasing before that date is a fair indication of the kind of investment which was taking place.

Loans outstanding at close of year (England and Wales only)

	1874–5 (£m.)	1879–80 (£m.)	1884–5 (£m.)
Urban sanitary authorities	33·74	61·68	80·58 [a]
School Boards	2·46	9·94	14·83
Harbour authorities	30·96	23·95	28·25
Metropolitan Board of Works	11·17	14·65	18·43
County and borough authorities	8·90	9·10	9·41 [a]
Total (including remainder)	92·82	136·93	173·21

[a] A small part of the debt of county and borough authorities was transferred in 1884 to the heading 'Urban sanitary authorities'.

[1] From 1893 to 1902 the figures are for expenditure out of money borrowed.

[2] For Scotland and Ireland the *Statistical Abstracts* give figures for all years except 1874–8, and for these five years interpolations on the basis of English borrowings have been made. For England and Wales in the years 1871–7 and 1879–81, the figures are for loans raised, so far as known, and include where necessary the loans authorized to be raised by Boards of Guardians under the Poor Law. For 1870 and 1878 an estimate had to be made on the basis of 'Receipts from Other Sources' (i.e. other than rates, tolls, dues, etc.) in adjacent years. The figure for 1882 is one of expenditure on capital account given in the Local Taxation Returns for that year; but the fall in loan expenditure can hardly have been so much as £6 m. (receipts from loans falling by only £4·5 m.), and this discontinuity should be kept in mind in analysing the aggregates of investment in Table 28.

Where there is any discrepancy between the estimates of receipts from loans given in the *Statistical Abstracts* and those given in the Local Taxation Returns, I have followed the *Statistical Abstracts*.

The loan expenditure of the Metropolitan Water Board and of the Port of London Authority has been omitted.

Table 28. *Loan expenditure of local authorities, 1870–1914*

Year	England and Wales (£m.)	Scotland (£m.)	Ireland (£m.)	Total loan expenditure (U.K.) (£m.)	Receipts from loans (U.K.) (£m.)
1870	5·22	0·25	0·06	5·5	—
1871	5·32	0·30	0·24	5·9	—
1872	6·97	0·15	0·17	7·3	—
1873	8·49	0·15	0·13	8·8	—
1874	11·92	+5%		12·5	—
1875	10·17	+6%		10·8	—
1876	12·52	+7%		13·4	—
1877	14·93	+8%		16·1	—
1878	(15·50)	+9%		17·0	—
1879	13·98	1·12	0·26	15·4	15·1
1880	13·35	1·03	0·40	14·8	14·4
1881	15·35	1·06	0·40	(12·8)	16·5
1882	9·37	0·90	0·40	10·7	12·0
1883	8·83	1·71	0·35	10·9	9·3
1884	10·45	2·09	0·30	12·8	13·3
1885	9·45	2·53	0·39	12·4	14·3
1886	8·51	1·80	0·48	10·8	11·6
1887	9·26	1·78	0·54	11·6	11·0
1888	6·99	1·50	0·71	9·2	9·2
1889	7·09	1·41	0·50	9·0	9·0
1890	7·19	1·76	0·55	9·5	8·5
1891	10·59	1·99	0·47	13·1	12·5
1892	10·60	1·93	0·78	13·3	14·8
1893	13·95	2·14	0·59	16·7	17·0
1894	13·38	2·32	0·68	16·4	18·2
1895	13·45	2·05	0·71	16·2	14·8
1896	13·81	2·78	0·88	17·5	17·3
1897	17·05	2·57	0·65	20·3	17·4
1898	21·50	3·07	0·59	25·2	23·4
1899	24·87	3·74	0·47	29·1	28·0
1900	27·95	4·49	0·94	33·4	35·5
1901	33·86	4·19	1·43	39·5	39·9
1902	36·09	4·09	1·03	41·2	39·8
1903	30·56	4·47	0·88	35·9	36·4
1904	31·39	3·73	1·29	36·4	38·3
1905	25·14	3·50	2·02	30·7	29·9
1906	23·06	3·31	0·94	27·3	24·2
1907	19·03	3·50	1·09	23·6	25·4
1908	17·97	2·82	1·29	22·1	24·0
1909	17·74	2·43	1·75	21·9	22·6
1910	17·33	2·25	1·70	21·3	21·3
1911	16·12	2·35	1·39	19·9	20·4
1912	17·49	2·25	1·49	21·2	20·6
1913	19·92	3·00	1·13	24·1	23·5
1914	(20·74)	3·33	1·23	25·3	26·5

It is clear that the building of schools and the carrying out of sanitary improvements were the most important items of expenditure. The chief influences behind both kinds of investment were legislative rather than economic. The loan expenditure of local authorities in the seventies was largely a matter of public policy, governed by Acts of Parliament rather than by interest rates. The Education Act of 1870 made it necessary to build schools rapidly, and the Public Health Act of 1875 gave a great impetus to improvements in sewerage, water supply and so on.

After 1884 the investment of local authorities becomes easier to analyse. Table 29 summarizes the changes that took place in the outstanding debt of English local authorities between 1884 and 1914. The figures are in £m. and are taken from the Local Taxation Returns.

Table 29. *Purposes for which outstanding debt of local authorities of England and Wales was contracted*

	1884–1885	1889–1890	1894–1895	1899–1900	1904–1905	1909–1910	1914–1915
Education	14·88	18·24	22·97	30·27	39·30	46·07	52·69
Highways, bridges, street improvements, etc.	30·95	33·92	36·56	42·97	58·59	61·03	67·02
Sewerage	16·57	19·35	23·73	29·33	37·61	41·82	44·27
Water supply	30·33	37·73	43·97	53·40	68·76	77·45	82·00
Electricity	—	—	1·38	7·85	25·64	29·54	31·53
Gas	13·77	14·85	16·93	19·82	23·83	23·25	22·51
Tramways, light railways	1·17	1·28	1·47	5·78	25·32	35·97	37·93
Harbour and dock	28·54	31·11	32·78	36·75	43·56	49·10	49·35
Total (including remainder)	173·21	198·11	234·48	292·95	416·94	463·26	493·94

In the eighties, borrowing was on a very small scale. The net increase in outstanding debt was little more than £60 m. in the ten years 1884–94, and over a third of the increase was due to borrowings for sanitary improvements. In the late nineties loan expenditure began to increase rapidly. More roads were constructed, more schools built, harbour and dock facilities were improved, tramway and electrical undertakings were started—there was hardly a single activity of local authorities for which more capital was not needed. This all-round increase in investment suggests that the heavy borrowing of the years 1896–1904 must be put down to the favourable terms upon which local authorities could raise money. Municipal stocks had risen steadily in public favour since the middle eighties, and especially at the time of

Goschen's Conversion Loan of 1888. According to Flux, the median yield on municipal securities was as low as 2·85 % in 1897, and did not rise to 3½ % until 1907.[1] These low rates must have been extremely tempting, especially when there was strong pressure on local authorities to take a wider view of their functions and compete more actively with private enterprise in the provision of transport and lighting services, house-room and so on. The falling off in borrowing by local authorities after 1904 was no doubt largely due to the sharp drop in the price of municipal stocks in that year, and to the continued fall in later years.

Legislation and interest rates had thus great influence on the loan expenditure of local authorities. There were other influences of equal importance. Of the huge increase in the debt of local authorities between 1894 and 1904 almost £50 m. was in respect of electrical and tramway undertakings. After 1907 very little debt was incurred for either of these. What happened was that a couple of inventions raised the productivity of capital enormously, and that ten years proved ample for the construction of most of the equipment that was necessary.

In addition to invention, emigration played an important part. The periods of active investment by local authorities coincide with periods of low rates of emigration. The provision of public utilities (certainly of schools) seems to have borne a close relation to population growth. Into this relation we will inquire more fully in a later chapter.[2]

There are few traces of cyclical influences in the investment of local authorities.

(d) Building

It is impossible to construct an entirely reliable index of building activity for the years before the first World War. There are, however, several different statistical series from which it is possible to form a general impression of the fluctuations that took place. By piecing together miscellaneous scraps of information, one can fashion an index of residential building activity; but the index is a summary of judgements rather than a summary of what did in fact happen.

(i) Unemployment

First of all, there is a continuous series, from 1860 onwards, showing the percentage of the members of the Amalgamated Carpenters and Joiners who were out of work at the end of each month. There is also, for a shorter period, a similar series for the plumbers. The membership

---

[1] Flux, 'Yield of high-class investments', *Trans. Manchester Statist. Soc.* 1910.
[2] See Chapter VIII, 'Investment and migration'.

of those two unions numbered only 56,000 in 1911, or about 6 % of those employed in the building industry, and the average rate of unemployment in the whole of the industry was about double that experienced by the carpenters and plumbers at the time when the unemployment insurance scheme was introduced.[1] Many of the members of the Amalgamated Carpenters and Joiners were employed in other industries such as shipbuilding, the manufacture of packing cases, and so on. Thus it is not possible to put complete reliance on the unemployment figures as a guide to building activity. They can be used with some confidence in tracing the *timing* of a change in the level of employment but not its *magnitude*.

(ii) *Employment*

There are no figures of employment in the building industry before 1908[2] except those given in the Census of Population. The census figures provide a useful check on long-term changes in employment and output. They have been sifted by Mr G. T. Jones so as to ensure comparability over the period from 1841 to 1921, and the figures relevant to our period are given in Table 30.

Table 30. *Numbers employed in the building industry in England and Wales, 1861–1911* [a] *(in 000's)*

Year	Bricklayers (including labourers)	Masons (including labourers)	Slaters and tilers	Carpenters and joiners	Plumbers, painters, glaziers, plasterers, paperhangers and whitewashers	Total
1861	79	86	5	177	95	462
1871	99	97	6	205	131	567
1881	125	97	7	235	170	690
1891	130	84	6	221	200	706
1901	213	96	9	270	270	953
1911	172	63	8	214	284	887

[a] G. T. Jones, *Increasing Returns*, p. 270.

[1] 'Report on the scheme for insurance against unemployment', *J. Inst. Act.* 1911, p. 460.

[2] From 1908 onwards, figures of employment on 'Constructional Work' are given in the *Abstracts of Labour Statistics* in tables relating to Workmen's Compensation. Later, the number of insured workers provides some measure of employment in the building trades.

There was a secular growth in employment in the miscellaneous trades given in the final column but no similar trend in the other trades. The divergence is probably to be accounted for by a rising expenditure of effort on the interior of buildings (e.g. on bathrooms), both during their erection and in their subsequent maintenance, and by some economy of effort in the construction of the outer shell. It would seem that, while the final column is the better index of the total volume of work done, the remaining columns correspond more closely to the number of new premises erected.

(iii) *Houses under construction*

The census also gives figures of the number of houses under construction at the date when the census was taken. These figures are a pointer to the number of houses built during the census year, both in the aggregate and in particular parts of the country. In England and Wales the definition of a house did not remain constant, and this may affect the comparability of the figures,[1] but in Scotland the definition underwent no change between 1881 and 1911.

The figures from 1861 onwards were as follows:

Number of houses in course of erection

Year	England and Wales	Scotland	Total
1861	27,305	—	—
1871	37,803	—	—
1881	46,414	4,990	51,404
1891	38,407	5,378	43,785
1901	61,909	9,062	70,971
1911	38,178	4,718	42,895

Thus the number of houses in course of erection was almost exactly the same in 1871, 1891 and 1911. It is likely, therefore, that the number of houses built during those years was also approximately equal. On the other hand, there was a rise of about one-eighth in the number of bricklayers, masons and carpenters between 1871 and 1911 (partly offset by an increase in unemployment) and perhaps a slight improvement in output per head. The volume of work done must have risen somewhat faster, therefore, than the number of new houses erected; the new houses were increasing in size, there was a rising stock of houses to maintain,

---

[1] The main change took place in 1911 when the practice of counting lodgers' rooms as separate houses was abandoned. This could have no effect on the number of 'houses' under erection.

and the proportion of building work that took some other form than house-building was almost certainly growing. Once the plumbers, plasterers and others are brought into the reckoning, the increase in numbers becomes much larger, 55–60 %. The increase in total building output, including both new construction and repair, exterior shell and interior fitments, was probably of the order of one-half to two-thirds.

(iv) *Building wages*

One way of checking the timing of fluctuations in building activity is to examine the movement of wages. On general grounds, one would not expect wages to be reduced at a time of rapid expansion, nor wages to be increased when activity had fallen some way from the peak. The value of information about changes in wages does not lie merely in its bearing on general fluctuations; it is as a symptom of *local* fluctuations— in particular towns and areas—that it is most useful. If, for example, figures of houses built are available for a few towns only, it is not easy to find evidence whether these towns were typical or not and data on wages may afford just such evidence.

The index shown in Table 31 is the mean of seventy-four rates for a variety of towns. I have not reproduced figures for individual towns, but data for Birmingham, Cardiff, Leicester, Liverpool, London and Manchester will be found in the Fiscal Blue Books.[1]

(v) *Production or consumption of raw materials*

There is unfortunately no information later than 1850 about the production of bricks.[2] The output of clay and shale, however, is given from 1895 in the Annual Reports on Mines and Quarries and from all appearances agrees closely with the output of bricks.[3] Figures of the output of slates go back to 1882 and provide one of the most useful indices of residential construction. As there was an extensive trade in

---

[1] E.g. in Cd. 1954 (1909), pp. 217–18.

[2] It is possible that the trade association collected information. Figures appear to have been submitted to the Committee on the Building Industry after the War (Cd. 9197, 1918).

[3] Compare, for example, the number of bricklayers (and labourers) in 1891, 1901 and 1911 with the output of clay in 1895, 1901 and 1911:

Year	Bricklayers (000's)	Clay (m. tons)
1891	130	9·80 (1895)
1901	213	14·16
1911	172	13·84

Table 31. *Indices of building activity, 1870–1914*

Year	Unemploy-ment[a] (%)	Wages[b] (1900 = 100)	Output of clay[c] (million tons)	Consumption of slates[d] (tons 000's)	Imports of sawn timber (million loads)
1870	3·7	—	—	—	2·93
1871	2·5	—	—	—	2·86
1872	1·2	—	—	—	3·09
1873	0·9	—	1·78	—	3·43
1874	0·8	81·1	2·44	152	3·84
1875	0·6	84·5	3·01	153	3·31
1876	0·7	87·8	3·97	157	4·12
1877	1·2	90·0	2·96	172	4·58
1878	3·5	88·9	2·71	169	3·64
1879	8·2	86·7	2·88	143	3·26
1880	6·1	85·6	3·06	153	4·12
1881	5·2	85·6	2·40	162	3·67
1882	3·5	85·6	2·86	437	4·20
1883	3·6	84·5	2·85	449	4·32
1884	4·7	84·5	2·70	416	4·05
1885	7·1	84·5	2·53	404	4·24
1886	8·2	84·5	2·39	394	3·79
1887	6·5	84·5	2·41	403	3·80
1888	5·7	84·5	2·56	408	4·36
1889	3·0	85·6	3·04	382	5·32
1890	2·2	86·7	3·31	362	4·78
1891	1·9	87·8	3·22	346	4·38
1892	3·1	88·9	3·10	348	5·09
1893	3·1	90·0	3·07	391	4·76
1894	4·3	91·1	3·26	418	5·45
1895	4·4	92·2	9·80	561	5·06
1896	1·3	93·3	11·34	597	6·03
1897	1·2	94·5	12·71	642	7·02
1898	0·9	97·8	14·74	711	6·36
1899	1·2	98·9	15·06	685	6·64
1900	2·6	100·0	14·05	618	6·63
1901	3·9	100·0	14·16	529	6·28
1902	4·0	100·0	15·30	558	6·68
1903	4·4	100·0	16·20	622	6·74
1904	7·3	100·0	15·95	621	6·07
1905	8·0	100·0	15·13	559	5·99
1906	6·9	100·0	15·29	508	6·69
1907	7·3	100·0	14·83	452	5·99
1908	11·6	100·0	14·40	423	5·49
1909	11·7	100·0	14·07	415	5·72
1910	8·3	100·0	14·09	429	6·00
1911	4·2	100·0	13·84	432	5·57
1912	3·7	101·8	12·81	383	5·77
1913	3·3	104·4	13·86	359	—
1914	3·3	—	—	305	—

(a) Average percentage (by number) of the members of the Amalgamated Carpenters and Joiners who were unemployed at the end of each month during the year.

(b) Mean of 74 rates as given in Cd. 1761 (1909) and continued in the *Abstracts of Labour Statistics*.

(c) In 1895 and subsequent years a large quantity of brick-clay returned under the Quarries Act is included; earlier figures include only mined clay.

(d) Prior to 1882 the figures are for mined slates produced; for the years 1882–1901 it has been necessary to estimate the weight of slates exported or imported, taking 700 slates = 1 ton.

slates, however, it is necessary to deduct net exports.[1] Less useful, although more frequently quoted, are the figures of imports of sawn and split timber, since the building industry was by no means the sole user of imported softwoods, and fluctuations in stocks may have been considerable.

(vi) *Building plans passed and the records of individual towns*

Returns of building plans passed by a number of urban districts were made to the Board of Trade from 1909 and published in the *Labour Gazette*. These show the relative importance of dwelling-houses, factories, shops, etc., in the total but cover too short a period to be of much help for our purposes, and, as the London County Council area is omitted, the sample is not an altogether satisfactory one.

The figures for some individual towns are available over a longer period. For example, those for Glasgow go back to 1862 and for Edinburgh to 1900. In 1934 I circularized the city engineers of a number of the larger towns in the hope of obtaining additional data but with largely negative results.[2] The records of many towns have suffered from salvage campaigns, but some might still be able to furnish from under the dust of half a century a glimpse of the course of building activity.[3]

This is true not only of figures of plans passed but of at least two other series: houses built and houses occupied and unoccupied. The latter figures often make their appearance in the Annual Reports of Medical Officers of Health, the Ministry of Health obtaining them from the local rating authority. They do not, of course, show directly the number of new houses built but only the net increase over a period of twelve months. Nevertheless, they are generally reliable as an index of buildings actually completed rather than planned or started. Unfortunately, the only continuous series at my disposal are those for Glasgow and Edinburgh.

London is the only town for which published figures of houses built are readily available.[4] Fortunately, the figures relate to Greater London and so cover about one-fifth of the population of England and Wales.

---

[1] Exports and imports were recorded by number up to 1902 and by weight thereafter. Imports were not recorded separately prior to 1895. Output was recorded by weight.   [2] The replies have since been lost.

[3] Recently Mr B. Weber has unearthed some most valuable data for several large towns but this data reached me too late to be made use of.

[4] They are given by Mr J. C. Spensley in his article on 'Urban Housing Problems', *J. R. Statist. Soc.* 1918. The M.O.H. Reports for Liverpool give figures back to 1876. Other towns for which nineteenth-century figures are given in M.O.H. Reports include Manchester and Birmingham.

In addition, I have had the good fortune to come across figures for the forty largest municipal areas of England and Wales included in a pamphlet entitled *The National Conference on Housing After the War: Report of the Organizing Committee.*[1] These municipal areas include Croydon, East Ham, Leyton, Tottenham and Walthamstow, but not the London County Council area and no part of Scotland. The figures relate to the number of houses erected in each of the years 1901–16, while the similar figures for London cover the period from 1871 onwards.

(vii) *Inhabited House Duty statistics*

It has been usual in the past to make use of the Inhabited House Duty statistics as a measure of fluctuations in residential construction. These statistics are, however, full of pitfalls, and the more I have analysed them the more distrustful of them I have become.[2] The one way in which the figures can be used with entire confidence is as a measure of the net increase in the number of premises of all kinds over a period of several years.

Of the total number of buildings charged to duty or exempt from it, only some 12–14 % were not private dwelling-houses. The number of houses demolished every year probably averaged about 10–15 % of the new houses erected. These two circumstances can be set against one another; and the 'net increase in the number of premises of all kinds' can then be identified with the gross absolute number of dwelling-houses erected. This does not provide an annual series but it gives a running total against which any annual series can be checked.

(viii) *Building prices*

The only available index of the selling price of building work is that constructed by Mr G. T. Jones. This index is highly insensitive and reflects building costs in the London area only, although the trend of

[1] Published by the Secretary, Mr Norman McKellen, Manchester, July 1917.

[2] See, for example, Stamp, *British Incomes and Property*, pp. 114, 132–3. There is, first, the difficulty of reassessment years—every five years in the Metropolis and every three years in England and Wales up to 1888–9 (thereafter every five years, except in 1910–11 when the interval was seven years). In these years increases in rent are given effect to while in other years only the decreases are entered in the returns. Changes in classification went on steadily between the years of reassessment; reductions in the annual value of residential shops, hotels, lodging-houses and farm-houses occupied by their owners might bring them into the category of exempt dwelling-houses. This difficulty is further increased by the constant transfers and retransfers between lock-up and residential shops. In reassessment years premises were often entered in one category until, after challenge, they were transferred to another category, or omitted altogether (e.g. farm-houses of less than £20 annual value).

building activity in that area was at times quite contrary to the trend in the rest of the country (for example, in 1878–81). Moreover, a reference to Jones's sources[1] makes it doubtful how far his index is one of selling price at all. Laxton's figures for selling price are a compound of labour costs and material prices with a rough addition (generally 15 %) for profit. There are many obvious cases of abrupt revision by the compilers, not reflecting any actual change in market quotations, and these abrupt changes are faithfully carried over into Jones's index of selling price. One can hardly be captious, however, when there is no other index to put in its place.

I have hesitated whether it might not be preferable to use the average cost per room in new houses built at Glasgow. This has the advantage of incorporating the upward trend in building costs associated with the greater amount of plumbing and other work done on each house. But the index is rather too erratic, and it fluctuates too violently to be typical of the country as a whole.

(ix) *Miscellaneous*

For some purposes it is useful to know the number of years' purchase at which property was selling. From 1894 onwards, figures are given in the Estate Duty statistics of the average for estates passing at death. For earlier years it should be possible to obtain figures, but I know of no published series. I have given elsewhere figures for Glasgow.[2]

There are no readily available figures of empty houses except for Glasgow and London. For the years 1870–82, however, figures exist of the reductions of duty made in England and Wales under Schedule A for unoccupied property and irrecoverable arrears, including allowances in respect of mills, factories, etc. Figures also exist from 1900 onwards for the annual value of empty houses not charged to duty in England and Wales. For Scotland figures of the annual value of empty houses not charged to duty under Schedule A exist from 1874–5 onwards. These figures are reproduced in Table 32.

Various other indices—of building material prices, bankruptcies of the builders, and so on—have been prepared. None of them seems particularly illuminating for our present purposes.

An index of residential building. For the years 1901–14 I have started from the figures of houses erected in Greater London and in the forty largest municipal areas in England and Wales. These are given in Table 33. I have then multiplied the total for the municipal areas by $2\frac{1}{2}$ to reach an estimate for urban areas outside London, and added a steady

---

[1] Laxton's *Builders' Price Book.*   [2] Above, p. 32.

Table 32. *Statistics of empty property in Great Britain, 1870–1914*

Year	England and Wales [a]		Scotland [b]	Percentage of unoccupied dwelling-houses	
	(£000's)	(£m.)	(£000's)	London [c]	Glasgow [d]
1870	139	—	—	—	2·14
1871	133	—	—	7·3	2·09
1872	127	—	—	5·9	2·12
1873	125	—	—	5·0	2·54
1874	130	—	134	4·7	3·99
1875	132	—	191	4·3	4·37
1876	141	—	311	3·9	4·91
1877	162	—	409	4·0	6·48
1878	201	—	540	4·2	7·94
1879	184	—	656	4·7	10·25
1880	210	—	677	5·2	11·22
1881	199	—	644	5·4	9·86
1882	214	—	593	5·8	7·84
1883	—	—	523	6·9	5·96
1884	—	—	503	7·7	5·17
1885	—	—	497	7·0	6·14
1886	—	—	499	6·6	6·56
1877	—	—	511	6·1	7·30
1888	—	—	495	5·9	6·72
1889	—	—	476	5·4	6·05
1890	—	—	408	5·0	4·69
1891	—	—	365	4·8	—
1892	—	—	336	4·6	—
1893	—	—	317	4·4	—
1894	—	—	356*	4·4	—
1895	—	—	334	4·2	—
1896	—	—	301	3·6	—
1897	—	—	271	3·1	—
1898	—	—	251	2·9	—
1899	—	—	235	2·8	—
1900	—	5·55	305	3·0	2·97
1901	—	5·68	283	3·1	2·66
1902	—	5·89	309	3·2	2·97
1903	—	6·34	369	3·5	3·82
1904	—	6·83	411	—	5·88
1905	—	7·57	489	4·7	7·51
1906	—	7·73	519	4·7	7·77
1907	—	7·65	611	5·3	8·28
1908	—	8·11	495	6·0	9·34
1909	—	8·36	527	6·6	9·48
1910	—	7·99	611	5·9	10·71
1911	—	7·60	577	5·3	10·72
1912	—	6·88	491	4·7	10·35
1913	—	6·14	411	3·9	9·25
1914	—	5·52	—	3·7	6·94

[a] The figures for the years 1870–82 represent the reductions of duty made under Schedule A for unoccupied property and irrecoverable arrears, including allowances in respect of mills, factories, etc. For 1900–14 the figures represent the annual value of empty houses not charged to duty.

[b] These figures represent the annual value (in £000's) of empty houses not charged to duty under Schedule A in Scotland. There is a discontinuity in 1894–5, and part of the rise in 1900–1 may be due to the inclusion of allowances by schedule (see J. C. Stamp, op. cit. p. 64). The percentage of empty houses (in Great Britain) was stated in the House of Commons to be 4·8 % in 1902–3, 6·3 % in 1909–10, and 5·9 % in 1910–11 (Stamp, op. cit. p. 133).

[c] Calculated by J. C. Spensley from Water Rate statistics (*J. R. Statist. Soc.*, March 1918).

[d] See above, p. 17.

20,000 a year for rural areas. The population of the forty municipal areas in 1911 was 8·8 millions, and for all urban areas outside London it was 21 millions, so that on a population basis a factor of 2½ is a little on the high side.[1] On the other hand, a lower factor would reduce the aggregate of houses built, and this is already slightly on the low side. For the ten years 1901–10 the number of houses built works out at 1·13 millions. The Inhabited House Duty statistics show an increase in premises of all kinds of 1·14 millions and of private dwelling-houses (including residential shops under £20) of 1·00 million. The Census of Population, however, shows an increase of only 840,000 houses, a change in definition operating to reduce the number of houses returned in 1911.[2] If we take the Inhabited House Duty statistics of the net increase in dwelling-houses at their face value, and accept the estimate in Table 33 of new houses built, the number of houses demolished between 1901 and 1910 was about 130,000 over the decade while contemporary estimates were of the order of 20,000 per annum.[3] It is for this reason that I regard the estimates as likely to err on the low side. A factor much in excess of 2½, however, would presuppose a bigger difference between the experience of large and small towns than is altogether likely.[4]

The estimate of a steady 20,000 houses for rural areas rests on the census figures of houses in course of erection. These were as follows:

Year	Urban areas	Rural areas	Total
1901	51,523	10,386	61,909
1911	28,319	9,859	38,178

I have assumed that in the rural areas it took about six months on the average to build a house and rather less in the urban areas. The total for 1901 is thus slightly in excess of twice the number of houses in course

---

[1] The total population of 36·1 m. was distributed as follows:

	Millions
Greater London	7·25
Other urban areas	20·91
Rural areas	7·91
	36·07

[2] Above, p. 147. For Scotland, where there was no change in definition, the net increase was 116,000 compared with one of 108,000 in the Inhabited House Duty statistics.

[3] *Report of the Land Inquiry Committee* (Urban), p. 80.

[4] The large towns, however, lost population fairly heavily by migration during this period (see above, p. 70).

of erection. The total for 1911 is slightly less than twice as great, but this might be explained by the rapid decline in house-building that was in progress in 1910–11.

For Scotland I have added one-eighth. There are indications that the boom at the beginning of the century reached bigger proportions in Scotland than in England and Wales, but the difference to the total resulting from more precise estimates would be small.

Table 33. *Residential building construction in England and Wales,*
1901–14

Year	Metro-politan Police District	Municipal areas in England and Wales	Municipal areas × 2½	Rural areas	Total	Total incl. ⅛ for Scotland
1901	27·2	32·8	82·0	20	129·2	145·4
1902	25·5	33·8	84·5	20	130·0	146·3
1903	26·4	34·2	85·5	20	131·9	148·4
1904	23·3	31·8	79·5	20	122·8	138·2
1905	22·0	32·2	80·5	20	122·5	137·8
1906	21·4	29·7	74·2	20	115·6	130·1
1907	19·2	27·5	68·7	20	107·9	121·4
1908	13·4	23·8	59·5	20	92·9	104·5
1909	13·3	22·8	57·0	20	90·3	101·6
1910	11·8	20·7	51·9	20	83·7	94·2
1911	10·0	16·5	41·2	20	71·2	80·1
1912	8·0	13·6	34·0	20	62·0	69·8
1913	8·6	13·1	32·7	20	61·3	69·0
1914	8·3	11·7	29·2	20	57·5	64·7

For the period between 1870 and 1901 I have started from the Inhabited House Duty statistics. I have assumed that about 70,000–75,000 houses were built in England and Wales in 1871 and 1891, and using these fixed points, I have then smoothed the Inhabited House Duty statistics in order to make the changes from year to year conform to the other evidence. At an earlier stage I tried to cling to the In-habited House Duty statistics in years other than reassessment years, interpolating for the latter; but I am now convinced that it is preferable to use only the net increase between revaluation years. For this purpose, however, the total has to be divided into its three constituent parts, the Metropolis, the rest of England and Wales, and Scotland. It is not too difficult to reach a rough approximation of the year-to-year changes provided the turning-points can be identified. For London itself, it is reasonable to assume that the inner area of the Administrative County

Table 34. *Index of residential building, 1870–1914*

Year	Inhabited house duty Increase in total number of premises				Estimated number of houses built			
	Metropolis	Rest of England and Wales	Scotland	Total	Metropolis	Rest of England and Wales	Scotland	Total
1870	—	—	—	—	4	60	14	78
1871 (a)	—	—	—	—	4	65	14	83
1872	—	—	—	—	6	70	14	90
1873 (b)	—	—	—	—	4	73	15	92
1874	—	—	—	—	4	78	16	98
1875	6·3	95·0	16·2	117·4	5	80	18	103
1876 (a, b)	5·6	87·9	34·1	127·6	6	85	19	110
1877	10·1	53·3	22·9	86·3	7	85	20	112
1878	12·6	83·3	29·3	125·1	9	80	19	108
1879 (b)	7·1	101·8	3·1	111·9	11	75	16	102
1880	15·2	71·6	10·8	97·6	12	73	12	97
1881 (a)	7·5	63·0	9·3	79·7	13	71	11	95
1882 (b)	13·2	78·1	13·2	104·5	11	69	11	91
1883	12·6	71·4	9·1	93·0	9	67	11	87
1884	3·7	62·9	9·1	75·6	7	64	11	82
1885 (b)	7·1	57·2	13·9	78·1	6	60	9	75
1886 (a)	1·6	66·5	11·5	75·6	6	65	7	78
1887	9·8	63·4	8·3	81·5	6	68	7	81
1888 (b)	9·5	75·8	5·5	90·9	6	73	7	86
1889	12·5	70·8	8·3	91·5	6	78	7	91
1890	−0·6	68·7	10·2	78·5	5	72	8	85
1891 (a)	12·4	75·1	5·7	93·2	6	65	9	80
1892	5·4	66·7	9·4	81·5	6	60	10	76
1893 (b)	6·3	45·6	7·7	59·6	6	62	10	78
1894	−0·8	75·6	14·3	88·9	6	66	11	83
1895	5·8	93·8	14·3	114·0	7	78	12	97
1896 (a)	1·7	108·8	20·8	131·3	8	95	16	119
1897	8·7	90·6	13·4	112·7	8	120	20	148
1898 (b)	17·0	121·3	21·3	159·6	9	135	25	169
1899	3·9	145·1	24·1	173·1	10	140	22	172
1900	9·0	132·4	19·6	160·9	9	125	18	152
1901 (a)	7·4	122·9	15·9	146·2	10	115	16	141
1902	11·0	102·6	15·1	128·7	9	120	17	146
1903 (b)	11·0	130·4	20·2	161·6	10	121	18	149
1904	14·6	117·2	17·8	149·6	11	113	16	140
1905	12·5	137·6	19·0	169·0	12	110	15	137
1906 (a)	4·4	109·7	14·9	129·0	11	110	15	136
1907	4·5	95·0	16·5	116·0	9	105	13	127
1908	4·1	107·9	0·2	112·2	5	95	11	111
1909	4·5	104·0	5·9	114·4	4	90	9	103
1910 (b)	3·1	32·8	13·1	49·0	3	80	8	91
1911 (a)	7·8	104·1	3·0	114·9	3	70	7	80
1912	4·7	64·2	4·8	73·8	3	65	6	74
1913	0·2	72·6	1·2	74·0	3	65	6	74
1914	2·0	77·5	3·7	83·2	2	60	4	66

(a) Revaluation Year, Metropolis.   (b) Revaluation Year, England and Wales.

Table 35. *Residential building, 1870–1914*

Year	New houses built (000's)	Selling price of new building	Index of size and complexity	Volume of residential building (1907 = 100)	Value of residential building (1907 = £28 m.)
1870	78	100	100·0	54·4	14·2
1871	83	103	100·5	58·2	15·7
1872	90	103	101·0	63·4	17·1
1873	92	109	101·5	65·1	18·6
1874	98	111	102·0	69·7	20·2
1875	103	108	102·5	73·6	20·8
1876	110	112	103·0	79·0	23·2
1877	112	110	103·5	80·8	23·3
1878	108	110	104·0	78·3	22·5
1879	102	109	104·5	74·0	21·1
1880	97	110	105·0	71·0	20·4
1881	95	107	105·5	69·9	19·6
1882	91	105	106·0	67·3	18·5
1883	87	101	106·5	64·6	17·1
1884	82	101	107·0	61·2	16·2
1885	75	100	107·5	56·2	14·7
1886	78	98	108·0	58·8	15·1
1887	81	97	108·5	61·3	15·6
1888	86	96	109·0	65·4	16·4
1889	91	101	109·5	69·5	18·4
1890	85	98	110·0	65·2	16·7
1891	80	95	110·5	61·7	15·3
1892	76	95	111·0	58·8	14·6
1893	78	90	111·5	60·7	14·3
1894	83	90	112·0	64·8	15·3
1895	97	91	112·5	76·1	18·1
1896	119	91	113·0	93·8	22·1
1897	148	93	113·5	117·2	28·5
1898	169	93	114·0	134·4	32·7
1899	172	97	114·5	137·4	34·9
1900	152	100	115·0	121·9	31·9
1901	145	103	115·5	116·8	31·5
1902	146	103	116·0	118·1	31·8
1903	148	103	116·5	120·2	32·4
1904	138	107	117·0	112·6	31·5
1905	138	107	117·5	113·1	31·7
1906	130	106	118·0	107·0	29·7
1907	121	107	118·5	100·0	28·0
1908	105	109	119·0	87·1	24·8
1909	102	107	119·5	85·0	23·8
1910	94	100	120·0	78·4	20·6
1911	80	100	120·5	67·2	17·6
1912	70	101	121·0	59·1	15·6
1913	69	106	121·5	58·5	16·2
1914	65	115	122·0	55·3	16·6

showed fluctuations similar to those in the larger area of the Metropolitan Police District.

The final estimates are given in Table 34, together with the crude Inhabited House Duty figures for the Metropolis, the rest of England and Scotland. They have been converted to a value series by assuming that there was a gradual increase of $\frac{1}{2}$% per annum, in the size or complexity of the average house, using G. T. Jones's index of the selling price of building work, and taking 1907 as a base. The resulting series shows a rise in the value of new dwelling-houses constructed from £15·7 m. in 1871 to £17·6 m. in 1911. Between those dates the number of dwelling-houses increased by over two-thirds, and outlay on repairs and maintenance (including alterations) may have nearly doubled. If the rise was from £13 m. to £25 m., the total value (and volume) of work done on dwelling-houses increased by approximately 50%. Allowing for a greater rise in industrial and other building, this is not inconsistent with the ratio of one-half to two-thirds estimated earlier.[1]

(e) Engineering

There remains engineering. I was at one time rash enough to make an estimate of the value of new machinery produced and to adjust it for exports and imports so as to arrive at net home consumption. In the process I had to manufacture an index of output without any figures of machinery produced and an index of machinery prices without any price quotations. I do not propose to put the results of these calculations to much use in this book; but as they may be of interest I have thought it worth while to reproduce them.

I ought, before doing so, to draw attention to the large amount of engineering work that is already included under the foregoing headings. Railways and shipbuilding represent two of the largest nineteenth-century users of machinery, and the local authorities, as the owners of large public utilities, were of increasing importance. Strictly speaking, therefore, it is only a part of the machinery retained for home use that should be added in order to form an index of new construction. Of this part, textile machinery was undoubtedly much the largest.

Although no figures are available of the output of textile machinery, there are various estimates of the additions made annually to the number of cotton spindles and looms, and it would probably be possible to find similar information (e.g. from Trade Directories) for other textile industries. Indeed, it might be possible to form a fairly accurate impression of the rate of increase of capacity in most of the larger industries. The figures for cotton-spinning show a marked cyclical fluctuation, a

[1] Above, p. 148.

rapid growth in capacity up to 1884, and a long lull until the beginning of a second prolonged period of expansion from about 1900 onwards.[1]

Apart from such direct indications of investment in machinery, one is forced back on a method suggested to me by Mr Colin Clark. From the consumption of pig iron less any increase in stocks deduct the pig iron consumed in steel;[2] then add the output of ingot steel to the

[1] See Table 37. Figures are given in four sources, which at times show considerable differences: Returns under the Factories and Workshops Acts (not always reliable) reproduced in the *Statistical Abstracts*; estimates made annually in Ellison's *Circulars* (reproduced in C. K. Hobson, op. cit. pp. 214–15); estimates for the Lancashire district based on the C.S.M. Directory by G. T. Jones, op. cit. p. 277; and estimates in *The Economist*, quoted by Professor D. H. Robertson, op. cit. p. 20.

[2] The consumption of pig iron per ton of steel produced was assumed to be as follows:

In the Bessemer acid process	105%
In the Bessemer basic process	110%
In the Acid open hearth process	70%
In the Basic open hearth process (from 1900)	75%
In all processes for spiegel and ferro-manganese	2·5% (1910–13 average)

For the years 1890–1900 a splice has been used. In years of acute depression the consumption of pig iron has been reduced (in the open-hearth process only) by 5%, to make provision for more extensive use of scrap.

After my calculations were complete I was assured by Mr D. L. Burn that the consumption of pig per ton of steel was greater before the first World War in the acid process than in the basic process. The difference made to my final results by a suitable correction, however, would be too trifling to make recalculation worth while.

Mr Burn is also extremely doubtful of the value of the British Iron Trade Association statistics of stocks of pig iron. So far as *public* stores go—for instance, those of Messrs Connal and Co.—the figures of stocks seem reliable enough. But details of *makers'* stocks were published only at the discretion of the makers themselves. The Cleveland Ironmasters made no returns after 1890, and up till 1880 there are no statistics for districts other than Scotland and Cleveland, although there must have been considerable stocks of hematite in Lancashire and Cumberland, and makers elsewhere must have had stocks of other sorts. There is no guarantee that the figures of makers' stocks published by the British Iron Trade Association for part of the period are reliable.

This lack of reliable statistics of makers' stocks is a serious defect. The very fact that stocks in public stores were visible, while makers' stocks could only be guessed, made it to the advantage of speculators to transfer stocks from the one category to the other. Thus the *Statist* pointed out on one occasion that 'the [Scottish] stocks are as high as they are because of the tremendous effort made by the bears to buy up all the unsold iron in the hands of makers, and that has all been crowded into store with the object of swelling the *visible* stocks' (8 April 1899, p. 538).

The statistics which I have used are as follows:

1870–80: Scotland and Cleveland (makers and public stores).

1881–95: British Iron Trade Association figures for Great Britain. (Source: *Annual Reports of British Iron Trade Association from 1878*; where copies unobtainable, Bulletins of the Association published in the *Iron and Coal Trades Review*).

1895–1914: Figures of stocks in the warrant stores of Scotland, Middlesbrough,

remaining pig iron (which would presumably be used in the manufacture of finished iron products) and treat the resulting compound as
an index of the consumption of iron and steel. From this two further
deductions fall to be made, one for iron and steel consumed in shipbuilding and naval construction[1]—so as to avoid duplication—and one
for the 'ingot equivalent' of exports less the 'ingot equivalent' of net
imports.[2] By 'ingot equivalent' is meant the number of tons of pig iron
or of ingot steel which would be required in the manufacture of finished
or semi-finished iron and steel products. Deductions for iron and steel
used in bridge-building by local authorities, in the production of steel
rails or locomotives for home use, in the construction of business
premises and public buildings, and so on, should also be made but are
incapable of exact estimation.[3]

The result is a total of 5·12 m. ingot tons consumed in 1907 in the
United Kingdom, the engineering industries (excluding shipbuilding)
taking about half. The total was made up roughly as shown on p. 161.

No index of the price of machinery exists, and there is very little data
from which one can be satisfactorily constructed. The best one can do
is to read through some engineering price-lists to form a general impression of the probable degree of fluctuation,[4] and consult the figures

and the west coast, and of stocks in the makers' yards in Scotland and the west coast.
Stocks of hematite in the Cleveland Warrant Stores are included only from 1895 to
1901. (Sources: *Ironmonger*, Metal Market Year Book, 1915. Supplementary estimates
will be found in the *Economist Commercial Histories* and, from time to time, in the
Statist.)

[1] The tons of iron and steel consumed per net ton of iron sailing vessels was taken
to be 0·7; per net ton of steamers, 1·075 for iron ships, 0·995 for steel ships. For war
vessels a three-year moving average of launchings was calculated and 20 % deducted
from the number of displacement tons thus obtained. For foreign warships a three-
year moving average was also calculated and the number of gross tons so obtained
was doubled. Where the figures of displacement tons were not obtainable, one-third
was added to the weight of armour in the hull. In order to arrive at the 'ingot
equivalent' of shipping consumption an addition of one-third was made to the weight
of iron and steel consumed. The requirements of ship-repairing yards were ignored,
but those of marine engineering are included in the figures just given.

[2] All exports were treated as finished iron and steel products (except in the eighties
when we were exporting blooms to America) and an addition of one-third was made
to the weight of exports to make provision for waste. (Pig iron, scrap, and old iron
were, of course, deducted from exports.) Re-exports and imports were divided into
semi-manufactured and finished goods, 10 % being added to the former and one-third
to the latter.

[3] The British Iron Trade Association published figures for the output and consumption of steel rails after 1877, but I have not been able to obtain a continuous
series beyond 1890, and for some years—e.g. 1889—the figures are far from plausible.

[4] There are some price-lists for the nineties in the British Museum (Press-mark:
PP 1660 da), but they are not particularly useful. Advertisements in technical journals
(e.g. *Iron*) have also been consulted.

Consumption of iron and steel, 1907

	Ingot tons (ooo's)
Output of finished machinery [a] (£60 m. at £40 per ton plus one-third for scrap)	2000
Repairs by engineering firms (£6·5 m.) ⎱	
Work done by firms on own plant (£16 m.) ⎰	200
Additions to work in progress (£5·7 m.)	200
Rails	670
Pipes, tubes and fittings	425
Structural steel	300
Wire	300
Railway tyres and axles	150
Tinplate	160
Chains, anchors, nuts, bolts, metal bedsteads	430
Miscellaneous (motors, bicycles, electrical engineering, etc.)	90
Imports of all kinds	200
	5125
Shipbuilding	1420
	6545

[a] Including locomotives and ordnance.

of export prices which began to appear in 1910. It is clear that many kinds of machinery—particularly advertised branded products—were very steady in price even in the most severe depressions and the most enormous booms. Machinery advertised at one price in 1896 can still be found selling at the same price in 1900, although iron and steel goods had risen by about 50 % in the meantime. In 1876 there were some types of machine which had not fallen in price in the past three years, although pig iron was fetching less than half its 1873 price and the fall in manufactured iron had been almost as heavy. There is reason to believe, however, that this steadiness of price was far from being shared in by the whole industry. For example, the average value per ton of exported machinery rose by nearly 10 % between 1910 and 1913, while the rise in the average value of exported manufactured iron was 23 %.

An important difficulty in forming an index of machinery is that of weighting. Different kinds of machinery move in quite different ways both in price and in output.[1] Changes in market quotations, even if they were known, would thus be a poor guide to changes in the average value per ton of engineering output.

[1] See, for instance, Colin Clark, *Fixed Capital Investment in Great Britain*, p. 17. In the years 1911–13, although there was a steady rise in the *average* value of exported machinery, there was a very wide dispersion of movement, some sorts rising while others were falling, some rising one year and falling the next.

Faced with these difficulties, I began by assuming that whatever changes in weighting occurred the average value of output moved in the same direction as the price of other iron and steel products. I made arbitrary estimates of the probable rise or fall in average values between the extremities of each boom and slump, and interpolated on the basis of the fluctuations in the average price of exported manufactured iron.[1] The index was given an upward trend so as to take into account the development of more complicated and more valuable sorts of machinery.

It is this unpublished index which has been used by some writers as an index of machinery prices. But in fact, of course, it is nothing of the kind. It is neither based on observation of changes in the price of machinery nor intended to measure changes in *prices* as distinct from average value per ton. I have since made some efforts to obtain data on machinery prices, first by approaching firms and secondly by examining the trade returns of countries which imported British machinery. For cotton-spinning machinery the records of the largest manufacturers of the period yield indices as follows:[2]

Year	Home	Export (f.a.s. English port)
1900	100	100
1901	102	98
1902	100	98
1903	104	100
1904	105	100
1905	108	100
1906	111	102
1907	110	103
1908	113	103
1909	114	105
1910	106	103
1911	109	(104)
1912	(107)	(104)
1913	(116)	(104)
1914	(126)	(104)

This is interesting as an indication of the variability of machinery prices and as a reminder that discrimination between home and export

[1] There is no satisfactory equivalent index of steel prices.

[2] I am indebted to Sir Percy Mills for the data from which these figures have been constructed. Figures for a second firm show a rise of 17% in home market prices and of 11% in export prices between 1904 and 1907.

markets is not a recent innovation. But it does not take us far towards a general index of machinery prices. The trade returns of continental countries are more hopeful, although more treacherous, as a source. Austria, France, Germany and Italy, for example, showed imports of machinery by weight as well as by value, the values being official values revised annually, not declared, or market values. If it were possible to have access to these official values they might allow a rough index of British export prices to be constructed, since Britain was undoubtedly the main supplier of continental markets in the nineteenth century. Without the details, one is left with aggregates that lump together locomotives and sewing machines, so that an increase in one may be concealed by a decrease in the other. I have examined the changes from year to year in the average import value of some of those broad aggregates. It would seem that machinery prices fell heavily from a peak in 1873 and in general followed fairly closely the index for the price of new ships given above (Table 23). But as I hesitate to launch one more spurious index of machinery prices I have not reproduced the calculations here.

I have reproduced calculations of the value of machinery retained for use in the United Kingdom. These estimates were made some years ago when I included them in the total for gross domestic fixed capital formation. I have since amended them, not for this purpose, but more as curiosities. The volume of iron and steel consumption has been multiplied by the average value of 'machinery' per ton, using a total of £50 m. in 1907 as a base. A deduction of 6 % has been made from the recorded value of exports, and an addition of 6 % to the value of machinery remaining at home, in order to provide for costs of transport and handling.[1] The result of this procedure is shown in Table 37.

The figures shown there fluctuate rather more than exports of machinery and rise in the nineties at a very rapid pace. They are also at variance with the unemployment figures for the seventies—unemployment increased steadily from 1872 to 1879 in all the principal unions—and would imply an increased investment in machinery after some of the major industries (e.g. cotton textiles) had begun to lose momentum. There are also various discrepancies in individual years between the 'machinery' and other series; for example, there is little in the unemployment statistics to suggest a swift recovery in 1902–3 or 1908–9 or a depression in 1911–12.

---

[1] It has been necessary to take account of certain changes in classification and to estimate imports of machinery before 1897. The base of £50 m. in 1907 is arrived at by deducting repairs (£6·5 m.) from the output of machinery (£54·5 m.) and making an allowance for accessories used in repair or exported (£2 m.).

Table 36. *Home consumption of iron and steel (tons 000), 1870–1914*

Year	Output of pig iron less net exports	Increase (+) or decrease (−) in stocks	Consumption of pig iron in steel	Consumption of pig iron in castings, wrought iron, etc. (col. 1 − col. 2 and col. 3)
1870	5251	+ 48	240	4963
1871	5626	−224	379	5471
1872	5512	−322	483	5351
1873	5499	− 36	589	4946
1874	5272	− 14	647	4639
1875	5465	+ 58	731	4676
1876	5679	+302	846	4531
1877	5771	+233	905	4633
1878	5486	+237	994	4255
1879	4798	+ 12	1022	3764
1880	6184	+ 42	1307	4835
1881	6718	+195	1799	4724
1882	6873	−159	2122	4910
1883	7004	+ 11	2019	4974
1884	6579	+140	1750	4689
1885	6493	+543	1819	4131
1886	6011	+139	2179	3693
1887	6440	+125	2950	3365
1888	7000	−190	3120	4070
1889	7203	−637	3359	4481
1890	6820	−558	3319	4059
1891	6628	−101	2827	3902
1892	5998	−420	2606	3812
1893	6182	− 3	2623	3562
1894	6658	+174	2813	3671
1895	6929	+228	2922	3779
1896	7707	− 24	3655	4076
1897	7753	−314	3937	4130
1898	7727	− 53	3951	3829
1899	8213	−211	4184	4240
1900	7713	−278	4188	3803
1901	7289	+ 78	4044	3167
1902	7803	− 73	4143	3733
1903	8006	+ 69	4373	3564
1904	8017	+ 73	4334	3610
1905	8754	+483	4973	3298
1906	8608	−149	5441	3316
1907	8275	−510	5472	3313
1908	7828	+176	4310	3342
1909	8500	+351	4822	3327
1910	8973	+197	5354	3422
1911	8493	+ 24	5319	3150
1912	7693	−555	5584	2664
1913	9350	− 29	6247	3132
1914	8365	+ 17	6404	1944

Table 36 (cont.)

Year	Output of steel ingots	Ingot equivalent of net exports	Ingot equivalent of shipbuilding consumption	Home ingot consumption of iron and steel [a]
1870	240	2501	453	2249
1871	364	2523	515	2797
1872	467	2453	627	2738
1873	573	2220	577	2722
1874	630	2095	743	2431
1875	708	1840	539	3005
1876	828	1568	403	3388
1877	887	1770	516	3234
1878	982	1617	580	3040
1879	1009	1728	548	2497
1880	1295	2334	649	3147
1881	1778	2716	827	2959
1882	2109	3034	1043	2942
1883	2008	2921	1180	2881
1884	1774	2615	732	3116
1885	1887	2537	525	2956
1886	2264	2693	421	2843
1887	3344	3320	500	2589
1888	3304	3420	740	3214
1889	3571	3482	1072	3498
1890	3579	3302	1031	3305
1891	3157	2744	1037	3278
1892	2920	2198	973	3561
1893	2950	2241	767	3504
1894	3111	1991	885	3906
1895	3260	2156	917	3966
1896	4132	2754	1037	4417
1897	4486	2794	921	4901
1898	4566	2327	1243	4825
1899	4855	2408	1391	5368
1900	4901	1955	1353	5396
1901	4904	1763	1359	4949
1902	4909	2067	1345	5230
1903	5034	1872	1071	5655
1904	5026	1895	1247	5494
1905	5812	2199	1441	5480
1906	6462	2677	1575	5526
1907	6523	3292	1420	5124
1908	5296	2497	869	5272
1909	5882	2814	908	5487
1910	6374	3085	1064	5647
1911	6462	2555	1604	5453
1912	6796	2581	1651	5228
1913	7664	2660	1812	6324
1914	7835	2449	1466	5864

[a] Pig iron not in steel, plus output of steel, minus consumption of iron and steel in shipbuilding and exports, plus consumption of iron and steel in imports.

It might be possible, with better figures for changes in stocks, and by eliminating structural steel, steel rails, iron castings for plumbing work, and so on, to obtain a more reliable index of machinery output. As matters stand, the figures in Table 37 can be used only in corroboration of other indications of trends in the production and consumption of machinery. They confirm the impression that investment was high in the seventies—though it would be hard to point to any *industry* of which this was conspicuously true. They also point to a high level of investment in the nineties; and for that period there is direct evidence of investment in machinery by some important industries. There was a boom in motor cars and cycles, in tramways, and in electrical products of all kinds. The older industries, too, were enjoying large profits and increasing their equipment. Chemicals, agriculture, textiles and the engineering trades themselves were all in need of more machinery. Thus there was an enormous increase in output, which, thanks to the requirements of the new industries, was well maintained during the years of declining home investment after 1905.

(f) Total home investment

The aggregate of the first four items of new construction analysed above works out at £80 m. in 1907. This total falls short of total new construction, which was approximately £140 m. I have thought that it might be of interest to blow up the series for building, shipbuilding, railways and local authorities in the ratio of 140:80, on the assumption that the items excluded fluctuated in much the same way as the items included. From what we know of the fluctuations in the largest item excluded—industrial machinery and plant—this is rather a large assumption; it is possible that industrial construction had a more pronounced cyclical rhythm than the total for the other items. The blown-up series (which is shown in Table 46) may, however, be a fair approximation to total new construction. This in turn is by no means the same as total investment, gross or net. In shipbuilding, for example, there is a world of difference between the value of new ships launched for British owners and the value of the increment in British shipping. Nevertheless, since the value of new construction is the chief determinant of net home investment, and since there is a small difference only between the two magnitudes for 1907—the first amounting to £140 m. and the second to £150 m.—it may be useful for some purposes to treat the two as identical.

Since the series for new construction consists of four items only, it is important that they should be given the right weight. Shipbuilding is clearly overweighted in relation to the other three items, in the sense

Table 37. *Home consumption of machinery, 1870–1914*

Year	Consumption of iron and steel [a] (1907 = 100)	Average value of 'machinery' per ton	Value of output of 'machinery' (£m.)	Net exports of machinery [b] (£m.)	Value of 'machinery' retained for home use (£m.)	Increase in cotton spindles (000's) [c]
1870	43·9	90·0	16·5	5·0	11·5	240
1871	54·7	91·6	20·9	5·6	15·3	400
1872	53·5	107·4	23·9	7·7	16·2	530
1873	53·1	115·0	25·4	9·4	16·0	940
1874	47·5	111·4	22·0	9·2	12·8	945
1875	58·5	105·5	25·7	8·5	17·2	607
1876	66·2	101·6	28·0	6·8	21·2	578
1877	63·1	99·3	26·1	6·3	19·8	400
1878	59·4	97·6	24·2	7·1	17·1	400
1879	48·8	96·0	19·5	6·8	12·7	100
1880	61·5	100·0	25·6	8·7	16·9	150
1881	57·8	95·8	23·1	9·4	13·7	350
1882	57·4	97·9	23·4	11·2	12·2	900
1883	56·3	96·8	22·7	12·6	10·1	1000
1884	60·9	94·5	24·0	12·3	11·7	1000
1885	57·8	92·7	22·3	10·4	11·9	—
1886	55·5	90·6	21·0	9·5	11·5	−300
1887	50·6	90·0	19·0	10·5	8·5	40
1888	62·7	90·3	23·6	12·2	11·4	—
1889	68·4	94·8	27·0	14·4	12·6	760
1890	64·6	100·0	26·9	15·4	11·5	250
1891	64·1	97·7	26·1	14·9	11·2	1000
1892	69·5	97·3	28·2	13·0	15·2	600
1893	68·4	96·1	27·4	12·9	14·5	−80
1894	76·4	96·5	30·7	13·0	17·7	—
1895	77·5	95·0	30·7	13·6	17·1	130
1896	86·3	96·3	34·6	14·8	19·8	−500
1897	95·7	98·5	39·3	13·4	25·9	—
1898	94·3	99·4	39·1	14·8	24·3	—
1899	104·9	106·4	46·5	15·4	31·1	300
1900	105·5	120·0	52·7	15·6	37·1	450
1901	96·7	117·9	47·5	13·4	34·1	479
1902	102·1	116·6	49·6	13·5	36·1	1475
1903	110·5	115·7	53·1	15·4	37·7	−26
1904	107·2	115·3	51·5	16·4	35·1	575
1905	107·0	115·0	51·3	18·3	32·8	777
1906	108·0	117·6	52·9	21·2	31·7	2350
1907	100·0	120·0	50·0	25·6	24·4	4263
1908	102·9	118·5	50·8	25·0	25·8	2633
1909	107·2	118·0	52·7	22·4	30·3	1808
1910	110·4	118·6	54·6	23·0	31·6	705
1911	106·4	119·1	52·8	23·8	29·0	271
1912	102·1	124·2	52·8	24·9	27·9	138
1913	123·4	130·0	66·8	27·9	38·9	341
1914	144·5	125·0	75·3	23·3	52·0	836

[a] See Table 36, final column.

[b] Exports and imports of sewing machines are excluded. A deduction of 6 % has been made from the value of exports for transport and handling charges.

[c] Up to 1900 from Ellison's *Circulars* (as given in C. K. Hobson, op. cit. pp. 214-15); thereafter from G. T. Jones, op. cit. p. 277, based on C.S.M. Directory.

that it is much less a *net* total and contains a large replacement element. On the other hand, investment in machinery and plant may have fluctuated in closer sympathy with shipbuilding than with any of the other items, and engineering output is underweighted in relation to building.

As a partial check on the figures of total new construction I have compared them with estimates of British capital at home for two dates

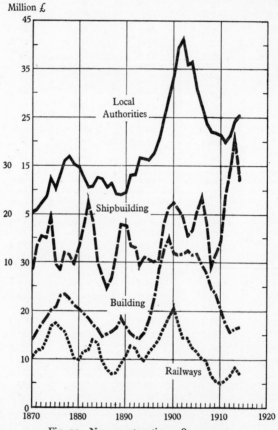

Fig. 13. New construction, 1870–1914.

that seem to admit of such a comparison. In 1875 and 1914 prices and interest rates were about the same. For 1875, Giffen's estimate (which I have slightly amended) of capital at home gives a total, excluding land, of about £5000 m. For 1914, Stamp's estimate gives a total, also excluding land, of about £9200 m. The increment over the period of forty years was thus some £4200 m. If we add up the annual totals for new construction in Table 38, we get an aggregate of £4800 m. for the

Table 38. *New construction, 1870–1914*

Year	Building (£m.)	Shipbuilding (£m.)	Railways (£m.)	Local authorities (£m.)	Total (£m.)
1870	14·2	8·6	10·5	5·5	38·8
1871	15·7	13·3	11·8	5·9	46·7
1872	17·1	15·3	11·8	7·3	51·5
1873	18·6	15·0	14·1	8·8	56·5
1874	20·2	19·3	16·8	12·5	68·8
1875	20·8	9·8	17·4	10·8	58·8
1876	23·2	8·5	16·4	13·4	61·5
1877	23·3	12·0	15·6	16·1	67·0
1878	22·5	11·6	13·2	17·0	64·3
1879	21·1	9·6	10·1	15·4	56·2
1880	20·4	13·0	9·9	14·8	58·1
1881	19·6	17·2	11·3	12·8	60·9
1882	18·5	22·7	11·8	10·7	63·7
1883	17·1	18·5	14·1	10·9	60·6
1884	16·2	9·9	13·3	12·8	52·2
1885	14·7	7·3	9·8	12·4	44·2
1886	15·1	4·8	8·0	10·8	38·7
1887	15·6	6·7	7·1	11·6	41·0
1888	16·4	11·5	7·2	9·2	44·3
1889	18·4	18·0	8·9	9·0	54·3
1890	16·7	17·6	10·4	9·5	54·2
1891	15·3	13·4	12·8	13·1	54·6
1892	14·6	13·1	12·2	13·3	53·2
1893	14·3	9·1	10·5	16·7	50·6
1894	15·3	11·2	9·7	16·4	52·6
1895	18·1	10·6	11·4	16·2	56·3
1896	22·3	10·1	12·6	17·5	62·5
1897	28·5	10·4	14·0	20·3	73·2
1898	32·7	18·0	16·3	25·2	92·2
1899	34·9	21·4	18·5	29·1	103·9
1900	31·9	22·4	20·6	33·4	108·3
1901	31·5	21·0	17·3	39·5	109·3
1902	31·8	19·8	14·5	41·2	107·3
1903	32·4	15·7	14·4	35·9	98·4
1904	31·5	16·6	12·4	36·4	96·9
1905	31·7	20·6	11·6	30·7	94·6
1906	29·7	23·7	10·2	27·3	90·9
1907	28·0	18·5	9·8	23·6	79·9
1908	24·8	9·1	6·9	22·1	62·9
1909	23·8	11·5	5·6	21·9	62·8
1910	20·6	14·1	5·0	21·3	61·0
1911	17·6	23·9	5·6	19·9	67·0
1912	15·6	29·4	6·6	21·2	72·8
1913	16·2	35·5	(8·3)	24·1	84·4
1914	16·6	27·0	(7·0)	25·3	75·9

same period. This total *includes*, while the lower total *excludes*, renewals of some fixed capital.[1] There is, therefore, no marked disagreement between the two.

3. THE STATISTICS OF FOREIGN INVESTMENT

This section consists partly of an attempt to revise Hobson's estimates of Britain's capital exports in the years 1870–1914, and partly of a brief account of the distribution of her foreign investments between different countries and types of asset at various dates over that period. I am conscious that the estimates in the following pages are subject to a more than usually wide margin of error and that they are presented too briefly and peremptorily. Nevertheless, I have thought it worth while to publish them as a kind of interim report to show the lines along which further research might usefully be done.

(a) The balance of payments on income account

Hobson's estimates[2] require revision at two points: his calculations of British shipping earnings and of interest from foreign investments are not altogether satisfactory.

(i) Shipping earnings

Invisible exports of shipping services have three constituents. First, there are the gross receipts earned by British ships in carrying British exports and imports[3] or in the cross-trades between ports situated abroad; from this total we have to deduct disbursements by British shipping abroad. Secondly, there are the passenger fares paid by foreigners travelling in British ships, less the passenger fares paid by British residents travelling in foreign ships. Thirdly, there are the disbursements by foreign ships in British ports. The first of these items is equal to the net earnings of the British mercantile marine from the transport of goods (net of disbursements abroad), and this in turn is equal to the net expenditure of the British mercantile marine in Britain (except that the one includes and the other excludes passenger fares). One straightforward way of calculating shipping earnings under the

---

[1] In the base year, 1907, net home investment, excluding additions to consumers' capital, was estimated above (p. 122) at £120 m. only, while the totals in Table 46 have as base a total of £140 m.

[2] C. K. Hobson, *The Export of Capital*, Chapter VII.

[3] British exports are entered f.o.b., so that the value of transport services subsequently performed by British ships is not included, although these services are paid for by foreigners. British imports are entered c.i.f., although part of the c.i.f. value is paid over as freight charges to British shipowners, and not to foreigners.

first two heads, therefore, is to add up the various items of shipping expenditure in the United Kingdom (including gross profits) and deduct passenger fares paid by British residents. Any payments by the British government in subsidies have also to be deducted.[1]

	Hobson (£m.)	Cairncross (£m.)
Wages and provisions (expenditure in U.K. only)	12	12
Stores purchased in U.K.	4	4
Bunker coal	11·75	7·5
Port and deck charges, pilotage	10	10
Loading and unloading	5	5
Management, office, taxes, etc.	5	5
Insurance, depreciation, repairs	24	24
Net profits [a]	8	10·5
	79·75	78·0
Less fares and subsidies	—	5·5
	—	72·5

[a] I have reckoned profits at 7 % on £150 m. compared with 5 % on £160 m. in Hobson's estimate (op. cit. p. 176). Giffen was prepared to put the capital value of ocean-going shipping as high as £192 m. (Evidence before the Committee on War Risks (1908), Q.2972 and Appendix VII.) Other estimates given before this Committee were those of S. H. Boulton (Q. 1513) of about £150 m., and of T. G. Bowles (Appendix III) of £160–170 m. The average first cost of all liner tonnage entered in the Liverpool and London War Risks Insurance Association in August 1914 was £18 per ton gross (*Final Report of Departmental Committee on Shipping and Shipbuilding*, p. 136) and would have been worth £11. 12s. if depreciation had been estimated at 4 % per annum. The book value of the fleets of the twenty-two principal liner companies, owning 70 % of all British liner tonnage, was £11. 6s. 9d. per ton gross in 1914. If we take a rather smaller average for 1907, say £11 per gross ton, and reckon tramps at £7. 10s. per ton, we get an average value for all steamships of £9 per gross ton, or £15 per net ton. Sailing ships were worth perhaps £6. 10s. per net ton. This gives a total for ocean-going ships of £147½ m. in 1907, say £150 m.

Using this method, Hobson reaches a total of £79·75 m., inclusive of fares by British residents and government subsidies. Other methods yield higher totals,[2] and he finally adopts a figure of £90 m., including

[1] Other methods of calculation are less satisfactory. Estimates based upon the excess of the value of world imports over the value of world exports are difficult to correct for insurance payments and commissions, for transit charges on non-sea-borne goods, for the fares of passengers and, finally, for errors and lacunae (always plentiful) in the import and export statistics themselves. Estimates based upon other methods generally make use of samples which are either unrepresentative (e.g. a few large passenger lines), or too heterogeneous in earning power (e.g. such companies as publish working accounts) to make the final result particularly reliable.

[2] Op. cit. p. 177.

disbursements by foreign ships in British ports. On the other hand, the Board of Trade's estimate for 1913, when earnings were a good deal higher, amounts only to £94 m. My impression is that the Board of Trade's figure is a little too low and that Hobson's figure of £79·75 m. for 1907, if it is intended to exclude disbursements by foreign ships, is a little too high.

In amending Hobson's figure, I have first excluded bunker coal bought by foreign ships. I have then deducted £1·5 m. for 'subsidies', and £4 m. for fares paid by British passengers. On the other hand, I have raised Hobson's estimate of shipping profits, for 1907 was a good year and a return of only 5 % in interest and dividends does not quite fit with other evidence. The two sets of estimates compare as shown in the table on p. 171.

For disbursements by foreign ships in British ports, I originally took a total of £12½ m. I have since reduced this to £10 m. made up as follows:[1]

	£m.
Port dues	4
Bunker coal	4
Loading, unloading, etc.	2
	10

Starting from these estimates for 1907, I have calculated the year to year changes in shipping earnings.

(a) *Disbursements by foreign ships in British ports.* I originally assumed that sailing vessels spent 4s. per ton cleared and steam vessels 10s. per ton, the total for 1907 working out at £12½ m. I should probably use a different method of calculation now, but it did not seem worth while to refine the previous figures and I have instead made a flat reduction of one-fifth throughout. The comparatively high figures for steam

---

[1] I regard £10 m. as on the low side but have been influenced by the estimates for the inter-war period (e.g. £9·5 m. in 1936). If freights in 1907 were about 10 % of the value of British trade and the proportion carried in foreign ships was one-quarter (as estimated by the Booth Committee), the gross earnings in freight of foreign ships on voyages to the United Kingdom amounted to £29 m. Adding in passenger fares, and taking one-third of gross earnings, we get at least £10 m. for disbursements in British ports. In view of the cheapness of British coal, it is hardly likely that the proportion of gross earnings spent in Britain was less than one-third. A second check, based on the outlay of British ships abroad per ton of British shipping entered and cleared in foreign ports, and on the assumption of a similar outlay per ton of foreign shipping entered and cleared in British ports, gives a total of £9 m., or, including Colonial vessels, nearly £10½ m. This method of calculation would be likely to err on the low side.

tonnage are intended to reflect expenditure on bunker coal in English ports.

(b) *Passenger earnings*. No figures are available of the passenger earnings of the British mercantile marine except for two inter-war years, 1931 and 1936. It is known that in 1936 receipts from passenger traffic amounted to about 16 % of gross receipts,[1] which in turn came to about £145 m.[2] Apart from this, all is confusion.[3] It is possible that in 1936 passenger fares were approximately as follows:

	£m.
U.K. residents in U.K. ships	10·0
Other passengers in U.K. ships	12·7 [a]
U.K. residents in foreign ships	2·0 [a]

(a) M. G. Kendall, loc. cit. p. 143.

Using these figures as a base, one might work out very rough estimates for the years before 1914. The results would, however, be subject to a wide margin of error, and in view of this and of the labour involved I have not made the attempt.

(c) *Freights*. If we ignore passenger earnings, we can use an index of freights as a measure of the price of shipping services and tonnage as a measure of volume. It is necessary to reduce sail and steam tonnage to some common denominator, to exclude coastwise shipping, and to make a correction for any secular improvement in speed and stowage, etc.

[1] H. Leak, 'The carrying trade of British shipping', *J. R. Statist. Soc.* 1939, p. 216. The only other estimate that I have seen is one by H. W. Macrosty of £26 m. out of £138 m. in 1925 (*J. R. Statist. Soc.*, 1926, p. 501). On the data given by Macrosty I should say that this was too high.

[2] M. G. Kendall, 'Merchant shipping statistics', *J. R. Statist. Soc.*, 1948, p. 141. According to Dr Isserlis ('Tramp shipping, cargoes and freights', *J. R. Statist. Soc.*, 1938, p. 71) the Chamber of Shipping inquiry yielded a total for 13·75 m. (out of 15·1 m.) gross tons of £120·7 m. for gross earnings, excluding passage-money paid by United Kingdom residents. This is roughly equivalent to £132·7 m. for 15·1 m. gross tons, so that the passage-money paid by United Kingdom residents may have been about £12 m. In 1931 an inquiry by the Chamber gave a total of only £6·9 m. (ibid. p. 68), but the number of British passengers to destinations outside Europe had risen by 20 % by 1936 and fares were probably also somewhat higher. The 1931 figure may also have been incomplete. I have assumed that Kendall's total of 'about £145 m.' means, in fact, £143 m., and that United Kingdom passengers paid £10 m. rather than £12 m. This assumption is consistent with the table given above.

[3] For example, Kendall first puts passenger fares by United Kingdom nationals in foreign ships in 1936 at £7 m. (*J. R. Statist. Soc.* 1947, p. 182) and subsequently at £2 m. (*J. R. Statist. Soc.* 1948, p. 143).

In calculating the 'volume' of British shipping, I have taken the equivalent, in terms of steamships, of the net tonnage on the British register employed wholly or partly in 'foreign trade', adopting the usual ratio of 3 tons sail, 1 ton steam. This has the disadvantage of omitting ships in the 'near-seas trade', i.e. ships trading between home ports and the continent between the river Elbe and Brest; but since all ships trading *partly* in the foreign trade are included, and since many of the ships trading between Brest and the Elbe were no doubt also recorded as taking part in the 'foreign' trade, the net error thus introduced is not likely to be serious.

I have made no correction for changes in speed or carrying capacity. Hobson puts the average improvement over the period, exclusive of any gain in carrying capacity resulting from the use of steam in place of sailing vessels, at about 60 %. I hesitate to introduce so large a correction when my results for the earlier years are already on the low side. It is possible that the fall in freights over the period was more drastic than that shown in the index used below or that outlay abroad increased relatively to gross earnings. It is also possible that port charges incurred in British ports fell progressively. Thus, while Giffen puts port charges, pilotage, etc., at £8½ m. for 1879, Hobson uses a figure of only £10 m. (or £15 m. including unloading) for 1907, when the net tonnage entered and cleared was 150 % higher. Whatever the explanation, shipping earnings do not appear to have increased appreciably *faster* over the period than my estimates imply, and I have refrained, therefore, from introducing a correction for speed.

An index of freight rates. There is no satisfactory index of freight rates. Rates fluctuated violently and there were wide divergences of movement between different routes. The only available indices for the period are those calculated by Isserlis[1] and by Hobson,[2] the former relating exclusively to tramps. Hobson's index is based on the series published by the Board of Trade, for the years 1884–1903, of inward and outward freights (including both tramp and liner freights). For the remaining years of the period 1870–1912, Hobson has relied mainly on tramp quotations.

The first difficulty about these indices is the weight which they give to coal freights. Isserlis uses an unweighted average without distinguishing inward and outward freights; about half the freight rates included are for coal outward cargoes. Hobson's own calculations of outward freights are exclusively in terms of quotations for coal cargoes. But total earnings on the carriage of coal exports were relatively small. In 1936 British tramps earned only £6·5 m. on the carriage of 20·6 m. tons of

[1] L. Isserlis, 'Tramp shipping, cargoes and freights', *J. R. Statist. Soc.* 1938, p. 122.
[2] Op. cit. p. 182.

coal, or less than 7s. a ton, and freights in 1936 were not very different from freights in the years immediately before the first World War. Although coal represented a very high proportion of the total weight of exports, it did not account for more than a modest proportion by value. In 1936 total earnings on British exports carried in British ships amounted to £25·6 m., while earnings on the export of coal were only £5 m. The total earnings of the British mercantile marine in 1936 were about £145 m. The carriage of coal accounted for less than one-twentieth of this total. Unless, therefore, coal freights were a sensitive index of outward freights both for tramps and liners, it would be wrong to use coal freights as a measure of fluctuations in receipts from the carriage of British exports in British vessels.

There is, in fact, some evidence that coal freights were rising in relation to other freights over the period. There was a rise, for example, in relation to inward freight rates. This was no doubt associated with the rapid increase in coal exports, which may have more than counter-balanced the growth in imports of tramp cargoes like grain, timber, ore, etc. It is unlikely that liner outward freights kept pace with freights on coal outward cargoes.

There is less reason to expect a divergence between liner and tramp freights on inward cargoes. Many goods could be carried either in tramps or liners. Moreover, the available freight rates cover a much wider range of goods. Nevertheless, it is desirable to make use of an index that combines tramp and liner quotations. For the period 1884–1903, this is possible by using the Board of Trade data. There are, however, no liner quotations for earlier or subsequent years.

The procedure which I have followed has been to make use of Hobson's index rather than Isserlis's, partly because Hobson's figures make use of the Board of Trade liner quotations and partly because he distinguishes inward and outward freights. I have, however, departed from Hobson's figures at two points. For the years 1870–84, Hobson uses only a small number of quotations to arrive at an index of inward freights. I have substituted a more broadly based index calculated from the data given by Isserlis. For the years 1884–1903 I have reworked the Board of Trade index for outward freights, so as to make use of liner quotations only, and have given a double weight to quotations for the Boston and Philadelphia routes. Throughout, I have given inward freights twice the weight of export freights. For the years 1912–13 I have used Isserlis's index of tramp freights but have damped down the changes in these two years by one-third.

Multiplying the resulting index of freights by the index of the volume of ocean-going shipping, we have a measure of British shipping earnings. Using 1907 as a base, we arrive at the estimates shown in Table 39.

Table 39. *Shipping freights and earnings, 1870–1913*

Year	Inward freights (1900 =100)	Outward freights (1900 =100)	Index of freights[a] (1907 =100)	Volume of shipping[b] (1907 =100)	'Shipping earnings'[c] (1907 £=72·5m.)	Disbursements of foreign ships in British ports (1907 =£10 m.)	'Shipping earnings' ($\frac{1}{16}$ of total British imports and exports (£m.)
1870	200	218	231	22·0	36·8	1·1	34·2
1871	202	210	230	23·7	39·5	1·4	38·4
1872	198	220	230	25·4	42·4	1·5	41·8
1873	226	234	257	25·7	47·9	1·7	42·7
1874	206	228	239	28·2	48·9	1·8	41·7
1875	194	194	218	28·2	44·6	1·8	41·0
1876	204	179	220	28·5	45·5	2·0	39·5
1877	212	176	225	29·9	48·8	1·9	40·4
1878	174	176	197	31·3	44·7	1·9	38·4
1879	164	183	191	32·6	45·1	1·9	38·2
1880	168	183	194	34·7	48·8	2·2	43·6
1881	178	168	197	37·5	53·6	2·2	43·4
1882	164	163	184	40·9	54·6	2·4	45·0
1883	146	162	170	44·0	54·2	2·5	45·8
1884	122	155	149	45·4	49·0	2·6	42·9
1885	107	138	131	46·0	43·7	2·6	40·1
1886	98	147	128	46·0	42·7	2·5	38·7
1887	95	156	129	46·7	43·7	2·6	40·2
1888	107	160	140	49·8	50·5	2·7	42·9
1889	125	168	157	53·3	60·7	3·0	46·4
1890	103	165	139	56·4	56·8	3·2	46·8
1891	104	135	129	59·1	55·3	3·4	46·6
1892	84	119	108	60·8	47·6	3·4	44·7
1893	85	109	104	62·5	47·1	3·3	42·6
1894	81	109	101	64·6	47·3	3·5	42·6
1895	75	102	93	66·7	45·0	3·6	43·9
1896	83	96	98	68·4	48·6	4·0	46·1
1897	82	104	100	69·1	50·1	4·5	46·6
1898	97	100	110	71·8	57·3	4·7	47·8
1899	84	98	99	74·6	53·5	5·8	50·9
1900	100	100	112	76·6	62·2	6·5	54·8
1901	69	101	90	79·4	51·8	6·2	54·4
1902	65	101	87	82·8	52·2	6·4	54·9
1903	67	106	90	85·6	55·9	6·7	56·4
1904	65	99	85	88·3	54·4	7·2	57·6
1905	68	106	91	92·4	61·0	7·8	60·8
1906	68	127	99	97·3	69·8	8·4	66·8
1907	71	127	100	100·0	72·5	10·0	72·7
1908	62	108	87	100·0	63·1	10·4	65·6
1909	67	105	90	100·3	65·4	10·4	68·4
1910	71	108	93	102·7	69·2	10·5	75·7
1911	75	121	101	106·5	78·0	11·1	77·3
1912	108	167	(124)	109·3	98·3	12·4	84·0
1913	—	—	(112)	112·0	90·9	14·1	87·7

(a) Inward freights are given twice the weight of outward freights.
(b) Net tonnage of British ships not engaged in the 'home' trade, steamships and sailing vessels being weighted 3:1. No correction for speed or efficiency has been made.
(c) Volume of shipping times average freights on a base of 1907=£72·5 m.

Giffen's estimates of shipping earnings. Giffen's estimates for 1879 and 1898 provide useful checks for earlier years. The figure for 1879[1]—£60 m.—is reached by several different routes, but is, to my mind, unquestionably too high. The rough approximation yielded by statistics of world exports and imports is £71 m. for the gross income of British shipping.[2] But this approximation is more or less valueless. It is reached without making any correction for earnings on non-sea-borne traffic to the difference in value between the aggregate exports and the aggregate imports of all countries. The imports of the United States are entered up in the total f.o.b. instead of c.i.f. The earning power of steamships is put at four times the earning power of sailing vessels per net ton, although Giffen's own figures support the usual ratio of 3:1. The proportion of total freights earned by British ships is taken on the basis of all shipping on the British and foreign registers instead of on the basis of ocean-going tonnage only. No provision is made for the fares of foreign passengers carried in British ships, nor for government mail subsidies. Lastly, the deduction of a sixth which Giffen makes from £71 m. for disbursements abroad is much too low and appears to be based on sail instead of on steamship disbursements (which were about twice as heavy). It is very doubtful whether, if the proper corrections could be applied, the net total would remain above £50 m., even though some of the corrections are in an upward direction.

Giffen's second method is to calculate shipping earnings directly from samples of the earnings per ton of steamships and sailing vessels. His samples, unfortunately, do not all refer to 1879 and are not too satisfactory from the point of view of size and representativeness. He estimates earnings at £15 per ton of steamships and £5 per ton of sailing vessels. This gives a total for 1878 of £47·4 m. Giffen's higher figure of £62 m. is due in part to his inclusion of coastal shipping, and in part to his use of 'tonnage on the register of 1880' as a multiplier.

Finally, Giffen uses the 'expenditure' method and obtains a total of £63 m. Again the inclusion of coastal shipping inflates the total. The table on p. 178 shows an amended calculation. Even this total is, I think, too high for 1879, when profits can hardly have averaged 7 % (Giffen puts them at 12½ %, but was possibly thinking of 1880–1, or of the decade 1870–80).

For 1898 Giffen gives an estimate of £88 m., obtained by deducting

---

[1] R. Giffen, 'On the use of import and export statistics', *J. R. Statist. Soc.* 1882, pp. 206 et seq.

[2] Giffen includes in British shipping about half the tonnage of colonial ships, on the assumption that about that proportion was in British ownership. It might be preferable to regard such ships as part of Britain's foreign investments.

20 % from earnings per ton in 1879.[1] The deduction seems much too small. Freights fell by over 40 % during the period 1879–98, and improvements in speed and in dead-weight carrying capacity were to a large extent offset by increased outlay abroad on coal. If earnings per net ton fell by 40 % and not 20 %, then shipping earnings must have increased from £47·4 m. in 1879 to £62·7 m. in 1898, both figures including passenger earnings and subsidies.

Earnings of ocean-going British ships in 1879

	£m.
Wages: at £1·1 per net ton sail × 3·21 m. tons	3·56
£1·5 per net ton steam × 2·1 m. tons	3·21
Provisions	6·0
Coal, port expenses in Britain, etc.	10·0
Insurance 7½ %⎫ On a capital of £84 m.	25·0
Profit 7 % ⎬ (sail, £10 per ton;	
Repairs, renewal, etc. 15 % ⎭ steam, £25 per ton)	
	47·8

An alternative calculation. In 1931 over three-quarters of the *net* receipts of British shipping (i.e. net of expenses abroad) came from voyages, one terminal of which was a British port; in 1936 the proportion was nearly 72 %. Before 1914 the proportion was probably not very different.[2] Moreover, in 1913 three-quarters of the goods entering or leaving British ports were carried in British vessels,[3] and before 1913 the proportion is likely to have been, if anything, greater. Hence the earnings of British shipping must have fluctuated closely with British exports and imports. In 1936, a fairly normal year, net shipping 'earnings' (excluding disbursements by foreign ships in British ports) amounted to £75 m. and total imports and exports to £1345 m. For 1913 the Board of Trade estimate for net shipping earnings amounted to £85 m.(?) and total imports and exports to £1404 m. These two years yield 5·5 and 6 % respectively for the ratio of net earnings to British imports and exports. These proportions are likely to be somewhat below the average for the period from 1870 to 1914 when British shipping played a bigger part in international trade. It might be not too far out for that period to offset the earnings of British ships in the cross-trades against the

---

[1] Giffen, 'The excess of imports', *J. R. Statist. Soc.* 1899, pp. 9 et seq. Deducting coastal shipping the total becomes £83·7 m.

[2] In 1912 the proportion by value of the goods carried in British vessels that entered or left a British port was about 63½ %; in 1936 it was about 65½ %. (H. Leak, loc. cit. p. 254.)   [3] Ibid. p. 226.

freights earned by foreign ships in trading to British ports and to equate British freights with the freights paid for the carriage of British exports and imports. Taking freight rates at an average of 10 % by value of exports (including re-exports) and imports and expenses abroad at one-third of gross freights, these assumptions would amount to taking $6\frac{2}{3}$ % of the value of British trade as equivalent to the net shipping earnings of the British mercantile marine.[1] The results of a calculation on this basis are shown in the final column of Table 39. They are not greatly at variance, except in individual years of high or low freights, with the earlier calculations. Where divergences do occur, they are an interesting pointer to the emergence of a new trend.

(ii) *Interest on foreign investments*

Hobson's estimate of interest on foreign investments is open to three criticisms.[2] First, he assumes that unidentified income from abroad (e.g. profits of concerns other than railways situated abroad but directed from Great Britain) increased at the same rate as the identified income. It is possible, however, that unidentified income increased in a greater ratio, and this was the view taken, for example, by the late Lord Stamp. Hobson's estimates are unlikely to require any considerable modification on this score.

First, the divergence between the rates of increase cannot have been large. It is probably true that in 1870 a much larger proportion of our income from foreign investments came from foreign bonds and other 'identified' sources. But there were countries like Australia, France, Austria and so on in which our investments in 1870 were to a much greater degree in concerns managed from London, etc., than in 1914. And the *spectacular* increases in investment during the period—in foreign rails, in colonial government and corporation stocks, and so on—were generally in securities in the 'identified' section.

Secondly, even if the actual increase in 'identified' income was in a smaller ratio than the increase in total income from abroad, the *apparent* increase in 'identified' income may not have been. There was almost certainly a gradual reduction in tax evasion during the period.

Thirdly, there were large blocks of securities which one would have expected to see assessed under Schedule C in 1870 but which were in fact assessed under Schedule D. Schedule C was 'merely a return from loan agents of the amounts they have paid income tax upon.... In the case of U.S. loans, where coupons are sold here for export, the possessor

---

[1] This ignores passenger earnings from non-United Kingdom nationals, but these were probably not very large.

[2] J. C. Stamp, *British Incomes and Property*, pp. 227, 235.

Table 40. *Export of capital (in £m.), 1870–1913*

Year	Total 'Shipping earnings'	Interest on foreign investment	Other invisibles (including ships)	Excess of imports	Net export of bullion and specie	Net export of capital	Balance of payments on income account
1870	37·9	42·0	18·0	59·2	−10·6	28·1	38·7
1871	40·9	45·0	19·2	47·4	+4·3	53·4	57·7
1872	43·9	48·0	23·9	40·1	+0·7	76·4	75·7
1873	49·6	52·0	26·8	60·3	−4·7	63·4	68·1
1874	50·7	55·3	23·4	72·4	−7·5	49·5	57·0
1875	46·4	55·7	21·5	92·3	−5·7	25·6	31·3
1876	47·5	52·8	20·0	118·3	−7·6	−5·5	2·1
1877	50·7	54·0	21·1	142·1	+2·6	−13·7	−16·3
1878	46·6	53·7	23·2	123·3	−5·7	−5·5	0·2
1879	47·0	53·8	22·1	114·2	+4·4	13·1	8·7
1880	51·0	56·2	24·3	124·8	+2·6	9·3	6·7
1881	55·8	57·4	28·0	99·9	+5·6	46·9	41·3
1882	57·0	59·8	30·2	106·3	−2·6	37·1	39·7
1883	56·7	63·5	30·4	121·5	−0·8	27·3	28·1
1884	51·6	65·2	26·4	94·0	+1·6	50·8	49·2
1885	46·3	69·1	23·6	99·5	−0·2	39·3	39·5
1886	45·2	73·0	23·6	80·9	+0·6	61·5	60·9
1887	46·3	77·5	25·9	81·9	−0·7	67·1	67·8
1888	53·2	82·5	27·9	89·0	+0·6	75·2	74·6
1889	63·7	86·0	34·8	112·0	−2·0	70·5	72·5
1890	60·0	91·5	35·3	92·4	−8·8	85·6	94·4
1891	58·7	90·0	30·7	127·1	−1·6	50·7	52·3
1892	51·0	91·0	27·6	132·2	−3·4	34·0	37·4
1893	50·4	91·0	28·3	127·6	−3·6	38·5	42·1
1894	50·8	88·0	26·4	134·5	−10·8	20·1	30·9
1895	48·6	90·5	27·9	130·9	−15·0	21·1	36·1
1896	52·6	92·5	31·8	145·4	+6·4	37·9	33·5
1897	54·6	93·0	32·4	156·8	+0·8	24·0	23·2
1898	62·0	98·5	35·9	176·5	−6·2	13·7	19·9
1899	59·3	99·0	38·9	164·7	−9·8	22·7	32·5
1900	68·7	99·0	40·7	177·3	−7·5	23·6	31·1
1901	58·0	103·0	40·4	183·3	−6·2	11·9	18·1
1902	58·6	105·0	36·5	185·0	−5·3	9·8	15·1
1903	62·6	108·0	36·8	186·5	+0·2	21·1	20·9
1904	61·6	108·5	36·4	184·4	+0·7	22·8	22·1
1905	68·8	121·5	37·8	162·8	−6·2	59·1	65·3
1906	78·2	130·0	47·1	155·9	−1·8	97·6	99·4
1907	82·5	140·0	53·3	137·8	−5·3	132·7	138·0
1908	73·5	146·0	45·0	146·9	+6·8	127·4	120·6
1909	75·8	153·5	41·2	161·1	−6·5	102·9	109·4
1910	79·7	166·0	49·4	152·9	−6·7	135·5	142·2
1911	89·1	171·0	46·2	128·9	−6·0	171·3	177·3
1912	110·7	181·5	51·3	152·7	−4·6	186·2	190·8
1913	105·0	194·0	(56·0)	144·9	−11·9	198·2	210·1

has to make his return under Schedule D.'[1] But it is not possible to identify these sales of coupons under Schedule D in 1870,[2] although they formed a very large proportion of our income from abroad; we had probably about £160 m. in United States government loans in 1870.

Finally, Hobson's figures for 1870–90 can be shown to be already rather low. A careful estimate by Nash in 1881 puts the minimum income from abroad at £52½ m., while Hobson gives £50½ m. for that year. Similarly, £50 m. does not seem excessive for 1873, nor £91·5 m. particularly high for 1890.

A second criticism which has been made[3] is that the income-tax figures used by Hobson are not all applicable to the current year, foreign *possessions* being assessable on the average of the past three years.[4] Except in the last ten years or so, this is unlikely to call for any very appreciable alteration in Hobson's estimates, and even for 1904–14 each year (except possibly 1908–9) would be affected upwards, at most by £10–15 m.

Lastly, Hobson takes no account of the Coupons Act of 1885, which had the immediate effect of reducing evasion.[5] I have made a correction for this, by extrapolating the items affected by the Act to 1884, and scaling up the figures for the previous years. For the period 1870–6 I have used rather different figures from Hobson, based upon statistics for those years given in the 1884–5 Report, and upon the probable increase in capital abroad after 1870.

(iii) *The balance of payments on income account*

For the remaining items in the balance of payments I have adopted without amendment the estimates given by Hobson. The final results are shown in Table 40. The net export of capital is shown in column 7 and the balance of payments on income account in column 8, the difference between the two being the net imports or exports of gold and silver, bullion and specie.

---

[1] R. L. Nash, *Short View of the Profitable Nature of our Investments* (3rd ed., p. 132). In 1870 only £3·2 m. of income from abroad was assessed explicitly under Schedule D. In 1880 the total was still only £10·7 m. Ten years later (partly as a result of the Coupons Act of 1885, and in spite of sales of United States government bonds) it had risen to £30·9 m.

[2] They seem to have been classed under 'Trade Profits'.

[3] Also by Stamp, op. cit. p. 235.

[4] Railways out of the United Kingdom are presumably also assessed in this way; but neither Stamp nor the Inland Revenue Reports give the basis of assessment.

[5] Stamp, op. cit. p. 227.

(b) The geographical distribution of foreign investment

Estimates of Britain's holdings of foreign securities at any particular date are necessarily extremely rough. Foreign securities are international securities, easily exchangeable and therefore easily sold to foreigners. Neither issue nor quotation on the London market ensures that a large proportion of the shares of a foreign company—much less the bonds of a foreign government—is held in Britain. Calculations of annual investment by the indirect method form some sort of check, and the Inland Revenue statistics of taxed income from abroad are also useful. But in all estimates mere guesswork is at one point or another quite unavoidable.

The apparently more ambitious task of tracing the geographical distribution of Britain's foreign investment is, surprisingly enough, much easier. Precise statistics are no longer essential, and the new issue market in London is a most obvious signpost to the trend of investment. The trade balances of the capital-importing countries are a further guide; and approximate estimates of foreign capital in these countries are sometimes not difficult to make.

Similarly with changes in the popularity of different *types* of investment. No one, for example, with even a slight acquaintance with the statistics of new issues, can be in doubt about the decline after 1875 in the proportion of Britain's holdings formed by the bonds of foreign governments. Again, although it may be impossible to determine the exact proportion of her foreign investments which helped to finance railway construction, it is easy to show that the proportion was high— about two-thirds in countries outside the Commonwealth.[1]

Table 41 shows the market value of Britain's foreign investments at the end of 1870 as estimated from a number of sources, of which the most important were *Fenn on the Funds* (12th edition) and Jenks's *Migration of Capital*. Her holdings of government bonds of all kinds were worth about £460 m., of which about a quarter was in the bonds of European governments, over a third in United States government bonds, and the remainder divided more or less equally between the colonies, India, South America and the Near East. A rather lower total, about £325 m., was invested in foreign, Indian and colonial railways and banks, in land and mortgage companies, telephone, gas, water and tramway companies, in mercantile establishments, mines, and other commercial enterprises. This estimate is particularly rough, data on Britain's holdings in continental railways being almost impossible to obtain. The aggregate of £785 m. is much below the *nominal* value of her investments, most foreign bonds being brought out at prices well

---

[1] Sir George Paish, *J. R. Statist. Soc.* 1911, p. 185.

below par. Assuming an average yield of 5½ % (which seems to fit the facts) Britain's income from foreign investments in 1871 would be £43 m., or almost exactly the income estimated in Table 40.

Table 41. *Government and industrial investments at the end of 1870*

Government bonds (£m.)		Joint stock companies, etc. (£m.)	
United States	160	U.S. rails	40
Russia, Italy, etc.	78·5	Continental rails, gas, water, etc.	50
Other European Govts.	30	South America	37·5
Turkey and Egypt	37·5	Foreign banks	10
South and Central America	47·5	Australasia	38·5
Australasia	34·3	Canadian rails, banks, etc.	20
Other colonies	16·0	Indian rails, etc.	105
India	55·0	Miscellaneous, say	25
	459		326

By the end of 1880 Britain's holdings must have risen by about £300 m., and by the end of 1885 by nearly £200 m. more. The distribution of British overseas investments in 1870 and in 1885 may have been roughly as follows (in £m.):

	1870	1885		1870	1885
India	160	270	United States	200	300
Australasia	74	240	Europe and the Near	230	175
Canada	20	113	East		
Cape and Natal	} 16	35	South America	85	150
Rest of the Empire		17			
	270	675		515	625

All through the seventies Britain was adding to her investments in India and Australasia, although aggregate foreign investment was no higher in 1880 than five years earlier. She sold off Russian and American government bonds and bought colonial securities in their place. Later she made heavy purchases of American railway bonds and added gradually to her investments in Brazil and Argentine. By 1885 fully half of her foreign investments appear to have been within the Empire against just over a third fifteen years earlier. This change affected all parts of the Empire, Australia being the leading borrower.

In 1885 Britain had already £150 m. in South and Central America, over £50 m. of this being in the Argentine. In the next five years over £100 m. was invested in the Argentine alone. Another £100 m. was lent to Australasia, and an equally large sum was applied to the purchase of American railway bonds.

In the nineties, South Africa was a prominent borrower. Gold- and diamond-mining were the chief industries requiring foreign capital. Britain still continued to lend to Australasia and the United States, but on a much smaller scale than before. Few other countries borrowed much in London. After 1900, indeed, there seemed every likelihood of an actual importation of capital. The building of London's underground railways was one of several enterprises to the financing of which the United States contributed.

When foreign investment was actively resumed after 1904, it was still to America and the colonies that the capital flowed. In 1911 as in 1885 half of Britain's investments were in the Empire, Canada having re-placed Australasia as the leading colonial borrower. Europe had sunk to a position of comparative unimportance. Investments in America, North and South, came to well over 50 % of the total as compared with not much over 40 % in 1885 and a rather smaller proportion in 1870.

I have brought together in Table 42 a number of estimates of Britain's investments in particular countries at dates between 1870 and 1914. Her investments on the Continent cannot be stated with sufficient pre-cision to be worth including in the table.

There is a considerable discrepancy between the increase in total foreign investments in the forty years 1871–1911 as estimated by the direct method and the increase indicated by statistics of the balance of payments. If Britain held £785 m. of foreign investments in 1871 and £3500 m. in 1911, we should expect her annual balances to total up to approximately £2715 m. Instead, the total is only £1830 m., or £885 m. less. Part of this difference represents investment in Britain by foreigners. Again, it is quite likely that Britain's income from foreign investments, especially in the years of buoyancy after 1904, is under-stated in Table 40.[1] It is also doubtful whether in his calculation of 'unidentified income' from abroad for 1907 Sir George Paish took sufficient account of income from capital placed abroad privately. Since 1907 has been used as a base year in estimating income from overseas investments, any revision of the estimate for that year carries with it a revision for all other years, and a corresponding revision in the estimates of the balance of payments.

There is a further possibility. Britain almost certainly made sub-stantial profits on her foreign investments through secular appreciation and through skilful speculation. These capital gains, whether due to the ploughing back of profits or to an improvement in the credit of the

[1] Above, p. 180.

Table 42. *British investments in foreign countries between 1871 and 1941* (£m.)

Beginning of year	U.S.A.	Canada	Australasia	India (including Ceylon)	Argentine	Brazil	South America (total)	Russia	Spain	Peru	South Africa
1871	200 [a]	—	73 [b]	153 [c]	5 [d]	11 [d]	—	50 [d]	15 [d]	17·5 [d]	—
1875	—	—	—	—	—	—	—	—	—	16·25 [e]	—
1876	—	—	133 [h]	—	35 [e]	43 [f]	(50) [g]	—	—	—	—
1880	—	—	—	180 [k]	—	—	—	—	—	—	—
1881	(100) [l]	—	200 [l]	260 [l]	—	—	—	—	—	—	—
1884	—	112 [l]	—	—	—	—	—	—	—	—	34 [l]
1886	—	—	—	—	46 [f]	46·6 [f]	115·5 [f]	—	—	5·6 [f]	—
1888	525 [m]	—	285 [h]	—	—	—	—	—	—	—	—
1899	—	—	—	—	—	—	—	—	—	—	—
1900	—	—	389 [h]	—	200 [n]	—	—	—	—	—	—
1902	—	205 [o]	—	—	—	—	—	—	—	—	—
1911	688 [p]	373 [p]	380 [p]	351 [p]	270 [p]	94 [p]	587 [p]	38 [p]	19 [p]	32 [p]	351 [p]
1914	755 [q]	515 [q]	—	379	319 [q]	148 [q]	722 [q]	—	—	—	—

(a) Hobson, op. cit. p. 132; sources quoted in Bullock, Williams and Tucker, 'The balance of trade of the United States', *Harv. Rev. Econ. Statist.*, Preliminary vol. no. 3.

(b) Coghlan, quoted by Roland Wilson, *Capital Imports and the Terms of Trade*, p. 108.

(c) Based on Jenks, op. cit. pp. 219, 225, 425; Hobson, op. cit. p. 136; Inland Revenue figures and R. L. Nash, loc. cit.

(d) Government bonds only: based on issues in London as given in Fenn on the Funds, 12th ed. (1874). (See also Ingall's *Foreign Stock Manuals.*)

(e) *The Economist*, 1 April 1876. Market value in April. Face value £25·5 m.

(f) *The Economist*, 23 January 1886. Market values. 1876 figures only approximate.

(g) Mulhall, *English in South America* (private capital only).

(h) Wilson, op. cit. p. 44.

(i) R. L. Nash, op. cit. p. 129: United States rails only (minimum estimate).

(k) Ibid. This estimate includes only £12 m. for British holdings of rupee paper and excludes private capital and unguaranteed railways.

(l) *The Economist*, 9 February 1884. Figure for India includes £30 m. of rupee paper and £60 m. for banks, plantations, etc.

(m) N. T. Bacon (*Yale Review*) for 1899). Estimate is for 1 January 1899 and includes life-insurance premiums.

(n) Tornquist and Co. (quoted J. H. Williams, *Argentine's International Trade*, p. 150). J. H. Williams (p. 103) puts foreign liabilities (nearly all to Britain) at $922·5 m. for 1 January 1892, i.e. nearly £200 m. 85% of this was borrowed after 1880 and 70% after 1885.

(o) F. Williams-Taylor ('public' investments only), quoted by Viner, *Canada's Balance*, p. 118.

(p) Sir George Paish, *J. R. Statist. Soc.* 1911.

(q) Paish, *Statist Supplement*, February 1914.

borrower, went to swell the total of Britain's foreign investments without being reflected in the balance of payments.

On the other hand, in 1870 there was some £50 m. outstanding against London on short-term account,[1] whereas in 1913 the balance was heavily in her favour.[2]

When all corrections have been applied, a large discrepancy remains. If we suppose it to be reduced from £885 m. to, say, £400 m., this still represents £10 m. per annum over the forty years. A consistent error of this order in calculation of the balance of payments by the indirect method is not by any means impossible. Commission earnings, tourist expenditure, government remittances, and so on, can only be known within wide limits. Receipts from emigrants may have been much greater than has been assumed. Import and export values may not have been correctly stated. Sales of ships may be put at too low a value. But such corrections have a way of cancelling out. For instance, imports, being in some cases dutiable, and in the aggregate of greater value than exports, are more likely than exports to have been understated. There was probably an unfavourable balance on tourist account. And so on.

I suspect, therefore, that either Britain had a larger total of foreign investments than £800 m. in 1871, or a smaller total than £3500 m. in 1911; all the more so since the figure of £3500 m. is not the market value but the nominal value of her capital in foreign countries. Some of Paish's figures have been challenged as rather too high—American railways for instance.[3] An error of, say, 10 % is quite feasible, and his calculations probably had an upward bias.

[1] R. H. I. Palgrave, *J. R. Statist. Soc.* 1873, p. 70, et seq., E. Seyd, *J. R. Soc. Arts*, 5 April 1878, p. 409.

[2] Sykes, *Banking and Currency* (7th ed.), p. 255. Paish's estimate of £300 m. for Britain's private investments overseas in 1911 can hardly include the whole of her acceptance credits.

[3] J. M. Keynes, *J. R. Statist. Soc.* 1911, p. 196; Bullock, Williams and Tucker, loc. cit.

CHAPTER VII

FLUCTUATIONS IN HOME AND FOREIGN INVESTMENT, 1870–1913

It is no part of the purpose of this book to write a history of industrial fluctuations. Yet something in the way of illustrative comment on the statistical results so far obtained may help towards a general understanding of the Victorian cycle. The statistics may be too often based upon conjecture for more than the most modest of conclusions to be drawn. But even these conclusions are of great interest, and provide a firm basis for the analysis of the Victorian economic system.

I wish first to deal with the connexion between home and foreign investment, treating the secular connexion and the cyclical connexion between the two as separate problems. Clearly, both the motives which prompted capitalists to place their money abroad and the consequences of their decision to do so were highly complex. There were a thousand and one special influences determining the attractiveness of investment at home and abroad: the guarantees and land grants offered to railway-builders, the chance projects brought to the notice of financiers, the military ambitions of foreign governments, the competitive position of British industries, the state of business sentiment, harvest yields, movements of population, and the like—all these must be inquired into. Or if we turn to the repercussions of the investment, and attempt to trace the propagation of cyclical disturbances in the trade statistics of the countries which were Britain's most important debtors, or markets, or sources of supply, our task is again no light one.

Rather than follow the subject down all the labyrinths into which it leads, I shall content myself here with a sketch of some of the main paths through it. The first point which I wish to make clear is that in the *long* run foreign investment was largely at the expense of home investment or vice versa. The great expansions in home investment in the late seventies and nineties, for example, coincided with stagnation in foreign investment; and when foreign investment was abnormally large, as in the eighties and after 1905, investment at home sooner or later fell away. This sensitiveness of home investment to the competition of the foreign loan market was not confined to any one branch, although building seems to have reacted most promptly.

In the *short* period, home and foreign investment generally moved together. This is well known and hardly requires statistical verification.[1]

---

[1] Cf. for example, C. K. Hobson, *Export of Capital*, p. 221; L. H. Jenks, *Migration of British Capital*, p. 333.

There is also plenty of evidence that it was foreign rather than home investment that pulled Britain out of most depressions before 1914. The boom of 1900 was perhaps the only one in which it was not foreign investment and the prosperity of the export industries that set the pace for domestic construction.

This antithesis between long period and short is fundamental to the argument of this chapter. The peculiar nature of Britain's trade with the countries in which she was investing capital is also of great importance.

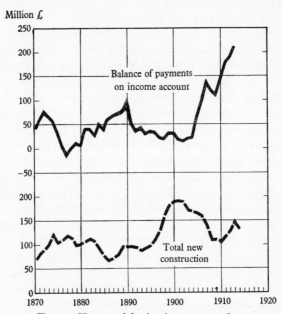

Fig. 14. Home and foreign investment, 1870–1913.

Up to 1870 (or even 1875), Britain lent chiefly to foreign governments, often European governments. The money was used to finance personal extravagances, budget deficits, wars, the construction of strategic railways and so on. Thus it tended to be the military preoccupations of her creditors rather than opportunities of profitable investment that led to fresh borrowing. After 1875 there was a quite pronounced change. Capital flowed more and more to the Empire and to America; British investors sold off their holdings of government bonds (especially Russian and American bonds) and bought railway stocks. Now the countries in which these railways were being built were Britain's chief sources of foodstuffs and raw materials; and they were not as yet serious competitors with her export industries, which were mainly engaged in supplying textile manufactures and capital goods of iron and steel.

Table 43. *Relative importance of markets for British exports and
sources of supply for British imports (in £m.)*

	British exports			Total British imports		
	1870–72	1890–92	1910–12	1870–72	1890–92	1910–12
British India	8·2	12·6	11·4	9·1	7·5	6·7
Australasia	5·0	9·2	8·9	4·5	7·1	8·2
Canada	3·7	3·0	4·8	2·7	3·1	3·9
Rest of Empire	7·1	8·8	9·8	5·6	5·2	6·2
United States	15·2	11·7	6·5	16·8	24·2	18·1
Germany, Holland and Belgium	20·3	14·4	14·6	13·4	16·6	17·4
France	6·9	6·5	5·3	11·0	10·4	7·3
Russia	3·0	2·2	2·9	6·9	4·9	5·8
Argentine and Brazil	4·1	5·7	7·2	2·8	1·9	6·4
Other foreign countries	26·5	25·9	28·6	27·1	20·1	20·0
All countries	100·0	100·0	100·0	100·0	100·0	100·0

One would expect to find, therefore, that during, or immediately
after, a fairly long period in which the terms of trade were relatively
unfavourable to Britain there would be heavy investment in the
countries supplying her with imports. A scarcity of raw materials or
a series of bad harvests in Europe would be likely to improve the credit
of Argentine and the United States. On the other hand, when capital
goods were expensive and foodstuffs were in over-supply, the continuance
of a rapid opening up of agricultural countries would be distinctly
surprising. What are the facts?

Calculations of the terms of trade during this period have been made
for a number of countries. The results of some of these calculations are
reproduced in Table 44. All such statistics must be treated with the
utmost caution. It is the easiest thing in the world to make two separate
calculations, using different weights or price series, and to arrive at
quite incompatible results. The figures, moreover, represent a price, not
a cost ratio. Import prices are inclusive of freights, while export prices
are not. Thus a change in the terms of trade favourable to Britain *need*
not involve a change unfavourable to other countries. Their costs may
have fallen, or freight rates may be lower.[1]

[1] The inclusion of imported raw materials in exports and the constant excess of
imports over exports introduce a freakishness into the statistics. Suppose, for instance,
that the price of raw cotton and wool rises by 10% and that this rise is passed on in
the price of finished textile exports. Then since textiles form a much higher proportion
of total exports than textile raw materials form of total imports, export prices may

In addition, the price series which are used are generally deficient. If market prices are taken (as Silverman has done), they exaggerate the fluctuations in realized prices; if average export and import values, the fluctuations are damped down because of changes in quality. The series for which continuous data are available are nearly always staple commodities, although a large proportion of British exports consisted of manufactured goods, many of them made for a special market, and less likely to fluctuate widely in price. On the whole, therefore, estimates of the terms of trade tend to exaggerate the true fluctuations.

Broadly speaking, between 1873 and 1881 the terms of trade were moving against Britain; between 1881 and 1895, or possibly 1900, the movement was in her favour; and after 1900 her terms of trade were either stationary or slightly less favourable. Broadly speaking, too, the same sort of changes took place in the terms of trade of France, and, after 1900 at least, of Germany. On the other hand, the terms of trade of Australia and Canada tended to move in the opposite direction to those of the industrial countries.

The statistics of capital export do not show the correspondence with these movements that one might expect. The unfavourable movement in Britain's terms of trade which began in 1874 was not followed by a renewal of capital export until 1878 or even later. This is not so surprising, however, when attention is paid to the abnormally sharp favourable movement in Britain's terms of trade before 1873 and to the numerous defaults (seldom by countries supplying her with imports) which brought foreign investment into disrepute in the seventies. A good deal of capital, in point of fact, was exported to Australasia and to India after 1873, but not, apparently, to the United States. That the United States took so long to recover was due largely to banking and financial difficulties, not to agricultural distress.[1]

Foreign investment was on a very large scale all through the eighties; even in the early nineties it was still active. Yet from 1881 onwards there was a gradual *improvement* in Britain's terms of trade. That it was in the

rise relatively to import prices, so that the terms of trade appear to have moved in favour of England. But textile raw materials are also used in manufacture for the home market, so that the terms of trade will in fact have moved *against* England.

[1] After the Jay Cooke panic of 1873 a large proportion of American railways defaulted on their bonds. The *New York Commercial Chronicle* (quoted in *Herapath's Railway Journal*, 5 February 1876) put the nominal value of the bonds on which default took place up till January 1876 at $784 m., of which $251 m. were estimated to be held abroad. In 1876 fully a fifth of the railway capital of the United States was reorganized (*The Economist*, 1877, p. 299). The difficulties of the railways were largely the result of competitive over-building and subsequent rate-cutting. Railway-building was not, however, at a standstill and first-class railway bonds appreciated steadily.

Table 44. *Terms of trade of capital-importing and capital-exporting countries, 1870–1913*

Year	Britain [a]	France [b]	Australia [c]	Canada [d]
1870	89	100	102	—
1871	97	103	124	—
1872	104	105	108	—
1873	112	107	113	—
1874	105	105	113	—
1875	101	105	120	—
1876	95	106	115	—
1877	88	105	110	—
1878	91	104	110	—
1879	89	102	120	—
1880	88	103	117	—
1881	83	107	117	—
1882	86	107	122	—
1883	87	109	120	—
1884	90	107	119	—
1885	99	108	114	—
1886	95	109	112	—
1887	95	102	114	—
1888	92	100	111	—
1889	96	99	108	—
1890	101	99	106	—
1891	99	100	101	—
1892	97	105	99	—
1893	96	108	93	—
1894	104	111	89	—
1895	104	107	92	—
1896	101	111	93	—
1897	102	110	89	—
1898	102	107	93	—
1899	107	104	117	—
1900	113	100	102	100
1901	111	107	100	108
1902	106	105	111	112
1903	104	101	115	110
1904	103	97	111	111
1905	105	96	120	111
1906	104	91	119	103
1907	108	97	118	104
1908	108	103	112	126
1909	98	100	113	128
1910	93	96	110	122
1911	97	97	105	123
1912	103	96	112	120
1913	107	95	111	115

[a] Calculated by Mr P. K. Debenham, corrected for imported materials used in exports.

[b] For 1870–9, from A. W. Flux, 'Price movements in the foreign trade of France', *J. R. Statist. Soc.* 1900; for 1880–1913 from H. D. White, *The French International Accounts*.

[c] Roland Wilson, *Capital Imports and the Terms of Trade*.

[d] From chapter III, Table 8.

'new' countries that she was investing there can be no possible doubt. Australia, Argentine and the United States were borrowing more heavily than ever before. Even the fact that the terms of trade reacted in favour of her customers in the years 1886–8, when she was lending particularly heavily, does little to solve the puzzle. The trend of borrowing was quite clearly in the opposite direction to the trend of the terms of trade.

Several explanations may be offered. First of all, there was a heavy fall in shipping and railway freight rates in the eighties. Farm prices fell much less than British import prices.[1] Thus, while the price of imported wheat fell from an average of 47s. 10d. per quarter in the years 1875–9 to an average of 33s. 6d. per quarter in the years 1885–9, the corresponding fall in the United States farm average was from 33s. 4d. to 25s. 1d. per quarter (that is, by 5s. less); while the fall in the farm average of six states west of the Mississippi valley was only from 27s. 7d. to 22s. 9d. per quarter.[2] This explanation, however, is of limited force. Australia, which was one of the chief importers of capital between 1883 and 1893, traded on less and less favourable terms during that period, import prices being measured inclusive of freight charges and export prices exclusive of them.

In the second place, the railway-building of the eighties was on such a scale that a fall in the price of agricultural products relatively to the price of industrial products was only to be expected. New land was being opened up at a tremendous pace. Costs in the fringe areas were far below costs in the older districts. The promise of additional traffic made railway-building profitable, and the provision of railway facilities made farming profitable. Moreover, once an increase in the farming population of the new countries had taken place, a fall in agricultural prices was long in bringing down the supply of farm products.[3]

The situation in the United States is of particular interest. After 1882 the area under cereal crops was practically stationary, although immi-

---

[1] Cf. M. Sering, *Die landwirtschaftliche Konkurrenz Nordamerikas*, pp. 512 et seq.; R. H. Hooker, 'Farm prices of wheat and maize in America, 1870–99', *J. R. Statist. Soc.* 1900; E. Atkinson, *The Railroad and the Farmer*.

[2] R. H. Hooker, loc. cit.

[3] The total railway mileage of the United States, Canada, India, Argentine, Australasia and Russia increased in the eighties by just over 100,000 miles, compared with an increase of only 60,000 miles in the seventies and 67,000 miles in the nineties. Russia was the only one of these countries in which the pace of construction did not quicken in the eighties. Yet paradoxically enough it was partly the increase in exports of wheat from Russia in the early nineties that was responsible for the depression in agriculture. For the relative importance of these countries as suppliers of wheat to Britain, see 'An inquiry into wheat prices' by R. F. Crawford, *J. R. Statist. Soc.* 1895, p. 81.

gration and **railway-building** were active (almost without intermission) from 1879 to 1893. Crops in European countries had been short all through the seventies,[1] and the years 1879–81 saw the worst harvests of any triennial period in the nineteenth century. Thus prices failed to respond to the steady expansion in acreage in the United States until 1883. The British wheat crop of 1879 ('the worst of the century') fetched a price little higher than that of 1878.[2] In the United States there were bumper crops from 1878 to 1881, and the value of wheat exports in these four years was higher than in any similar period before 1914. From a minimum of $69 m. in 1877, exports of wheat and wheat-flour leapt to $226 m. in 1880 and $213 m. in 1881.[3] When at last European crops began to be above normal, wheat prices naturally fell heavily and did not recover until the late nineties. The price of other cereals followed a similar course.

Thus the mere maintenance of the area under crops in the United States would have been sufficient, normally, to have depressed the price of grain of all kinds. It happened that, simultaneously, there was an expansion in exports of wheat from Russia and India. In both cases the railway-building of the seventies and a heavy fall in freights seem to have contributed to this expansion; India had the additional advantage of a depreciating currency. It is possible, though it is difficult to judge, that the fall in grain prices in the eighties forced the Russian peasants to market more wheat in order to pay their taxes, rent, etc. In India wheat is too much a commercial crop for this explanation to apply.

In the United States, as is clear from Table 45, the area under crops expanded rapidly whenever grain prices rose. What is more to the point, however, there was an expansion west of the Mississippi even when prices were falling. This was offset by a contraction of acreage in the eastern states. Between the period 1879–83 and the period 1889–92 the area under cultivation in eight states east of the Mississippi fell from 14·1 m. to 11·7 m. acres, while in seven states west of the Mississippi the area under cultivation rose from 12·1 m. to 15·2 m. acres. In Kansas and the Dakotas the rise was from 2·66 m. to 7·64 m. acres. Now the terrific railway-building of the eighties took place chiefly in the states west of the Mississippi—41,000 miles out of 73,000. In Kansas and the

[1] Except in 1874 and 1878. In 1878 there was a famine in India, and this, in spite of a bumper crop in the United States, checked the fall in wheat prices.

[2] The *Gazette* average was only ½d. higher in 1880 than in 1879 and was less in 1879 than it had been in 1878. As the quality of the 1879 crop was poor, the true change in price was probably upwards.

[3] The mileage of railroad in operation rose from 79,000 at the beginning of 1878 to nearly 115,000 at the beginning of 1883—that is, by almost twice the present length of the English railway system (not counting multiple track) in five years. The area under cereals expanded simultaneously.

Dakotas, the main low-cost areas, 9000 miles of rail were brought into operation.[1]

It would appear, therefore, that what took place in the United States was the consolidation of an advance in agriculture made before 1882 and not resumed until the late nineties; that this consolidation took the form of town- and railway-building; that it was financed largely by British capital and carried through with the help of British immigrants; and that it was held up in the seventies by monetary difficulties in America and distrust in London.

Table 45. *Area under cereals in the United States, 1870–1910*

Average of years	Area under corn (m. acres)	Area under wheat (m. acres)	Area under oats (m. acres)	Area under corn, wheat and oats (m. acres)	Price of winter wheat in New York
					s. d.
1869–1871	36·61	19·37	8·87	64·85	42 2 [a]
1874–1876	44·97	26·33	12·06	83·36	42 3 [a]
1879–1881	59·22	36·08	15·23	110·53	43 1
1884–1886	72·84	36·82	22·58	132·24	32 4
1889–1891	75·50	38·04	26·49	140·03	33 11
1894–1896	75·23	34·52	27·49	137·24	23 7
1899–1901	85·59	45·66	27·41	158·66	27 6
1904–1906	94·33	46·41	28·95	169·69	34 5
1909–1911	106·21	47·32	36·24	189·77	—

[a] Gold prices. The *nominal* equivalent prices were 52s. 3d. in 1869–71 and 47s. 5d. in 1874–6.

It is not possible here to discuss the similar puzzle of the meat supply in the eighties.[2] The wet seasons of the late seventies, improvements in meat packing and transportation, industrial depression, and the opening-up of low-cost areas provide the kernel of a full explanation. It is also impossible to discuss the forces encouraging investment in other agricultural countries in a period of agricultural depression. There were countries like Argentine where heavy investment at that particular time seems to have been largely accidental.[3] But this was obviously not true of all agricultural countries, and the example of the United States suggests that, whether or not farming was profitable, opportunities of investment in these countries had been accumulating since the

[1] R. F. Crawford, loc. cit. pp. 100 et seq.
[2] See R. H. Hooker, 'Meat supply of the United Kingdom', *J. R. Statist. Soc.* 1909.
[3] H. Osborne O'Hagan, *Leaves from my Life*, vol. I, pp. 377–8. Cf., however, D. H. Robertson, op. cit. p. 86.

seventies, while opportunities of investment in Great Britain had been rapidly exhausted in the seventies.

To a very large extent the course of investment in the eighties was governed by movements of population. There was heavy emigration from the industrial countries in the eighties, and correspondingly heavy immigration into the agricultural countries. In part, this movement was the result of better opportunities of employment in America and the colonies; in part, it reflected the depression in agriculture in Europe. Once begun, it aggravated the changes in investment out of which it arose. I shall return to this point in the next chapter.

Apart from the eighties, the facts seem on the whole to support the hypothesis advanced above, that the attractiveness of foreign investment varied with the terms of trade. The boom in foreign investment was finally brought to an end by a sharp break in the price of foodstuffs and raw materials in the early nineties. About 1903, when the terms of trade had ceased to move in Britain's favour, foreign investment revived. The great burst of investment after 1906 coincided with a period of rising import prices and practically stationary terms of trade.

In the short period British home and foreign investment might be expected to move in parallel. The areas of the world that were in course of rapid development relied on British capital and on British manufactures for those spurts in development that we now call booms. When investment increased in one such area, the consequent expansion of incomes in that area resulted in increased purchases from connected areas until they, too, became centres of investment. Given the close links between Britain and overseas development, it was inevitable her export industries should be sensitive to the general tempo of development in the 'new' countries and that any acceleration should be communicated through the export industries to the home market and to domestic investment. If the United States started to build more railways, Britain sold more steel rails and locomotives, or more textiles to American workers. Those sales increased the profits of British steel works, engineering establishments, and textile mills and gave manufacturers an inducement to extend their plant. Fewer houses stood empty, fewer ships were laid up, railway receipts increased. Investment in Britain rose. So also did savings—chiefly out of the increased profits. Britain was thus in a position to finance not only railway-building in the United States but also new construction at home.

It is conceivable that the chain of causation might run in the reverse direction, and that a boom beginning in Britain might spread to other countries. Increased activity would raise the demand for imported food and raw materials, improve the scope for agricultural development, and create a demand for Britain's capital in order to promote that development. If home investment were already in the lead, however, the financial problem of supporting a simultaneous expansion in foreign investment would be likely to prove a formidable one, and the rise in foreign investment would be more subdued than in booms initiated from without.

The imperfections of our statistical material make it difficult to be quite sure what did happen in the short period. It is clear, however, that home and foreign investment fluctuated cyclically, 1906–7 being the only boom in which both did not rise together. The fluctuations in home investment tended to lag behind those in foreign investment and were apparently somewhat less violent.

The only boom in which the rise in home investment was much more pronounced than the rise in foreign investment was that of 1900. There was no preliminary rise in foreign investment—indeed, there was a fall—and when the rise did come it was comparatively small. This was the nearest approach to a purely domestic boom. All other booms from 1870 onwards seem to have been communicated through the export trades from America and other centres of investment.

The response of the export industries to fluctuations abroad is illustrated in Fig. 15; a similar diagram shows the movement in the main groups of imports.[1] The figures from which these diagrams were constructed were twelve-month moving averages expressed as a percentage of the trend. They help to bring one the amplitude and priority of fluctuations in different groups of exports and imports.

The metal industries were naturally the most sensitive, fluctuations in exports of pig-iron, machinery and iron and steel manufactures being extremely violent and preceding, as a rule, fluctuations in home investment and employment. At times—as, for instance, in 1873—the value of exports of metals and hardware seemed to decline rather late; but the *volume* of such exports was always a good index of slump or revival.[2]

---

[1] These diagrams are taken from K. Zweig, 'Strukturwandlungen und Konjunkturschwingungen im Englischen Aussenhandel in der Vorkriegszeit', *Weltwirtschaftliches Arch.* 1929.

[2] Exports of pig and puddled iron fell from 1·33 m. tons in 1872 to 1·14 m. tons in 1873; exports of railway iron fell from 0·95 m. to 0·79 m. tons. The fall was chiefly in exports to the United States and to Germany, and the sharp fall in exports of textiles in 1873 was also due in the main to a contraction in these two markets. When there was at last a revival in the second half of 1879, exports of iron and steel again played a large part. The United States, whose good harvests had encouraged railway building, took 721,000 tons in 1879 as compared with 159,000 in 1878. Exports to the United States played a similar role in the revival of 1886. When they declined rather suddenly in 1888, the Argentine came forward as a customer and carried on the boom until 1890. It should be pointed out, however, that exports of textiles to India contributed to the recovery in 1886 (as they did again in 1894 and 1896).

Fig. 15 shows very clearly the comparative stability of textiles and the slight lag which generally separated them from exports of iron and steel manufactures. To some extent, both the stability and the lag were the result of steadier and later-moving prices. But volume figures would nearly always show similar results.

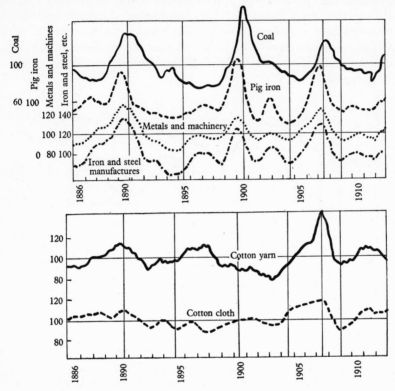

Fig. 15. Fluctuations in the value of British exports, 1885–1913.

In the short period, therefore, an increase in activity abroad, generally associated with an increase in foreign investment by Britain, pulled the country out of pre-1914 slumps by improving the prospects of the export industries. If the investment was on the Continent, the textile industries gained; if in America or the Colonies, the metal industries expanded. The demand for textiles from India—which depended more on harvest yields than on investment—was a rather random factor which seems also at times to have been of assistance.

Partly as a check on the statistics, partly as a measure of the variability of savings and investment, I have expressed net investment as a percentage of national income and compared it with the average unemployment percentage. The two series are shown in Fig. 17. For net investment I have taken the sum of new construction[1] and the balance of payments on income account and for the national income the series published by Mr Prest. The unemployment percentage is the average for all trade unions making returns, and since most of those unions were engaged in the capital goods and export industries their experience was not altogether representative.[2] The smoothness of change and the fair agreement between changes in the unemployment percentages of different unions makes it certain, however, that the smallness of the sample does not greatly damage the Trade Union figures as an index of year to year variations.

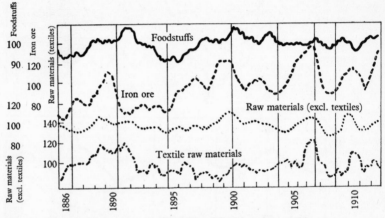

Fig. 16. Fluctuations in the value of British imports, 1885–1913.

In general there was a fairly definite inverse correlation between the two percentages. When unemployment was high, investment formed a lower proportion of the national income. This was true, both cyclically and, so far as one can judge, over longer periods. From the middle seventies to the middle nineties unemployment averaged over $5\frac{1}{2}$%; from then until the outbreak of war the average was about $4\frac{1}{2}$%. Over the same period the ratio of investment to national income rose from 11 to $12\frac{1}{2}$%. This is not very much to build upon, given the uncertainty of the data, but it is at least plausible.

If one accepts the figures, it would seem that savings reached a major peak in 1872–4 and that this peak was not subsequently surpassed,

---

[1] See above, p. 166.

[2] The total membership covered by the Trade Union figures did not reach 100,000 until 1872. In 1893 returns were made by 23 unions with a membership of 300,000; and by 1912, 800,000 workers were represented. (J. Hilton, 'Statistics of unemployment', *J. R. Statist. Soc.* 1923, p. 155.)

although 1913 came close to it. For some reason, 1900 comes out lower than any other cyclical peak, although unemployment would seem to have been on a smaller scale in 1900 than, say, in 1907.

It is, however, quite clear that the figures of investment are not reliable for individual years. In the earlier years particularly, the ratio of investment to national income fluctuates erratically when one would expect a fairly smooth curve. One important source of these erratic fluctuations lies in the lack of adequate data; there are just too many guesses in the estimates of new construction. A second lies in the logical jumps from a partial index of construction to an index of total net investment. The movement of stocks, for example, was not always in the same direction—much less to the same extent—as new construction.

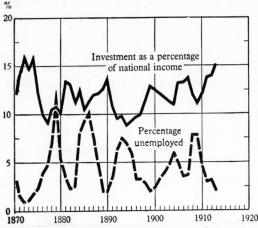

Fig. 17. Investment and unemployment, 1870–1913.

If the figures of unemployment and investment are closely compared, it is obvious that the two series show a number of divergences, especially in the earlier years. In nearly every boom the unemployment percentages appear to reach a turning-point a year or so earlier than total investment. A similar lag is traceable also in the upturn of investment in years of slump (e.g. in 1894 and 1909). There are several possible reasons for such a lag. One is the movement of prices. If prices went on rising after the peak of the boom, the volume of investment might turn down before the value of investment, and the volume of exports before the value. Secondly, near the top of a boom, unemployment and employment might move in the same direction; or there might be a small increase in unemployment in the industries for which figures exist at the same time as employment was still increasing in other sectors of the economy. Thirdly, a running down of stocks might produce a divergence between the movement of economic activity, as reflected in the statistics of unemployment, and the movement of imports and exports, as reflected in the balance of payments; foreign investment might continue to rise while employment was already falling. Fourthly, harvest fluctuations would have no direct effect on employment statistics (there were no agricultural trade unions) but would react on import requirements and so on the balance of payments. A favourable crop, if it happened to coincide with the peak of a boom, would help to maintain foreign investment beyond the peak. There are plenty of other possibilities which might be of interest to those who take a literal view of the multiplier, the propensity to consume, and allied concepts, but which are of little relevance here unless they can be linked with actual events.

Whatever the explanation in peak years, the divergences between investment and employment at other times were often associated with erratic fluctuations in imports and with harvest fluctuations. In 1884, for example, unemployment rose sharply from 2·6 to 8·1 %, while 'investment' showed a surprising increase, entirely because the balance of payments improved by some £20 m. This happens to be the exact amount by which imports of grain and provisions fell in comparison with 1883.[1] The British wheat crop did not alter much in the years 1882–4, but in 1883 imports had been abnormally great, the United States having had a bumper crop in 1882, and prices fell very sharply during 1883–4. It is only reasonable to suppose that the apparent rise in foreign investment in 1884 was more or less offset by disinvestment in grain stocks held in British ports, and that total investment fell fairly heavily.

In 1880, on the other hand, the apparent rise in 'investment' is probably an understatement. 1879 had been a year of harvest failure, and although imports of wheat did not increase in the following year, imports of other cereals did. There was probably also additional investment in stocks of textile raw materials, imports rising from £88·5 m. to £100·2 m. while exports of textile manufactures rose by very little more—from £99·2 m. to £112·8 m.[2]

In 1878 the apparent rise in investment is very largely due to a falling-off in imports from the abnormal level of 1877. Foodstuffs had risen in price in that year but, in spite of falling employment, the volume (and, a fortiori, the value) of imports had increased. Imports of sugar, tea, tobacco, etc. (tropical produce) rose by £7 m. in 1877 and fell by £9½ m. in 1878. Imports of grains and provisions increased by £12·1 m. and fell by £2·2 m. in the same years. It is impossible to believe that

---

[1] The totals were: 1883, £89·3 m.; 1884, £109·6 m.

[2] The rise in the selling price of cotton cloth in 1880 was practically in the same *ratio* as the rise in the price of raw cotton (using G. T. Jones's estimates).

the consumption of foodstuffs increased very much in 1877 or fell abnormally in 1878; and since there is little evidence of a deficiency in the home supply of foodstuffs in 1877 or of a surplus (until after the harvest) the following year, there must clearly have been an increase in investment in stocks of foodstuffs in 1877 and a decrease in 1878.

The dynamic relationships are perhaps more adequately expressed in Fig. 18 which compares the annual increments in new construction plus exports with the annual increments in national income. It would be unwise to attach too much significance to this comparison, given the imprecision of the estimates—and, *a fortiori*, in annual increments in

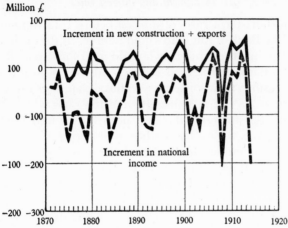

Fig. 18. Changes in national income, new construction and exports.

them. Even so, the figures suggest that there was a relationship between the two increments, national income undergoing larger and later changes than new construction plus exports. In three years and three only did the two increments move in opposite directions—in 1876, 1883 and 1886—and on no occasion was the magnitude of the divergence large. Nor was this correspondence of movement one more reflexion of the dominance of the trade cycle; new construction and exports often moved in opposite directions so that the increment in the aggregate of the two could not be known in advance to conform to a cyclical pattern.

I have shown in Table 46 the capital expenditure of public authorities so far as I have been able to estimate it. The figures headed 'Public investment' include the capital expenditure of local authorities (for the earlier years, *receipts* from loans) and expenditure on naval work (repairs as well as new construction). The trend is fairly steeply upwards, the biggest increase being between 1892 and 1902, when the total almost trebled. There is little sign of any cyclical pattern. In the first half of the period there are some signs of a falling-off in the total in peak years and of an increase in times of depression. That the sophistication of a public works policy had no part in this coincidence is obvious, however, from the most casual study of the second half of the period. The facts can be explained in terms of the response of local authorities to influences similar to those governing new construction of other kinds.[1]

I should like to conclude this chapter by touching briefly on the connexion between investment, wages, the terms of trade, and interest rates, without attempting a detailed analysis of the mechanism of pre-1914 cycles.

(a) Investment and interest rates

Movements in short-term rates of interest before 1914 were dominated by the state of the Bank of England's gold reserve. If the exchanges were at gold export point, the bankers who sold gold for export found their balances at the Bank of England reduced, and were forced to call in short loans to restore their customary ratios. Call loan rates stiffened, and later there was a rise in bank rate and the rates which by custom moved with it. Bill brokers who had been forced into the Bank cut down their discounts, the exchanges began to improve, and gold ceased to flow abroad. Sometimes the Bank took the initiative, for instance, by selling Consols and buying them back for the account or by borrowing at call from the Joint-Stock Banks.[2]

Changes in short-term rates were not always accompanied by changes in long-term rates in the same direction. The long-term rate tended to move *nearer* to the short-term rate, rising towards it if the short-term rate was already higher, or falling if the short-term rate was below it.[3] In the years in which this rule did not hold there was generally some exceptional event—a war or debt conversion—to explain the divergence. Yearly averages, it should be observed, show the connexion between the two sets of interest rates much less satisfactorily than monthly data.

Changes in short-term rates were largely cyclical. They rose in the boom and fell in the slump. They even lagged slightly behind fixed capital investment, no doubt because of the increased pressure to be liquid towards the end of the boom. Long-term rates oscillated about their trend in a rather similar but much less violent way. In the boom of 1873 the long-term rate actually fell (1870–72) and then remained

---

[1] See above, pp. 144–5.

[2] For a full account of such devices see R. S. Sayers, *Bank of England Operations, 1890–1913.*

[3] Cf. T. T. Williams, 'The rate of discount and the price of Consols', *J. R. Statist. Soc.* 1912. The short-term rate used by Williams is one of the rate on good three months bankers' bills in London.

Table 46. *Investment and national income, 1870–1914 (in £m.)*

Year	Total new construction[a]	Exports	Increment in cols. 1 and 2	Increment in national income[b]	'Total investment'[c]	'Public investment'[d]
1870	68·0	199·6	—	—	106·7	7·5
1871	81·8	223·1	+37	+58	139·5	7·6
1872	90·2	256·3	+42	+54	165·9	8·7
1873	99·0	255·2	+ 8	+92	167·1	10·9
1874	120·5	239·6	+ 5	—	177·5	15·0
1875	103·0	223·5	−33	−48	134·3	13·4
1876	107·7	200·6	−18	+ 3	109·8	16·3
1877	117·4	198·9	+ 8	+ 5	101·1	18·6
1878	112·7	192·8	−11	−22	112·9	19·6
1879	98·5	191·5	−16	−51	107·2	17·6
1880	101·8	223·1	+35	+53	108·5	17·1
1881	106·7	234·0	+16	+40	148·0	15·2
1882	111·6	241·5	+12	+43	151·3	13·4
1883	106·2	239·8	− 7	+28	134·3	13·8
1884	91·5	233·0	−22	−48	140·7	16·1
1885	77·4	213·1	−34	−18	116·9	17·8
1886	67·8	212·7	−10	+17	128·7	15·2
1887	71·8	221·9	+13	+29	139·6	15·3
1888	77·6	234·5	+18	+82	152·2	12·5
1889	95·1	248·9	+32	+87	167·6	13·5
1890	95·0	263·5	+15	+66	189·4	16·0
1891	95·7	247·2	−16	−13	148·0	19·6
1892	93·2	227·2	−23	−25	130·6	18·6
1893	88·7	218·3	−13	−31	130·8	21·0
1894	92·2	216·0	+ 1	+47	123·1	22·0
1895	98·6	226·1	+17	+65	134·7	23·3
1896	109·5	240·1	+25	+28	143·0	26·1
1897	128·2	234·2	+13	+49	151·4	26·9
1898	161·5	233·3	+32	+82	181·4	33·6
1899	182·0	264·5	+52	+71	214·5	38·6
1900	189·7	291·2	+34	+84	220·8	44·6
1901	191·5	280·0	− 9	−32	209·6	50·8
1902	188·0	283·4	—	+14	203·1	52·8
1903	172·4	290·8	− 8	−24	193·3	51·1
1904	169·8	300·7	+ 7	+28	191·9	50·8
1905	165·7	329·8	+25	+76	240·0	43·6
1906	159·3	375·6	+39	+121	258·7	39·0
1907	140·0	426·0	+31	+96	278·0	34·7
1908	110·2	377·1	−79	−109	230·8	33·1
1909	110·0	378·2	+ 1	+47	219·4	34·8
1910	106·9	430·4	+49	+90	249·1	37·7
1911	117·4	454·1	+34	+77	294·7	36·0
1912	127·5	487·2	+43	+128	318·3	38·5
1913	147·9	525·2	+58	+100	358·0	42·3
1914	133·0	(430·7)	(−109)	−102	—	44·4

[a] Total given in Table 38 increased in ratio of 14:8 on a base of 1907 = £140 m.

[b] From estimates of Mr A. R. Prest in *Econ. J.* 1948, pp. 58–9.

[c] The sum of new construction in col. 1 and the balance of payments on income account (Table 40).

[d] Capital expenditure by local authorities and expenditure on naval work.

absolutely steady for two years, while bank rate rocketed about between 3 % and anything up to 9 %. It is possible to argue, however, that since there was a distinct downward trend in long-term rates in the seventies, the interruption of the fall in 1873–4 was equivalent to a stiffening of long-term interest rates. This line of argument is hardly adequate to explain away the very rapid fall of 1879–81, but the very low level of short-term rates in these years makes them rather exceptional. In 1882–3 the long-term rate, being below the short-term rate, at last began to increase. Thereafter each boom witnessed a regular oscillation of the long-term rate of interest about its trend.

The behaviour of interest rates at the peak is perhaps less interesting than the coincidence between rising bill rates in the London money market and rising foreign investment in the first year of recovery. There was an acyclical rise in short-money rates (accompanied by a loss of gold from the bank) in 1877–8, 1886–7, 1903 and 1910, in marked contrast to the quite regular movements in other years. What is the explanation?

In each of the years mentioned, the rise in short-term interest rates was accompanied by an increase in foreign investment. Apart (possibly) from 1877–8, this increase in foreign investment ushered in a revival of trade and employment. In practically every case foreign securities rose in price.[1] It seems probable, therefore, that British investors were buying foreign securities faster than the export industries were furnishing the foreign exchange for the purchase of these securities; just as, in a recovery of home trade, a rise in share prices generally precedes a rise in employment. The improved liquidity preference of investors took the form of an increased demand for foreign securities.[2]

It is noteworthy that the 1900 boom—primarily a home investment boom—was the only one which was not heralded by a preliminary oscillation in short-term interest rates. The temporary rise in 1893 (a year of crisis in America and Australia) was accompanied by a fall in the price of foreign securities and no great loss of gold. The increase in foreign investment during the year, therefore, may safely be put down to temporary accommodation of foreign money markets rather than to the financing of fixed capital investment abroad.

Speculations of this kind, however, require much more elaborate investigation than can be attempted here.

[1] Home securities also rose in price in 1910.
[2] On the other hand, since foreign issues took an upward jump as early as 1902 and 1908, it is just as likely that foreigners were transferring funds borrowed at an earlier date.

(b) Investment and the terms of trade

The connexion between investment and the terms of trade during the cycle is too familiar to need elaborate discussion.[1] Export prices, being the prices of manufactured and of capital goods, tended to fluctuate more violently than import prices which were chiefly the prices of foodstuffs.[2] In the boom, therefore, the terms of trade generally moved in Britain's favour, and in the slump against her. Import prices, however, depended upon random factors—particularly harvest yields—and sometimes rose sharply in years of high investment. On the other hand, there were some depressions in which the fall in import prices was abnormally great and the terms of trade, therefore, unexpectedly favourable. The best example of high import prices coinciding with high investment was in 1880–2, while low import prices and low investment occurred together in 1894–6. Normally, a rise in export prices and a favourable movement of the terms of trade made the high investment of the boom very much easier. The profits of capitalists formed a levy at the expense of other countries (and sometimes of the British investor, if there were purchases of equipment to be made in Britain) and were largely saved and invested. Money wages being slow to change, the working class did not share in the gains until near or after the peak. Imports did not expand greatly and foreign investment was free to increase.

(c) Investment and wages

It is well known that money wage-rates did not reach their maximum in pre-1914 fluctuations until the beginning of the slump. Employment was declining in 1874, 1883–4, 1891, 1901, 1907 and 1914, when wage-rates had hardly ceased to rise. Similarly, it was usual for wage-rates to go on falling after employment had begun to increase. The fluctuations in money wage-rates were smooth and not (apart from the coal industry) particularly violent. Most of the figures which exist in any state of completeness are for wage-rates in the export industries,[3] and these naturally respond to changes in export prices. Now export prices were the most unstable of all, and wage-rates in the export industries, therefore, are by no means a good index of changes in *average* wage-rates. They do show, however, that wage-rates moved in sympathy with, and

[1] It was pointed out by Giffen as early as 1880 (Cd. 2484, p. 9).

[2] The prominence given in most calculations of export prices to semi-manufactured iron and steel products makes the terms of trade seem even more sensitive to industrial activity than they were.

[3] And in the constructional industries (e.g. shipbuilding), which were even more unstable.

Table 47. *Wages and prices, 1870–1914*

Year	Money wages [a]	Cost of living [b]	'Real wages'	Export prices [c]	Import prices [c]	Terms of trade [c]
	1914 = 100			1885–1900 = 100		
1870	66	110	60	144	150	89
1871	69	113	61	143	145	97
1872	74	120	62	161	153	104
1873	79	122	65	168	153	112
1874	80	115	70	156	149	105
1875	79	111	71	146	143	101
1876	78	110	71	134	139	95
1877	77	110	70	128	143	88
1878	74	104	71	123	132	91
1879	72	101	71	117	125	89
1880	72	105	69	121	133	88
1881	72	103	71	116	132	83
1882	75	102	73	118	131	86
1883	75	102	73	115	127	87
1884	75	97	77	111	119	90
1885	73	91	81	106	112	99
1886	72	89	81	101	105	95
1887	73	88	84	100	103	95
1888	75	88	86	101	106	92
1889	80	89	90	102	109	96
1890	83	89	93	108	106	101
1891	83	89	92	107	108	99
1892	83	90	92	101	103	97
1893	83	89	94	99	101	96
1894	83	85	98	95	93	104
1895	83	83	100	91	89	104
1896	83	83	100	93	91	101
1897	84	85	98	93	92	102
1898	87	88	99	92	92	102
1899	89	86	104	97	93	107
1900	94	91	103	113	102	113
1901	93	90	102	108	99	111
1902	91	90	101	104	99	106
1903	91	91	99	105	100	104
1904	89	92	97	107	101	103
1905	89	92	97	107	102	105
1906	91	93	98	114	107	104
1907	96	95	101	123	112	108
1908	94	93	101	118	109	108
1909	94	94	100	112	111	98
1910	94	96	98	119	119	93
1911	95	97	97	123	123	97
1912	98	100	97	124	119	103
1913	99	102	97	131	121	107
1914	100	100	100	—	—	—

[a] A. L. Bowley, *Wages and Prices in the United Kingdom since 1860*, pp. 30 and 34. For the seventies I have interpolated on the basis of wage-rates in agriculture, engineering, building, coal-mining, cotton and printing.

[b] Ibid. pp. 30 and 121.

[c] From unpublished calculations of Mr P. K. Debenham. The index of the terms of trade has been corrected for imported raw materials used in exports.

a year or so later than total investment. Fluctuation in money earnings followed a similar course.

Real wage-rates (real hourly wages) tended to move with the terms of trade. Money wage-rates followed export prices, and the working-class cost of living followed import prices, imports forming about half the total supply of foodstuffs. Now fluctuations in the price of imported foodstuffs depended on many random factors and had not the same cyclical regularity as the fluctuations in export prices. Real wage-rates,

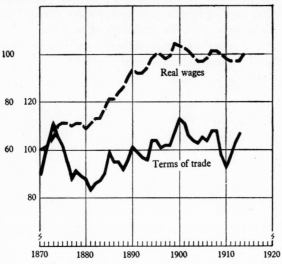

Fig. 19. Real wages and the terms of trade.

therefore, tended to rise and fall with industrial activity. In the seventies and early eighties, when real wages in Britain were less closely linked to the cost of imports, and harvest fluctuations were a more than usually disturbing factor, the phenomenon of real wages falling in times of depression is less readily observable.

In a closed system we should expect real wage-rates and output to move in opposite directions. But if one part of the system specializes in the manufacture of capital goods, and if the price of capital goods fluctuates more widely than other prices, there is no reason why, given appropriate harvest fluctuations, real wage-rates in that part of the system should not move with investment and output. And these conditions describe the situation in which Victorian Britain was placed.

In the analysis which we have just concluded two points stand out. An understanding of the role first of investment, and secondly of the terms of trade, is fundamental to any study of industrial fluctuations in

Victorian Britain. It was upon investment—home and foreign—that income and employment ultimately depended; and it was upon the terms of trade that the distribution of investment between home and foreign, as well as the course of real wages, ultimately depended. The openings for investment were seldom long exhausted; and Britain's trading relationships made a switch from home to foreign investment (especially in the boom) a matter of comparative ease. The conditions of the period seemed to work together for the unstable maintenance of stability. A qualified stability admittedly, for there were repeated and severe depressions; and an insecure stability, since it required the constant opening up of new fields for investment and the free movement and rapid increase of population which these new openings encouraged; but none the less, by inter-war standards, stability.

CHAPTER VIII

INVESTMENT AND MIGRATION

In this chapter I wish to discuss the relation between the migration of labour and the migration of capital from Victorian Britain. I hope to show that the apparent smoothness of capital transfer (from the point of view, at any rate, of Britain) was largely the outcome of a simultaneous labour transfer to the capital-importing countries.

In the first place, periods of active emigration were also periods of heavy borrowing by foreign countries. Table 48 shows that in each decade emigration and capital export rose and fell together—and to much the same extent. In the seventies and nineties there was comparatively little emigration, and not much foreign investment; but in the eighties and from 1905 to 1913, both took place on a very large scale.

Table 48. *Export of capital and migration from Britain, 1871–1910*

Decade	Export of capital [a] (£m.)	Net loss by migration from Great Britain [b] (000's)
1871–1880	266	257
1881–1890	561	819
1891–1900	286	122
1900–1910	721	756

[a] Above, p. 180.　　　　　　[b] *Statistical Abstract.*

Changes in the short period showed a similar resemblance. Emigration and foreign investment were both cyclical phenomena, increasing during the boom and falling away in times of depression. Apart from the eighties, and considering the possible margin of error in the estimates of capital export and of emigration, the two moved in fairly close agreement with one another (Fig. 20).

Moreover, the countries which borrowed most in London tended to be the countries which received most emigrants from Britain. If the statistics of passenger movements are any guide, about two-thirds of all emigrants between 1870 and 1900 sailed for the United States, her chief debtor.[1] In the same way, British settlers and British capital were provided simultaneously to whatever empire countries were in favour. The most spectacular example of this coincidence of flow is afforded by the rapid development of Canada after 1900. British capital in Canada rose between 1900 and 1914 by well over £300 m., while more than a million persons emigrated from Britain to Canada. There were, of course, exceptions—India and Argentine, for example—but it is noteworthy that in such cases there were generally heavy purchases in Britain out of the borrowed funds, and/or large numbers of immigrants from European countries.

These movements of labour had a considerable influence on investment in the countries gaining population as well as in Britain. That influence was twofold. A greater labour force in capital-importing countries kept down the cost of investment and facilitated rapid development; and, in addition, it led to 'secondary' investment because of the fixed capital requirements (housing, transport, etc.) of the new population. On the other hand, in Great Britain there was a greater shortage of labour during booms and a greater surplus during slumps. There was thus additional pressure on money wages, upwards or downwards, and still greater pressure on export prices. At the same time, the check given by emigration to population growth reduced home capital needs—particularly the need for houses. The situation summed itself up in the migration of unemployed building workers from Britain to Canada (where there was a building boom) between 1909 and 1914. So far as can be judged from the unemployment figures, and other data, this migration must have been on a considerable scale.

In earlier years, most emigrants appear to have come from country areas. The losses by migration of the rural districts were generally great enough to cover the whole of net emigration from Britain and the gains of the chief urban areas as well. It was only in the decade 1901–11 that the net loss by migration of the rural areas fell below the net loss of England and Wales.[2] It is conceivable that in earlier years the net gains of the towns covered a wholesale emigration to America and the colonies which was more than offset by rural immigration. Some of the older towns and many of the industrial areas certainly lost population fairly heavily in the eighties. But it seems reasonable to suppose that only

[1] These emigrants were chiefly Irish. The number of Scottish and English emigrants was more commensurate with the importance of the United States as a borrower.

[2] See above, p. 70. Much the same conclusion could probably be applied to Scotland. Greenock was the only town of more than 50,000 inhabitants to show a more rapid rate of increase after 1901 than in the previous decade. In Glasgow, Edinburgh and Dundee, the population was practically stationary. Clearly, town artisans must have been emigrating in large numbers. Before 1900 emigration from the towns was probably on a much smaller scale.

a limited proportion of agricultural workers moved to the towns, while emigration of town workers increased as America and the colonies became more and more industrialized.[1]

This point may be made a little clearer, and the incentives to migration may be illustrated, by a study of Fig. 20. The real wages of industrial workers never rose faster than in the eighties, yet it was in the eighties that emigration reached a peak. On the other hand, after 1900 real wages were falling or stationary, and yet emigration again increased. This suggests that there may have been a change in the type of emigrant over the period.

Changes in real wages tended to reflect changes in the terms of trade; and it will be remembered that the countries with which Britain did most trade were, on the whole, her debtors. A change in the terms of trade favourable to Britain raised real wages, and, unless 'agricultural' costs were falling rapidly, deteriorated the borrowing power of 'new' countries. There was thus a falling off in the openings for investment and employment abroad, and a state of depression in British agriculture which encouraged migration of agricultural workers to the towns. This was the sort of thing that took place in the nineties; the opposite happened after 1900. First there was urbanization and little emigration; then the towns emptied as agriculture recovered and prospects in foreign countries improved. In the eighties the fall in the prices of agricultural products did not prevent Australia, the United States and Argentine from borrowing heavily in London. The combined force of depression in British agriculture and expansion abroad resulted in a tremendous rural exodus, not so much to the towns as to America and the colonies. Some migration to the towns there must undoubtedly have been, since real wages were rising; but jobs were scarce—scarcer probably than in the nineties—and emigration, however troublesome, spared the necessity of a change of occupation. To the unemployed artisan also,

---

[1] The evidence of the occupation statistics given in the annual *Statistical Returns Relating to Emigration* is rather ambiguous. Of the adult male *passengers* (of 12 years of age and upwards) who embarked from Britain in the years 1875–9, no less than 30 % were returned as 'general labourers'; the majority of these were probably, but not certainly, rural workers. A further 12 % consisted of 'agricultural labourers', 'farmers', 'graziers', etc., and 19 % did not state their occupation. The most important section of the remainder, 'gentlemen, merchants, etc.', came to 14 %, and included many who were not really emigrants at all.

In 1913, when a new type of classification was in use, 20·6 % of the British and Irish *emigrants* were engaged in agricultural work, 18 % were general labourers, 31·4 % were skilled workers, 19·1 % were in commerce or the professions, and the remainder, 10·9 %, either did not state their occupation or were engaged in unclassified pursuits. For Great Britain alone, the proportion of skilled workers amongst the emigrants in 1913 was rather higher (it was over 40 % for both Wales and Scotland) and the proportion of agricultural workers and labourers was lower.

emigration must have been attractive; but the town workers who kept their jobs had little incentive to move so long as real wages continued to rise.

The movements of population during the period are reflected in the statistics of rent and of empty houses. Average rents increased between 1870 and 1873 fairly rapidly, and in the next three years there was

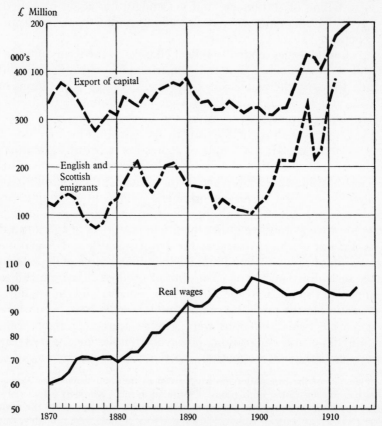

Fig. 20. Emigration, foreign investment and real wages.

a further sharp rise. About 1876–7, in the middle of the building boom, the rise came to an end. It is probable that in the depression of 1878 and 1879 rents on the average were falling, and that, apart from a slight improvement in the early eighties, the rise was not resumed until 1889. From then on, until about 1904, and particularly in the years immediately after 1890 and immediately after 1900, there was a steady increase. In spite of a fall in the price of fixed-interest securities, investors were

Table 49. *Factors affecting residential building, 1870–1914*

Year	Rents in England and Wales	No. of years' purchase of house property	Residential construction (1907 = 100)
1870	100		54
1871	100		58
1872	101	14·3	63
1873	102		65
1874	103		70
1875	104		74
1876	105	17·0	79
1877	106		81
1878	106		78
1879	105		74
1880	105		71
1881	105	13·5	70
1882	106		67
1883	106		65
1884	107		61
1885	107		56
1886	107	12·8	59
1887	107		61
1888	107		65
1889	108		70
1890	108		65
1891	109	13·0	62
1892	109		59
1893	110		61
1894	110		65
1895	111	14·50	76
1896	111	14·96	94
1897	112	15·36	117
1898	113	15·50	134
1899	114	15·61	134
1900	115	15·75	122
1901	116	15·79	117
1902	117	15·40	118
1903	118	15·13	120
1904	118	14·67	113
1905	118	14·61	113
1906	118	14·65	107
1907	118	14·09	100
1908	117	13·50	87
1909	117	13·23	85
1910	116	13·87	78
1911	116	13·86	67
1912	116	14·29	59
1913	116	14·00	59
1914	117	14·42	55

content with a lower and lower yield on house property—apparently in the expectation of a subsequent rise in rents.[1] As late as 1906 house property was valued at a higher number of years' purchase than in 1895, although British municipal bonds were selling at nearly 20 % less. After 1904 rents began to fall. From 1910 to 1914 they were again rising.

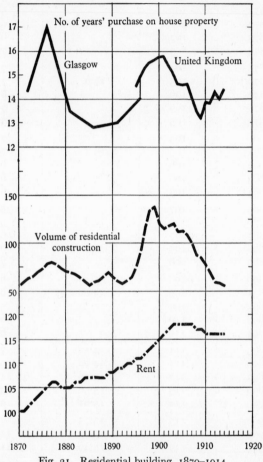

Fig. 21. Residential building, 1870–1914.

These changes reflect corresponding changes in the supply of, and demand for, house-room. In the seventies the towns were growing rapidly, partly as the result of new facilities of travel (tramways and suburban railways), partly because of agricultural depression. Real wages increased steadily up till 1876, and emigration—after 1873 at

[1] The fall in the percentage of empty property in the nineties (and also, no doubt, in arrears of rent) may have contributed to raise the number of years' purchase on house property by increasing the chances of finding tenants.

Table 50. *Rents in England and Wales (excluding Metropolis),*
1873–1910

Period (end of years named)	No. of houses of less than £10 gross annual value in middle of period (000's)	Abnormal decrease in such houses in years of revaluation. (Index of changes in rents) [a] (000's)
1873–1876	2521	91
1876–1879	2551	−7
1879–1882	2606	20
1882–1885	2640	32
1885–1888	2660	7
1888–1893	2719	81
1893–1898	2683	70
1898–1903	2659	114
1903–1910	2580	−57

[a] These figures show the number of houses of less than £10 gross annual value estimated to have been revalued at more than £10 gross annual value in 1876, 1879, etc. The numbers require to be decreased, however, by an unknown amount equal to the number of demolitions not recorded until years of revaluation. The large *increase* in houses of less than £10 gross annual value in 1910 may be due to the allowance of many reductions in rent by schedule only in the years 1903–10 (Stamp, op. cit. p. 53), although this is in conflict with the information given by Stamp.

A rough index of changes in rents can be constructed (on the assumption that demolitions not recorded until years of revaluation were small) if we suppose all houses below £10 in gross annual value to be evenly distributed over the range £5–10 and to be equally affected by changes in rents. The rise in rents in the years 1873–6 would then be 0·60 % per annum, and the rise in 1898–1903 would be 0·43 % per annum. These rates are probably rather too low, but it should be remembered that they represent, not changes in average rents per room, but changes in the rent charged for houses already old and growing older.

any rate—was low. Bricks and mortar were a solid security, flattering to the sense of prudence of investors who had come a cropper in speculative foreign securities. The rise in rents, combined with this feeling of security, was all too encouraging to investors in house property. Real wages ceased to rise, houses began to stand empty in increasing numbers, and reductions in rents began to be made.

In the eighties there were three conflicting tendencies. There was first of all emigration on a large scale; there was a remarkable rise in the rate of real wages (although unemployment was rather abnormal); and there was comparatively little new building. The depressing effect of emigration seems to have been just outbalanced by the rise in real wages and the falling off in construction. Rents rose slightly and the number of houses standing empty declined.[1]

After 1890 net emigration fell off. Real wages continued to rise, and new construction was still low. The result was a sharp increase in rents. It was only a question of time until a new building boom should begin. The heavy fall in interest rates and in the price of imported foodstuffs in 1894–6 gave building a final stimulus. The boom lasted for a full ten years (the absolute increase in the adult population was at its maximum) and did not finally break until 1906. Long before the end, the number of empty houses was rising fast and the upward movement of rents had been arrested. Again there had been over-building, and again it took several years for building to recover. On the eve of the war there were signs of renewed activity. In spite of emigration on an enormous scale, houses were more easily let and at better rents. The natural increase of population and the fall in unemployment were apparently more than enough, in a period of building stagnation, to counterbalance the removal of large numbers of artisans and their families to foreign countries.

The more mobile people are, the greater is likely to be the demand for house-room.[2] There will be, on the average, a larger number of houses standing empty, either because the owner expects that tenants will eventually come to the district, or as a result of unexpected movements of population to other districts. Thus if, in any period, mobility increases, while emigration does not alter, the building industry will nevertheless be more active. It is of interest to inquire, therefore, whether movements of population *inside* Great Britain were of more common occurrence at one time than at another.

It is not possible, unfortunately, to give statistics of short-period movement. But it is fairly certain that mobility increases when there are more openings for employment—that is, during the boom. This conclusion is borne out by the statistics of migration between *countries*, and by some figures for Sweden published by Professor Myrdal.[3]

Table 51 gives the balance of persons leaving or arriving in certain towns and districts in England and Wales in the three decades after 1881. Mr Welton, upon whose work the table is based, divided the

[1] In Scotland (and Glasgow) after 1880; in London after 1884. There are unfortunately no statistics for the rest of England and Wales, but there is little reason to suppose that the changes there differed from those in Scotland.

[2] I have left this section as it stood in 1935 because it happens to contain some interesting data on the flow of migrants by age and sex; but I do not find the argument very convincing.

[3] In his essay on 'Industrialization and migration' in *Economic Essays in Honour of Gustav Cassel*.

Table 51. *Gains and losses by migration of nineteen groups of districts in England and Wales, 1881–1911*

	Males	Females	Total
1881–1891 : Gains	133,069	241,714	374,783
Losses	548,483	443,681	992,164
Net emigration	415,414	201,967	617,381
1891–1901 : Gains	306,426	404,767	711,103
Losses	423,359	342,204	765,563
Net emigration	116,933	62,473 [a]	54,460
1901–1911 : Gains	147,304	145,115	292,419
Losses	460,284	338,921	799,205
Net emigration	312,980	193,806	506,786

[a] Net immigration.

country into 160 areas, each more or less homogeneous, and grouped these areas into nineteen categories—ten large towns, nineteen old towns, nine colliery districts, and so on. I have taken the balance of movement from or to each of these nineteen groups, and summed all the net gains and all the net losses. The result is a rough index of the number of persons in Great Britain moving more than a certain distance. The areas forming any one of the nineteen groups did not always show exactly the same migration structure, some gaining population when the majority lost, or losing population when the majority gained. But this lack of homogeneity was rather exceptional and the corrections to be applied are unimportant. Again, the original data does not represent actual movements of population, but balances of movement; and unless the drift was strongly in one direction, the totals of positive and negative balances may be quite misleading indices of total gain and loss.

Taking the figures for what they are worth, we can draw one or two interesting conclusions. The mobility of the population was much less variable than emigration, although it varied in the same direction. The loss of nearly a million persons by declining areas in the eighties was reduced to one of three-quarters of a million in the following decade, and rose by over thirty thousand in the next. Secondly, there seems to have been a secular decline in mobility, taking into account, of course, the increase in population. The growth of towns and the filling up of 'new' countries are probably sufficient explanations; there is a limit both to urbanization and to colonization. Thirdly, the statistics of *gains* (i.e. of movement within the country[1]) show fluctuations rather less violent than, and partly compensating, those of net emigration. The very large jump in the nineties is well brought out. The chief gainers were the large towns, the colliery districts, and the residential localities. It is important, however, that the colliery districts gained fewer men than usual, while the industrial towns (other than those engaged in the manufacture of textiles) gained more than usual or gained where there was normally a loss. These facts, taken in conjunction with the statistics of home consumption of machinery and other data, suggest that in the nineties new industries (cycle manufacture, electrical industries, etc.) were springing up in the towns, while city life was becoming more attractive.

A more accurate picture of internal migration is given by Table 52, in which migrants are divided according to sex and age grade. Some areas gained women and lost men, or gained persons of one age and lost persons of another.[2] The totals in Table 52 take some account of these possibilities but are less complete—owing to the omission of children under 15—than those in Table 51. It would appear that the rise in internal migration in the nineties is rather exaggerated in the figures of Table 51. This is partly due to the exclusion of children from Table 52, however, for there was a large net immigration of children in the nineties. The greater movement in that decade was most marked amongst men of from 35–50 (where mobility is usually low), and it was in the same age grade that emigration fell most heavily.[3] It is also worth while noticing that changes in the migration of the two sexes were approximately equal, although after 1900 the number of women leaving one of the nineteen selected districts for another or for abroad declined, while the corresponding number of men increased;[4] and at the same time the proportion of women leaving for other districts rather than for abroad was abnormally low.[5] The general similarity of movement of males and females makes it safe to base conclusions about the demand for housing on figures of total movement; movements of domestic servants for whom no additional accommodation might be necessary were probably fairly steady.

It is clear, therefore, to sum up, that in the nineties there was not

[1] Including immigration from other countries.

[2] Unfortunately, Welton does not give the necessary data for 1901–11 or for 1871–81.

[3] The change of most importance *absolutely* was in the fall in emigration (indeed, net *immigration*) of women in the age-group 20–35.

[4] In the rural areas the change was quite the reverse; net emigration of women fell much less heavily than net emigration of men, although in the previous two decades it had moved parallel to male migration.

[5] Residential places were practically alone in showing a gain in the female population. The large towns, for the first time in their history, lost heavily.

Table 52. *Gains and losses by migration of nineteen groups of districts in England and Wales, by age-groups*

Age-group and sex		+ items		− items	
		1881–1890	1891–1900	1881–1890	1891–1900
15–20	M.	32,066	34,729	71,398	61,047
	F.	84,861	89,008	103,453	85,599
20–35	M.	105,968	141,020	362,351	316,126
	F.	184,445	262,502	194,591	159,706
35–50	M.	11,984	50,107	60,735	28,288
	F.	7,042	20,255	123,147	87,290
50–	M.	14,447	35,468	38,964	15,539
	F.	16,506	30,105	48,165	35,485
Total (adults only)	M.	164,465	261,324	533,448	421,000
	F.	292,814	401,870	469,316	368,080
		457,279	663,194	1,002,764	789,080

only a greater increase in population than in the ten years preceding or in the ten years following, but there was also more movement of population from place to place within the country. Much the same could no doubt be proved of the seventies. The building booms of Victorian Britain seem to have depended not only on an increase in the aggregate demand for house-room, but also upon changes in the incidence of this demand. On the other hand, the fact that the net loss by migration of 'declining' areas was generally less than the natural increase of population damped down the influence of migration on the building industry. Local overbuilding, when emigration was on a small scale, must have been due, as a rule, to other forces than unexpected reshufflings of population. Local overbuilding of rural cottages was unheard of; and when the villager migrated to the town it was the increase in the rent he had to pay quite as much as a 'change of residence' that caused new construction to be undertaken. Still, greater mobility within the country—especially when combined with more rapid urbanization—must clearly have been favourable to building activity.

The reasons for responsiveness of the building industry to changes in foreign investment should now be abundantly plain. The more foreign countries borrowed, the more men we sent them to carry out the work of new construction for which British capital was wanted. The emigration of these men left houses empty in this country. There was thus less certainty of finding tenants for newly built houses, and more difficulty in letting houses at customary rents. The decline in demand naturally hit the building industry. Simultaneously, builders had often to put up with worse terms of credit; or investors ceased to buy house property altogether and purchased foreign bonds instead.

Once the rentier had had his little flutter, and been scared by some major panic abroad, he was more ready to make prudent loans on mortgage or to building societies, and had less difficulty in finding reliable borrowers. If foreign investment came to a standstill, emigration was certain to be equally low, and this gave a fillip to the demand for house-room. The distress sales of agricultural products in the English markets, which were the not unnatural outcome of the decline in investment in these countries, raised real wages and tempted agricultural workers to make for the towns at the first opportunity. So long as employment in Britain fell in sympathy with the contraction of her export markets, the high real wages of the towns could have little influence on building, and rural immigration was held up. Once the building industry did get going, however, it was obvious that all things would work together to provide a market for the new houses built. That a start was ever made in the seventies and nineties was due partly to extraneous impulses. But even apart from gold discoveries, new inventions, Public Health Acts, and so on, the elements of recovery were already there. A reduction in foreign investment was enough of itself, by bringing gold to London, to cheapen credit. Investors, too, were more willing to lend to the building industry at whatever rates happened to be ruling. Finally, those who kept their jobs and earned higher real wages would not want the sort of house which those who were out of work were trying to vacate.

The building industry was not sheltered from great fluctuations in employment by the sort of harmony that has just been described. But those who worked in the industry and could move to other industries were less badly hit than they might have been. Total investment was stabilized and total employment must also have been steadier. If, when foreign investment increased and there were more jobs to be filled in the export industries, these jobs did not go to unemployed carpenters and bricklayers, they must have gone to other unemployed workers or to juveniles who might have entered the building industry, or to workers from other industries to which builders might be suited. If the builders lost—and a steady growth of population without sudden bursts of emigration and foreign investment would naturally have been more to their liking and to the nation's advantage—their loss was mitigated by a gain to others.

The connexion which has just been traced between migration and the building industry can readily be paralleled by a study of other branches of investment. The railways and public utility services were closely dependent upon the rate of growth of population and of cities. The emigrants of the eighties, had they stayed at home, might have been employed in the extension and widening of railway track, the building of waterworks, the operation of tramways. Their removal from the labour market and the consequent retardation of the growing demand for transport services and public works made home investment less advantageous and less urgent. The railways, the local authorities and the building industry, responded to similar incentives.

CHAPTER IX

DID FOREIGN INVESTMENT PAY?

Public opinion has almost always been biased in favour of investment of capital at home and against investment in other countries. Even in England, from the eighteenth century onwards, there has generally been an undercurrent of feeling against the right of investors to hazard capital freely in the bonds of foreign governments or in enterprises situated abroad. As early as 1730 the issue of a loan to the Emperor Charles VI on the London Stock Exchange was prohibited by the government.[1] In the nineteenth century, it was partly the desire to encourage home investment which lay behind the government's refusal to bring pressure upon defaulting countries. Default was regarded as a useful reminder of the imprudence of foreign investment. If capitalists lacked that nice blend of self-interest and high-mindedness, which, by the grace of Providence, led men to invest at home, then it was not the business of the government to rescue them from their well-merited misfortunes. Thus, Palmerston, in a circular to the British Diplomatic Representatives in 1848, declared that 'it has hitherto been thought by the successive governments of Great Britain undesirable that British subjects should invest their capital in loans to foreign governments instead of employing it on profitable undertakings at home, and with a view to discouraging hazardous loans to foreign governments who may either be unable or unwilling to pay the stipulated interest thereupon, the British Government has hitherto thought it the best policy to abstain from taking up as international questions the complaints made by British subjects against foreign governments which have failed to make good their engagements in regard to such pecuniary transactions. For the British Government has considered that the losses of imprudent men who have placed mistaken confidence in the good faith of foreign governments would prove a salutary warning to others, and would prevent any other foreign loans being raised in Great Britain, except by governments of known good faith and ascertained solvency.'[2]

[1] Poley and Gould, *History of the Stock Exchange* (4th ed.), p. 14. At that time, however, the bias was against foreign borrowing rather than foreign lending.

[2] Quoted by Max Winkler, *Foreign Bonds*, p. 136. The qualification introduced in the last sentence is superfluous. In 1848 few governments 'of ascertained solvency' had borrowed or wished to borrow in London—except the British!

It must not be thought either that a policy of non-intervention was rigidly adhered to, or that it was prompted solely by concern for investment at home. Palmerston was quite ready to give instructions for a note to be sent to a defaulting country

It is not easy to say how far this bias is justified. Questions of investment are so wrapped up in human institutions—in private property, in
capitalism, in imperialism and in war—that judgements of national
advantage cannot be based simply upon money yields. Those who
encouraged the French rentier in his folly may have thought the
cementing of a political alliance vastly more important than the
sacrifice which they were foisting on him, or the profits which they
were able to net for themselves. It is not even possible to say that there
is a necessary money advantage or disadvantage in the export of capital.
The experience of different countries—and of different generations—
has varied too widely for any definite presumption that foreign investment does or does not pay to be established. It is only possible to offer
a catalogue of some of the circumstances in which foreign investment
should be looked upon with favour or disfavour; or to try, from a recital
of the gains and losses of some particular country at some particular
time, to form a balanced judgement of probable gains and losses at
some future time. This chapter, as its title indicates, is intended as a
recital rather than as a catalogue.

The dangers of foreign investment can readily be illustrated from
French experience. By 1914 France had embarked close on £500 m.
in Russian bonds bearing 4 and 5 %.[1] It was known—although not to
the French investor—that the Russian government was spending half
of its borrowings on armaments,[2] and that it was relying to an increasing
extent upon profits from the sale of alcohol in order to meet its ordinary
expenses.[3] It had, in fact, been more or less on the verge of bankruptcy

stating 'that the patience and forbearance of H.M.'s Government...have reached
their limits, and that if the sums due to the British...claimants are not paid within
the stipulated time and in money, H.M.'s Admiral commanding on the West India
Station will receive orders to take such measures as may be necessary to obtain justice
from the —— nation in this matter' (Hertslet, *Recollections of the Old Foreign Office*,
p. 84).

The main grounds for non-intervention seem to have been, first, that 'those who
invested their money in the bonds of other countries in order that they might obtain
a higher rate of interest for it, knew perfectly well that they were running a great risk
of losing their capital'; and, secondly, that intervention 'would subject the government to the liability of being involved in serious disputes with foreign powers, on
matters with regard to which the government of the day might have had no opportunity of being consulted' (Jenks, *Migration of British Capital to 1875*, pp. 124–5).
These grounds were accepted from the start by the Corporation of Foreign Bondholders. Some illuminating remarks on the whole question will be found in Jenks,
especially at pp. 115–25.

[1] Feis (*Europe: the World's Banker*, p. 51) gives a total of 11·3 milliard francs. Lysis
(*L'Escroquerie Russe*) puts the total at 16 milliards in 1910!   [2] Lysis, op. cit. p. 35.

[3] Ibid. p. 38. The alcohol monopoly brought in a third of the ordinary revenue,
and the consumption of alcohol per head increased by a third in the years 1902–10.
One calculation of the Russian national income put it as low as £6. 10s. 0d. per head.

ever since the nineties. A war or a revolution—and neither was altogether unforeseen—would bring certain default. In the event, the loans were repudiated outright and not a penny of the whole £500 m. has ever been recovered. The loans which France had made, with equal craziness, to Turkey, Greece, Austria-Hungary, the Balkans and South America, were also repudiated. In all, France lost two-thirds of the net total of her foreign investments, or about six times the amount of the German indemnity of 1870.[1]

The individual investor simply had not the information on which to base a sound judgement. The financial columns of the large dailies were leased to financial writers privileged to conduct their columns with complete liberty.[2] It was estimated that only 25 out of 186 financial journals had any claim to independence, and only two or three of these could be said to be thoroughly honest in their comments on new issues.[3] Misrepresentation was carried to extraordinary lengths both in the Press and in prospectuses;[4] there was no legal requirement that the statements made should be accurate.

The investor had for long relied upon the advice of his local banker, whose preference was usually for the securities of firms with whose standing he was familiar. With the amalgamation or extinction of the local banks, the investor was left at the mercy of the Paris issuing banks who were much less scrupulous tipsters than their predecessors, and often recommended the issues which were most profitable to themselves.[5] In practice, these issues were generally large loans to foreign powers. Thus it was mainly in the interests of foreign investment that the credulity of the investor was exploited.

The interest received, in spite of the difference in risk, was not appreciably greater than the market rate on similar French securities.

[1] H. D. White, *The French International Accounts*, p. 275 n.

[2] White, op. cit. p. 280.

[3] Even the English financial press was not altogether free from corruption. In the seventies *The Times* was sometimes called the 'Jews'-harp' because its city editor boosted Rothschild stocks (L. H. Jenks, op. cit. p. 399). For other cases see O'Hagan, *Leaves from My Life*, vol. I, p. 37, and Peters, *The Foreign Debt of the Argentine Republic*, p. 24.

[4] See, for instance, the case of Paraguay, White, op. cit. p. 281 n.

[5] Lysis, *Contre l'oligarchie financière*, pp. 9 et seq., H. D. White, op. cit. p. 279. These profits on issue were decidedly generous. On some loans they were alleged to come to as much as 17 % or even more; they probably averaged about 4 %. If a class gain of this kind is associated only with the raising of capital for *foreign* investment and is thought just as undesirable as outright loss, then these profits do not affect the balance sheet of gain and loss to the French nation. But if the business of issuing is regarded as an export industry with peculiar opportunities for profiting from foreign investment, then the high prices charged by issuers for their services can be construed as a change in the terms of trade in favour of France.

It has been estimated that in 1899 the yield on domestic securities at the price of issue averaged 4·28 %, while the yield on foreign securities was no more than 3·85 %. At the *market* price in 1900 the yields were 3·23 and 3·84 % respectively. The difference, whether positive or negative, was trifling.[1] It must be remembered, too, that the type of investment in which France specialized—bonds of European governments[2]—paid the lowest interest. The French rentier—the most cautious of capitalists and the most credulous—was content with a gilt-edged return on securities in which no self-respecting gambler would have dabbled. He was financing the warmongers for a mere pittance. He was starving French industry of capital.[3] And he was doing little or nothing to promote French commerce or to reduce the cost of imported products.[4]

On the other hand, there is at least a *prima facie* case for believing that British investment in other countries has been economically advantageous to the investors themselves and to the nation as a whole. In the nineteenth century there were constant defaults—chiefly by South American countries[5]—but, for the most part, with the exception of those of the twenties and seventies, of a comparatively minor character. The return, in profits and interest, was substantial. And the opening-up of new countries with British capital—the building of railways, the provision of banking and insurance facilities, the financing of public utilities of all kinds, the operation of mining ventures and so on—was attended with solid advantages to this country over and above the pickings of judicious investment. There were, of course, many 'unsavoury incidents'—exploitation of the weakness and credulity of foreign peoples and governments, and of the ignorance and folly of investors. But political injustice and polite fraud were not peculiar to *foreign* investment, and would presumably exist in the absence of any investment

[1] White, op. cit. p. 107. The yield of 3·85 % is calculated on the basis of all foreign securities listed on the Paris Bourse: on securities actually held in France the average yield was rather higher—perhaps, 4·2 %.

[2] In 1914, 60 % of all French foreign investment was in European countries—chiefly in government bonds.

[3] Cf. White, op. cit. p. 300: 'It is possible that the French attitude towards experimentation, towards new ventures, new methods would have been different had French capital more eagerly sought opportunities for domestic investment.'

[4] Cf. White, op. cit. p. 295 n. Between 1880–4 and 1905–9 imports into France from the countries most indebted to her either fell, sometimes heavily, or, as in the case of Russia, rose by no more than 10 % (although prices were higher).

[5] In the eighteenth century the Abbé Terray was denounced for his 'unlimited immorality' when he recommended that each state should default at least once every hundred years. In the nineteenth century one can well imagine him elected to the Council of Foreign Bondholders and sent on a mission to South America to convert the natives from their unfortunate belief in decennial defaults. Guatemala was perhaps the most fanatical of the defaulters; see the long recital in Winkler, op. cit. pp. 41–4.

whatever. And it was remarkably rare—everything considered—for any of the countries most heavily indebted to us to find in its reliance upon foreign capitalists a source of irritation or a matter for regret.

Uncertainty about the composition of the British portfolio makes it difficult to give any accurate estimate of the profit on each type of investment. We were constantly buying and selling—sometimes in huge quantities. These changes were generally profitable, especially when we 'nursed' the securities of debtor countries until their credit improved. But there were times when we bought at the peak or made panicky sales near the bottom of the slump.[1] Moreover, there was a gradual change over the whole period in the distribution of our investments between different types of security. In 1870 the loans and guarantees of foreign governments were easily the most important item, and our investments were chiefly on the continent of Europe. By 1914 railway loans were the predominant form of investment, our holdings of the bonds of non-empire governments were of minor importance, and our investments in Europe were also comparatively small.

In addition to this difficulty of weighting, there is the problem of finding an appropriate basis of comparison for securities which are not equally risky. The investor judges uncertainty for himself. Even if foreign investments offer a consistently higher return, he may rest content with Consols. It may be possible to convince him on the basis of results that he earned less than he might have done; but there can be no certainty *when he makes his choice* that he is acting imprudently. On the other hand, actual yields cannot by any means be assumed to offer a satisfactory index of risk. In the market some securities, through ignorance, or skilful advertising, or patriotic sentiment, or anticipation of government backing, or mere miscalculation of gain, enjoy a quite adventitious esteem. Thus, while a difference in return *may* correspond to a real difference in uncertainty—as judged by well-informed and unbiased persons—it may equally well be the result of market aberrations. A statistical investigation of actual yields may still be of some help, therefore, in deciding upon the merits of foreign investment.

Such information as is available suggests that the earnings on our foreign investments were on a par with the return on risky investments at home. Sir George Paish put the average return on our 'public'

---

[1] Our purchases of French government and railway securities during the panic on the Bourse in 1830, and of American railway bonds during the Wall Street crisis of 1907 were both extremely profitable (Hyde Clarke, *Theory of Railway Investment*, p. 30, and C. K. Hobson, *Export of Capital*, p. 155). On the other hand, we probably lost heavily through the purchase of Turkish bonds from France after 1870, and through the re-sale of American securities in the United States during the Civil War and the depression of 1893–6.

investments in other countries at 5·2 % for 1907. The lowest return was on Indian Government Loans, which yielded 3·21 %.[1] Indian railways yielded 3·87 %, and colonial and provincial government loans 3·71 %. All the other headings given by Paish, except 'finance, land, and investment', averaged at least 4 %, and altogether eight groups, amounting to almost exactly 50 % of our 'public' foreign investments, showed yields of between 4 and 5 %.

A further source of information is Lehfeldt's inquiry into the rates of interest offered by home, colonial and foreign borrowers on large issues in the years 1888, 1893 and 1898–1914. The following table shows the return (including yield on redemption) promised by each of these groups of borrowers in the two five-year periods 1900–4 and 1905–9:[2]

	Home	Colonial	Foreign	Colonial less Home	Foreign less Home
1900–4	3·18	3·33	5·39	0·15	2·21
1905–9	3·61	3·94	4·97	0·33	1·36

It is clear that colonial borrowers could raise their loans on terms almost as favourable as home borrowers, while foreign borrowers required to offer about 1½ % more. If we were to omit British Government Loans, the rate paid by other first-class British borrowers would probably be greater than that paid by colonial governments.[3] On the other hand, to make a quite different comparison, foreign borrowers were paying practically twice the yield on Consols. Consols were yielding approximately 2·7 % in the period 1900–4, and foreign borrowers offered 5·39 %; in the period 1905–9 Consols were yielding, say, 2·88 %, while the average yield on foreign issues was 4·97 %.

Lehfeldt's data is also interesting as casting light on the problem of default. On large issues of nearly £41 m. by foreign borrowers in 1888 the rate of interest promised was 5·61 %. The rate actually obtained over the next ten years was 3·49 %. Obviously there had been many important defaults—chiefly by South American borrowers. Now the rate promised (and paid) by colonial borrowers on £25 m. raised in 1888 was only 3·43 %, i.e. actually less than the average received on all foreign borrowings. Home borrowings were too small to affect the comparison.

[1] The yield on Consols in 1907 was approximately 3 %.

[2] Of these two periods the second was the more normal, large issues of war loan driving down the average rate on home borrowings between 1900 and 1904, while the rate on foreign borrowings was kept up by the disfavour with which foreign investment was regarded.

[3] To judge from the prices of *existing* securities, Home Railways and Municipalities were still ranked (on the average) above Indian and Colonial Securities in 1910 (cf. Flux, 'Yield of high class investments', *Trans. Manchester Statist. Soc.* 1910).

Had Lehfeldt taken twenty years instead of ten, the defaults on loans raised in 1888—and it would be difficult to pick a worse year between 1875 and 1914 for such a test—would have appeared even less serious.

A more elaborate calculation can be made for the ten years 1870–80 on the basis of data in R. L. Nash's *Short View of the Profitable Nature of our Investments*. The seventies were probably the least remunerative decade in the sixty years before the war. There were many defaults, the most important being those of Turkey, Peru, Spain, Honduras and some of the smaller South American Republics, and there is little doubt that the losses made were sufficient to deter the majority of investors, for some years, from sending their capital abroad. The exposure of a number of frauds and bogus loans (Giffen called them 'disguises to plunder the public'[1]) in the Report of the Committee on Foreign Loans in 1875 heightened the bad odour of all loans to foreign governments. But the loans dealt with in the Report—all issued by South American Republics—came to a mere trifle. The cash subscribed by the public cannot have been much over £7 m., and the average return on this sum—in the absence of default—would have been over 10 %, together with a substantial premium on redemption.[2] Not all of the £7 m. was ever remitted to South America.[3]

The worst cases of default were not investigated by the Committee.[4] But the leading authorities were agreed that in all a comparatively small amount—perhaps £60 m.—was all that was at stake.[5] The face value of the defaulted loans might be as much as twice the actual money subscribed,[6] and the money which was ultimately paid over to the borrowing country was, of course, still less, since there were fat commissions to be paid to the contractors and other intermediaries. The more disreputable the loan, the fatter the commissions.

[1] Giffen, *Economic Inquiries and Studies*, vol. I, p. 107.

[2] The face value of the loans was £9·2 m. and the average price of issue 81. The price at which the loans were actually disposed of to the public cannot readily be ascertained.

[3] San Domingo received £38,000 on an issue of £757,700. The Costa Rican government claimed that it received only £½ m. on a loan of £2·4 m. issued in 1872. Paraguay and Honduras received a rather larger proportion of the proceeds of their loans. 'It becomes a question', says Hyde Clarke (*J. R. Statist. Soc.* 1878, p. 321), 'whether these are to be regarded as foreign loans, or as loans from the public to the persons concerned in their concoction.'   [4] Cf. Hyde Clarke, loc. cit. p. 307.

[5] Cf. Hyde Clarke, loc. cit. and Ernest Seyd, ibid. Opinion on the Stock Exchange on the subject of our losses by default was divided. Compare, for instance, the evidence of G. W. Medley and L. L. Cohen before the Royal Commission on the Stock Exchange, 1877 (Q. 3239, Q. 8567, Appendix X, etc.).

[6] The average issue price of Turkish loans was 58 (D. C. Blaisdell, *European Financial Control in the Ottoman Empire*, p. 39). In 1874 a Turkish loan for £16 m., bearing 5 % interest, was issued at 43½. Turkey defaulted in the following year.

Table 53. *Yield on foreign investments, 1870–1880*

	Market value of investments (£m.)	Yield in dividends (%)	Yield in capital value (%)	Total annual yield (£m.)
(i) *Government bonds*				
United States	160	6·1	1·4	12·00
India	55	4·25	0·15	2·42
Colonies	50	5·0	0·4	2·70
Russia	50	5·9	—	2·95
France, Holland, etc.	30	5·4	1·6	2·10
Turkey	20	5·5	−7·5	−0·40
Egypt	17½	7·7	−2·2	0·96
Peru	17½	3·3	−9·3	−1·05
Spain	15	8·0	−4·7	0·50
Brazil	11	5·6	0·6	0·69
Italy	7½	7·6	4·4	0·90
Portugal	6	8·8	5·7	0·87
Argentine	5	7·0	−0·4	0·33
Chile	4	5·8	−1·0	0·19
Honduras	3	2·8	−8·7	−0·18
Mexico	3	—	−5·0	0·15
Other South American	4	5·0	−6·0	−0·04
Total	458½	5·6	−0·15	25·11
Total (omitting United States)	298½	5·4	−1·0	13·11
(ii) *Railways*				
Indian Rails	80	4·8	1·5	5·04
U.S. Rails	40	5·7	3·6	3·72
Continental Rails	35	5·1	0·4	1·93
South American Rails	10	5·3	3·4	0·87
Canadian Rails	10	1·9	0·15	0·21
Total	175	4·9	1·8	11·77
(iii) *Miscellaneous*				
Telegraph, cables, etc.	15	6·6	−1·3	0·80
Colonial Banks	10	8·4	4·0	1·24
Foreign Banks	5	7·2	−1·5	0·29
Land, Mortgage Coys.	5	10·0	6·0	0·80
Total	210	5·4	1·7	14·90
Grand Total	843½	5·4	0·7	51·78

It must be remembered, too, that the defaulted bonds had sometimes paid very high interest for some years: in 1870, for example, Turkish and Egyptian loans were yielding over 10 %, and Spanish loans over 12 %. Nor was default always complete. Something like 20 % of the capital in defaulted Turkish loans—and not all were in default—was finally recovered.

In Table 53 I have attempted to make a rough estimate of the return, taking into account defaults and capital appreciation, on two main classes of foreign investments in the seventies: government bonds and foreign and colonial railways. The distribution of our holdings between different countries in 1870 can only be made very approximately, and subsequent changes, except in the figures of yield, have had to be ignored. Full allowance is not made for defaults, since some important issues, made after 1870, were afterwards in default, and the weights given to defaulting countries are consequently rather low. On the other hand, the rough estimates of yield do reflect any defaults on post-1870 loans. These estimates are approximately equal to the mean return on all issues given by Nash, i.e. all issues up to 1875. In the absence of the necessary data for mines, tea plantations, etc., it has been necessary to leave the table incomplete.

Government bonds, even omitting the United States, yielded 4·4 % per annum between 1870 and 1880. This figure is the balance of interest payments and profits on redemption over net capital depreciation through default, distrust, etc. Now the return on Consols during the period was no more than 3·26 %, which, together with an annual capital appreciation of 0·58 %, gives a net return of 3·84 %. Thus an investor who was determined to hold government securities would have done rather better to buy a batch of European and South American government bonds on which he would have earned well over 4 %, rather than Consols on which he would have earned 3·84 %. If he had bought only Indian, Colonial and United States bonds, his earnings would have been very much greater. Moderate risks, as Nash points out, were the ones which paid.

But while the return on foreign government bonds, as one would expect, was greater than on Consols, it was less than could be earned on good industrial issues at home. The investor could have earned 4·3 % in dividends and 1 % in principal from a representative purchase of Home Railway debentures, 4·7 % in dividends, and 1·8 % in principal from Home Railway preference stocks, and a much larger sum, nearly 6 % in dividends and over 3½ % in principal from Home Railway Ordinary stocks.[1]

[1] Taking ten of the biggest (Caledonian, Great Eastern, Great Northern, Great Western, Lancashire and Yorkshire, London, Chatham and Dover, London and

The proper comparison, however, is not between Home Railways and foreign government bonds but between Home Railways and Foreign Railways. The return on Foreign Rails of 4·93 % in dividends and 1·79 % in principal is rather better than that on Home Railway preference stocks. Considering the exceptional rise in popular favour of Home Rails in the seventies, and the excellent security offered by guaranteed Indian Rails or first-class American mortgage bonds, the comparison is by no means unfavourable to foreign investment. The figures for banks and mortgage companies suggest that there may have been some kinds of foreign investment—of a sort which a well-informed investor might choose—which paid even more handsomely than foreign railways. But the market for home industrials was probably equally imperfect, and the number of 'plums' which the investor in foreign securities could pick must have been very limited in 1870, or even in 1880.

The redistribution of our holdings between different types of security after 1875 was all in favour of a higher rate of return. Government bonds, the least remunerative of our foreign investments, shrank steadily to little more than a quarter of the total at the outbreak of war, and very little of this quarter consisted of the bonds of continental countries. The bulk of it was in the more or less gilt-edged stock of empire governments. Private investments in shipping and mercantile establishments, foreign banks, and so on increased rapidly before the war, and may fairly be assumed to have earned large profits. Investments in rubber estates, oil companies, jute mills, gold and diamond mines, land and mortgage companies also formed an increasing proportion of our foreign investments, and paid, on the average, high rates of dividend. Foreign and colonial railways, in which the bulk of our capital was sunk, were with few exceptions consistently profitable.

In all, British capitalists earned some £4000 m. in just over forty years in interest and dividends on their foreign investments. An average income from overseas of almost £100 m. a year was a tidy contribution to the National Dividend, which at that time was ranging between, say, £900 m. in 1870 and £2300 m. in 1913. During the period, moreover, there was a steady improvement in the credit of our debtors and in their power to buy back (at enhanced prices) their own bonds. There was a secular capital appreciation to add to the high dividend yield.

North Western, London and South Western, Midland, and North Eastern), an equal sum invested in the ordinary shares of each would have brought in 5 % in dividends and 4⅓ % in principal. Or if the investment had been weighted in accordance with the market value of each company's ordinary stock in 1880, the return would have been 5·7 % in dividends and 3·6 % in principal. In each case the total return would have been 9·3 %.

The actual return on our foreign investments is something quite definite. The earnings on the home investment that (presumably) would have gone on if foreign investment had been less popular, are altogether incalculable. How far the rate of interest would have fallen one can only guess; how much more rash investors would have become is also a matter for speculation. The available statistics do not show any very pronounced change in the trend of interest rates when there was a burst of foreign investment, but this cannot by itself be taken to prove that the demand for capital for investment at home was highly elastic. There may have been a simultaneous decline (e.g. because of emigration) in the demand *schedule* for capital for home investment; or a very rigid, and more or less unanimous, view of the future course of interest rates.

Some check to the National Dividend would certainly have taken place. The earnings of capitalists would presumably have been less, because of a lower rate of interest, or because of a check to accumulation, or for both reasons. These earnings being the main source for the provision of fresh capital, the check to the National Dividend might have been cumulative. Indeed, a gloomier view may be taken. The alternative may have been to accumulate capital abroad or none at all. Our foreign investments were made largely in times of boom out of the abundance of high profits, and when nearly the whole employable population was at work. Is it certain that, if there had been no convenient 'sinks' for British capital in foreign countries, the income from which that capital was provided would ever have been created?[1] It is only those who think of savings (or of investment) as something apart from the income-creating process who can lightly deny that the depressions of the Victorian age would have dragged themselves out, or that the wealth of Great Britain would have been little augmented had foreign investment been unpopular or impracticable. We might have had to put up with a lower level of world investment, and of employment and income in Britain, if the difficulties in the way of foreign investment had been greater.

This is largely a matter of speculation: the gain to our export industries was one of simple observation. There was an expansion of buying power in their markets, increased orders for equipment, with the prospect of additional orders later for replacements, and increased sales to consumers. Now, in many of the export industries, there were economies of scale—both in marketing and production—whereas in the chief import-competing industry, agriculture, there were few economies. There was thus a national gain to be derived from an extension of the

---

[1] For an early expression of the point of view which looks on foreign investment as a sink, see Fullarton, *Regulation of Currencies* (1844), p. 162.

export industries, quite apart from any increase in employment or rise in export prices that might result.

A second source of gain lay in the spread of information of profitable openings for investment. The commercial ties of Britain with other parts of the world opened our eyes to the credit-worthiness of borrowers, enabled us to take sane risks, and gave us the inside track in the negotiation of attractive propositions. Moreover, the projects which traders sought to finance brought good customers to our export industries. Companies promoted here, however controlled, were often staffed by British engineers or British managers who, through goodwill, prejudice, or actual arrangement, tended to specify British machinery for new construction and for replacement.[1] Thus the market imperfections which allowed us to dominate the business of exporting capital (for industrial purposes, at any rate) worked also in the Victorian age to put large sections of our export industry in a semi-monopolistic position.

We gained also through a cheapening of imports. The heavy fall in the price of imported foodstuffs between 1880 and 1900 was largely the result of railway-building with British capital in the United States, Argentine, India, Canada, and Australasia. In 1870 there were no more than 62,000 miles of track in these countries. By 1900 there were 262,000 miles of track.[2] In the seven years 1907–14 Britain provided £600 m. for the construction of railways in countries supplying us with foodstuffs and raw materials.[3]

At a time when the population was increasing rapidly it was vital that foodstuffs should be obtained as cheaply as possible. By 1870 the home supply was clearly approaching a limit, and our dependence on imports was increasing. For an improvement in the standard of living the rapid opening-up of fresh sources of supply was obviously imperative. The change took place rather abruptly in the seventies,[4] and from then on the course of real wages in Britain was dominated by the terms on which we were obtaining imports. These terms in turn depended upon what sums we had placed abroad in new countries in the recent past. The course of real wages was thus closely dependent upon our willingness to finance railway building abroad.

On the other hand, in 1914 the future prospects of foreign investment were by no means rosy. Those governments whose credit had improved could re-borrow on progressively better terms. What was more important,

[1] Tacke, *Kapitalausfuhr und Warenausfuhr*, passim.

[2] Sir George Paish, 'Export of capital and the cost of living', *Trans. Manchester Statist. Soc.* 1914, p. 77.   [3] Paish, loc. cit. p. 78.

[4] 'In 1868 the United Kingdom still produced four-fifths in value of what the inhabitants consumed of grain, meat, dairy produce and wool.... In 1878 the United Kingdom supplied her inhabitants with scarcely one-half' (Jenks, op. cit. p. 330).

the chief sanction on which British investors relied for the enforcement of their claims—namely, the financial power of London—was certain to become gradually less effective in bringing recalcitrant debtors to heel. So long as foreign countries found it necessary to pile up debts to Britain, there was some guarantee that they would honour these debts: but once the time came for repayment and no fresh debts were being contracted, they might not be so scrupulous. Companies owned by British capital might with more impunity be harassed by heavy taxation or by discriminatory legislation. The chief bargaining counter in trade agreements might become the observance rather than the conclusion of loan contracts.

It would be a mistake to suppose that all our foreign investments were in this precarious position. We had an enormous sum (probably £700 m.) in the United States—a rich country unlikely to stoop to default. Half of our investments were in the Empire, in which default was practically unknown. Much of the remainder was in foreign companies, controlled by the citizens of foreign countries, and not particularly open, therefore, to discriminatory treatment.

Secondly, a latent divergence of interest between workers and capitalists was coming more and more to the front. Though capitalists had not been alone in gaining from the export of capital, the working class participated more by accident than design. It was only by a rare coincidence of interests that the most profitable risks happened to fructify in cheaper and cheaper foodstuffs and raw materials. Capitalists were ready enough, at a price, to finance schemes of less advantage to their countrymen—the building of sultans' palaces,[1] the mining of diamonds, the purchase of warships, the construction of strategic railways. At the same time, a rising standard of living amongst wage-earners was not entirely dependent upon reductions in the cost of imports. More investment at home would have meant better houses, better travelling facilities, and better public amenities of all kinds. Had the rate of interest fallen, there would have been, in addition, a redistribution of income in favour of wage-earners, and it is possible that the slowing down in the rate of capital accumulation would not have been great.

The more new countries were opend up, the more apparent did the sectional conflict become. The likelihood that foreign investment would reduce the cost of British imports was less overwhelming, the fear that industries competing with our own would be fostered was more intense. Cheap capital for other countries and improving terms of trade and real wages were no longer synonymous. Foreign investment, it was apparent, might lower the standard of living instead of raising it.

[1] Cf. Nassau Senior, *Journal Kept in Turkey*, p. 115.

Finally, there was the danger that capital abroad might be lost through revolution either in Britain or in the country in which the assets were situated. There was no guarantee that, if the export of capital gave way to an export of capitalists, the title-deeds to foreign property could be easily seized or would be readily honoured. Tangible assets at home can be lost to the nation only through invasion, destruction, depreciation, or obsolescence. But assets abroad may be beyond the reach of expropriation.

Up till 1914 there was a sufficient coincidence of private profit and social gain in Britain's export of capital to prevent the government from exercising more than a minimum of control over investment. Broadly speaking, British foreign investment paid. But it was far from evident that uncontrolled investment would be equally advantageous in the future.

CHAPTER X

THE VICTORIANS AND INVESTMENT

A pedigree can nearly always be found for unorthodox economic theories. Some happy-go-lucky crank of a century ago can be crowned with the laurels of more than usual penetration or sturdy common sense, and paraded by the *nouveaux riches* of the intellectual world as a pledge of their respectability. Ancestor-hunting is a popular sport. It can also be a very instructive one. Theories which were rejected or forgotten may have been right even at the time, but may have failed to influence policy because of some inadequacy in their statement or because of some perversity in the economic thinking of the age. If a post-mortem can reveal something of these inadequacies and perversities, it will be helping to free modern thought from the trammels of past controversies and to secure the more ready acceptance of once-discarded views. Or if these views can be shown to have been based upon a mistaken reading of the facts, then attention will be focused with advantage upon the change in economic life which has made traditional opinion out of date.

Our task in this chapter is more modest: it is one of disinterment, not of conducting a post-mortem. Victorian thought on investment and unemployment is still so much buried in pamphlets, lengthy tracts and commercial journals that it may be of interest to bring together here some specimens which I have unearthed in the course of excavations directed to rather different ends. These specimens of opinion are chiefly from the writings of men of affairs—journalists and business men and politicians—who were more or less unanimous on matters of 'pure theory' but held widely different views on monetary problems. It would hardly be correct to label any of these views unorthodox, for there was no body of thought on money and investment—at any rate until the end of the century—which was regarded as undeniably orthodox. There were simply a series of controversies—over the Bullion Committee Report, over the 1844 Act, and over Bimetallism and the question of the standard generally—in which economists, if they were sufficiently interested, took sides. In these controversies there were certain strands of thought which met with more success than others—the quantity theory, for example. But until the time of Marshall the strands were not woven very closely together.

The quantity theory did give unity to the views of a very large group of economists. It focused attention upon the price-level, and upon the money supply as the chief determinant of the price-level. But it gave no clear account of the *mechanism* by which changes in the quantity of money reacted upon the price-level. Nor did it give any clear definition of the terms in which it was phrased. The supply of money was sometimes defined in terms of cash, sometimes in terms of credit, sometimes in the most ambiguous ways.[1] The demand for money was analysed very superficially.[2] It was thought obvious that people would only want more money if prices were to rise. Employment was assumed to be more or less constant,[3] and the rate of interest was regarded as of minor importance.

Later in the century, however, the quantity theorists gave more prominence to the role of interest rates. The crude theory of Overstone, which assumed that prices would respond automatically to additions to the money supply (strictly speaking, to the supply of notes), was abandoned, and emphasis was placed more and more upon the Bank of England's discount policy as a means of control over the money market and over the price-level.[4] The odds and ends of a theory of interest rates began to accumulate and had been sorted out by 1900 into the two comparatively elaborate theories of Wicksell and Marshall.[5]

---

[1] Mill excluded from his definition of the quantity of money all cash 'kept as a reserve for future contingencies' (*Principles*, Ashley edition, p. 490)—a very vague qualification which might exclude *all* money. He came near to identifying the quantity of money with expenditure.

[2] Mill defined the demand for money as 'the whole of the goods in the market' (loc. cit. p. 491). If, instead, he had written 'output', his theory would have been more intelligible and comparatively modern.

[3] It is interesting to find Wicksell, who had a high regard for the Currency School, speaking of unemployment in normal times as no more than 1 % (*Geldzins und Güterpreise*, p. 132), and deliberately assuming that abnormal profits will not lead to a marked increase in output (pp. 82, 131, etc.).

[4] Even Lord Overstone shifted his ground. 'How charmingly', commented James Wilson (speaking of one of Overstone's letters to *The Times*), 'how charmingly he persists in a high rate of interest as the only security, which is just what he never dreamt of before when the fluctuation in the circulation of notes was to do everything, and when those opposed to the mere currency theory insisted that it was the rate of interest only that could regulate the money market' (quoted by T. E. Gregory, *Select Documents and Statutes*, vol. I, p. xxxii).

[5] Wicksell, *Geldzins und Güterpreise*; Marshall, Evidence before the Gold and Silver Commission, especially Q.9686 (*Official Papers*, pp. 51-2). The ideas strung together by Wicksell were already familiar in England in an unconnected, and sometimes rather muddled, form. The ideas of 'forced saving', of a divergence between natural and market rate and of an increase in the quantity of money forcing up prices via an increase in investment (e.g. Ernest Seyd, *J. Soc. Arts*, 5 April 1878, p. 411), can be found here and there before 1900. After 1900 the ideas began to be expressed more lucidly. There is an interesting passage in D. H. Robertson's *Study of Industrial Fluctuation* (1915) which puts some of Wicksell's points very neatly:

'Any temptation to over-investment', he says, 'will be aggravated by an increase

But it was still round the price-level that discussion centred. Economists of the Currency School seldom stopped to inquire *why* the price-level should be of such peculiar importance. They were content to take for granted the maintenance of a stable rate of exchange and deduce the undesirability of fluctuating prices. The danger of financial panics, not of unemployment, was uppermost in their minds. They might, of course, throw in a hasty postscript to the effect that rising prices meant rising profits and an increased demand for labour. But this was a half-hearted afterthought, not pursued and not always insisted upon. Or, in the long run, when stable exchanges failed to prevent prices from rising and falling with the tides of gold, they might grieve over the concealed tax upon fixed incomes or the general unprofitability of business. They were not blind, that is to say, either to the effects of fluctuating prices upon output or upon distribution. But since changes in output were regarded as subsidiary, and changes in distribution as important chiefly in the long run, it is difficult to see why there should have been such a fuss over the price-level. There was a vague feeling that panics and slumps were somehow the aftermath of rising prices. So the quantity theorists set themselves to explain the rise in prices, and imagined that in doing so they were explaining panics and slumps. Their simple diagnosis, their 'fool-proof' remedy, and the lack of other positive proposals ensured them a good hearing. The device of concentrating upon the price-level secured a prestige which the opponents of Peel's Act could not shake off and which stuck for nearly a century.

Nevertheless, there were many economists—generally of the Banking School—who made little mention of the price-level in their explanations of industrial fluctuations. There was, for example, Tooke—a bitter opponent of the quantity theory—who developed a psychological theory of trade fluctuations. There was James Wilson—another of the Banking School—who put forward a scarcity-of-capital explanation of crises. There was Fullarton—still another of the Banking School—who held that there was a chronic tendency to over-save. And there was a large body of opinion which had a firm belief in 'dormant' or 'unemployed' capital and connected this unemployed capital rather hazily with industrial depression. In the popular mind all of these explanations were hopelessly jumbled together.

---

in currency. For in the first place the transference of resources to business men is a transference to those who are most prone to use resources in investment; and further ...the fact that the rising price-level lowers the real rate of interest actually demanded below the rate which savers mean to demand is particularly unfortunate at a time when the expected future productivity of constructional goods is abnormally high and when only the exaction of a high rate could prevent an unduly rapid absorption of resources in investment' (loc. cit., pp. 215–16).

Broadly speaking, the main division—in Victorian times as at the present day—was between those who were preoccupied with booms and those who were concerned to explain slumps. Those who arrived at some explanation of the boom tended to look on the slump as the inevitable reaction from a debauch and as something which called for sound nursing and careful abstinence from quack prescriptions. Those who claimed to explain the slump looked upon depression as a chronic complaint of the existing system and upon booms as aberrations of healthiness. The former spoke in terms of over-investment; the latter in terms of over-savings. In addition, of course, there was the usual army of cranks and pamphleteers, willing to put down depressions to anything from the issue of free railway passes to the withholding of the franchise from women;[1] and the inflationists-on-principle who were uneasy because prices were falling, and attacked the standard as a preliminary to stopping the fall.

The 'depressionists' were a motley group. Malthus must have been one of the first;[2] Sismondi, Rodbertus, and later Marx, were of the number. The popularity of their views may be gauged from the comment of Mill on his famous proposition that 'demand for commodities is not demand for labour'. 'Even among political economists of reputation', he said, 'I can hardly point to any, except Mr Ricardo and M. Say, who have kept it constantly and steadily in view.'[3] Yet by 1889 J. A. Hobson was able to declare that Mill's doctrine that 'saving enriches and spending impoverishes the community along with the individual', though 'strenuously denied by the educated world, supported by the majority of economic thinkers, up to the publication of Ricardo's work', was now 'reiterated and restated...from the daily papers to the latest economic treatise, from the pulpit to the House of Commons...till it appears positively impious to question it'.[4] In academic circles the economic system was thought to be obviously self-adjusting: 'if anything goes wrong with the working, there is a system of checks and balances which will be sure to set it right again, or, at any rate, prevent the evil from becoming serious.'[5] But it was hardly to be expected that *everyone* would be taken in; the facts of unemployment and depression were too well known, the inquisitiveness of business men and reformers too persistent. Whatever the Victorian's

[1] D. H. Robertson, *Study in Industrial Fluctuation*, p. 1.
[2] J. M. Keynes, *Essays in Biography*, pp. 142–3.   [3] Mill, op. cit. p. 80.
[4] Mummery and Hobson, Preface to *Physiology of Industry*, p. iv. These authors put down the acceptance of this dogma to the inability of economists 'to meet the now exploded wages-fund doctrine'; confused thinking about interest rates (from which Hobson is not free) must have contributed. It is probable that Hobson, in his eagerness to play the heretic, exaggerated the unanimity of the public.
[5] Ibid. p. 101.

capacity for self-deception and metaphysics, he claimed to have—somewhere—a conscience.

The theory of over-saving recurs constantly. It was put forward, for example, by John Fullarton, in his tract *On the Regulation of Currencies*, published in 1844. Fullarton's views are worth quoting at some length:

Without entering into the abstract question so much debated among economists [he says] as to whether such a thing as an over-supply of capital be possible, I may venture, I think, to state, without much fear of contradiction, that, under the present constitution of society in this country, what with the annual savings from income and the large fortunes in constant course of remittance from the colonies, the amount of capital seeking productive investment accumulates in ordinary times with a rapidity greatly out of proportion to the increase of the means of advantageously employing it. The subjects of investment which are chiefly in favour for their safety and convenience, such as the public stocks, are either stationary in amount or in a gradual process of diminution. There is only a certain fund to be divided; and the effect of any new capital being invested in it is merely to alter its distribution, without in the least adding to its quantity. The competition inevitably raises the price.... The Government is enabled to reduce the interest on its funded debts, and landed proprietors to renew their mortgages on easier terms. The capitalist finds his income reduced perhaps by a third; and after waiting for several years in expectation that matters may take a favourable turn, he loses his patience, and...becomes disposed to listen with avidity to any project which holds out the expectation of a better return for his money. His scruples on the score of security insensibly give way before the splendid visions of gain which are spread before him....

From the Bubble year downwards, I question much if an instance could be shown of any great or concurrent speculative movement on the part of capitalists which had not been preceded by a marked decline of the current rate of interest.... Indeed, one would almost be tempted to suspect that a periodical destruction of capital has become a necessary condition of the existence of any market rate of interest at all.[1]

These views are not supported by a reasoned analysis either of saving or of investment. To Fullarton they must have appeared self-evident.

That a wild spirit of speculation and adventure is not only essentially promoted by any long-continued depression of the market rate of interest, but that the difficulty of procuring secure and productive investments for capital is at the root of nearly all those violent paroxysms of speculative excitement which occasionally convulse the money market, is a truth which, if it had not been questioned by very high authority [Tooke?], I should have thought indisputable.[2]

The main points in this theory—the chronic insufficiency of openings for investment, and the divergence between actual and anticipated yields

---

[1] Fullarton, *On the Regulation of Currencies*, pp. 169–72.   [2] Op. cit. p. 168.

set up by a fall in bond rate, are clear enough.[1] But there is no hint of the *mechanism* by which a deficiency of investment is transformed into industrial depression, and the theory of interest rates put forward—in spite of an interesting aside on the Scottish building boom of 1824—is highly unsatisfactory. 'Were all speculations based on sound principles', he says, 'doubtless the fluctuations of interest would have very little share in producing them. But what I am speaking of is not sound or rational speculations, but speculations extravagant and monstrous.'[2]

Economists had, in fact, made little progress beyond the observed fact that 'abundance of money and low rates of interest have always the effect of stimulating trade and promoting speculation'.[3] The influence of bank rate was supposed to be confined to 'speculation' or to foreign lending. The more sophisticated of the quantity theorists tended to lay emphasis on 'speculation', the Banking School on foreign lending. When the balance of payments was under discussion the one group thought of international price-levels and the other of international capital movements.[4] But thought on interest rates was still so confused that Tooke was able to argue—not consistently—that a low bank rate, by reducing costs, would cause prices to *fall*![5]

Views similar to those of Fullarton crop up repeatedly in the nineteenth century. Even Mill was influenced by them.[6] So were Giffen, Leone Levi, and many others.[7] But they were never, after the time of Malthus, systematically defended by any British economist until the

---

[1] 'John Bull will stand many things, but he will not stand two per cent', was a common saying in the nineteenth century.   [2] Op. cit. p. 170 n.

[3] *Currency Self-Regulating* (Anonymous, 1855), p. 71.

[4] For the views of the Banking School see particularly James Wilson, *Capital, Currency, and Banking*, pp. 17–24 and Art. XV; Hubbard, *Currency and the Country*, p. 42. These economists were by no means so fatalistic in their outlook on trade fluctuations as Fullarton and Tooke. Their account of the *modus operandi* of bank rate shows considerable acuteness.

[5] Tooke, *Inquiry into the Currency Principle*, chapter XIII.

[6] Mill, op. cit. pp. 641–2.

[7] Thus Levi remarks (*History of British Commerce*, 2nd ed., p. 302): 'In truth, capital in England ordinarily increases more rapidly than the means of safe and profitable employment; and consequently, from time to time a great competition arises between the owners of capital for the means of investing their surplus stock.' Giffen declared (*Stock Exchange Values* (1878), pp. 141–2) that 'the great rise (in security prices) since 1870 especially appears to show that there is hardly any limit to the force of saving in the great communities of modern times, and that the creation of good solid securities cannot keep pace with it. People lay past every year more than they can employ profitably in a reproductive manner, although every year new reproductive employments are created....Pending the discovery of wants in society, for which fixed capital is required, there is no way of converting circulating into fixed capital profitably, and the means available for this conversion may also be increased so rapidly that if a new way is found, the void is at once filled up. Consequently there

publication of Hobson's *Physiology of Industry* in 1889.[1] Here at last a protest is raised against the view that a market is created *pari passu* with production and in favour of the Malthusian contention that the demand for labour depends upon the sales proceeds of industry. Mr Hobson's arguments are familiar, and call for no lengthy exposition. Total income is shown to be identical with the sales proceeds of current output.[2] Now depression can be defined as 'a general reduction in the rate of incomes'.[3] Depression, therefore, must be due to an insufficiency of demand for the factors of production, that is, of demand for final output, *that is,*[4] of consumption. A reduction in consumption caused by the saving of the thrifty will cause all incomes to fall, and this fall will proceed until the least thrifty section of the community begins to spend its capital.[5] This capital will be acquired by the savers and equilibrium will be restored.[6] The whole thing is as plain as a pikestaff—'we venture to assert, unassailable'!

The main defects in Hobson's theory have long been recognized to be his failure to give a satisfactory account of interest rates and his neglect of the influence of monetary policy. These two defects were common to a great deal of Victorian thinking. Of the two, the lack of a proper monetary theory was the more fundamental. Time and again, concentration on the problems of an ideal, real-exchange economy made them forget or explain away the peculiarities of a monetary economy. This preoccupation barred the way to a proper theory of trade depression—for *repercussions* of unemployment cannot occur where people are *first* spending their income and then handing over what they do not consume for purposes of investment.[7] It led instead to theories of rational contraction in output rather than in employment,[8] or to loose thinking on wage theory.

is almost always a surplus pressing for investment, which appears never to be destroyed except in the rare case of a great war....'

This line of thought was usually associated with the doctrine of the tendency of profits to a minimum (*alias* the declining marginal productivity of capital as the ratio of capital to other factors of production increases).

[1] This volume is interesting also because of the acute excursus on the imperfections of competition in chapter v, and because of the stress which it lays upon the divergence between individual and social interest in the supply of capital.

[2] Op. cit. pp. 88 et seq.

[3] Op. cit. p. 96.   [4] My italics.   [5] Op. cit. p. 184.

[6] Hobson gives no indication of having thought out the nature of the equilibrium position.

[7] Professor Pigou's theory of 'synthetic' repercussions in a real-exchange economy (*Industrial Fluctuations*, p. 61) depends ultimately upon commodity A having the properties of money.

[8] Cf., for instance, Professor D. H. Robertson's *Study of Industrial Fluctuation*, pp. 125–6.

There were, however, some economists who achieved a crude theory of repercussions. For them the problem was one of under-employment rather than of over-saving. They had some glimpse of the truth that the level of investment may determine, rather than be determined by, the level of saving. Torrens, as early as 1808, had set down as the 'chief advantage of the poor laws' that 'on sudden interruptions of trade, by affording relief to the manufacturer [i.e. wage-earner], they keep up, in a great degree, the effectual demand for the farmer's produce, and thus render temporary that want of employment which, if the land proprietor's revenue suffered diminution, must necessarily be lasting'.[1] Relief would have to continue until the landed proprietor acquired new desires, 'the gratification of which shall create a new demand for labour'. Torrens describes in detail the chain of repercussions that he supposes would follow the cutting off of part of the supply of imports (and presumably also of exports).[2] 'A universal stagnation would ensue.... The incomes that should purchase the home-made [instead of imported] luxuries cease to exist', unless farmers, being rich, dis-save and continue to pay rent while their products are unsaleable. Torrens suggests as remedies the accumulation of capital (public works?)[3] and Government intervention (dole?).

In Hyde Clarke's *Theory of Railway Investment* (1846) prominence is again given to the idea of under-employment. Arguing against what has since been nicknamed the 'Treasury View' of investment, he suggested that

with sensible men it must be held impolitic to talk of circumscribing the bounds of railway investment and apportioning and applotting the distribution of the national resources.... The love of defining, of setting bounds, is strong in weak minds. They would set bounds to the Godhead.... We may safely lay down, as a principle, that the whole labour of railways might be done by the present means, in addition to the usual labour of the country. The general truth of this anyone's observations will teach him.[4]

The saving to finance the additional investment would, in fact, be forthcoming out of increased income: 'partly from the increased resources of the country and partly from the greater energy of existing means.'[5] Much of the cost was simply a *transfer* of capital—land, for example,[6] and the wage-equivalent of poor relief.

[1] R. Torrens, *The Economists Refuted*, p. 61.

[2] He appears to have been thinking of the Berlin decrees.

[3] The remedy of public works is, of course, almost immemorial. A scheme of exchange-depreciation-cum-public works was put forward by Misselden in his *Free Trade* (pp. 106–7) in the reign of James I. The idea is probably much older.

[4] Op. cit. p. 9. Hyde Clarke was an anthropologist and philologist, editor of the short-lived *Railway Register* and Secretary of the Council of Foreign Bondholders. He was writing in the middle of the railway boom of the forties.

[5] Op. cit. p. 18.   [6] Ibid. p. 14.

Our whole population, under the institution of the poor laws, must be fed....Although the feeding of the population is provided for, there is no provision for the effective application of its labour....Were there any adequate organisation in a period in which other employments were slack, the national industry would be employed in improving the dwellings and public buildings, in draining the soil, in embanking the rivers, recovering lands, promoting fisheries and mining, making harbours, and otherwise adding to the yearly production of permanent plant.[1]

Even Mr Lloyd George could not have been more emphatic.

It is only occasionally in Victorian literature that one encounters ideas like those of Hyde Clarke and Colonel Torrens. The theory of repercussions was given a new vogue by Bagehot in his *Lombard Street*,[2] and in the hands of Giffen developed into what was practically a theory of investment.[3] But very few people got beyond the simple conception of 'dormant' or 'unemployed' capital, or connected under-employment of capital with under-employment of labour. Unemployed capital was mixed up with stocks,[4] or—what was much worse—with land; or it was identified with hoarding.[5] Unemployed labour was a matter for the Charity and Poor Law Commissioners—a problem of poverty, not of wealth.

The 'Treasury View' was far more popular. It can be traced through a long series of 'scarcity of capital' ancestors, back to Ricardo. The theory had its representatives in the versatile Banking School—for example, James Wilson, once referred to by Torrens as 'the most formidable opponent of the Act of 1844'.[6] Wilson puts the argument as follows:

It is clear that [investment] cannot be undertaken, except with the surplus provisions, or capital which is left over and above the quantity required for regular reproduction, and that this quantity must always limit the power of a community to increase its capital.

...It is, therefore, not difficult to see that it becomes a most essential thing to the continued prosperity of a country, that its *floating* capital, on

[1] Hyde Clarke, 'On the debts of sovereign and quasi-sovereign states', *J. R. Statist. Soc.* 1878, pp. 319–20.　　　　[2] Pp. 125–6.

[3] See especially *Economic Inquiries and Studies*, vol. x, pp. 101–3, where the depression of the seventies is analysed in terms of the collapse of foreign investment in 'new countries'.

[4] As by Blake, *Observations on the Effect Produced by the Expenditure of Government* (1823), pp. 60–70; and by G. Dixwell, *Premises of Free Trade Examined* (1881), pp. 8–10.

[5] E.g. W. Joplin, *A Letter on the Fluctuations in the Money Market* (1853). This pamphlet contains an interesting analysis of credit creation and contraction. The idea of 'hoards' as unemployed capital is very ancient.

[6] R. Torrens, *Principles and Practical Operation of Sir Robert Peel's Act*, 2nd ed. (1857), Preface, p. xi. Wilson was a Scottish Cabinet Minister who founded *The Economist*. His monetary theory has a modern ring.

which the continued reproduction of commodities of everyday use depends, as well as the continuous employment of labour, should not be withdrawn from those necessary purposes, and converted into *fixed* capital, in a greater degree than the surplus accumulation of the country... will admit.[1]

Hence a crisis 'is not a question of deficient *currency*. It *is* a question *only* of deficient *capital*,[2] or, in other words, of commodities; and anything that does not include quantity of commodities can be of no use whatever. It must either be, therefore, by increased economy...or by the creation of new commodities that any relief can be afforded.'[3]

Giffen, who has already been quoted as a 'depressionist', expressed a similar point of view.[4]

Confusion may be caused [he remarks] by engagements to invest beyond the savings of a community, but the investments themselves cannot be made. To a certain extent, however, it would seem that they can be made. Unawares, a portion of the means of a community required for consumption may be diverted to fixed investments. To restore the equilibrium, it becomes necessary to create more consumable articles than formerly in a given time; while this is being done a certain portion of the invested capital gets to be on offer for the purpose of obtaining articles of consumption.[5]

There were other explanations of the crisis. It was sometimes put down to a psychological relapse, sometimes to a shortage of money. Tooke, who denied that the banks possessed the power to stimulate (home) investment but was willing to speak of a 'factitious increase of nominal monied-capital coming into competition with pre-existing real monied-capital seeking investment',[6] seems to have regarded trade

---

[1] James Wilson, *Capital, Currency and Banking* (1847), p. 127.

[2] Wilson—like many Cabinet Ministers—was fond of italics.

[3] Op. cit. p. 208.

[4] So, too, did Mill. But both Giffen and Mill keep their 'depressionist' views in a separate compartment. They seem to have confused over-savings with 'the tendency of profits to a minimum', i.e. gradually falling interest rates. Giffen, for instance, thought it 'obvious, that if there is a surplus pressing for investment...it will by competition help to lower the yield obtainable by all capital in securities' (op. cit. p. 142).

[5] Giffen, *Stock Exchange Securities*, p. 21. Compare also W. Austin, *On the Imminent Depreciation of Gold* (1853), pp. 27–8; and James Maclaren, op. cit. pp. 31–2. For these authors see R. S. Sayers, 'The standard in the eighteen-fifties', *Econ. Hist.* January 1933, pp. 580–1.

[6] Tooke, *State of the Currency*, p. 83. But it is doubtful whether he had a theory of fluctuations in the *total volume* of trade at all (cf. T. E. Gregory, *Introduction to Tooke's History of Prices*). However vague Tooke may have been on the subject of output, he was extremely illuminating on the subject of the price-level. Compare, for example, the following passage:

'The cost of production will determine whether and to what extent the supply will be continued, but the extent of the effectual demand, in a given state of supply, will

fluctuations as the fruit of illusion. Giffen (a good journalist, familiar with all points of view) found a limit to the rise in prices both in monetary and in psychological factors. An expansion of credit would be brought to a stop if bank reserves were depleted, for instance, by an internal drain of cash 'into the hands of non-banking classes'.[1] And the rise in security prices, which would set a premium on new issues,[2] would be arrested by the bearishness of investors and speculators who thought that prices were 'above the average'. 'The disposition to keep money uninvested cannot be reckoned permanent, but occurring as it does, when the natural limits to credit rises are being approached, the anticipation has a great effect.'[3]

There was, in fact, very little of the modern theory of investment that one or other of the Victorians failed to 'put across'. The ideas of a shortage of capital, of a demand for money varying with prices and money-incomes, of repercussions, of the relation between expenditure and prices, of foreign investment as a sink for 'the frozen income of the super-rich',[4] had all been given expression before the end—one might almost say the *turn*—of the century. But they were mere *obiter dicta*—fragments of a complete theory which no one had pieced together, and no one could piece together without a less cumbersome, or less abstract, or less pessimistic theory of interest rates. Instead of giving us such a theory, the economists of the later nineteenth century followed the Currency School up the *cul de sac* of the quantity theory and purged their economics of monetary forces. The pamphleteers threw themselves with zest into an interminable squabble on the standard. And the public was left with the impression that monetary theory was merely a statement (in a couple of sentences) of the causes of fluctuations in prices, and an elaborate exposition (in a couple of chapters) of their consequences.

be measured by the prices which the consumers may be able and willing to pay. Now the power of purchase by the consumers depends upon their incomes; and the measure of the extent and of the exercise of such power is, as has just been observed, in that portion of their revenues which is destined for expenditure in objects of immediate consumption.... Any increase of incomes... of which wages constitute the largest part, will raise general prices, and a fall of wages will depress them, supposing no alteration in the cost of production' (*Inquiry into the Currency Principle*, pp. 71–2).

Wicksell (*Geldzins und Güterpreise*, pp. 40–1) declares that 'Dieser Erklärungsversuch hoffnungslos in einem Zirkel bewege': since (*a*) incomes depend upon prices just as much as prices upon incomes, and (*b*) costs and incomes must be equal and each must total up to 'the sum of the prices of produced and consumed goods'.

[1] Op. cit. p. 32.
[2] Ibid. Giffen did not connect new issues with the creation of income.
[3] Op. cit. pp. 34–5.
[4] Holsinger, *Mystery of the Trade Depression* (1929), p. 359. Compare Fullarton, op. cit. p. 162, and Hobson, *Imperialism* (1902), pp. 77–8.

INDEX OF SUBJECTS

INDEX OF NAMES